LIFE
IN THE
LIGHT
TIANSHIRE

James Hendershot

Order this book online at www.trafford.com
or email orders@trafford.com

Most Trafford titles are also available at major online book retailers.

Printed in the United States of America.

ISBN: 978-1-4907-2093-7 (sc)
ISBN: 978-1-4907-2094-4 (e)

Trafford rev. 12/04/2013

Trafford PUBLISHING® www.trafford.com
North America & international
toll-free: 1 888 232 4444 (USA & Canada)
fax: 812 355 4082

Dedicated to my wife Younghee, with thanks for financially providing for our family during my days and nights of writing, and to my sons, Josh and John and daughters, Nellie and Mia and my publishing consultant, Love Blake, check-in coordinator Stacy Canon and book consultant Tanya Mendoza.

CONTENTS

CHAPTER 01

DARKNESS FELL UPON THE LANDS

Our world underwent many changes in its long history. It too, like most of the life from other planets in this solar system had a life that was destroyed, as the planets were destroyed, then reformed again. Saturn fell first, followed by Jupiter and Mars after which was Earth, which is now starting to cool down and reform. It should be ready for life if our world is also destroyed once more. I have heard about the children of Mars and Earth from stories as told by my father. They were such contrasting worlds, as Mars was so spiritual and rebelled against the throne and Earth rebelled against the thrones.

Oi, my brother whom is as much of my soul as is I, as we always searched for the wrong that these creations had, and spent most of our lives explaining what these creations did wrong and how to avoid the inevitable doom or removal from the light. We steered our eyes to the heavens and never wavered, for we knew the price of disobedience is death or absence of the light. We at no time worried about any punishment for disobedience; we knew that we not, at any time, live without our light and never cared about all the trials and tribulations that followed every step of our flesh test. We knew that which we touched was not to be forever, for it was in the dark and actually hiding the light. If we touch it or it touches us, it is a part of the struggle to the light. It is as air and water. When disobedience is added to the air, it becomes heavy and changes form. When life is sucked into it, the life will die. Only life born from within water may live within the water. Water must be purified by the fire of our sun and pulled apart through separation until it once again becomes air. The wise way is to stay in the air and not suffer the sun's baking heat to be made pure again after disobedience.

Oi and I discovered that remaining pure as the air was a choice and that this choice would lead to eternal light in the sea of love. Our world faced greater obstacles than the others that our small solar system did. We were an experimental planet, in that the Queen of the Dark finally accepted the light, and was given our New Venus as a first mission. As such, dark would not permit this without the greatest battles of the unseen world. The dark eventually suffered titanic losses as their powers in our universe sank so low that their only chance of survival was to infiltrate the light and lay as dormant cells; however, that is another story. The point, which I am trying to share, is that dark attacked all who lived on New Venus day and night, with their greatest armies after Oi and me. My view is enhanced now that I am in the light and can see all that was in my path. The heavens have given me scrolls that I may eat thereof and speak their words. The scroll of the beginning is the first one that I ate. As these annex my spirit, I am paralyzed seeing that which I never knew. This is what I knew not; however, it just now has magnified the glory of the light that I chose to be served.

The magnitude of emptiness within our throne's borders, or as others call it the Milky Way, overwhelms me. There are so many worlds, which are only occupied by spiritual temples. They are filled with places in which the saints may praise the throne. They fill the unseen world with such peaceful harmony. I also see so many armies of angels fighting to remove the demons. The Milky Way is as well a black hole for demons as they voluntarily are sucked deep into its clutches. I do not understand why so many come into our kingdom. Why do they focus so much on the Milky Way? My scrolls tell me to worry not for that truth will also be revealed.

I currently continue watching my scrolls as their light burns both outside and within me. This is the truth of the ages that my mouth, might now speak, and record for those to read from before, now and yet to come. As in all that I have seen, when darkness covers light, and light does not yield, their light will burn in the darkness, which will fade into the light. I now stood on the great seashore with my feet sinking into the sands of time. The waves of knowledge turned into light as they escaped from the darkness of the night and sea, which appeared as one. I can see but a few spots of white against this curtain of black as it tries to remove the light around me. Shadows of dark slowly push against me from all sides, yet I fear not, for I have within me the light and with the light, I shall not fall to the dark but today take the knowledge it has tried to conceal for so long. Without warning, rising from the sea came one who had large powerful eyes.

I must search longer to find the words to describe her. She wears a black dress and has dark butterflies on her hand. Her mouth lives on the left, yet is decaying on the right. Her lower-right nose is dark, yet all her skin that I see is a light pure azure, which means of the purist living light. Her hair pours as rivers of life-giving blue. She motions for me not to speak. I can feel only good and purity flowing from her, as the dark stays behind her. This is a level of virtuousness, which I have never known. I can only wonder, "Who is she and why is she coming forth from the dark sea?" For her to come out of the dark and still be of light is a sign of her great power. The music in my soul is now trying to find words to mate yet, as with each tone vibrates, the words flash as if between light and dark. The words are searching for and trying to find their order. I heard one word that felt good to my soul, and I now am searching for that word since I lost it. No other word knows the word I am searching. I now look at the light in the light and ask her, "Who are you and where is the word I am searching to find?" She answers me, "I am one who was with you on your journey, who had to leave you and have for so long searched for you." I asked her, "If you know me, tell me about the path I have traveled." The woman straightaway tells me, "You are the granddaughter of a queen, the daughter of a demon and whose father was the only to eat the forbidden fruit. You now rest in a small throne with your brother and your sister in faith Queen Boudica." I ask her, "Who are you?" She tells me, "I was a queen of the dark; however, I am now the queen of queens of the greatest righteousness ever to be." I then asked her, "If you are the queen of queens in the finest throne of righteousness. Why do I not know you?" She told me, "It is not your time to know. I am with you now to help show you the greatest mysteries so that when your time comes you will know the path to choose.

Fear not my love for I shall never depart from you as we shall transform history, for I shall have all four and not only two." I said to her, "Queen of Queens, what are the two that you have and the two you have not?" She then smiled and said, "Fear not for I am with you now. I shall give unto a saint from your heavens who will share the visions with you and tell you if they be of light or dark." I then asked, "Who is this Saint?" The queen told me, "He is from the old Earth, and is a judge for any who tries to enter your throne."

I now saw that the Light among the sheep made a great slaughter among them in their pasture, until they cried out to him, in consequence, of that slaughter. Then he departed from the place of his habitation, and left them in the power of lions, tigers, wolves, and in the power of foxes, and of every beast. Afterwards I began to cry out with all my might, imploring the Light of the sheep, and showing him how the sheep were devoured by all the beasts of prey. Nevertheless, he looked on in silence, rejoicing as they were devoured, swallowed up, and carried off; and leaving them in the power of every beast for food. He called also seventy shepherds, and resigned to them the care of the sheep, that they might overlook them; saying to them and to their comrades, "Every one of you henceforward overlook the sheep, and whatsoever I command you, do; and I will deliver them to you numbered." As I listened to these words, memories of some great teachings that I heard during my eternal duties as a queen began to manifest themselves. I needed to hear some more to be sure, thus he began to talk again, "Of all the destruction brought about by each of the shepherds, there shall be an account. According to the number, I will cause a recital to be made before me, how many they have destroyed of their own heads, and how many they have delivered up to destruction, that I may have this testimony against them. I may know all their proceedings; and that, delivering the sheep to them, I may see what they will do, whether they will act as I have commanded them, or not. Of this, however, they shall be ignorant; neither shall you make any explanation to them, neither shall you reprove them; even so, there shall be an account of all the destruction done by them in their respective seasons.

Then they began to kill, and destroy more than it was commanded them." I now know who this Saint was as he began to manifest all but his face. I then cried out, "Is that you Enoch?" He answered, "Yes, my queen; I have come to you as per the wishes of the great one of the Empires of Good and Light. He then told me, "A greater light could join the lesser light, for only darkness can divide them. Our walk shall be in the purest of lights as I share great mysteries with you. You, who have labored, shall wait in those days, until the evil doers are erased, and the power of the guilty be annihilated. Wait, until the darkness passes away; for their names shall be blotted out of the holy books; their seed shall be destroyed, and their spirits slain. They shall cry out and lament in the invisible waste, and in the bottomless darkness. There I witnessed, so to speak, a cloud that could not be seen through; for from the depth of it, I was unable to look upwards. I beheld also a flame of fire blazing brightly, and, to some extent, glittering mountains whirled around, and agitated from side to side.

He said, "There, in that place which you behold, shall be thrust into the spirits of darkness and the wicked; of those who shall do evil, and who shall pervert all, which light has spoken by the mouth of the prophets; all, which they ought to do. Respecting these things, there shall be writings and impressions above in the heavens. That the angels may read them and know what shall happen both in darkness and to the spirits of the humble, and those who have suffered in their bodies, but have been rewarded by Light. Those who have been injuriously treated by wicked men, who have loved Light, who have been attached neither to gold nor silver, nor to any good thing in the world; however, I have given their bodies to torment, to those from the period of their birth who have not been covetous of physical riches. Nevertheless, they have regarded themselves as a breath passing away. Such has been their conduct; and much has the Light tried them; and their spirits have been found pure, that they might bless her name. All their blessings have I related in a truth; and she has rewarded them, for they have been found to love heaven with an everlasting aspiration."

The Light has said, "While they have been trodden down by wicked men, they have heard from them slandering and blasphemies; and have been cruelly treated, while they were blessing her. Now will I call the spirits of the righteous from the generation of light, and will change those who have been born in darkness, who with glory, as their faith may have merited. I will bring them into the splendid light of those who love my holy name: and I will place each of them on a throne of glory, of glory peculiarly her own and they shall be at rest during unnumbered periods. Righteous is the only judgment of Light. Dark shall forever be in emptiness and dark, as she will shatter them into all the universes never to be joined again. For to the faithful she shall give faith to the habitations of uprightness. They shall see those, who have been born in darkness into darkness shall be cast, while the righteous shall be at rest. Reprobates shall cry out, beholding them, while they exist in splendor and proceed forward to the days, and periods prescribed to them. These are the leaders of the chiefs of the thousands, those that preside over all creations, and over all the stars; with the four days, which are added and never separated from the place, allotted them according to the complete calculation of their year. Respecting them, men greatly err, for these prodigies truly serve, in the dwelling place of the world, one day in the first gate, one in the third gate, one in the fourth gate, and one in the sixth gate. The harmony of the world's becomes complete in every three hundred state of it."

For the signs, she showed me; the Queen of Queens appointed over all the galaxies. Of heaven of the heavens, and in the worlds that they might rule in the face of the sky, and appearing over the galaxies, become conductors of the days and nights: the suns, the moons, the stars, and all the ministers of heaven, which make their circuit with all the chariots of the heavens. Thus, she showed me gates open in the circuit of the chariots of the suns in the heavens, from which the rays of the suns shoot forth. This proceeds heat over the worlds and the secret passage to the greater universes, when they are opened in their stated reasons. They are for the winds and the spirit of the dew, when in their seasons; they are opened, opened in the heavens at its extremities. Tens of thousands gates I beheld in the heavens, at the extremities of the worlds, through which the suns, moons, and stars, and all the works of heaven, proceed at their rising and setting. Many windows also are open on the right and on the left. One window at a certain purpose grows extremely hot. Hereafter, also are there gates from which the stars go forth as they are commanded, and in which they set according to their number.

She showed me, likewise, the chariots of the heavens, running in the world above to those gates in which the stars turn, which never set. One of these is greater, which goes around the unabridged worlds. Moreover, at the extremities of the creations, I beheld the gates open for all the winds, from which they proceed and blow over of creation biospheres. Some of them are unclosed in the front of the heavens, some in the west, some on the right side of the heavens, and some on the left. The first are those, which are towards the east; the second are towards the north, and the third is behind those which are upon the left, towards the south, and lastly on the west. From them proceeds, winds of blessing, and of health, and from others proceed winds of punishment. When they are sent to destroy the darkness, from the heavens above, all its inhabitants, and all which are in the waters, or on dry land. The first of these winds proceeds from the gate designated the east, through the initial gate on the east, which inclines southwards. From this proceeds obliteration, famine, torridness, and punishment. From the second gate, the middle one, proceeds equity. They issue from it rain, fruitfulness, health, and dew; and from the third gate northwards, proceed cold and drought. After these proceed, the south winds through three principal gates, through their first gate, which inclines eastwards, proceeds a hot wind.

However, from the middle gate proceeds grateful odor, condensation, deluge, vigor, and existence. From the last gates, which are westwards, proceeds dew, rain, blight, and destruction. After these, there are winds to the north, which are called the aquatic. They proceed from the gates. The first gate is that which is on the east, inclining southwards; from this proceeds precipitation, volley, affliction, and devastation.

From the middle direct, gate proceeded rain, dew, life, and health. In addition, from the third gate, which is westwards, inclining towards the south, proceed mist, frost, snow, rain, damage, and blight. After these in the fourth quarter are the winds to the west. From the first gate, inclining northwards, proceeds dew, rain, frost, cold, snow, and chill, from the middle gate proceeds rain, health, and blessing, and from the last gate, which is southwards, proceeds scarcity, destruction, blackening, and inferno.

The account of the gates of the four quarters of the heavens is ended. All their laws, all their inflictions of punishment, and the health produced by them, have I elucidated to you. The first wind is called the eastern, because it is the original. The second is called the south, because the Most High there descends, and frequently there descends she who will be blessed forever. The western wind has the name of diminution, because there all the luminaries of the heavens are diminished, and descend. The fourth wind, which is named the north, is divided into many parts; one of which is for the habitation of man; another for seas of water, with valleys, woods, rivers, shady places, and snow; and the third part contains paradise. Seven high mountains I beheld, higher than all the mountains of the world, from which frost proceeds; while days, seasons, and years depart and pass away. Seven rivers she beheld on each of her worlds, greater than all rivers, one of which takes its course from the west; into a great sea, its water flows. Two come from the north to the sea, their waters flowing into the sea, on the east. With respect to the remaining four, they take their course in the cavity of the north; two to their sea, and two are poured into a great sea, where also it is said there is a desert. "And the mountains shall be molten under Him, and the valleys shall be cleft, as wax before the fire, and as the waters that are poured down a steep place." She took and brought me to a place in which those who were there were like flaming fire, and when they wished, they appeared as men.

They then brought me to the place of darkness, and to a mountain, the point of whose summit reached into the heavens. In addition, I saw the places of the luminaries and the treasuries of the stars and of the thunder and in the uttermost depths, where was a fiery bow and arrows and their quiver, and a fiery sword and all the lightning. They took me to the living waters, and to the fire of the west, which receives every setting of the suns. I came to a river of fire in which the fire flows like water and discharges itself into the great sea towards the west. I saw the angels have hermaphrodite higher-dimensional bodies; they have no need for reproduction, for they live forever, and have been created with the necessary psychological and mental male and female components that make them complete. According to this, evil spirits are what remain, when the bodies of those descended from the wicked angels die; this does imply that humans have an ethereal spirit, popularly, and occult, called the "soul," the foundation of spiritualism. We saw the treasuries of all the winds: I saw how she furnished with them, the whole creation, and the firm foundations of the worlds. I saw the cornerstone of the ultimate power; I saw the four winds, which bear the firmament of the heavens. I saw how the winds stretch out the vaults of heaven, and have their station between the heavens and biospheres.

These are the pillars of the heavens. I saw the winds of heaven, which turn and bring the circumference of the suns and all the stars to their setting. I saw the winds on the worlds carrying the clouds. I saw the paths of the angels. I saw the ends of Mars, Venus and so many other worlds in the Milky Way. I now looked at Enoch and asked, "How can this be?" Enoch spoke saying, "The Mountains that they did climb and the rivers from where they drank were from the dark, and darkness spread so deep and wide that the great lights had to save the smaller dying lights from within our Milky Way. When a light must destroy so much dark, it shall become faint; and is ultimately consumed by the darkness. Yet, if a greater light shines on it, the lesser light shall become at one with the greater light." I then asked again, "What does this truly mean?" He now looked at me and spoke again, as his eyes of love sent new energy into my troubled soul, "It is not the time for you to know, for first you must tell your story and when the time is chosen, I will come for you. Fear not, for you shall be saved. You may speak this truth to no one, for she shall hide it deep inside you so the mystery shall not be discovered. She has chosen you, as you have searched for and elected her." I then asked, "When did I chose her, for I have only chosen the throne for which I have loved since my soul was created?" He said to me, "When the mystery is revealed, you shall discover that the light inside you shall never change, for it will effortlessly be given more light so you may fight darkness."

I now turned back to that which had surrounded me, and I saw the firmament of the heavens above. I proceeded and saw a place, which burns day and night, where there are seven mountains of magnificent stones, three towards the east, and three towards the south. As for those towards the east, was of colored stone, and one of pearl, and one of the jacinth, and those towards the south of red stone. Nevertheless, the middle one reached to the heavens like the throne of Good, of alabaster, and the summit of the throne was of sapphire. I saw a flaming fire. Beyond these mountains is a region meeting the end of the great heavens, there the heavens were completed. I saw a deep abyss, with columns of heavenly fire, and among them, I saw columns of fire fall, which were beyond measure corresponding to the height and towards the depth. Beyond that abyss, I saw a place that had no firmament of the heavens above, and no firmly founded world beneath it: there was no water upon it, and no birds, but it was a devastated and horrible place. I saw there seven stars like great burning mountains, and to me, when I inquired regarding them, she said, "This place is the end of the heavens of your Milky Way, this has become a prison for the stars and the host of heaven.

The stars, which roll over the fire are they, which have transgressed the commandment of the Light in the beginning of their rising, because they did not come forth at their appointed times. She was wroth with them, and bound them until the time when their guilt should be consummated for tens of billion's years." She said to me, "Here shall stand the angels who have connected themselves with women, and their spirits assuming many different forms were defiling mankind and shall lead them astray into sacrificing to demons as gods. For here shall they stand, until the day of the great judgment, which they shall be judged until they have made a termination. The women also of the angels who went astray shall become sirens." In addition, we saw the vision, the ends of all things, and no man shall see as we have seen. We saw the mountains of the darkness of winter and the place whence all the waters of the deep flow. We saw the mouths of all the rivers of the worlds and the mouth of the deep. We saw the treasuries of all the winds. We saw how she furnished with them, her whole creation, and the firm foundations of the worlds. Moreover, I saw the cornerstone of the biospheres, "We saw the four winds which bear the firmament of the heavens. In addition, we saw how the winds stretch out the vaults of heaven, and have their station between the heavens and worlds; these are the pillars of the heavens. We saw the winds of the heavens, which turn and bring the circumference of the suns and all the stars to their setting.

We saw the winds on the biospheres carrying the clouds; we saw the paths of the angels. We saw at the ends of the worlds the firmament of the heavens above. We then proceeded and saw a place, which burns day and night, where there are seven mountains of magnificent stones, three towards the east, and three towards the south. Notwithstanding, as for those towards the east, was of colored stone, and one of pearl, and one of the jacinth, and those towards the south of green stone. Nevertheless, the middle one reached to heaven like the throne of the gods, of alabaster, and the summit of the throne was of cerulean. We saw a flaming fire. Beyond these mountains is a region the end of the great world; there the heavens were completed. We saw a deep abyss, with columns of heavenly fire, and among them, we saw columns of fire fall, which were beyond measure alike towards the height and towards the depth. Beyond that abyss, we saw a place, which had no firmament of the heavens above, and no firmly founded world beneath it: there was no water upon it, and no birds, but it was a waste and horrible place.

We saw there seven stars like great burning mountains, and to me, when we inquired regarding them, the angel said, "This place is the end of your heaven and world; this has become a prison for the intergalactic and the host of heaven. The stellar, which roll over the fire, are they, which have transgressed the commandment of the Ancient One in the beginning of their rising, because they came forth at their appointed times. She was wroth with them, and bound them until the time when their guilt should be consummated for ten thousand years.

We proceeded to where things were chaotic. We saw there something horrible; we saw neither a heaven above nor a firmly founded world, but a place chaotic and horrible. There we saw seven stars of the great heaven bound together in it, like pronounced mountains and burning with fire." Next Enoch asked, "For what sins are they bound, and on what account they have been cast in here?" Then one of the holy angels pronounced, who was with us, and was chief over them, "Why do you ask, and why art thou eager for the truth? These are of the number of the stars of heavens, which have transgressed the commandment of the Spirit of the Queen, and are bound here until a thousand vigintillion years; the time entailed by their sins, originally to be consummated by the lake of fire, now to be vanished from all who are. From thence we went to another place, which was even more horrible than the former, and we saw a horrid thing; a extreme fire there which burnt and blazed, and the place was cleft as far as the abyss, being full of great descending columns of fire; neither its extent or magnitude could I see, nor could I conjecture.

Then I said, 'How fearful is the place and how terrible to look upon!' Subsequently she answered me, one of the holy angels who was with me, and said unto us, "Why hast thou such as fear and so afraid?" I answered "Because of this dreadful place, and because of the spectacle of the pain." She said unto me, "This place is the prison of the angels, and here they will be imprisoned until they shall be erased forever." I then asked, "Why after that is there such a place if they are to be erased?" The holy angel said to us, "These places existed in the time before the queen of queens desired that no seed of evil to exist, even in exile, among her sacred children."

Then we went to another place, to the mountain of hard rock. There were in it four hollow places, deep and wide and very smooth. How flowing are the sunken places, far down, and dark to look at? Then an angel answered, one of the holy angels who was with us, and said, "These hollow places have been created for this very purpose, that the spirits of the souls of the dead should assemble therein, yea that all the souls of the children of men should assemble here. These places have been made to receive them until the day of their judgment and until their appointed period, until the great judgment approaches upon them." We saw the spirit of a dead man making spirits, and his voice went forth to the heavens and made a spirit. I asked the angel the holy angel who was with us, and I said unto him, "This voice, which makes spirits, whose is it, whose voice goes forth and makes spirits to the heavens?" He answered me saying, "This is the spirit, which went forth from those righteous who were slain by evil. Moreover, they make their spirits against them until their seeds are destroyed from the faces of the worlds, and their seeds are annihilated from among the seeds of men" Then I asked regarding it, and regarding all the hollow places, "Why is one separated from the other?" He answered me and said to me, "These three have been made that the spirits of the dead might be separated.

Such a division has been made for the spirits of the righteous, in which there is the bright spring of water. Such has been made for sinners when they die, and are buried in the worlds, and judgment has not been executed on them in their lifetime. Here their spirits shall be set apart in this extreme pain until the great Day of Judgment and punishment, torment and erasing of those who curse forever and retribution for their spirits. There she shall bind them perpetually. Such a division has been made for the spirits of those who make their testimony, who make disclosures concerning their destruction, when they were slain in the days of the sinners. Such has been made for the spirits of men who were not righteous but sinners, who were complete in transgression, and of the transgressors, they shall be companions, but their spirits shall not be slain in the Day of Judgment nor shall they be raised from here." Then we blessed the Lord of glory and said, "Blessed be our Lord, the Lord of righteousness, who rules forever." From thence, we went to another place to the west of the ends of the biospheres. We saw a burning fire, which ran without resting, and paused not from its course day or night but burned regularly. I asked saying, "What is this, which rests not?"

Then one of the holy angels who was with us answered me, and said to me, "This course of fire, which you have seen is the fire in the west which persecutes all the luminaries of the heavens." From here, we went to another place of the atmospheres, and he showed me a mountain range of fire, which burnt day and night. We went beyond it and saw seven magnificent mountains differing each from the other. The stones thereof were magnificent and beautiful, magnificent as a whole, of glorious appearance and fair exterior, three towards the east, one founded on the other, and three towards the south, one upon the other, and deep rough ravines, no one of which joined with any other. The seventh mountain was in the midst of these, and it excelled them in height, resembling the seat of a throne: and fragrant trees encircled the throne. Among them was a tree such as, I had never yet smelt neither was any among them nor were others like it. It had a fragrance beyond all fragrance, and its leaves, blooms, and wood withered not forever. Its fruit is attractive, and its fruit resembles the dates of a palm. Then I said, "How beautiful is this tree, and fragrant, and its leaves are fair, and its blooms very delightful in appearance." It then answered one of the holy and honored angels who was with us and was their leader saying, "Tianshire, why dost thou ask me regarding the fragrance of the tree, and why dost thou wish to learn the truth?"

Then I answered him saying, "I wish to know about everything, but especially about this tree." He answered saying, "This high mountain which thou hast seen, whose summit is like the throne of the gods, is her throne, where the Holy Great One, the Lord of Glory, the Eternal King and Queen, will sit, when they shall come down to visit their worlds with blamelessness. As for this fragrant tree, no mortals are permitted to touch it until the pronounced judgment, when they shall take vengeance on all and bring everything to its consummation forever. It shall then be given to the righteous and consecrated. Its fruit shall be used for food to the elect; it shall be transplanted to the holy place, to the temples of the gods. Afterwards shall they rejoice with joy and be glad, into the holy place shall they enter; its fragrance shall be in their bones, as they shall live a long life on their worlds." I then asked him, "Why do they not end time now?" He answered me saying, "For they are still saving those who wish to be saved. All times in all the dimensions shall end at the appointed time. Next they shall live long lives in their worlds such as Enoch's fathers lived, and in their days shall be no sorrow, plague, torment, or calamity touches them as now the queen of queens have given to her children." Then we blessed the God of Glory, the Eternal King, for the queen I know not, who hath prepared such things for the righteous, and hath created them and promised to give to them.

We went from there to the middle of the old biospheres, and I saw a blessed place in which there were trees with branches abiding and blooming. There I saw a holy mountain, underneath the mountain to the east, there was a stream, and it flowed towards the south. I saw towards the east another mountain higher than this, and between them, a deep and narrow ravine; in it ran a stream underneath the mountain. To the west thereof, there was another mountain, lower than the former and of small elevation, and a ravine gaping and withered between them; and another deep and dry ravine was at the extremities of the three mountains. All the ravines were deep and narrow; being formed of hard rock, and trees were not planted upon them. I marveled at the rocks, and I marveled at the ravine, yea; I marveled very much. I then said I, "What object is this blessed land, which is entirely filled with trees, and this accursed valley between?" Then one of the holy angels who was with us, answered and said, "This accursed valley is for those who are doomed forever; here shall all the accursed be gathered together who utter with their lips against the Lord unseemly words and of his glory speak hard things. Here shall they be gathered with each other, and here shall be their place of judgment. In the last days, there shall be upon them the spectacle of righteous judgment in the presence of the righteous forever, here shall the merciful bless the Lord of glory, the Eternal King and his great servant. In the days of judgment over the former, they shall bless him for the mercy in accordance with which He has assigned them their lot."

Then I blessed the Lord of Glory, set forth His glory, and lauded Him gloriously. After that we went towards the east, into the midst of the mountain range of the desert, we saw a wilderness, and it was solitary, full of trees and plants. Water gushed forth from above. Rushing like a copious watercourse, which flowed towards the north-west, it caused clouds and dew to ascend on every side. Then I went to another place in the desert, and approached to the east of this mountain range. There we saw aromatic trees exhaling the fragrance of frankincense and myrrh, and the trees also were similar to the almond tree. Beyond these, we went afar to the east, and we saw another place, a valley full of water. Therein, there was a tree, the odor of fragrant trees such as the mastic. On the sides of those valleys, we smelt scented cinnamon. Beyond these, we proceeded to the east. We saw other mountains, and among them were groves of trees, and there flowed forth from them nectar, which is named Samara and galbanum.

Beyond these mountains, we saw another mountain to the east of the ends of the old biospheres, whereon aloe trees and all the trees were full of their harvests, being like almond-trees. When one burnt it, it smelt sweeter than any fragrant odor. After these sweet smelling odors, as we looked towards the north over the mountains, we saw seven mountains full of choice nard and fragrant trees and cinnamon and pepper. Behold the day cometh, that shall burn as an oven; and all the proud, yea, and all who do wickedly, shall stumble; and the day cometh shall burn them up.

Thence we went over the summits of all these mountains, far towards the east of the old biospheres, passed above a great Sea, went far from it, and passed over the Angel Zotiel. We came to the Garden of Righteousness, and from afar off trees more numerous than these trees and great-two trees there, very pronounced, beautiful, and glorious, and magnificent, and the tree of knowledge, whose holy fruit they eat and know pronounced wisdom. That tree is in height like the fir, its leaves are like those of the Carob tree, its fruit is like the clusters of the vine, very beautiful, and the fragrance of the tree penetrates far. Subsequently, I said, "How beautiful is the tree, and how attractive is its look!" Then one of the holy angels, who were with us, answered me, and said, "This is the tree of Wisdom. Those who are advanced in years, and thy aged mothers, who were before thee, have eaten, and they learnt wisdom and their eyes were opened, and they knew that they were naked, and they were driven out of the garden of the aged creations, as such was not the story only on behalf of New Venus. We gave fruit from this tree to you and Oi, that yours messages onto those who followed you should be great."

From there, we went to the ends of the biospheres and saw their great beasts, each differed from the other, and we saw birds also differing in appearance and beauty and voice, the one differing from the other. To the east of those beasts, we saw the ends of the biospheres wherein the heavens rest and the portals of the heavens open. We saw how the stars of heaven come forth, and we counted the portals out of which they proceeded, and wrote down all their outlets, of everyone star by itself, according to their number and their names, their courses and their positions, and their times and their months, as the holy angel who was with us showed us. He showed all things to us and wrote them down for us, their names he wrote for us, and their laws and their companies. From there, we went towards the north to the ends of the biospheres, and there we saw a great and glorious device at the ends of the whole biospheres. Here we saw three portals of heaven open in the heavens, through each of them proceed north winds, when they blow there is cold, hail, frost, snow, dew, and rain. Out of one portal, they blow for good; however, when they blow through the other two portals, it is with violence and affliction on the biospheres, and they blow with violence.

From there, we went to the west to the ends of the old biospheres, and saw there three portals of the heaven uncovered such as, I saw in the east, the identical number of portals, and the same number of outlets. From thence, we went to the south to the ends of the biospheres, and saw there three open portals of the heavens, and there come dew, rain, and wind.

From thence, we went to the east to the ends of the heaven, and saw here the three eastern portals of heaven open and small portals above them. Through each of these small portals pass the stars of heaven and run their course to the west on the path, which is shown to them. As often as we saw, we blessed always the Lord of Glory, and we continued to bless the Lord of Glory who has brought great and glorious wonders, to show the greatness of His work to the angels, to spirits, and to people, that they might praise His work and all His creations. They might see the work of His might, praise the great work of His hands, and bless Him forever.

The second voice I heard blessing the Ancient One, and the elect ones who hang upon the Lord of Spirits. The third voice I heard prays and intercedes for those who dwell on the biospheres and beseech by the name of the Lord of Spirits. I heard the fourth voice scourging off the Demons and Devils and forbidding them to come before the Lord of Spirits to accuse them who dwell on the worlds. After that, I asked the angel of peace who went with me, who showed me everything that is hidden, "Who are these four presences which I have seen and whose words I have heard and written down?" He said to me, "This first is Michael, the merciful and long-suffering. The second, who is set over all the diseases and all the wounds of the children of men, is Raphael. The third, who is set over all the powers, is Gabriel, and the fourth, who is set over the repentance unto hope of those who inherit eternal life, is named Phanuel, whose name means the face of God. The four voices that we heard in those days are the four angels of the Lord of Spirits." I now confessed to Enoch that I did not know about these four angels, having never met them all my days on the throne.

He explained that in the heavens with the Saints, they serve. I then asked why we were sometimes told about a King and Queen of Queens, afterwards only a King and a King and his mighty servant. He then explained that different judgments took place in the distinctive thrones. Our vision was from unlike places and at distinct times. I then asked him, "Why have they shown this to me?" He explained, "As you tell your story, you may see things now that you saw before but did not know. You must be careful when you speak about the Lord of New Venus." I wanted to know why and Enoch told me, "Since her spirit has vanished, the eternal laws of the heavens will not let us speak of her. You may speak about her in your story, yet only about recorded events or personal feelings." I next confessed, "This vision has confused about my mind, for one minute I am seeing rich blue rivers and seas, subsequently I am looking, deep down, into valleys.

Will I ever put it together and discover a truth?" He told me as he was preparing to leave, "The truth changes as more is seen, the truth of yesterday died and a new truth for today lives. Die not with the truth of yesterday, but share the truth of today. It will come together when our Queen of Queens saves us. Speak for no person or spirit about this vision today, not even our Lord." I asked why I could not tell our Lord, and he told me, "If you tell our Lord, you could risk their salvation and new throne as greater than they wish them not to fall slaves to be evil. Speak not of this anymore." I at no time wanted anything bad to happen to our throne another time, as they deserved to be saved from the darkness that gave us only sadness and defeat, thus I agreed not at any time to speak of this once more, until we meet again.

As they all departed into the sea, I found myself drifting back into emptiness. Somehow, I was traveling through time, as if now to become trapped within it as I was during my days of soma. So many things were flashing before my eyes as I could see my story was soon to begin. I could only see those images that appeared unto me, for I could not speak with those within them. I so wonder why my story would be important, for others also suffered hard for our throne.

Then a voice spoke unto me saying, "Worry not of the value of your story, for those who sit upon the thrones have commissioned you. This story you give so that other children of our Lord may feast upon the wisdom of your words." I then asked, "Where do I begin?" They divulged to me with words of thunder, "Began with was we give unto you." I then answered, "I do this only if it brings glory to our Lord." Now, a crowd of voices shook my foundation by saying, "It brings great glory to our Lord." As their words finished, I fell into a deep sleep.

Chapter 02

The Before That Befell, And Oi

I now slowly began to revive from my deep sleep. I looked all around me and could see nothing. All was empty and cold. Subsequently, I could feel a strong wind pushing at me, and lights flash by as if arrows with tips of fire. Instantly, I was in the center of many circles of stars. I wondered what these could be, thus going against the wind I pushed towards the nearest cluster. Soon, I could determine it to be as a spiral wheel of many lights.

I saw a solid bolt of lightning strike down deep inside one of the spokes in this giant spiral. Voices from within me were saying, "Thou heavens are created; we shall now go forth and create the worlds for your image to be tested." I followed what appeared to be as a lightning bolt into the clusters and saw our sun's heat being adjusted and the planets being formed. All the small balls of flame were being cooled as a huge breath old cold wind blew over them, pulling all save one from its prodigious grip. I could see giant white creatures, such as. I have never before seen, pulling the other worlds out to their newly determined circles.

Once in position, these creatures spun them, as would proceed a ball, and placed them in these circles of energy that they called orbits. Just four of the small balls of flame that circled it were now having life blown upon them. At this time, one of the creatures came towards me and revealed, "Fear not Tianshire, for you are in a vision from, He who sits upon the Throne. We have been commanded to reveal unto you what it is that we are doing. We now prepare four worlds for life, and shall prepare the world you came from, New Venus, which will replace the current one, and place yours in the contemporary circle that holds the world, which was called Earth.

However, that will be executed much later. What we do now is create all that shall be here and program the age it will appear and how it will progress. Four worlds will have their circles close to the warmth from the sun in which life my form. Life shall go as follows; Jupiter shall be given fire-life beings of fire, called the Difemoun. Saturn shall be given bodies, such as talking guerrillas, called the Makak. Mars shall be given angels of the anointed Cherub (morning star). Jupiter fell, thus their fires were joined by the great fire of the sun. The Makak feel having within them no love for the Lord. Great plagues destroyed them as the Lord put rings around Saturn to warn others never to enter for the plaque still lives among the rocks therein. Mars was scarred with many meteors greater than those were of the judgments on the Old Earth.

Those fallen angels, who were the most sophisticated and picturesque of all the Ancient Ones' creations, became wolves dressed in sheep's clothing to fall upon humanity of the Earth. Their original purpose was to accuse those who walked the Earth, as a method to prevent any future surprise raids upon the throne. This failed, as instead they become the teachers of the forbidden fruit and was the deceivers.

The first Earth shall be given humanity in the image of our God inside and the fallen from Mars. The New Earth shall only be given the righteous images of God. Your New Venus shall be given humanity in the image of our God, and a Lord has chosen by He who sits upon the Throne. These images, who die in righteousness, shall join those on the new Earth living for eternity with all the righteous images of God." I understood this, while serving as a Queen. Eve told us many stories and actually was the one who introduced me to Enoch.

What I never truly understood was the breathing in the life into dust portion. These guides started to explain this, as I watched another type of beings who were quite advanced racing through our solar system. They said to me, "You now see the planters, who were sent by the Ancient One to store flesh upon very few select worlds. These are those who were spoken of by Mempire's messenger of the past, "The king put my existence into an instrument, which I can always be and shall ever not be, as long as I serve inside his instrument allowing him to share his message with all who were of the planters." Some worlds will receive the breath of the Ancient One, while others will evolve as animals. Earth and New Venus received these shells. The ones stored on Venus, and Earth were placed deep inside to keep them from decomposing, as their appointed times have not arrived. I saw two placed on each, and to my amazement on Earth, a man named Adam received one shell and my Lord, while still stained with evil, was placed on the other. I asked, "Why does only one receive the breath?" They answered, "That is the way through the ages. The spirit of your Lord was pulled from Lamenta, being deceived by the horrendous deceiver. She was later released, and a woman made from his rib named Eve was made the mother of the Earth." I told them, "This thing I know, yet Eve never told me why she came to New Venus to once again be a mother to humanity." The messengers told me, "Those who were her children on Earth greatly disappointed her in their abundance in their volumes of evil and hate that they manifested.

Upon your world, the two planted by the planters died while only having Eve as a child. The heavens feared when she was born that with such hatred and murder already in the blood that the future generations would be worse than that of Earth. Thus, in order to prevent their total destruction, your Lord begged the throne to breathe Eve into the new child. Eve agreed, and the child was given her spirit. A few seasons had passed when the angels asked the Ancient One, "How can only Eve create the new generation from her sisters?"

The Ancient One asked Eve if she wanted to have her family that would be flesh of her flesh. She gladly begged the Ancient One, "I must bear fruit in my womb. Can you put a seed in my womb?" The Ancient One then told her, "The seed will need a father, thus I shall make a man for you from your ribs, and he shall be called Aman and shall be righteous in his ways." I knew their story so very well, as my father, the father of sin told how his brother, the father of righteousness became the slave of an evil goddess.

My father may now walk among the heavens with great honor of his son Oi and myself were among the greatest lovers of the word ever to walk upon New Venus. We currently began to review the days of my life.

The first view reveals me talking to my brother, and I hear the words as recorded by the Lord of my World, "Then she replied: "My brother is no longer living on this world; he is living with the Lord now, and his name was Oi. "Tianshire prayed beside Oi every minute she could, and Oi often told her that her love for the Lord was as deep as his was. When Oi ascended into heaven, Tianshire kept her faith and lived owning nothing . . . she had all of his writings memorized, and would quote them from her memory and through her heart. One never had to fear demons when Tianshire was among them, because the angels would manifest themselves, almost daily around her . . . there was no mystery of the spiritual word for her as she saw Oi ascend to the heavens. Of course, Oi would aid her occasionally and congratulate her for the outstanding ministry she had established . . . all could see a decent fight against evil and all believed that "good" would win. They believed the power came from Oi who was saving the people who saved him. For Oi could never do anyone wrong. Could this Saint be better? . . . these scouts saw Tianshire's inordinate works. They knew with every fiber of their bodies that she was doing the Lord's work, and all had heard from Oi how the Lord had great mercy . . . build temples for the Lord God and teach your young the things that Oi, and I have taught you . . . Tianshire said unto them: "Ask the Lord to pick one, and he shall tell you who he has picked." I must now leave you. Then did they say, "Blessed is Belcher, for he is the father of Oi and Tianshire." Oi was a miracle, yet to add Tianshire from the same father was absolutely a blessing that no man outside the garden had ever enjoyed . . . The teachings of Oi and Tianshire was only one of the skills they developed . . . the black land's tribe had been the victim of intense evil and the temporary homes of two of the greatest saints to live outside the garden, Oi and Tianshire.

No can ever argue the holiness of Oi and Tianshire, being the pride of this land's claims to prophets and saints . . . We must strive each day to be worthy to live in the land that once Belcher, Oi & Tianshire worshiped the Lord on . . . Go and bring great pride to the Heavens in the name of your Lord and Oi and Tianshire and for the Lord's people . . . As the beast of the sky headed for the Queen's temple she demanded that all stand fast and pray to the Lord that he bring the temple with them as they enter the heavens to be with Oi and Tianshire . . . Oi and Tianshire never said they were wrong for the way they believed, for they were a peace loving people . . . Remember that Oi and Tianshire loved the Lord more than life, for if you love your life more than the Lord you will parish as did the Garden of Eden . . . Then among the chosen elders who had assembled around the thrown, did Queen Tianshire, one of the three Supreme Queens say unto all, "I elect Queen Boudica to go forth and fight this battle."

Then did Oi say aloud: "Queen Boudica will guarantee us a victory . . . Then did Queen Tianshire and Oi say unto the Lord: "Let us call her into the heavens and ask her. We shall put her in hell for a few hours before she comes before you and tells her that would be her eternity. After that did the Lord in sadness agree, for even the Lord God knew that Queen Boudica would save the throne and Venus . . . subsequently and Tianshire dropped the lovely Queen into the harshest pits of Hell. However, as she burned in a pain that only evil would know about, all could see a smile upon her face, as she sang praises to the Lord. This did anger demons also imprisoned there, yet no matter what they did, she would not stop singing her praises to her Lord God.

All in heaven were so amazed, saying, "We have only seen this kind of love from Saint Oi and Supreme Queen Tianshire . . . Supreme Queen Tianshire and Saint Oi agreed, as heaven rejoiced . . . the galaxies were singing great praises as they were being shown the mighty credentials of a queen no one had ever heard of before. Nevertheless, when all considered that she was a child of the Supreme Queen Eve (through Belcher), from the same nation as Saint Oi and Supreme Queen Tianshire the grandchildren of the Supreme Queen Eve, became even more amazed."

Oi begins black land tribe's mission

I was very much surprised by the many tales that the Lord had recorded and asked these messengers if I could have some time to reflect on these great memories. I remember that everywhere I went all would speak to my brother. We traveled through Belcher's prison in a crisis and later the black lands. We faced so much vulnerability in our home lands that we were forced to leave. The demons tormented our audiences and us so that we could see no hope for our ministry; therefore, we escaped into the black lands.

The initial days were not favorable as we were received for what we represented and when they discovered who our mother was we were then in extreme jeopardy. We were imprisoned, stoned, and beaten in public, with crowds demanding our execution. We did not resist nor speak out against them. This impressed some of the military guards who decided to take us deeper into the nation for our protection. When we arrived at our first town, we were placed in a temporary secret prison. When the people discovered us, they came and destroyed the prison taking us out into their open streets to stone us to our deaths; however, this time things were different. As each stone came to us, it dropped before us. Soon the entire village was trying to stone us, yet none could succeed. The guards came and tried to take us to safety, yet Oi refused and instead began talking about the people.

He told them that the hate inside of them would destroy them. He then asked, "Who is the wicked here, the ones being hit by the stones, in which the heavens protect, or the ones who throw the stones, giving their hearts to the evil that they worship?" When some elders heard this, they through down their stones and walked in another place. Soon, the others began to walk aside. Oi then cried out, "Do you not want to hear the good news that I bring to you?" A few stayed to listen, one of which was a sightless old man. Oi asked him, "Why are you unsighted?" The old man told him, "I am blind to the evil that my parents did." Oi told him, "Your parents did not do evil, thus you are not blind." When Oi told the old man these words, the elderly man could see again. He ran through the village telling everyone that the stone stoppers had given him back his sight. All the people rushed to Oi and me, as we were still outside the village talking to the guards who now refused to take us to a prison saying to us, "We will not put well in where the bad are to be." This was strange to us, in that we had always heard how evil the black land's people were, yet they had an unwritten moral system far beyond that of my mother's servants.

The people rushed back out of the village and asked, "Did you give back this man his eyesight?" Oi answered, "How can I give back that which I did not take?" They after that asked, "Did you give him his eyesight?" Oi then answered, "He claimed that his blindness was for the evil that his parents had done, I saw no evil in them, thus told him he could not be blind. He then accepted the eyesight than the Lord had given him upon his birth. It was him freeing himself from the chains of evil that restored his eyesight." They then said, "We know that only the righteous can do miracles for the good, for if evil does it their empire will fall. We now know that you are of righteousness and ask that you forgive us." Oi then said, "Neither, I or my little sister has any bad feelings towards you. We both may enjoy much peace." Then one woman said, "You speak many wise words, will you share more with us so that we may know the righteous and bring them no harm?"

Oi then said, "That is why we came to your lands, so that you may all be righteous and suffer not from the evil of the forbidden lands." They all knew Belcher's prison as the prohibited lands for whosoever would enter and return would be cursed with blue skin. Oi added, "My Lord, the Lord of the Garden of Eden, has seen much suffering in your lands and now wants to prepare the road that you may all be saved and someday your children may live as the Lord wants for them." They then asked, "What can we do to get this safety for our new generations?" Oi said, "I shall teach all in the black lands how to seek the Lord."

As we traveled from one small village to another small village, many would come to listen to us teach. I also taught much of the same things as I recorded each message he shared with us. Soon, the valleys would be packed with people who were so hungry for safety from Rubina's raids.

One time while he spoke many demons flooded the area screaming out that all who were there would be eaten alive. Oi looked up and said, "Oh God of Eve, deliver those who are here today in your name whom we may serve your many more days." At that time, all the demons began burning and begged Oi to have mercy on them. Oi said unto them, "You shall have the mercy in which you have given." They all burned and fell upon the ground, as none in the group had suffered, not even a scratch. From those days forward, the demons no longer bothered us while in the black lands. Instead, they forced Rubina to send her soldiers, who in order that those of the black lands would cast out Oi and me, would torture and kill all that they could find. Rubina found herself dismayed how these actions forced the black lands to engage in war against her troops.

Those who ventured in too far for steady supplies never returned. They now, in defense of their lands would lay an ambush to Rubina's troops, as they would raid. These ambushes would never plan to survive, as less than twenty could be counted upon to kill up to one hundred invaders. This also made the invaders restless, not knowing when the next ambush would come, as no route was ever safe for them to invade. This caused many commanders to move at a turtle's pace taking every precaution. They could travel through no hills or mountains, as the black land's archers would pick them off randomly from distances too far ever to catch them. The black land's would also starve wild beasts and then release them on the raiding armies. Nevertheless, Rubina continued to raid, both by land and by sea. The sea soon found itself prey to unforeseen dangers, as the black lands would send divers to the ships after the raiders had reached shore, and burn the ships. Rubina's marine force would be trapped and thus try to wiggle back to their homelands past all the ambushes. Some never returned. Those who did speak of terrifying things, as the black land fighters would dissect the dead enemy and plant their body parts along the return routes.

This added a sense of fear in the escaping raiders. The people had asked Oi once, "What should we do? Should we fight or turn our other cheeks?" Oi told them, "An evil as great as this must be fought, for not to do so will only force others who are righteous to stumble and surrender to be evil. I would never fight unless I knew the Lord was on my side. You can believe that as long as you fight the evil of Rubina, the Lord shall be on your side. This will be a long fight, as you are now only beginning your journey. I shall tell you that one day; one among us shall lead your people to victory." They then asked, "Will those be you, oh great prophet chosen by the God of Eve?" He looked at them and said, "It shall be one who is greater than I am." I never knew from that time he was talking about me, as neither did any in the crowds who asked him these questions.

Their lands suffered much from famine, as it had ravaged them for many years. They were filled with too much fear to grow crops, as the raiders would search for fields of crops and then kill all in the area, searching until they found them. They believed that crops were evidence that people lived near them. Oi told the people that. "We must trust him without fear the days of our lives. Without this trust, our days will be few." He now told the people to plant the crops in smaller fields away from where they lived. A horse can help bring the food to them. The people who lived outside the area had to plan where to put the fields as to enable them to establish strong and secret ambushes. Those who stole food could never be allowed to get that food back into Belcher's prison. Having smaller fields spread out would weaken their ability to protect themselves. They also had to ensure that no-good fruit were on any trees along their raids, as he often heard his mother talk about feeding those on her ships from the fruit of the lands.

The black land's people had discovered ways to dry the fruits, so they could eat them over a prolonged period. This new war strategy would allow them to save the fruit they striped from the trees and eat them while they waited for the crops to harvest. Oi told them, "An invader who is hungry must return home early and may not invade deeper into their lands." The people spread this strategy to all their tribes. The people were now doing something; they had never before done, and that was working together and talking with each other. In the past, they were so filled with fear that they avoided each other thinking larger groups would lead them to greater dangers. They were still too afraid to form armies. Oi would never see them overcome this great fear. So much of his teachings was about fear, which gave me the solid foundation to rally the battle cry towards the end of my ministry.

I remember him consistently saying, "The Lord is my light and my salvation, whom shall I fear and The Lord is the stronghold of my life, of whom shall I be afraid?" The people invariably loved when he told them this, as he could tie in the Lord being the light for them and their salvation, and thus who could ever defeat one who was in his light. They would ask him, "How can we make the God of Eve the stronghold in our lives?" They knew we had done so by being among them with no fear. Oi also clarified that they should not fear, for the Lord was now with them, and he would strengthen them and uphold them with his righteous right hand.

He told us he asked the Lord were such things as, "He might dwell in the house of the Lord all the days of my life, to gaze on the beauty of the Lord and to seek him in his temple. For in the day of trouble he will keep me safe in his dwelling; he will hide me in the shelter of his temple and set me high on a rock." This was their foundation, which they would always use to justify building temples." They asked, "How can we dwell in the house of the Lord when we have no temples to gaze upon his beauty?" He qualified, "The Lord knows you have no temples, thus until you are free from the demons on the other side of this large land, all the black land shall be his temple." Therefore, when the days of trouble arrive, he may sit you in the high places among the rocks and hide you in these lands. For they shall look upon you and see you not, as our God is our refuge and strength and always present with help when we are in trouble."

The people wanted so much to war against Rubina and asked Oi if he blessed them. He told them not to be anxious about anything, but in everything seek an answer in prayer being always thankful for what they had received, for the peace of God would transcend all understanding and guard their hearts and minds. We know that the time had yet to arrive that the black lands can fight an evil such as Rubina in her courts. Is it now wiser to protect what the Lord has given us to include the wives and children? Life is more than food and the body further than clothes."

Consider all the beautiful wild flowers, and how they grow. They do not labor nor worry. They grow, share their beauty, and fade away for the winter, yet when spring arrives the once again create their beauty. Let us now share the beauty of the wonderful words our God is giving us. We shall use these words to make the soil that we are planted in order to rise again in greater numbers and finer beauty."

I was always moved as much as the crowds that now followed us. I never truly understood why Oi and I was the only among our siblings to follow our father. We would go through the forests to some secret places of our father, and there he would tell us so many wonderful stories. He warned us about the evil that was growing in our mother. She was a commander of the most heartless killers in the early history of New Venus. They would raid all over the planet killing and stealing. We often asked him, "Why did you marry her?" He told us that in all the years he suffered here alone, she was the only female ever to appear. She had given him many sons and daughters and for this, he was thankful. None of my sisters followed him, for they like all my other brothers, save two followed my mother. Oi and our younger brother Tsarsko loved our father. Tsarsko saw how the other brothers would try to beat on Oi and thus would only join us when we went out during the nights for some special meetings. I truly began to believe in our Lord when I witnessed how he protected Oi. My other brothers could never defeat him, as even when they hit him, they would end up with a broken hand and Oi not in spite of a small bruise. This always angered our mother so much.

Belcher, our father, warned us how evil can destroy even the strongest man. It can make you blind, and take away your mind then easily deceiving you. When it takes your mind, it will do some terrible evil thing that you will receive the punishment. He was naturally talking about how the spider had tricked him into eating the fruit. He warned that if evil tries to touch you hit it hard and ask the Lord to curse it, because once evil gets inside you, the Lord can, then only see the evil when he looks at you. The Lord will not bless or protect evil.

Our father spent all his days begging the Lord to forgive him and allow him to return into the garden. Oi once told me that the Lord could not let him return into the garden for the evil that was inside Rubina. Belcher was a righteous man, as he would take Oi, myself to the borders with the black lands. He told us that Oi, and my future lay among those tribes. He also warned that if something happened to him, for us to flee into the black lands immediately. I asked him about Tsarsko. He told me not to worry about him, for the Lord had told him that Tsarsko would be saved.

I often found myself struggling to follow Oi when he would travel the cities in Belcher's prison. My sisters worked so hard to prevent me from joining him. Notwithstanding, the Lord would find ways to help me pass them. Most of the time it simply involved putting deep sleep on them. Then I would merely walk past them. This initially did not deter the demons. The demons tried to capture and torture us; however, the Lord would punish them brutally. They soon were extremely afraid to pester us, and avoided us. They were too ashamed to tell Rubina, and therefore, gave us an alibi saying we were doing some evil somewhere. This always pleased Rubina, as she never wanted to disturb anyone doing evil.

We were so saddened by what we saw in our homeland. Our people were suffering from our mother's raiders and the demons. Rubina taxed the people greatly, many times taking half their harvest and livestock. She would then ship the harvest to overseas markets to purchase slaves for her demonic sacrifices. The harvests also feed her armies and small navy. She only had a little secret navy, as Belcher demanded that she not build navies. He did not want her evil to spread beyond his prison. She always had her sons watching their father, as she wanted to know all that he did. Belcher at no time traveled any throughout the nation and never knew about all the people who had come here to escape the Flexsters, only to fall into another of their secret traps. I remember as if it were yesterday a song he would sing at our meetings. "My soul yearns, notwithstanding faints, for the courts of the LORD; my heart and my flesh cry out for the living God. notwithstanding the sparrow has found a home and the swallow a nest for herself, where she may have her young, a place near your altar, O Lord Almighty, my King and my God.

Blessed are those who dwell in your house; they are ever praising you." He explained why he never worried about where to sleep next, for he wanted no home upon New Venus, instead he wanted a home with his Lord where he could worship in the heavens. In my view, it was as if he could look at the heavens and see these great wonders. He told the people always to see the birds when they looked up into the sky, for they have homes and we believe shall have homes. We soon departed from the Baracs and moved on to our second great mission in Tolna.

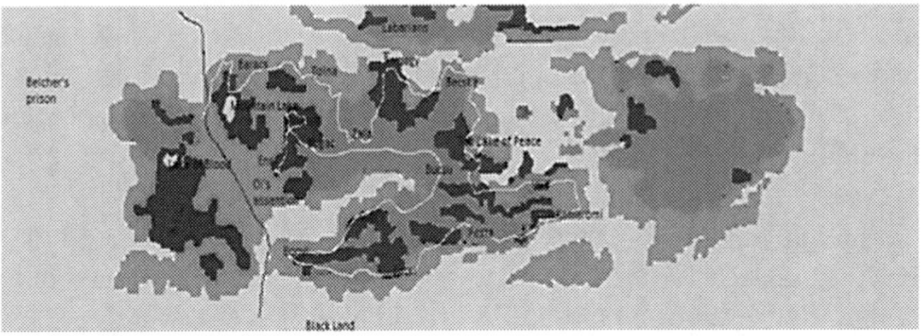

The Baracs were people who could exist on their desert lands, mountains and at times surviving on the great Mountain Lake, as they lived on the green lands and would use their small boats to journey out on the sea. The Baracs were the tribe that suffered the most from Rubin's horrible invasions.

Considering the misery that they suffered, the other tribes would send them food and extra archers. Archers fared well in the Baracs lands, as they would form along the mountain cliffs that Rubina's killers would flow through the grasslands. They would also light large fires, by shooting arrows into pre-planted brush piles. These smoke fires would alert the people in the green lands who would hide in the deserts or the nearby mountain ranges. Rubina's warriors would finally fill their mission goals; however, these cost Rubina's time and warriors, to the degree that she decided to raid through the mountain ranges bypassing the Baracs.

When we first arrived in the lands of the Tolna, they greeted us with a humongous crowd. The priests pulled Oi to the side on our way to greet these crowds. The priests confessed to Oi that they wanted to put away their gods and follow the one from the Garden. Oi had them explain their doctrines and was able quickly to blend the God of the garden over their deities, as they so eerily matched the functions of the God of the garden. They worshiped seven gods who would join into one.

Their seven functions were encompassed inside seven great spirits. Nógrád the spirit of wisdom, which they called upon to show them how to do things inconsiderate. The lives they lived could only continue if they had prudence and walked in astuteness. This led them to record all the messages that we gave the people in our ministries beyond the Baracs. I had recorded the highlights of our ministries in Baracs, and filled in the details, which they so passionately craved. They recorded mine as it began after Oi's assenting.

They also had Pétervásárai the spirit of understanding. They learned that understanding rises above the natural reasons, which is concerned only with the things we can sense to the world around us. Our world gives us signs each day that we must study so that our days may be more. Thus, understanding is concerned with intellectual knowledge and real-world knowledge, because these will help us to harmonize the actions of our lives toward our end, which is God. Thorough understanding, we may see the world and our life within it in the larger context of the eternal law. Oi told them that such a spirit was good. As we breathe in the invisible air to keep us visible, for without the invisible, we would walk no more. We should never lean unto our own understanding. Moreover, with all our heart, we must seek understanding.

The next spirit they introduced was Fedémes, the spirit of counsel. They told how they would never make plans without seeking advice. They also told us that Fedémes told them that if they are to wage war, they must seek guidance. The priests believed that Oi could give them the guidance they needed. Oi told them that first, they would need many priests who knew the minds of our heavenly spirits. Oi told them that where there was no counsel, the people will fall, but in the multitude of counselors, there is safety. Any who will not be counseled can be helped. Many receive advice; however, only the wise profit from it. Oi believed that they would follow the counsel that the Lord gave to him.

Oi spoke to the priests about the greatness of knowing wisdom and instruction, and how they joined in discerning the understanding of sayings. "We must use wisdom and understanding to receive righteousness, justice, and equity; to give prudence to the naive, to the youth knowledge and discretion. A smart man will hear and increase in learning, and a man of understanding will acquire wise counsel. To understand a proverb and to figure the words for the wise and their riddles

The next spirit they told him about was of might Geszteréd. Oi agreed that such a spirit was needed as the righteous can only survive with the might of power to defeat the demons. Oi taught that, "We must let faith that is right to make our might; and in that, faith will allow us, to this end, dare to do our duty as we understand it. In war as in life, it is often necessary when some cherished scheme has failed, to take up the best alternative open, and if so, it is madness not to work for it with all our might. I only wish that our farmers and herders had an limitless capacity for doing harm; then they might have an unlimited power for doing well. Just when we exceed men's might will we dwell among the gods within us." They asked Oi, "How can we exceed men's might?" Oi told them, "It is better to follow the light and use the might of the light, which is greater than any man or demon. Follow me and I shall share the words that our Lord has given me."

They have now introduced the spirit of Téti, who is the spirit of knowledge. Oi taught them that, "Knowledge comes by eyes always being open and working hands; and there is no knowledge that is not power. Knowledge is power. There is no knowledge that is not power. In a time of turbulence and change, it is truer than ever that knowledge is power, for without knowledge, we can never defeat Rubina."

The last spirit they told Oi about was the fear of their master spirit Ózdi. Oi further taught them, "Let all on New Venus fear our Lord, and let all the inhabitants of the world be in awe of him. The fear of the Lord is to hate evil. There is no fear in love, for flawless love casts out fear, because fear has to do with punishment. The one who fears is not made perfect in love." They asked Oi, "How can we not have fear of Rubina, for her demons hunt us daily to torture and kill us?" Oi told them, "When you have filled yourself with the word and knowledge of our Lord you shall have no fear, for you will know that greater is he that is within you than the demons of Rebina."

They now asked Oi, "How can you know to do much about the Lord we serve?" Oi then said, "We worship the same Lord, who has only shown himself in a different manner to you. He is now releasing all his knowledge and power so you will have an understanding and be able to defeat the evils of Rubina. You shall someday follow a great one filled by the power of understanding who will free you from the evil grips of Rubina." They all rejoiced in this pronounced news. I asked Oi how he knew this, and he told me he had seen the seven faces of our Lord, and told me that the heavens had told him the truth. The spirit of the Lord rested upon him, the spirit of wisdom and understanding, the spirit of counsel and might, the spirit of knowledge and of the fear of the Lord. The hearts for the people from these lands were pure. It was not fair that they had suffered so much, yet the Lord would ensure they were rewarded."

I felt good knowing that our Lord was also talking to others in this world, as I always wondered why he would not do so. I now felt more at peace knowing that these people shared a lot of the same love that Oi and I shared. It was strange that we had to go into the forbidden lands to find others who wanted the identical Lord. It is hard for me now to realize that the worship that Tsarsko, Oi my father, and I gave was enough to justify the forgiveness of our entire nation, even though mostly in the southern part had come from the brown lands. Once they came here, Rubina would not let them return. She would leave tax harvests along the borders to lure more to cross into her lands. Once in, only about three out of four were allowed to settle in the green lands between the mountains and the ocean. The remaining, she fed to her demons.

The priests now completely supported Oi and eagerly mixed his teachings into all the temple documents. They spread the word throughout the black land tribes that it was time to build up their faith and prepare for a war against Rubina. Just before we began to speak this day, messengers told us that Belcher had died and now Rubina was going to take the entire lower islands and make them feeding grounds for her demons. Her armies and navies began to sail for their new war; however, plagues swept through them reducing their numbers. The plagues even killed the demons who feasted upon them. She quickly left those suffering from the plagues in the black lands and brought the others back, quarantining them until she knew they were good. She now demanded that the demons obtain more power or leave as she reduced their human sacrifices forcing them to take her commands seriously.

I asked Oi if we could return to seeing our father properly buried. He told me that the Lord had told him in a vision, "Do not return to your mother will seek to kill you as she did your father." It was so hard for me to believe that my mother had finally stooped so low as to kill our father. I always figured her to be too weak to do so, fearing the God of the garden. She was furthermore so deep into her evil now to turn back or ever to be free from the greed that haunted her day and night. Just knowing that two of her children were traveling to other lands on this small continent preparing the people to fight her tormented her.

Oi now went to meet the crowds as the priests were leading them in songs. It would be so much better now that what they had learned could be used with what they knew to save their nation. Oi talked to the Tolna about hard times being ahead. He wanted all the people to know that the times of troubles were at hand. The woman of the black land tribes had pain through the delivery process, as only those in the Garden of Eden were currently exempt. He began by telling them that, "The angel of the Lord encamps around those who fear him, and he delivers them. Taste and see that the Lord is good; blessed is the man who takes refuge in him. Fear the Lord, you his saints, for those who fear him lack nothing." They rejoiced as he explained that the angels of the Lord would stay with them, as long as they feared him. One man asked, "If we love the Lord will we not be free from fear?" Oi explained that he was talking over the things about this world, for they were not important as we take from this world what we bring into it. The things we can have no fear, nor fear the evil that Rubina has cursed these lands.

He also told them that Rubina cursed her people more than they were. He clarified; this fear is different from the fear of the Lord, which is the beginning of all wisdom. Never be foolish enough to think it is wise to fall into the hands of an angry God. Rubina and her demons may look happy now, yet their hearts are filled with great pain and misery. They do not see what they do or have. They only see their miserable defeat, and that, which they do not have. We see more peace and joy in one hour than they see for many years. We must rejoice, for our rewards are greater as we are walking along a road that leads to the throne of our Lord. We shall have peace and joy for eternity. They will be punished greatly for what they now do. What they are receiving from us is in no way equal to the punishment we shall give them. He told them that they would cry under the altar of our heavenly father for revenge and justice to be served onto Rubina and her demons. He told them to be thankful that they were not one of her demons and while before such a mighty God to hear our cried for justice. He stressed that we were the ones who were truly blessed. We will lack nothing if we walk in his love and laws.

Oi further told them that the same God who took care of him would supply all their spiritual needs from his glorious riches. Now faith is being sure of what we hope for and certain of what we do not see. You shall someday see your nation saved from Rubina. I tell you we must have the faith to defend our lands before we can ever dream of defeating her. I will tell you a great truth that you will forget about when it happens; notwithstanding afterwards, you will remember, and that is that you will suffer no death when you enter Rubina's Empire to destroy it. We suffer deaths now because we are babies in our faith. It must must grow in our faith and destroy as many invaders as we can. I tell you, no Empire can survive that is losing its blood. For as a body can bleed to death, so will an Empire die as its body bleeds to its death? Each raider we kill today cannot invade tomorrow. We can hide in our faith and use that faith top strike our enemy. I also tell you, that whosoever dies in the defense of this land against Rubina and has known about the Lord as his or her God shall be saved and live with our Lord in his heavenly mansions forever and ever.

Oi told them that only a faith and knowledge that rested upon the hope of eternal life, which God, who does not lie, promised before the beginning of time. This knowledge has set you free, liberated to defend your Lord and your homes from the evil of Rubina. We now journeyed over the mountains of the Somogy. Rubina's armies seldom went past these mountains, and they hated the desert, which had almost one-hal their lands. Rubina depended upon her navies to raid the coasts of these black land tribes and those tribes on the neighboring islands.

We now walked through the desert lands of the Zala. The first day was very hazardous to us as the winds blew without mercy and the sand cut as small needles. Then as we came close to one of their villages, the winds stopped and the warm sun took away the chills of the winds. Oi after that told me that all the middle lands were like this and only a few openings at varied times to the green lands. This was their defense as it had taken them a long time to find these passes. I was surprised to see some fields with crops in them. Oi explained that the inner deserts were spotted with springs of water in which they used for their fields by digging ditches, which acted as small streams to get the water to the crops. Rubina had never discovered these middle lands and as such, these people had lived in a secluded peace. They know of the evils of Rubina as told by their priests. Priests were all trained in temples throughout the tribes; however, once ordained were sent to the missions throughout all the lands based upon need.

These people lived in tents, as they would move throughout the year. Each village of tents would rotate for turns to go into Somogy for fruit that they could dry and eat while preparing for a new harvest after the cold winter had passed. The winters in the desert lands were much more at calmer than the remainder of this small continent. Nevertheless, it did get cold enough to freeze the vegetation, so this forces them to start the new season's crops in early spring. They could get two harvests during the year. They would trade the excess crops to the neighboring tribes who needed this food, especially the Tolna and the Baracs. The priests from the temples had alerted the priests in the Zala of the people's needs. The Zala knew that they had to help the Tolna and Baracs in order to maintain some sort of resistance to Rubina as she would only continue to raid deeper into their lands.

Oi began by thanking them for the great sharing they had done and for their strong will to survive. Oi told them that everyone is born of God overcomes the world. This is the victory that has overcome the world even though our faith. You must be on your guard and stand firm in your faith. You are people of courage and must be strong. However, you who are the people of God, have fled from all this, and pursued righteousness, godliness, faith, love, endurance and gentleness. Nevertheless, you must know that you cannot be careless in your ways, or the demons who travel in the skies may find you. You have thus been spared because you share with your needy brother's in the other tribes. The longer that you give them, the more that our Lord will give you defense from the demons who can someday discover your passes and bring Rubina into the riches that our Lord has bestowed on us. Then one of the men asked him, "Why do the demons only attacked while Rubina's soldiers are near?" Oi told this man, "You are very wise in knowing this thing, and thus I will tell you a great secret. These demons are also bound by laws on how they may act between us. They have shown Rubina great enchantments, charms, magic, sorcery, augury, and witchcraft to break these laws. However, I tell you that no demon may harm us, unless she or a representative is near. This is why I have told the priests that each of her soldiers that we can ambush will give her representational less power to give to the demons. Each day, we must have a victory, as now when the raiding armies entered, they were being ambushed going in and while going out. Resist them, standing firm in your faith; because you know that, your brothers throughout the black land tribes are undergoing the same kind of sufferings. Is it now wiser to cut off the hand of one who is coming to steal from you before he arrives? Is it not better that your faith might not rest on men's wisdom, but on God's power?" They were amazed at his knowledge about the heavens, and all began to praise his Lord, which had always also been their Lord. We then returned through a temporary peaceful exit into the lands of the Somogy.

The Somogy welcomed us with their arms up begging to let us sleep in their temples. This was the first tribe to have stone buildings and forts. They had the forts positioned above the passes that allowed them to guard against any unwanted visitors. They had met one of Rubina's armies and inflicted such high losses that the commander retreated as Rubina ordered that they no longer attack through the mountains. They could sink some ships that tried to make it through the narrow strait between them and the Labarians. Their lands were bursting with wildlife, which gave them plenty of food to go along nonstop fruit trees. In order to survive, they had removed the other types of trees and replaced them with fruit trees. This helped keep the desert tribes from killing their beasts as food.

Their priests told Oi how they believed that by having extra food for your neighbors kept their neighbors from taking their food. Oi agreed that they had done well in that we should all try to feed the hungry and clothe the naked. He told them that sometimes the Lord would appear as poor or a naked stranger to test us on how we treat them. If we feed them, we will be blessed. Oi told them that the Lord had told him many things about helping the poor, "He who is generous will be blessed, for he gives some of his food to the poor. He who is gracious about a poor man lends to the Lord, and He will repay him for his good deeds. When you give a celebration or a dinner, do not invite your friends, your brothers, or your relatives or rich neighbors, in case they also invite you in return, and repayment comes to you. However, when you give a reception, invite the poor, the crippled, the lame, the blind, and you will be blessed, since they do not have the means to repay you; for you will be repaid when you join the Lord in his heavens.

The righteous are concerned about the rights to the poor; the wicked does not understand such concerns. He who oppresses the poor reproaches our Lord, who made them, but he who is gracious about the needy honors Him. I know that the Lord will maintain the cause of the afflicted, and justice to the poor, for you have been a defense for the helpless, a defense for the needy in his distress. Those same, helpless, and needy shall join you against the wickedness of Rubina.

Blessed are you who are poor, for yours in the kingdom of God. Blessed are you who hunger now, for you shall be satisfied. Blessed are you who weep at present, for you shall laugh later. The poor are truly blessed, for as you see my little sister, and I have nothing nor want nothing in this world for we know of the riches our Lord is giving us in his heavens." The people greatly applauded his words and rejoiced at the greatness of his teachings.

We now moved on to the lands of the Becske. The Becske also knew of the temporary portals that lead into the desert lands. They depended on these and the nearby mountains as their refuge against the sea invasions. Their greatest concentration of people was along the northern shores of the Lake of Peace, which they shared with the Tabil. They had a long history of fighting with the Tabil, who bordered them along the green lands, and mountains. The Tabil held fast in the mountains below the Becske and only through agreements made by the priests could they enter the mountains if Rubina was raiding. In exchange, the Becske agreed not to harm or alter the Lake of Peace, which the Tabil depended on for fresh water fish. The Becske would bring sea life from the oceans and place in the Lake of Peace. Many times, these species would flourish, as their natural enemies were not present to control their populations.

Oi continued by telling them, "It grieves my heart when I hear about the battles you fight with your brothers in the black land tribes the Tabil. Each body that dies in these battles is one more victory for Rubina, as it also makes her prey easier to harvest. Therefore, brothers, in all our distress and persecution we were encouraged about you because of your faith and will have to love our Lord more than the hate in your heart. Our Lord has loved you, even in the times of your greatest sins and will forgive you, as we believe you will also forgive your brothers in the Tabil. I ask you to look at the heavens when you kill your brother and to see that which you forfeit including a peaceful future for your children. I will tell as I also will tell the Tabil, who is right or wrong is of no value here, for now the Lords of your priests are living among you, so you may someday have a victory over Belcher's Prison. Do not be among those who kill as Rubina does, for when the Lord destroys her, he will also destroy all others who are wicked. If we cannot love and cannot forgive than we cannot join the kingdom of our Lord, for he will cast us out to live with others who cannot love or forgive. If I tell you all mysteries and give you knowledge, and if you have a faith that can move mountains, but have not loved, you are nothing."

We could clearly see how this message was growing deep in their hearts, as the mothers did want to chance anymore of their children dying. Therefore, their tribal leaders agreed in a written treaty that they gave to Oi to give to the Tabil that they would no more launch a war against them and rather than fighting would rather share the blessings of the God of the garden with them. This brought great joy to the priests, as they no longer wanted to see the young kill themselves in this foolish feud. Rubina had a few very successful raids in this land and Oi feared that she would continue to return unless plans for ambushes were established. The Becske could not fight to the sea if they were also fighting to their backs. We now walked to the Lake of Peace where the priests had assembled the crowds on the western shore. We had to pass a small mountain range to the west of the lake that the priests knew of many caves, which guided us through to the southern lake.

Oi began by talking to the tribal leaders about the peace treaty he had. They agreed to end their war, so that they could join in the war against Rubina. Oi began by blessing them, "Blessed are the peacemakers, for they shall be called the children of our God. Every life that you save in your peace will give you many more lives, for in this you shall see many additional sons and daughters. Now, in peace plant the seeds to give your tribes peace from the evils of Rubina. I have heard that you are a very industrious people, as you have learned to live among the mountains and your dangerous green lands, which are covered on three sides by the ocean. I tell you that someday your friends shall visit you from these very seas as you shall rejoice in those times by the ocean." We noticed that there were no buildings, and that they lived as nomads. They have always lived on the run, so they could fight against the Becske and at times the Bucsu, which they had made peace with years earlier. Oi told them, "You have collected your dead off empty battlefields leaving only their blood on the ground as witness whom they once were. You have seen their enemies sleeping beside them. They now speak to your sons and not you. I say to you that it is better than you sleep beside your sons and daughters. Peace will give this to you. Therefore, you need not to go before the Lord with a heavy heart filled with great pain and misery. You have given this to yourself. Now, when the demons come to take your younger sons and daughters, your burdens will be too great for you to bear. You will them end up in the hands of evil, who will take all of you and those you love. I say that it is wiser to fear the Lord than the enemies you have made. I see a day when you shall rest beside your enemies with peace and love into your heart. On that day, you will have shame for the hate you gave that cheated you out of such good friends.

Chapter 03

Oi's Mission Continues

Dying and crying in the wilderness

After finishing our time with the Tabil, we went down the mountain range, crossed the bitter desert, and traveled through a pass into the next set of mountain ranges. This was among, if not, the longest mountain range on our continent. It was not deep; however, it was tall and provided a lot of defense for the people living in this bottom peninsula. We were heading south until the priests stopped on one peak and told us it was time to go east. When we finally started to see the foothills, we were greeted by a large crowd, which was mostly composed of the Priests of Vas. They had many concerns they wanted to talk with Oi over. They began by telling him, "Oh mystery prophet; we have come to determine if you indeed walk with the Lord. Is this okay with you, so that we may allow you to minister unto our people? Oi then told them, "I care not if you approve or disapprove, for they are not your sheep. The Lord has given them to me. I pity any false prophets who would take them from the Lord. They shall be fed to the demons of Rubina." They now stood up and demanded that Oi fall to his knees and beg for forgiveness.

Oi looked at them saying, "I beg not Rubina's demons nor shall I beg you." The priests told Oi that their sheep greatly loved them and their teachings and would follow no other prophet. Oi said to them, "You have taken from your sheep for your own riches and glory here on New Venus. I tell you, you shall not enter the kingdom of the God of Eve, for your greed has made you too heavy to lift into the skies." Then one priest asked, "Oi, how can we enter the heavens of the God of the garden?" Oi told them they must first sell all that they have and give that money to those who are hungry. Do you not hate Rubina for taking your food? How can your sheep not discover the wolf that is taking their food?" This priest now said to Oi, "I shall sell all that I have and give it to my poor, yet may I first fill my spirit with your wise words?"

Oi then told him, "Yes, my fellow shepherd, yet first remember I cannot claim these words as mine, they are the words which the God of the garden has placed upon my heart. If I tell them not, my heart will burn, as later my soul." The priest then casts down his garments, and covered himself only with the some rags from his belongings and gave his clothes to Oi who in turn gave them to the priests who came with him and told them to sell these and give the money to the poor so that they may eat. Oi afterwards told me, "Little sister, we shall see this man walk with our Lord in his heavens." Oi then looked at the other priests and told them, "I tell you today, this man has stored riches greater than what can be found in all the black land's tribes, in his new mansion in heaven." The priests looked at their comrade and said, "You are a fool." Oi then looked at the group and said, "Having eyes they could not see, having ears they could not hear as neither could the Lord see them or hear their pleas for mercy when he judged the wicked and the righteous."

The priests now asked him, "If we catch a man steeling, should we cut off his hands as our laws teach us?" Oi then said to them, "Has the Lord cut off your hands for stealing from his sheep? No, instead, he sent his prophet to warn you, one stopped stealing, and he gave him eternal life with him. A thief must be punished, yet I say to you ask the Lord what punishment to give, for only the Lord can judge. I do know that Rubina cut off the hands of thieves, should we be at her. If you cut off his hands, he may no longer work in the fields to harvest his food, thus he can only steel to live. I truly tell you, that in this matter as all matters, I must ask the Lord, so then I will know the true judgment." They now brought before him a prostitute and told Oi, "We have caught this woman selling her body to men for her own profit. What shall we do? Oi then asked them, "Where the man who gave her unto him sold her gift from the Lord?" They looked at him and said, "We care not about the man." Oi subsequently looked at the woman and said, "Then I care not about the woman."

He looked at and said, "The Lord has forgiven you, so go and sell your body no more." Oi then looked at the priests and asked, "If a man comes into a house at night and steals your most precious jewels without first asking the master; however, leaves a small amount of money as the price the master's servant agreed to, what would you do with the thief?" They are yelling, "We would put him in prison and demand that he returns the jewels." Oi next asked, "What if he had destroyed the jewels?" The priests yelled, "Then he would forever remain in prison." Oi then asked them, "Is this not the same as the woman you brought to me, as she is the servant, the Lord is the master, and the man is the thief. The man took a jewel from the Lord, who can never be returned, taking it without the master's permission by only paying a small sum to the servant who held that gift for the Lord?"

The priests now left in great anger and promised that they would warn their people not to listen to his words. The servants of the priests refused to return to their temples saying, "You have stolen too much from our sheep, and we will no longer follow you." They sent messengers to tell the people about the great words of Oi.

We now began to walk over the Plain of the Pains. Here we were met by our first crowd of the Vas. The people surrounded us, as we could feel fear in their hearts. They asked us, "Do you come from the demons or from the Lord?" Oi then asked them to search for the answer to that question in their hearts, for if the Lord tells them he comes in his name to stay.

Those who cannot hear that voice should leave now." They all stayed, since they did not want the shame of not telling others, they could not hear the voice. Then an old woman comes forward with her son following her carrying a little girl. The little girl was my age and had such a beautiful smile. I went up to her, and she told me her name was Tvář Lásky, which she told me means face of love. I held her hand and felt so good.

I asked her if she wanted to play. I seldom play, for I could not find another tyke that I was attracted to, and felt this strange peace flowing from her. She then held my hand and with a warm, smile said, "I am so sorry Tianshire, I have no legs." I looked down and saw she had no legs below her kneecap. I then asked her, "How do you know my name?" She told me that a good angel in her dream told her my name. This brought sorrow to my heart, for she was so virtuous and blameless. Oi came to me, wiped my tears, and gave Tvář Lásky a kiss on her cheek. The old woman now spoke to Oi, "Oh great prophet from the Lord, will you ask the Lord to have mercy on Tvář Lásky, for she lost her legs when demons bit each of them putting their poison in her body, and thus to save her, we had to cut off her legs." Oi looked at the people and then laid Tvář Lásky on the ground putting a blanket over her missing legs.

Oi then asked the people, "Do you have faith that our Lord can give Tvář Lásky back her legs? If you have faith in our Lord, she can walk once more and her pain on this Plain of the Pains may be released from her shoulders." The people yelled out aloud that they 'believed the Lord would heal her.'" Oi then asked Tvář Lásky, "Do you believe?" Tvář Lásky told him, "I have seen the Lord do this, so today I will walk." The Oi said, "Tianshire remove the blanket from Tvář Lásky." When I removed the blanket, Tvář Lásky, without looking, stood up on her legs. I gave her a big hug and asked her to stay with us until we left the Vas. Her mother gave her permission, and she sat beside me as I prepared myself to record Oi's message.

The people all rejoiced when they saw Tvář Lásky walking and jumping. They said, "Surely a prophet is among us. He does great work by the name of the Lord. A man of evil will not take away their works of pain." Oi told them that, "It was your faith that gave back Tvář Lásky's legs. You now have seen what great works your faith can do. I tell you that Rubina shall continue to torture you not only on the Plain of the Pains but along many areas, you suspect not. However, with your faith, you can strike back at her and her demons. You may not feel that your strikes are of benefits, yet each one you kill destroys a body that Rubina's demons can possess. We must rebuild our lives with one small victory at a time."

As he continued to talk, an exceptionally malicious storm approached over this crowd. Soon, all was black and it was as if we were all blind. The winds blew across us, and the rains began to pour upon us. The rains poured so hard that Oi could see people falling to the ground. Oi stood up and said, "Spirits in the rain, I command you to hold the rains from this land." Then we all saw; the rains pull up from the ground and return to the sky about ten feet above our heads. A bright light appeared behind Oi; therefore, all could see him. Never before had any seen such a thing as this. All the water remained above them and flowed down the sides of this invisible shield. I heard a man say, "He has surely been sent by the Lord for even the spirits of the world obey him." Then the rains ended, and the shield lifted itself into the clouds. Oi tried to finish his message; however, they refused to leave. Oi thus said to them, "As in all lands, there are among us wicked, greedy, clusters for riches, and evil men. You know who they are, for they said to you, 'The Lord has said, 'give to me, give to me,' man of God, flee from all this, and pursue righteousness, godliness, faith, love, endurance and gentleness.

For those who say, 'the Lord says and the Lord has not said it shall be punished.' Your heart will warn you against such evil men, and it will tell you to run. I tell you to run as fast as your legs can and do not look back. If you look backward, you are giving evil another chance to deceive you. That is the same as putting your head in front of flying arrows and asking the arrows not to hit your head. We have seen from the thirst in your souls that you so much want to serve our Lord." Then one asked, "Oh prophet Oi, "Is he not your Lord?" Oi after that answered, "My friends, he is our Lord, and that is why he sent me to tell you that your day of freedom will someday arrive. Stay righteous, keep your wonderful love and faith, and endure." Then he looked out among the large crowds and saw how all were famished. We did not realize that he had taught for two days straight, repeating all he had taught in the earlier tribes. He was not confident that the Vas priests would share the teachings that the other priests had given them. Then Oi asked them, "Who among you is hungry?" They all told him that they were starving. Oi then told them to catch the fish as they fly by. The crowds now began to laugh thinking Oi was too tired from all his hard work.

An old woman began to scream, for all around them were the largest fish they had ever seen, and they were flying. As they would pass by and as someone touches them, they would fall to the ground with no life in them. They were then able to round up the loose brush that had miraculously appeared on the ground. They gathered the brush and made small campfires which the cooked the large fish portions on. While cooking, strange white fluffy bread chunks began to fall from the sky. So much fell that the villagers had to send back over one hundred wagon loads of fish and bread. All were filled and had plenty for their journey's home. Many claimed this to be the best fish they had ever eaten.

The elders sent the Saints among them to greet the priests of Komaromi and tell them the great things we did. Oi elected to visit with some Saints in Vas for a few days to give me time to play with Tvář Lásky. We had so much fun just being crazy little girls. We found some boys to throw rocks at, which turned out to be a bad idea as the boys had much more practice than we had, and thus we took a few bruises. We did not care, for it was fun. We stood beside each other showing the world that we would stick together and not the betray each other. Fortunately, for us, the Lord sent some small girls to us who taught us how to play some girl games. I had never had an adventure such as this. The other girls were now more excited than they had ever been before, for currently there was a taste of hope in their future.

They told me about some terrifying encounters they had with the demons. For some strange reason, the raiders attacked the little girls hard in this portion. Tvář Lásky told me that her father told her the demons and raiders figured to force the men to fight and sacrifice themselves to save their daughters and at the same time to inflict the greatest grief. I did not want to think about that now, nor did I ever remember having other youngsters to play with. None of my sisters would talk with me; all they actually did was to try to prevent me from sneaking out with Oi in the nighttime. They never figured out that there was no way of catching me. As I would go to them, the Lord would put them in a deep sleep until after I returned.

I always felt sorry for my sisters many times, as our mother would beat them for falling to sleep. Finally, she started sending my brothers until they also fell to sleep. She would not beat her sons, so she once again started having my sisters watch me. They could never figure it out, nor as my oldest sister told me, that 'she did not want to know.' The less she knew; to a lesser degree the demons would torment her. They were hated by everyone since they were Rubina's daughters. The demons hated them because they refused to behave as our mother did with them. Belcher ensured that they did not touch his daughters. He cared about them, yet knew that Rubina was too far gone to bring back. The demons were helpless when Belcher was among them, so they worked hard to avoid him. Now, sadness once again came upon me as my three days of playing Tvář Lásky ended. I could not ask for more time as Oi had given me an extra day. I never again saw her until we met once again in heaven. I could, at no time, forget the great love and enthusiasm she had at heart and from the miserable life that the Lord had rescued her.

Oi and I once again continued his ministry, this time with the tribe of the Komaromi. We now moved into the green lowlands of the Komaromi, as they planted many fields of crops among their lands. They were the most fierce guerrilla fighters among the tribes, guarding the entire coastline with multiple layers of trenches. They were famous for ambushing from trees, as the raiders would try to pass the empty trenches. They also would hide in their fields and kill the raiders as they tried to destroy their crops. They actually had a five to one kill ratio, which would even witness Rubina's ships passing far from the coast. They would swim out, and go underwater breathing through hollow vegetation and take their axes and beat holes into the undersides of the ships. They could travel in small rafts, and brought back large harvests from their green colonies on the nearby islands. They traded much of their harvest to the Pesta and Bucsu, as the Bucsu would passed much on to the Zala. They knew now that there would be more raids that Belcher was no longer alive, thus they had stored plenty of grain to feed the tribes for up to ten years. This would make them riches above all other things, as the hungry would pay all; they had to get some grain. The new hope and sharing that Oi was teaching did not go well with the future plans of the Komaromi, consequently Oi hit hard from the beginning.

Oi began to speak to the first large crowd saying, "For it is by the charity you have been saved, through faith, and this not from yourselves, it is the gift of God. I warn you to use this gift wisely, for not to do so can cause our Lord to take back his charity. I ask you, what is the profit of your grain if you are eaten by a demon? How much of your grain would you share to get the demons to set you free? I hope you do not believe that the demons make deals, for they do not need your grain, they need your flesh and soul.

Can you tell me how you produced the grain? Did you not put a seed into the soil and give it water while the sun feeds it? Who made the soil, sun, and seed? Should not the creator also receive some profit? I tell you that once there lived a man who had a poor neighbor. This neighbor begged him for money to build a new spear factory. He also asked the man if he helped him in the factory, and as more people wanted his swords, he asked the man if his wife and children could also help.

He promised to pay him back plus for all the wages as soon as he paid for the large inventory that he had purchased for the business. One day while they were working a stranger came into the business to speak with the owner. They went into his private office and talked for some time. The owner soon emerged with a nice heavy bag and quickly exited leaving town. Later, that day the man who gave the loan and still had wages due to him, and his family discovered that the owner had sold the business and left their area with the money. I ask you, what judgment should that man who took the money and departed to receive?" The crowds all screamed, "He must be punished." Then Oi asked them, "If the Lord gives you the land, sun and creates the seeds and through his work produces the grain, and one of his servants whom he also created now faces starvation, what should he do with the owner of the grain who will not share the Lord's grain?" No one in the crowd would answer until one man cried out, "The farmer planted the seed and harvested it. Why should his work go to feed another who did not produce it?" Oi then asked the man, "By what magic did the farmer produce the grain?" I tell you that everyday around us our Lord does great magic, for he created the heavens and New Venus. We must take time each day and thank the Lord for what he has given us. He gives us beautiful flowers to enjoy, cool waters from the springs and streams, and air that we may breathe. For without air we would quickly die.

We are closer to death than to our next meal. In death, we all will be judged, as our master will open his record of all deeds. He will know all that we have done. As I tell all the tribes I visit, "The Lord will bless those who feed his hungry children. In addition to all this, you must take up the shield of faith, with which you will be capable of extinguishing all the flaming arrows of the evil one. Without the shield of faith, Rubina will carry you to her dungeons for a trip to misery and slow death. Our shields of faith will stop all things of evil that Rubina will hurl at you. Clearly, no one, not even me, is justified before God by the law. The righteous will live by faith, and we will use this faith to give glory to our God so that he may free us from his law." Then one man asked, "Are you telling us that we do not have to obey the laws of God?" Oi afterwards said, "If you are righteous and love the Lord with all your heart you will break no laws, yet as all people stumble, if you stay in the faith you will walk again by the Lord's mercy and grace." Oi next asked the man, "Do you love the Lord with all your heart?" The man after that said, "I truly love the Lord with all my heart. I only asked the question so you would give more details so some, here would not try to take the easy way?" Oi then asked the man, "Do you give to the poor?" The man said, "I give one-third of all I receive to the poor, and one-third to our temple, and use the remaining third for my family."

Then Oi said to him, "You are truly a righteous man, and I tell you that when we all get to the Lord's throne he will bless you abundantly for eternity. Does anyone among us understand eternity?" All in the crowd just looked at him, thus Oi said, "My friends, eternity makes the time of our life here as a small drop in all the oceans and rivers and other sources of water on New Venus. I understand that many fear my words about the war, which most alive here today shall see, therefore I want you to know even one hundred years of terrible torture is nothing compared to eternity, which only has a beginning. The people who have this vision, does the righteous things based on faith, and lives by these shall spend eternity with our Lord. Rejoice, for the enemy you fight will be punished by our Lord. It is better to have them torture you than to have the Lord Judge and punish you. I tell you that the whole world is a prisoner of sin, nevertheless, our faith and love of the Lord will set us free." At this time, they brought forward an old blind man and put him in front of Oi. They asked Oi, "What should you do to this sightless man?" Oi then told them, "How can I care about him being blind if he does not know the Lord?"

The old man cried out, "I need not to see your world, for the world that I see has a magnificent Lord sitting on a great throne calling out, "Ajkai, come to my altar that we may fill your tired soul with love." Oi looked up and saw the same vision. Oi then asked the Lord, "Oh mighty Lord would you give Ajkai his sight and forgive him of his sins?" Later we all saw a bright white-light flash and heard, "Ajkai, thy sins are forgiven, go and enjoy your site." Ajkai fell to the ground as those around him splashed water on his head to wake him. He awoke and stood up, leaving his canes behind walked deeper into the crowd where he stopped and yelled out, "Blessed is the Lord, for he shall lead us to victory." All were amazed that the blind man could see again, and the Priests yelled out, "Our sacred Lord has given us a miracle. Praise the Lord." Oi stood there with his arms raised praising the Lord. Then Oi spoke out, "Ajkai has blessed us here today with the spirit of love. I shall share with you what the love we are receiving from our Lord is. Love is patient, as we can and will endure until the day that the Lord gives us the leader who will free us from the clutches of Rubina. Love is kind, as we saw how the Lord gave Ajkai his eyesight while sharing his love with him.

Love does not envy. Through our Lord's love, we are free from the hate that jealousy and greed, which can destroy others and ourselves. Love does not boast. We must understand how dangerous excessive pride and self-satisfaction about ourselves can destroy. Pride will make us stumble. Do as I do. I lay my pride before the Lord and submit myself, for I take great pride in my Lord. Humble yourself in all things before the Lord, since Love is not vain. Love does not need to be proud, as, we only our proud of our love for the Lord. Love is not rude. Bad-mannered people are hated by evil, who only endeavors to take them to the pit.

We must be polite to all whom we meet, for we know not if they are an angel sent to test us. Love is not selfish. That is why our Lord and I thank you for the grains, which you save to share with the other tribes in our great war against Rubina. Love is not easily angered. We have all unfortunately been around people who are quick to anger. They do not think, and most times hurt those who love them. Even angry words can hurt the ones you love. Speak to others as you would speak to the Lord, who is going to deliver you from the evils of Rubina. So many senseless murders have been committed by those who are quick to anger. The danger of an action in that split second of destroying someone's life is too great. How can we have peace when our love is shattered by a fool's anger?

I now tell you another great mystery, and that is what our Lord does with the sins, he forgives us. These sins are removed from are books of life and thrown into the sea of forgiveness where the Lord may never again know about this. They are not only forgiven; they are forgotten. I know so many times that we forgive; nevertheless, we begin to watch the forgiven one, as we cannot forget what they have done. I tell you that if you do not forget, you cannot forgive. Remember, we are forgiving the children of our Lord, as the Lord forgives us. Therefore, Love keeps no record. Love, like the Lord, does not delight in evil. I wonder how some can say they love someone, yet have great joy when misfortune strikes the one they claim to love. Let me tell you, if you delight in the misfortune of others, you shall get a taste of a greater misfortune. When you delight in their misfortune, you have made wickedness your brother. For when the Lord strikes evil, he will also strike you.

I tell you there is there is more glory in rejoicing in the truth. I wonder if you could delight in a Lord, who does not speak the truth. We must have truth to be the foundation of all love, as the shadow of the truth will remain behind you, yet the shadow of a lie will tell your enemies where you are. When you are in the truth peace will fill your soul as you may rejoice in front of the Lord, for the shame of a lie will not force you to hide. Rejoice, rejoice, for we are loved by the truth of the Lord, and our Lord is served by those who rejoice in the truth."

Oi was going strong now, as I could see his eyes sparkling. So much love was flowing through him that those who were in the front rows of our congregation began to faint with large smiles on their faces as they were laughing and praising their Lord. The priests had done a wonderful job of spreading the word about our Lord to the tribes, accordingly, now when we arrived in the tribes, they had already taken possession of the Lord as their Lord. At this time, a strange light appeared behind us. It was a large light, the size of five men. The light began to change colors as it was spinning around within itself. We all moved out of its path, as the swirling would try to suck us into it. Then the light and swirling began to slow down. Slowly, we could see a spirit that was the color from pure white. Oi said to him, "Who are you?" The spirit then said, "I am James, the son of Zebedee, and I am one of the Lord's disciples and also one of the twenty-four elders." Oi afterwards asked, "Why do you come today?" James, the son of Zebedee answered, "We were listening to our great words about love and could feel your love reaching into the throne. I asked the Lord if I could come and share some more things that love is. He granted my request."

Oi then said to the crowd, "Let us rejoice greatly today, for the Lord has sent one of his chosen twelve to share his feelings about love. I beg that this wonderful guest; therefore, share his message with us. James, the son of Zebedee began by saying, "The always protects. Consider it a joy whenever you face trials of many kinds, because you know it is a test. Evil is testing you to make you look bad before the Lord, stand up, and show the Lord the power of your love. The Lord God cannot be tempted by evil, nor has he ever tempted anyone. If you want the protection of his Lord, you must not let yourself be dragged away by your own desire and be enticed. When desire has conceived, it gives birth to sin, and sin, when it is full-grown, gives birth to death.

Love always trusts. Look at Rubina, for not a word comes from her mouth that can be trusted, her heart is filled with malice. Her throat is an open grave, with her tongue telling lies. Do not trust in your arrows and small tools of war, but trust in the Lord our God. Place your trust in the Lord our God. Rubina has many woes, but the Lord's unfailing love surrounds all who trust in him. Woe unto them, which trust in their wealth, and boast of their great riches.

Nevertheless, your God, will bring down the wicked into the pit of decay; the bloodthirsty and deceitful will not live out half their days. However, as for me, I trust in our Lord. Whenever I was afraid during my days on the old Earth, I always tried hard to put my trust in our Lord. When you put your trust in the Lord, you will not forget his great deeds and will keep his commands. Blessed is anyone who trusts in the Lord. Ask the Lord to teach you good judgment and knowledge so you can trust his commands. Do not put your trust in princes or any other human being, for they cannot save. The Lords kingdom is an eternal kingdom. He is trustworthy in all his promises and faithful in all he does. I know you have some great trials and temptations on the road you now travel. Trust in the Lord and you will see the day when one among you here currently shall deliver you from the hands of Rubina. I must now return to our father." Moreover, with these words, he vanished from us. I so very much enjoyed his words, as we were not only listing to Oi as he could see into the heavens, but we were seeing a spirit in which the Lord had given a high position. Oi now decided to speak again.

Oi spoke saying, "We have been greatly blessed today with the words from James, the son of Zebedee. The Lord has felt the power of our Love, and it has given him great pleasure. Our pronounced humbleness gives our Lord great pleasure in us. Love always hopes. Hope is our dream for a better today and tomorrow. You will be secure, because there is hope; you will look about you and take your rest in our safety after the war has finished. However, the eyes of those who serve Rubina will fail, and escape will elude them; their hope will become a dying gasp. At least, there is hope for a tree, if it is cut down, it will sprout again, and its new shoots will not fail. Integrity and uprightness may protect me, because my hope, Lord, is in you. Your unfailing love may be with us, Lord, even as we put our hope in you. For that who is evil will be destroyed, on the contrary, those who hope in the Lord will inherit this land. The desire of the righteous ends only in good, but the hope of the wicked only in wrath.

Love always perseveres. This is how we will survive until the day that our Lord delivers us from the great evils of Rubina. However, those who hope in the Lord will renew their strength. They will soar on wings like eagles; they will run and not grow weary, and they will walk and not be faint. Nevertheless, as for me, I watch in hope for the Lord; I wait for God my Savior; my God will hear me.

Love will never fail us. Not even in our times of need. Love will be the power that will unite us in the Lord as we drive Rubina from this world." He continued to talk about love as a great peace had fallen on them. Be joyful in hope, patient in affliction, and faithful in prayer. Now these three remain faith, hope, and love. Nevertheless, the greatest of this is love." We now left our new friends and with our large following, which with the Komaromi had grown so much larger followed us into the Pesta tribe's lands. The Komaromi brought many wagons of extra grains, enough to feed trice the following for at least four months, as we had eight more tribes to visit.

We walked for many days; as Oi would stop and have all pray to the Lord, then continue. He once again delivered the flying fish to our group, as their faith had grown so much. Oi marched us to the foothills of the middle mountain range in this tribe that had very little green lands. The deserts along this southern shore did not need the border winds, as these lands had many caves and mountain ranges. These were the largest crowds we spoke to, as the small crowds would be no more. The priests all along the southern tribes were very much more focused on the Lord. Rubina seldom put her navies in the south, for during the times of Belcher, as she had mostly small boats. These boats did not sail well in the turbulent waters of the southern oceans. Therefore, Rubina's small boats concentrated on Death Bay. Most of the green lands in Death Bay were uninhabited. Only vacant fields spotted the verdant landscape. The brown desert lands that bordered the southern ocean were a mystery to so many people. Irrigation streams could be dug to bring the waters in and create a wonderful green land.

The Pesta did not want to cultivate this land until after Rubina was removed. They used this land now for ambushes, as the raggedy multi-shades of brown vegetation made close ambushes very easy, as well as the small rocky chestnut hills gave archers all they needed to hit with great accuracy. Some fighters bragged about how the limited paths through the thorny vegetation even made it possible to follow the raiders at the end of their columns and spear them in their backs while hold their mouths closed then simply slide the body under the brown vegetation and start picking off more of them. Rubina always lost at least three out of four while raiding these parts, thus she stopped and would instead set the dried vegetation on fire, more of a harassment and a reminder; the Death Bay was still available. Though not properly identified on maps, the tremendous small rolling foothills, which flowed into the tall mountains, then rose along the deeper inlands. This large empty place can create loneliness. It teases me with such a big challenge as if to say, 'make me into what you want, for we are near the bottom of the world, and no one else cares what you do here, as the hilltops cast down their deep shadows across the plains.

Oi began his message for the Pesta on a much more timid note than he did on the previous couple of tribes. The Pesta was known as a peaceful tribe and to walk away from fights in which the other tribes would try to start. They were; however, very famous for the way they fought off the raiders. Oi considered the thing they could bring to the new family of tribes would be the patience and ambush skills. Oi began, "I consider it a pure joy to speak with the Peska, who are truly my brothers and sisters as we have faced so many hardships of many kinds. We know that testing of our faith produces dedication. Let your dedication finish its work so you may be mature and complete and lacking nothing. I have asked our Lord to give anyone who lacks wisdom to pour out on the Peska, for he will give it to all who want it generously without finding fault as this wisdom will be given to you.

Nevertheless, when you ask you must believe and have no doubt, because the one who doubts is like a wave on the sea, blown and tossed by the wind. Doubters should not expect to receive anything from the Lord, for such a person is double-minded and unstable in all they do. Those of you who belong to the Lord in humble circumstances ought to take pride in their high position. However, the rich should take pride in their humiliation, since they will pass like a wild flower. The sun rises with scorching heat and withers the plant; its blossom falls and its beauty is destroyed. In this same wall, the rich will fade away even while they go about their business.

This shall be the case of Rubina, for her riches cannot save the defeat someday she shall suffer. To our great hope and joy, she will fade away. Blessed are those who persevere under trials because, having stood these tests, they will receive eternal life with our Lord and travel around in his heavens. When we are tempted, we cannot say that God is tempting us. For our God cannot be tempted by evil, nor does he tempt anyone. We become tempted when we allow ourselves to be drug away by our own evil desires and to be induced.

When this desire is born, it birth to sin, and when it is matured, it gives birth to death. Rubina, when as a young girl in a small peaceful village in the Flexster's lands saw youthful boys go off to the raids and return with great tales of their brave deeds, of which most were only tales. Even though false tales, they gave way to a desire in a little girl who then had to fight hard to make it in this male-only organization. This forced her to hate harder, hit brutally, and fight each day as if a tomorrow would never come. It was her ability to hate and deceive that the Flexsters gave her first ship to command. She had to stand, as a brick wall while controlling the men on the ship as even one small sign of weakness would result in mutiny or her being cast into the sea for the sharks to eat. Her mission was not as the others since she had made too many promises to the demons who now wanted to put her somewhere in a land of sin where others would avoid. To our great misfortune, they selected Belcher's prison, not knowing that Belcher, even thou abandoned by God refused to abandon God.

Belcher kept his faith; he endured all his tribulations, trials, and temptations, having more faith than any other does on New Venus when he died. He had destroyed all evil desires in her heart and thus walked into death with the Lord welcoming him home. Rubina, on the other hand, became a slave to her desires, as these desires now blossomed into withered flowers and each placed heavier burden on her. She currently faces the torment and horror each day as she commits crimes that even the Lord can never forget, for the blood of her victims cries out for justice. As she matures, there shall come that day when she sees our armies riding up to where she is hiding and take her life from her. I see that day, as she burns in a fire that we made. Her screams shall be released into the ages for those who she caused to suffer that they may hear and rejoice as vengeance and justice are served.

Do not be deceived my friends, for every good and perfect gift is from above, coming down from our Lord and does not change such as shifting shadows. He chose to give us birth through the word of his truth that we may be a kind of first fruit of his new creation on this southern land. We all must be quick to listen, slow to speak, and unhurried to become angry, because our anger does not produce the righteousness that our Lord desires. Therefore, we must get rid of all moral filth and the evil that is so widespread and humbly accept the word that is planted in you. This word can and will save you. Do not merely listen to the word, and so deceive yourselves. Do what these words tell you to do. Many have worked hard to record my messages so you can have the meat you need to build your new spiritual bodies, therefore, revealing to you what must be done to save yourselves and your families. He who merely listens is the word and does not do what it says.

Anyone who listens to the word but does not do what it says is like someone who looks at his face in a mirror and after looking at himself, goes away, and immediately forgets what he looks like. Nonetheless, whoever looks intently into the perfect law that gives freedom, and continues in it, not forgetting what he heard, but doing it, will be blessed in what they do. Those who consider themselves with conviction and yet do not keep a tight rein on their tongues deceive themselves, and their conviction is worthless. A conviction that God our Father accepts as pure and faultless is this, to look after orphans and widows in their distress and to keep oneself from being polluted by the world.

We shall defeat Rubina by doing what we say through the power of the words that we now have knowledge therein. Remember, that those who are needy were created by our father, as were you. Our conviction will be ours until the day we depart these bodies to live with our Lord. Rubina's demons are speedy to speak, and swift to anger, and quick to fight. How can we ask favors if we act as they do? Let them see the Lord in us, by the way; we live. When they see we are the children of God, they shall know that when they strike at us, we will strike back with the power of our father on the throne. We are the wise ones, for we do not hide our knowledge, we take our knowledge and put it in our hearts and hands, for we not only know righteousness, but we follow righteousness as it guides our hands and our legs. We now departed the southern desert of Pesta and went into their southern mountains to cross into the grassy lands of Encsi. The Encsi was very famous for sharing with the Gyori and Bonyl since they lost much grain in the green lands along Death Bay.

Rubina would steal as much of the harvest as possible to trade with the middle islands that circled New Venus. The Gyori and Bonyl were lucky to salvage about one-half their needs and depended on the Encsi for the remainder. The Encsi gladly kept them alive, for fear that if they all came into their lands, Rubina would shortly thereafter follow suit. The Encsi harvested about three times what they needed each year, giving one-third to the temples who stored it in the mountain caves in case a great famine would strike the black land tribes, and one-third to the Bonyl and Gyori and Encsi. Oi was very impressed with the ways these tribes worked together. In exchange for the grain, the Bonyl and Gyori worked hard building up a solid line of forts and temples in the mountains, which all three tribes would use in a raid from Rubina.

The tribes had only begun working this hard together for the past decade as the raids along the Death Bay had increased. The Encsi had placed many sharp rocks under the shallow muddy waters along the southerly coast that made trying to land any medium size or larger ships on the shores, and a safe quick exit impossible. Rubina dare not risk taking grain from the southerly coast's fields as it would weigh her boats down and trying to move it over land was too dangerous due to the unlimited ambushes. The Encsi had one vice that the other tribes complained about and that was kidnapping women from the other tribes. The Encsi had a strong 'secret' sex slave market, which so many disapproved. Oi began by asking the Encsi, "What good is it, my brethren, if someone claims to have faith but has no deeds? Can such faith save them?

What if there was a brother or sister, who was without clothes or daily food? If one of us says to them, 'go in peace, keep warm and eat well, but do not give them clothes or food, what good is it? This is same as with our faith by itself, if it is not accompanied by action, it is dead. The underfed stay hungry until fed, and the naked stay uncovered until clothed. One cannot say, I have the faith while another says I have the deeds. Show me your faith without deeds and I will show you my faith by my deeds. You believe there is a Lord. That is great, and I will tell you that even Rubina's demons believe in the Lord and shudder when they see him. Do you need evidence that faith without deeds is useless? You must see that a person is considered righteous by what they do and not by faith alone. Those people who say that I have healed many people do not tell you the whole truth. I do not heal them; it is their faith by their deeds that reward them with their healing.

I will now tell you a story about a tribe who lived on the old Earth many ages ago. They had been made slaves in a foreign land where the ruler hated them and made them work hard on buildings that would glorify him. They suffered for around four hundred years when the Lord delivered them from this prison and miserable life. The Lord did many miracles to secure their freedom and led them into a desert land that was in the path to their new promised land. Within a short time in the desert, as their leader was on a nearby mountain receiving their covenant from the Lord, they made a false god and defiled themselves upon this golden calf. The Lord punished many that day, yet he also gave many a chance to choose righteousness before his punishment. Those who chose the Lord walked to one group, the fools who wanted to return to their prison of torment stood on the other, and the Lord destroyed them.

Those who were saved, through their deeds walked to join the Lord's people. Faith, without works is dead. If you break one of the Lord's laws, expect to be punished. Nevertheless, remember, our Lord is a merciful Lord, thus beg for your forgiveness. Even so, returning to our story, the tribes, who were the Lord's chosen people, finally made it to their promised land, and now it was time for the Lord to make a way for them to claim this land, as the sinners who occupied it had to be removed. Their first challenge was a giant fortified city, which had walls that could not be taken without a great war and much bloodshed. Subsequently, the Lord told this leader that a rope would be hanging from a window of an apartment along the wall's top and to have some men climb that rope and enter that apartment, go into the city and open the gates, so their army could enter therein and conquer these sinners.

Three men, in faith walked along this long dark monstrous wall until they saw a rope hanging. They did not just check a few feet and complain, 'oh the Lord has forgotten us.' No, they walked until the rope was before them, and then they climbed the wall and entered into an apartment belonging to someone who belonged to this city famous for their evil and great tortures. They entered into their faith and with the work of placing themselves in unknown danger did as the Lord had told their leader to tell them. They entered into the room and found therein a beautiful woman, and they spoke for a while, and then learned she was a prostitute. Did they curse the Lord for having a prostitute save them? No, they told her to climb down the rope and return to their tribe, so she may be saved. They then went down to the wall and opened it. Our Lord's chosen people entered and destroyed all the sinners and in such removed a great danger to themselves. The leader declared the prostitute righteous, as her faith in what was to all in that land an unknown God, with her actions of listening and doing what the Lord had asked her to do, allowed the Lord so to save many of his chosen people.

I am saying today to pray for those whom you think are fallen, and share the blessings the Lord has given you. I have spoken before about prostitutes selling a gift that belongs to God. I am telling you today that he who sells the prostitute is seven times for guilty than the prostitute, for she is only trying to survive, yet the person who sold her is selling something that belongs to our Lord for their own greed and personal profit. To sin from one's personal choice is between that person and God. To cause another to sin is between the one who caused the other to sin and God. For if the Lord trusted his chosen people's safety with a prostitute, what other great works may he have her do for him. As I have often told you, the Lord so sometimes sends his angels to us in a human form to test us. They search to see if we feed the hungry and care for the needy. That woman you steal to make a prostitute could be an angel. Are you prepared for that angel to take you to the throne of our Lord today and accuse you? You cannot say, 'oh Lord, I gave much grain to the temple and expect the Lord to excuse you.' Do not be foolish enough to think that you can steal from the Lord since you also give to him. My brothers and sisters, if the Lord chooses to have a prostitute to do his work, except this as the Lord's will.

Do not simply say to the prostitute, 'you are sinning and stop now for you have your freedom.' Will you protect her when her master comes to punish her? Will you give her shelter and food until she can return to her family? Will you protect her from her master while she travels home?

This faith must be matched with many deeds. However, I tell you, that whosoever sees a prostitute who wants to be free and does not free her is now a part of her sins and will suffer accordingly. As I am told, any woman, at any time for any place in the three southern tribes could be captured and sold as a prostitute. As you save someone, someone may someday save you. Our Lord loves the poor and needy, the crippled and old, as he also loves all people. It is my desire that we all be righteous and that the Lord will not look into Rubina's Empire to give his blessings. The thing I cherish the most about the Black Land Tribes is that when they receive knowledge about a wrong road that they travel, they immediately turned around and walk in the Lord's path. Rubina shall suffer at the hands of your tribes then her tortured and abused people."

With this Oi then went and talked with the people and the priests. Oi specifically told the priests that the temples must stop this capturing and selling innocent people as sex slaves. "If one becomes a prostitute of her own free will, then we will let God judge that case. However, for one to be stolen and sold, we must free her and capture her master. I want the masters nailed with six nails to a wooden cross and left to die. We must remove this cancer before destroys our hopes for a victory. I warn you that the Lord is very angry at this and has declared it must stop." We ate our meals and rested the night in the temple. They had wonderful temples, which the priests explained that the temples were built about two hundred years earlier while the area worshiped other gods. I was curious and asked them, "Why did they convert, and who told them about the Lord?"

They told us that Belcher always witness about the Lord, and the angels would walk with Belcher while doing great miracles during his ministries. The converts then wondered throughout the tribes' speaking of the seven-headed God. Little details were blurred as parts of their local legends were blended within the version of that tribe. We began to standardize our beliefs after Rubina's demons started raiding our lands." I thanked them for this precious story as Oi and I both smiled, taking pride in our father, who even though he felt betrayed by the Lord, he still ministered to others, which he wanted them saved. He looked at others as all being lost or with a plague that he had the cure. I am only saddened that more of our siblings did not choose to stand with our father. They just did not want to believe that our mother was evil, in their delay to decide; the evil got them, and they shall someday die.

We now moved on to Bonyl in which Oi wanted to have the meeting on the green plains a safe distance from Death Bay. As we started to leave the mountains, a giant army of demons came over us pulling all of us off the ground. Oi commanded them to release us, and they did. Fortunately, for us, we were only a few feet from the ground. Oi then asked the Lord to punish them. We immediately saw one-half the demons explode and cry in torment as they vanished. Oi then asked the Lord why he had not destroyed all the demons. The Lord told him, "Their time has not yet come." Oi then thanked the Lord for destroyed as many as he had, which I would estimate around five thousand. The Lord afterwards told the crowd and demons, "You who serve evil may not touch those who serve me." The demons then took twenty-two people, as they screamed for the Lord to save them, and devoured them in the sky above us. Not even one drop of blood hit the ground.

Oi straightway told us, "The demons will not let one drop of blood hit the soil, lest these people cry out for justice. The blood of all who are murdered, Saint or wicked, may cry out for justice once their blood touches the Earth or manmade surface covering the ground." Oi now looked at the demons and asked them, "By what authority did you take these twenty-two people from me?" They answered, "They were not righteous, as they were our feeders and therein servants of Rubina." Oi then asked the Lord, "Is this real oh Lord?" The Lord next told Oi that it was true. Oi now asked the Lord to protect those who were following him and receive the messages as he received them.

The Lord then commanded the demons not to touch any who followed Oi or was going to any of his functions. The demons have now raised themselves another forty-five feet. Then the Lord placed a shield that we could see through between the demons and us. This caused many to attend this meeting in the open green lands. Oi then stopped and gave a short sermon as most who were going to attend his message for the Bonyl. He began, "Oh great righteous of Bonyl; we have been tested and found to be righteous. I hope you noticed that it was evil who did the judging for they know who serves the Lord. They will not touch the

Lord's servants for fear the Lord would punish them. The Lord does not protect any evil. Evil will not let one go once they have a chance to take them, for fear that, they would turn to the Lord. They took their feeders. I had to ask the Lord what feeders are. He told me that they secretly captured unimpeachable people and for a profitable, trade sold them to the demons. The Encsi sell women as sex slaves, and now the Bonyl are selling innocent people to the demons.

The Lord has demanded that the feeders be captured and executed in public. They will be easy to capture since they are now blind, deaf, and have a red X tattooed on their forehead. I have heard from their spirits that they were saving their friends by feeding the demons other people. Oh, my fellow Saints, God does not show favoritism and a demon can never become full of human flesh and blood, for their stomach is as a bottomless pit when it comes to blood. Remember, demons do not eat or drink, and the taking of the blood is in pretense, as the soul is what they are capturing. They are casting them into their prison, so they may torment them. When someone makes a deal with a demon, he or she will lose his or her life. There will be no exceptions ever. When evil comes to you, as it did me today, call upon the Lord to save you. This is why the Bonyl meeting is in the open green field.

Our faith will keep us safe, even though many have this faith by seeing the miracle shield, it is still faith, and we are free to worship our Lord for he is greater than all the demons combined. You will no longer have your loved ones taken from you by your neighbors as those who did these evil deeds shall never again hear or see in the flesh. They truly do not want to see the prison that they are being contained. When evil comes to you call upon the Lord, and you will be saved, or at worse, you will be taken to be with the Lord in his heavens where the demons may not seek you. We shall now go to the meeting place the Lord has selected and receive his message for your tribe."

We now journeyed to the meeting place. We noticed many small fields of the crops sort of tucked inside patches of weeds. They told us they would spread the crops out among the weeds so the raiders could not find them easily when they raided. The Bonyl would hide in the weeds and ambush the raiders. This made them very precocious in the weeds and time-consuming to harvest the entire field, as they would have to search for each plant thereby leaving themselves exposed to danger. They were forced to do this, as the Death Bay was a favored place for the demons and raiders to search. Therefore, they had to work hard for what little they could harvest and depended on the Encsi to survive. Thus, they had to do the work for their slim harvest and work for a product to trade that usually entailed a special craft. Many times the men would work four months each year in Encsi and then eight months in their homes. As we arrived, Oi quickly got into his message, for even he did not like all these beasts buzzing over his.

Oi began by saying, "Today, we meet as a victor over evil, as evil is above us, and we are in the Lord's bosom. These same demons may very well perish when we drive Rubina from this world. My brothers and sisters, believers in our Lord, we must not show favoritism. He, like all personalities has selected some to do his will. He has three types of wills, first is predestined in that these people were tasked with a function before they were born, the second is personal, in which the circumstances promote opportunities that are pleasing to the Lord's eyes. The third will is his permissive will, in which he will allow a Saint to do a mission in which that Saint has his or her heart set upon.

If a man enters the temple with many fine jewels and badges showing he is wealthy and famous, and a poor man in filthy old clothes comes in you must treat both the same. If you rush the rich man to the best seats in the temple to be in view of the priests and say to him, 'these are our foremost seats,' yet say to the poor man, 'you stand there or sit on the floor in front of the temple's door,' you have differentiated among your yourselves and become judges, and your thoughts are evil.

The Lord created both men. They both are serving the Lord. I tell you the least must be made the greatest, for our Lord, who is the finest made himself the minutest before his father so that we may become a part of his kingdom. Listen, fellow babes in the milk of the word, has not the Lord chosen those who are poor in the eyes of the world to be rich in his throne and with him inherit the kingdom he has promised us for eternity. I tell you few rich will be in heaven, yet many poor will be. Therefore, is it not more of a blessing to be poor while in this world and rich for eternity?

The rich were given more as a test to see that if they became slaves of greed and evil, or help the Lord fed the poor and care for the needy.

If you show favor the rich, who can be as a double-edged sword and cut you both ways when they swing at you, you are breaking the Lord's laws. If you stumble over one part of the law, you are guilty of breaking all of it. We know that if we steal, we have sinned, and if we murder an innocent person, we have sinned. If you do not steal, yet murder, are you not guilty of sinning? Judgment without mercy will be shown to anyone who has not been merciful. Mercy triumphs over judgment. We know this to be true, for it is our Lord's mercy on us that we have a future someday of being free from Rubina's terrible judgments. As I have spoken too many of the other tribes, I am still concerned about taming our tongues. Few of you should become teachers, because you know that we, who teach, will be judged more strictly.

We all stumble in many ways. Anyone who is never at fault in what they say is perfect, able to keep their whole body in check. Tianshire and the priests work very hard to give you the teachings the Lord has given me. This manner makes teaching no more than allowing the student to read the words and using your love of our Lord gives them understanding so they will not be ignorant. When we put bits into the mouths of horses making them obey us, we can turn the whole animal. Alternatively, take Rubina's large ships as an example. Although they are so huge and are driven by strong winds, they are steered by a very small rudder wherever the captain wants to go. Likewise, the tongue is a little part of the body, but it makes great boasts. Consider that the dry plains in Pesta are set to fire by a small spark. The tongue also is a fire, a world of evil among the parts of the body. It corrupts the whole body, sets the complete course of one's life on fire, and is itself set on fire by hell. All kinds of creatures are being tamed and have been tamed by humanity, but no human being can tame the tongue.

It is a restless evil, full of deadly poison. We have seen our daughter sold as sex slaves and our neighbors selling our children to demons to feed. These processes needed the tongue to control the actions and steps within these transactions. Evil men stand in the temple and blaspheme the Lord. He is struck down by the priests. The evil man's tongue from not being tame destroyed his whole body. The love of our marriages is formed and maintained by the words of our tongues. We shall form our armies to drive Rubina from these lands with the power of our tongues. Our tongues can also allow us to praise the Lord and thus, receive eternal life. If we had no tongue, then would be as animals. We have the wisdom to control our tongue. Who is wise and understanding among you? Let them show it by their good life, by deeds done in the humility that comes from wisdom.

Nevertheless, if you harbor bitter envy and selfish ambition in your hearts, do not boast about it or deny the truth. Such 'wisdom' does not come down from heaven but is from humanity, unspiritual, and demonic. For where you have envy and selfish ambition, there you find disorder and every evil practice. However, the wisdom that comes from heaven is, first of all, pure' then peace loving, considerate, submissive, full of mercy and good fruit, impartial and sincere. Peacemakers who sow in peace reap a harvest of righteousness. I tell you many things about evil, for evil has attacked you as hard as it attacks the Barac and Ensi tribes. This is why you must guard your faith, as faith is being sure of what we hope for and certain of what we do not see.

Be on your guard; stand firm in the faith; be men of courage; be strong. However, you, men of God, flee from all this, and pursue righteousness, godliness, faith, love, endurance and gentleness. Resist Rubina, standing firm in the faith, because you know that your fellow tribes throughout this new nation are undergoing the same kind of sufferings so that your faith might not rest on men's wisdom, but on God's power. Now faith is being sure of what we hope for and certain of what we do not see. We truly hope for our freedom from these demons that torment us daily. If I have the gift of prophecy and can fathom all mysteries and all knowledge, and if I have a faith that can move mountains, but have not loved, I am nothing. We must love all our brethren, rich or poor, unless condemned by our Lord, whom they must perish. We must open their eyes and turn them from darkness to light and from the power of Rubina to the Lord. Hence, that they may receive forgiveness of sins and a place among those who are sanctified by faith in me. For it is by grace you have been saved, through faith, and this not from yourselves, it is the gift of God. In addition to all this, take up the shield of faith, with which you can extinguish all the flaming arrows of the evil one. We know that the testing of your faith develops perseverance.

We strive that at the end of our days we can say, 'I have fought the good fight; I have finished the race; I have kept the faith.' We now went to the court of the elders where we saw the feeders, which were collected. The Lord had currently commanded that we burn them on special poles in the middle of the green fields so that all the villages could see the smoke. This smoke rose up to the shield and went through it. We could see the demons screaming as the smoke hit them, and they were flying away in an injured condition. Oi asked them why they were screaming and the Lord told him that he had put a special pain in the smoke that only affected the evil demons. Of this smoke, approximately twenty percent died, or an additional 1,000 demons. That made now 6,000 fewer demons to prey upon the Death Bay. I am smart enough to know that more demons will arrive to supplement them soon satisfactorily. As we were walking in the mountains of Gyori, we saw two villages sitting on the mountains beside us. As we approached, some of our followers who had been scouting for us came back and told Oi, "We cannot pass through this valley, lest they kill all of us."

Then Oi heard the Lord tell him to stay where he was, and he would destroy the two villages because of their wickedness. One of the followers heard Oi say this to the priests as they were preparing to make camp here. The follower begged out to Oi, "Oh great prophet, will you ask the Lord to spare these cities if we find ten who are righteous." Oi then asked the Lord and the Lord said yes and for the follower to enter the cities and find the ten moral people. He took with him three of his friends. About three hours later, he came running back alone telling us that his three friends were dead. He had most of his clothes removed and had bruises all over his body. Oi asked him if he found what he was looking for. He told Oi that those whom he was looking for were no longer alive, and that he could find no righteous in these cities. Oi then looked up and said, "Oh Lord, thy will be done." Immediately, giant balls of flaming fire came from the sky and destroyed both cities instantly. Oi told the priests the Lord said for them to stay here for the night as the wind would be blowing through the city, and the smoke would be going away from us. Oi then asked the priests to meet with him and explain what these cities were. The priests told him that demons had possessed the wicked in these cities and that everyone avoided this path. Oi asked them if there were any more cities like this.

They told him that these were the only two, that their defenders would drive people who are possessed with demons to these cities. Oi then told them, "From this day forward, we shall take the person to the Lord and let the Lord handle the demon." They all agreed. Oi then continued, "How many times have I said, "We must be pure in faith and breaking no laws in order to assure our victory over Rubina. We would have been sad if our sons and daughters were on the battlefield fighting today and the Lord had turned his back on us. We must take this seriously." The next day they proceeded to his designated meeting place with the Gyori, which would be in the foothills of the northern most mountaintop. The people assembled and Oi began his talk, "My message to the Bonyl declared that if one breaks a part of the law, they break the entire law.

We can never be sometimes sinners. Each must decide which road to journey, and we must stay on that road. The Lord has chosen to give us a new hope, a new life free from the evil of Rubina, so that we may no longer cry at the death of our family members by the evil hands of Rubina, which even I have suffered. The wages of sin is death, but the gift of God is eternal life with our Lord. The wages of the righteous is life, but the earnings of the wicked are sin and death. Whose sin does this refer? Does this only apply to Rubina's sins and not to ours because the Lord likes us? Sorry, as with your judges, when we break the law, we are punished. We do the crime we do the time. When our Lord talks about sin, he means every sin, original sin, actual sin, every kind of sin, lesser and greater. These sins have not been forgiven, as forgiven sins are no longer sins. When we speak of death, all who sin dies the physical death. It is what happens thereafter, which is of the most concern. The righteous accept their eternal reward; those whose name is not recorded in our Lord's book of life are cast from his throne. They lose their being gift of being created in the image of our God, as sin strips this from them.

Sin is as a plague in that it completely takes the life of the one, it is being given refuge within. Remember, all have sinned. It is what they did after than sin, which is at issue. Did they return to our Lord in his grace and receive their salvation? Maybe they played the most dangerous game, there is, and that is playing with sin. They may have thought, wow; this sin was fun, so I will have some more fun before I return to that boring life of the righteous. Why is this game threatening? It is dangerous because they are also playing with evil, which many times are as a wolf in sheep's clothing. As we have seen in the two villages, the Lord just destroyed, once wickedness gets in the front door, it destroys everything and everyone in that home. Remember, sin is evil and evil is sin. Please do not say that since I believe in the Lord, that I am sinless.

Every one of the 10,000 demons who tried to stop us in Bonyl believed in the Lord, yet 6,000 of them are no more. Please, get those sins out of your life before evil gets into your life. You must think of sin as a deadly poison, that once you decide to keep it, it will destroy you. Cannot we see the destruction that Rubina is doing to her people and the people of the black lands? Since she has crossed the line into evil, she must now be destroyed for those sins. I do feel sad, because sin stole a mother from little Tianshire and myself. I can only give great thanks to my sisters in the Lord, who have cared so very much for little Tianshire as she works endlessly with the priests trying to make sense out of my ramblings."

I looked at my big brother and winked at him, because I know how much he loves me and how safe I am around him, even though he is on the front lines of what will most likely be the greatest spiritual battle of our times. Oi, as if he were reading my mind said, "We are quickly moving towards the greatest unworldly war that we shall see in our lifetimes, as even within this last week 6,000 demons died and two villages of human slaves to sin burned alive. You all depend upon the Lord to give you a strong leader for this war. Do you want a sometimes sinner, sometime not leader? What would happen to your families under such a ruler?

Sin is committed against our Lord and thus deserves to be cast away from his presence. I do not tell you these things to be a pest or accuser; I am only telling you what the one who shall later come to save you will not lead sinners against sinners. This leader will merely lead the righteous so that the Lord will join them in destroying their common enemy, evil. It shall be a war of righteous against evil. Our Lord, sometimes, allows us to sin with a gap before receiving the punishment. Beware of the sin unto death as I have spoken to you so often. This is willful, deliberate, unrepentant, continuous sin.

Exercising much more patience than would any parent, our Lord will reach his boiling point, which the next unrepentant sin becomes the straw the broke the horses back. I shall now talk about compassion, which we will treat the other creations of our Lord, whom we live with daily. We must strive to get our eyes as the Lords, where we can see as the Lord sees, and apprehend insight, as each of us will develop two qualities, wisdom, and compassion. Wisdom and compassion are two wings that work together to enable flying, or two eyes that work with each other to see deeply. We all search hard for wisdom; however, without compassion, when you see the wisdom, you will not know it.

To sail the high skies of wisdom we must also crawl on the ground with compassion. Rejoice when you see the needy, for above them is wisdom if you are in compassion. Rejoice with those who rejoice, and weep with those who weep. For you must work hard to lessen suffering wherever it happens. I ask you, do the evil ones try to lessen the suffering of the afflicted. They do not, and are we not opposite of them, so we should, as we will do. Do not the wicked ask, 'what profit will they receive?' Therefore, should we not ask instead, "How much can we give?" I tell you that whatever I see evil to do; I strive to do the opposite, and if I do not know whether I am correct, I ask the Lord. I see no harm in giving too much, yet the great danger in giving too little. To sum up, let all be harmonious, sympathetic, brotherly, kindhearted, and humble in spirit. Nevertheless, whoever has the world's goods, and beholds his brother in need and closes his heart against him, how does the love of God abide in him? Be gracious to me, Oh God, according to Thy loving kindness, According to the greatness of Thy compassion blot out my transgressions. He who is considerate of a poor man lends to the Lord, and He will repay him for his good deed." With this, Oi closed out the meeting and went to speak with the priests. His heart was heavy for these last three tribes as so much evil was among them. He warned the priests that many people could be saved; however, it would take much work on their parts. If evil is going to fight hard for souls, then so shall we. The war was now raging on the small peninsula and Oi did not want to take many casualties. He told the priests, "We have the Lord on our side, so why should we lose yet even one soul?" We now traveled what they called the Peaceful Path. The wind blew hard on both sides of this path, yet not on the path while over the green lands and gave a comfortable cooling wind while crossing the desert area. I said to my brother, "They have many peculiar things in these southern lands." He told me, "Tianshire, our father told me that the mates from the Five Tribes of the Sisters always told stories about strange things happening on the lands to the far north. Maybe, this is only the way of the worlds." We now passed a small section of green lands until we entered the deserts belonging to the Bucsu. The Bucsu was a warlike tribe, yet never fought with the other tribes. They had fought off some serious invasions from both their eastern and Death Bay shores as Rubina had tried hard to capture their lands, so she would have the southern tribes separated from the northern tribes. They had no temples, or any form of building as they only lived in small tents, that they could take down and put up quickly. They had an amazing network of underground tunnels that allowed them to appear almost at will anywhere they chose. Rubina's armies believed they were fasting many large armies, when, in fact, they were only fighting one small-scattered army. The tribes depended upon the Bucsu to keep the nation untied, especially as the Death Bay cut so deep inland. The Bucsu held about ninety percent of the nation's grain reserves in their tunnels in special side tunnels they had opened so as not to obstruct the movement of the army. We actually went through secret tunnels all the way to the Bugac's mountain range. I told my brother that I could not imagine people digging this many underground spacious tunnels and especially as they were deep and had a sophisticated air network without compromising their security. They explained that the ancient people dug the tunnels with their jaws from the sky. Belcher always told us how Eve spoke of archaic advanced civilizations that had underground empires hidden throughout the cosmos. As legend goes, one of the Bucsu ancestors had a special dream in which he was shown the entrance to this amazing network. They also had some unique lights that would shoot lines of hot light, as we would be an arrow and whatever this light touched, it would be destroyed. These lights had the range of a four-hour walk. They would pull them out at times and do some long-range demon shooting. They were effective enough to keep Rubina's raiders of the northerly shores of Death Bay and shed always raided east by way of the northerly or central green lands going around the mountains. The Bucsu was also able to keep the Zala protected from southern raids and to move their populations across long distances in the desert when needed.

Never too low for the Lord to go

The Bucsu is slightly different from the other black land's tribes, although this difference can be attributed to their security concerns. In the tunnels, they could enjoy additional freedoms that those above on the surface could. These freedoms naturally did not extend beyond the hard rock that reinforced the tunnel walls. Their freedoms came with the ability to co-exist with each other with no fear of demons swooping down and capturing them. Children could play and actually make as much noise wanted, although the tunnels provided the restrictions. They had some children's games that I had never known. I think most of them; they created because of the tunnel shaped environment. They taught me a special game in which they called, 'Rock Shirts.' In this game we would pick a side tunnel and through a rock that was scrapped in a shirt into the tunnel.

Then we would all rush into the dark tunnel to find the rock shirt. Whoever found it first was the victor. No one could stand up until the shirt was recovered. I asked Oi if I could play rock shirts with the other girls. He was visiting with some priests in of their open underground caverns. The priests told him it was safe and not to worry about it. Oi then told me, "Tianshire, just be careful, because you are all the family I have left. So, go and be a little girl before you turn into a big girl." I thanked him and off; we went. I heard him talking to the other priests about how I needed some more playtime." I was glad he thought like that, because every moment, I had with Tvář Lásky still was fresh in my mind, as I would pretend play with her a lot. I sometimes felt guilty for wanting to play, when we had such important work to do for the Lord, nevertheless, Oi told me that previously the Lord revealed to him once he was human born the same as everyone else. Oi actually told me that the Lord told him to ensure that I had some play time and to let me be a little girl often." This really made me feel good, for I do not control how my mind and body learn about each other. One case in point, about how fun it is to throw rocks.

Such a non-productive action, nevertheless, it is fun. Throwing rocks are not feeding the poor nor giving clothes to the needy, this is just plain fun and what is better, and by crawling in the tunnels, we will get our knees dirty. The girls tell me they found a unknown tunnel to play in. It had just been a small hole before; however, they have been working hard to remove the rocks so to you a new hole for rock shirts, which is usually the first official human function of a new discovery. We had one of the mothers toss the rock shirt in for us. The girls told me that mothers and even sometimes daddies watched the first couple of times the children go into a new tunnel. That was a little scary for me; nevertheless, the girls told me that no one had ever yet been hurt in a rock shirt except some bruises and cuts on their legs. The mother then had us drop to our knees in a straight line and said go.

Off we went, into the darkness. The other girls (Zala and Tolna) have lived long enough in a tunnel environment, so they appeared to know how to keep orientated; nonetheless, I kept running into a wall. When I ran into this current wall, I could feel some rocks become loose. I now considered that a new side tunnel discovery would be better than the rock shirt, in which the other two girls had me defeated already, so I started wiggling out some more rocks. I can get them to wiggle, yet I just cannot seem to get them put pop out, so I decided to kick the bottom center one out, and that should give me a strong enough grip on the others to verify my new discovery. Therefore, I wiggle around in the dark, and get my feet in front of me and kicked at the rock to loosen it. Ouch, that hurt my foot.

Maybe a better approach would be to push it with my feet. In addition, push away I did, and the rock moved ahead of my foot and after that only dropped as I could hear it rolling down something going somewhere. Afterwards, just before I was to announce my discovery, the other rocks that I had loosened came crumbling down on my foot. I tried to pull it out. The darn thing has a lock on my leg. Hence, I began to yell for help. The mothers yelled in order to tell me they were on their way and Zala, and Tolna yelled to tell me they were also on their way to me. The mothers had a lit torch with them, and I could now see them rushing to rescue me. When they arrived, one of the mothers positioned the torch while the other one started removing the rocks. She wiggled one out and sat it beside me. I then told her that she only had to push the rocks in, and they would fall away. She looked at me strangely and pushed the next rock. It fell inside as we both could hear it rolling down some sort of hollow opening. The other mother jumped in beside her and started pushing the higher ones, telling us, "We need to move these high ones out first so they will not fall on her leg."

Zala and Tolna had now returned, and they started pushing the rocks into this hole. I believe everyone was having fun making the rocks roll. We then started bragging about whose rock made the loudest sound when it ended. This was so much fun, and before we knew it, the hole was opened, and I could easily pull my leg out. After that, Zala and Tolna screamed out, 'There is a big room and this is its door." Their mothers repositioned the torch and then Zala's mother said, "You all had better step back and let me get some men in here so we can make sure this is safe." Zala then said, "What is different from this than the other places?" Her mother told us, "This one is to a large opening and could be unstable or dangerous. We need not to take any chances." Then Tolna's mother agreed and had all three of us stand behind her. She turned facing us and drummed up some kid chit chatter to pass the time, which actually was not that long.

The men arrived with ropes and all the tools they used while exploring in caves. Soon all the rocks were removed from the opening, and they lowered a torch into the hole. In the meantime, some other women cleaned my leg and wrapped it in some white cloth they had. A short time thereafter, I heard some cheering. I looked at Tolna and she revealed to, "Tianshire, you have discovered a new civilization." I then asked her, "Where are the people, so Oi and I can share the Lord with them?" Tolna afterwards said, "Oh no Tianshire, they are all dead." I next asked her, "Who killed the people I discovered?" Zala after that told me, "No one did Tianshire, and we will now wait until the men tell us what they have discovered. This might be our greatest discovery, so they have sent for your brother to join us." It was nice for someone to say 'they have sent for your brother,' which gives me a sense of belonging since it seems like such a long time ago we were with our father. It has only been a few years, yet it felt like a lifetime ago. My brother is coming to get me. I like that, so at least I belong to something. I wonder whether he will be mad about this or will be in a hurry to leave. I would like to stay around for a little while. Oi arrives and once he sees me, starts running to me, picks me up, holds me tight and then asks me if everything is alright. I think to myself, 'what has gotten into this young man who can face 10,000 demons and not waver.' I can tell, by the way, that he is holding me that he is holding something important to him, as we each would gladly give our lives for the other, if I were old enough to know that concept. I saw my mother hurt ample people, so I believe I have seen enough that I do not want to see it again. Oi then says to me, "Little sister, I hear you have been very busy," as he is looking at the wrapping on my leg." I later told him, "My friend told me I found some new people, yet someone has already killed them, and you would explain to me why." He sat me down and told me, "Tianshire; we do not know everything yet; however, you have discovered an opening into the secret homes that people who lived many ages ago.

Do you think we should go down and study it?" I told him, "Tolna's mommy said no kids were allowed down there." Oi then said, "That is right, unless they have a big brother whom the priests say can escort them." A nearby priest, who was listening said, "Oh course, follow me." I looked over, saw Zala's sad look, and asked Oi, "Oi, May my two best friends join us." Oi looked at their mothers' who smiled and shook their heads yes, and in an instant Zala and Tolna were holding my hands, and off, we went. I never was around the unsaid language and interactions between adults and their children. The mothers shaking their heads were the ultimate absolute, non-reversible approval. Zala told me that daddy's sometimes change their minds when mommies get mad; however, mommies never change their minds when the daddies say no. This must be true, because the priests did not even question it. Soon, each of us little girls rode down a big person's back as down the long rope, we went. The men had already set up many lanterns to provide as much light as they could. When we arrived down on this lower surface a priest came up to Oi and said, "Oi, your sister must surely be blessed of the Lord, for he has opened a door that was closed so many ages ago. We cannot even begin to comprehend how long this has been here.

We do know that these rocks are not like any in all our tunnels." He pointed up as we saw perfectly square marble rocks covering the ceiling. We could see where some steps may have once reached up to that ceiling, yet now we are falling down. The priests said, 'This was most likely due to earthquakes, which attest to how strong these walls are. They believed the ceiling was covering another route to the surface. No one wanted another way to the surface for that would also mean another way for the surface to come here. As I look around, I see what looks like small upside-down mountain rocks flowing from the ceiling to the ground. We walk over and touch them, yet even as we run our hands over them, no dirt comes loose. These are not stacked rocks. The priests tell us that they are most likely a support system to keep the room from caving in, in the same manner the tribes used to support the temple roofs. These supports held up much more weight than the ones in the temples. These also blended in well with the open area, creating a natural look, which is the only look any of us knew from down here. They were clearing up what few rocks had fallen; of which many were what we pushed on trying to free my leg. There were three openings in the floor, which led down into the darkness below us. I particularly liked the nice rock fences they had used to mark off these holes in the ground.

Some more priests came rushing to us saying, "Tianshire, would you like to see some of the beautiful places at the end of these extended hallways?" I looked up at Oi, and he shook his head yes, thus I reached out for the priest's hand, and away we went down one of the hallways. I asked the priest, "Why are their only priests down here?" He told me, "Since we had promised to serve our people, we like to go into the unknown first to make sure they will be safe when it is their turn." I thought, 'this is wonderful; the shepherds are protecting their sheep.' The Bucsu priests were the only ones who took oaths not to have possessions. Therefore, they could be trusted because anything they found, they would give to the temple who would give it to the people, in rank of need. I can tell how relaxed Oi is here, and I can feel how he may want to stay here for a while. We only have three more tribes after the Bucsu, and he still has not told me what we will do next. I told him it would be nice to visit all the tribes again, and he told me, "Tianshire, you will visit all the tribes again." I rather have a strange feeling about the way he said it; however, he is always saying peculiar things, so I will worry about that when my brain gets bigger and can handle complex operations such as this.

We now see some priests running to meet us. They ask, "Where did all you pretty little girls come from? Zala and Tolna, who are my shadows currently since they figured I knew how to work around the big people, told the priests, "We have always lived here." The priests winked at me and then said, "Tianshire; we now believe that these people also had a network of tunnels and from the maps, we see, they may actually extend throughout this entire world." Zala looked and me and said, "Wow Tianshire, that is a whole bunch of places to play." They were carrying strange sticks that did not burn, hitherto still gave light and a lot of light. One priest had a whole bag of them. I asked him, "Fellow servant of our Lord; what kind of light is that?" The priest looked at me and said, "Tianshire; we do not know; we found one by accident and shook it, and the light came forth. We are going to get some other priests to collect some more, as these people had giant rooms packed with them. We will have everyone use these since the air will next stay cleaner, and we will have better light." I afterwards said, "That is great, for our people need a strong light to guide them through the darkness." All the priests looked at me, and then one said, "Very true and wise Tianshire."

Then off those priests went, as we shook our sticks and had light. We each only took one since we were going past one of the storage rooms anyway. Then Tolna asked me, "What did you say that the priest said was very true and wise? Every time I tell them something, they tell me to go home and study some more." I answered Tolna, "I do not know what I said, except that with all the darkness down here, we needed better light." Zala then said, "Perhaps they are being nice to you because of your brother." I looked at Zala and said, "Maybe you are the one that is intelligent." The two priests who were with us now said, "Will you very wise young ladies continue with us?" We all looked at them and said together, "Oh yes; we do not want to be in this hallway without you wonderful priests." We continued to walk past many rooms, until we could see only the hallway. The priests recommended that we go back and look into the rooms. I asked them if we could continue as I had a curious feeling. They asked me about my odd feeling, and I told them, "I cannot really describe it, except something special is not too far from here." The priest asked me, "Do you think it is good?"

I told him, "I do not know if it is of my mother or my father." I just know it is close, so either way I would feel much better knowing. The priests then agreed not to want anything that could harm the people being close, so we all continued. As we got closer, the feelings became better, until I could identify it as not being from evil. I thereby told the priests, "It is not from my mother, as I can feel my father telling me it is safe." Zala and Tolna now asked me, "We do not see your mother and father, and besides how can they talk to you? Furthermore, why do you speak of them being from different places?" The priests then told Zala and Tolna, "Tianshire's father lives with our Lord, and you are too young to know about her mother; however, Tianshire and Oi are going to help us kill her someday." Oi had always spoken about seeing our father in heaven, as the sinner who was forgiven. Zala and Tolna rushed to my sides and screamed out, "Do not worry Tianshire; we will help you protect your mommy."

I then told them, "Zala and Tolna, I have no mommy, for the demons took here and the only way we can save our world is to destroy her. If we do not do this, she will destroy all the people in our world." I could at this moment in time see tears flowing down their little cheeks, and I told them, "It will be okay; that is why my brother and Lord are taking care of me at the moment." "We hugged each other as these two innocent children, in which life was playing rock shirts and having their mothers scrub their kneecaps got their first dose of the pains and miseries of evil. The priests were now comforting them when suddenly a blue light appeared before us. When we walked towards it, the light was dancing ahead of us, as if telling us to follow it. This was kid's stuff here, which brought Zala and Tolna back to their world full of play and nice pretty things. While we continued to walk, more lights of many colors began to appear.

We saw before us a sight of unbelievable beauty. Never had any of us been so stunned in our lives. There was a beautiful colored lake reflecting the colored stones above it. The opening was clearly not from nature as some of the stone cuts were smooth and long. They were at least the length of a man. It still had the same design as the first opening I discovered and the large funnel shaped rock column dropping into the lake. The colored rocks were not just colored; they were as our lights and shinning. One of the priests shocked me when he said, "These lights might have actually been shining for over one million years. What kind of people could create such a heavenly lake so deep inside Venus?" At first, I wondered why he said Venus and not New Venus until I realized he meant even before New Venus. Without hesitation, I started to feel like this is truly special. I had not seen that much of our world, although I had seen much more than many other children who lived on this divided continent.

The air was so warm. We could see so many tunnels flowing out from this small port, as it had some tiny boats tied to some posts in front of us. The priests felt the boats and told us, "These boats are not made from wood, for if they had been, they would be underwater long ago. It feels sturdy, although we should go get the gang and do some more inspection. We do want to make sure it is not an illusion from evil." One of the priests volunteered to go back and get some help. I asked him, "Please ask Oi if he comes with you." The priest then said, "Tianshire that is one request you can believe will be asked." I smiled at him as Zala and Tolna commented, "The priests sure are nice now." I told them, "They are excited just like you. They may at times disappoint you with their words; however, they must tell you what the Lord tells them. You are much more benefited by them punishing you rather than the Lord punishing you." The priest, who was leaving, picked up some small pieces of the colored rocks and put them in his pocket. I would say he did this, to provide evidence of this discovery. The four of us sat patiently until we could take it no more.

The remaining priest noticed the nice smooth walkways that were along the lakeshores and suggested that we very carefully walked around. The three of us guaranteed him, as well as any three toddlers could guarantee an adult, that we would be very cautious and we all went off together. Actually, we had decided to be careful since we did not know what this really was, except for being wonderful and beautiful. We soon discovered that a system of identifying our ports was needed as they; all looked the same except in some minute variations in their colors. Our priest took us back to our port, removed his outer garment, and put it safely on the ground. Zala and Tolna both told us, "We always wondered what you guys wore under your robes." The priest then smiled, as he was still completely clothed with a lighter robe afterwards told us, "I hope you girls will keep this a secret from your mommies and daddies." Next Zala said, "My daddy told me to tell him if any boys took their clothes off in front of me." I after that asked her, "Why would he tell you something like that?" The priest then said, "He did not mean when the boy had other clothes on; however, we will tell your father. Now, do you want me to put my robe back on, and we get lost down here and never see your daddy and mommy again?" Zala subsequently commented, "I was only teasing you. We all later began to laugh, as the priest put his jacket back out. He then picked up some stones, and after we would pass each beautiful port, he would put four stones down in a row close together in the middle of the path.

He told us this was necessary because it would help us to return, and that the rocks had to be put the same way for each station to keep us from getting lost. We looked at each other, and then Tolna said, "We are lucky to have a priest with us; because they are the smartest people in the whole world." Our priest just looked at us and smiled. He afterwards put a chill down all three of our backs when he said, "I only pray to our Lord each day that I can be one-tenth as smart as Tianshire shall be someday." Zala and Tolna next looked at me and said, "When you get all that smart, will you remember us?" This touched my little heart so much, as I needed to have their world in mine, as they now wanted my world into theirs. I told them, "I honestly do not know how I can let you go." Our priest now seemed as if he understood all our hearts and then said, "You three should not be separated. Let me talk to your brother and see what can be done in our Lord." Zala and Tolna after that asked me, "Why would you want to stay with us, when you have so much?" I then told them, "I do not have what you two have and that is each other." They looked at each other and said, "She must be talking big people talk." We currently continued on our mission to discover the unknown, especially when it looked this fun. I even now wondered about this place, as we would pass a special giant perfectly round colored stones in the middle of an extended opening. These simply were just too big for any man or large group of men to make. They each had some special words on them.

They were too far in the water in our eyes to determine what they said. Our priest told us that others in boats would have to discover what they said. Since we have come a long distance, our priest told us we could return. I wish I knew his name. Oi told me most tribes would not let the priests keep their names, as a name belonged to the world, and they were supposed to belong to the Lord. We soon were getting close, as we could hear Zala and Tolna's mothers screaming out for them. Our priest then yelled back, "They are with me." He afterwards looked at us and said, "They got here faster than I expected. I may need your help girls with your mothers." Zala and Tolna told him, "We will help you." I could now see some men rushing to us, and to our priest's great merriment, one of them had his robe. Almost immediately, our priest had his robe back on and we all started telling about our new discoveries. I looked over and saw some men in a boat passing us.

One of the priests who just arrived told us that this discovery had been opened to all the scientists, teachers, and anyone else who could be able to help with their knowledge and skills. We soon met back up with my friend's mothers and Oi. At first, the mothers were somewhat disturbed to say the least; however, Zala and Tolna calmed them down by complaining how strict the priest was. They later explained to me that if the kids complain about an adult being too strict, then the parents knew the kids had not enjoyed themselves. I asked them how they knew this, and they told me all kids knew this. I did not know this. When I complained to my mother about being too strict, it would be for such things as stabbing too much or shooting too many arrows in our backs. When we complained, we had the bodies to prove it. Our priest then asked Oi, the mothers and fathers who were now present, and we girls to join him for a meeting in some boats. We walked over a few ports, grabbed the boats, and went into this beautiful what looked endless lake. Our priest began by saying to Oi, "Young Tianshire needs to have some special friends her age to help her develop more like a human than a spirit." I was surprised when Oi agreed by saying, "What you say is true; notwithstanding, I could not leave her with our mother." Our priest, as I call him since he is as if my advocate next looked at the mothers and said, "These three girls really do enjoy each other so much."

The mothers looked at him and began crying, "Oh, please do not tell us the Lord wants to take them from us." Then Oi looked at them and said, "Our Lord would never take them from you, for he gave them to you?" Our priest later said, "I was thinking more along the lines as spending some time with Oi's ministry, only for a little while." They subsequently looked at Oi and said, "So long as you at no time take them into Belcher's prison, and you make sure they are safe at all times." Oi after that told her, "Fear not mothers, for I never shall again go into Belcher's prison, and they shall be back with you one year from today. I will ask the Lord to have one thousand angels protect them." The mothers currently gasped saying, "One thousand angels, wow, would he do that?" Oi next said,

"Let me ask him now." Oi afterwards called out to the Lord, "Oh great and honor Lord of all love and he who understands all needs. Tianshire is such a wonderful gift that you have given us, yet she is but a child and as a child must sometimes do the things of a child, as you created her. If these mothers allow their daughters whom you gave them to serve you as a child for Tianshire will you guard these children with one-thousand angels?" At this instant, all the lights in this underground kingdom went dark as one bright white light appeared.

This light now walked to us, as we all trembled at the power that came from him. He then spoke saying, "I will not have one-thousand angels protect them." We all kept on praising him for we knew without a doubt the Lord was now among us. Many of the priests began begging the Lord that he would forgive them. The Lord now said, "Did not Oi teach you that you may only be forgiven if you have transgressed." Oi then said, "Forgive them Lord; I must have omitted that from our ministries." The Lord afterwards commanded, "From this day forward all shall know Tianshire as my daughter and shall say, behold we have among us the daughter of the Lord. And I shall protect her at all times with ten legions of angels and for Zala and Tolna; if they serve beside the daughter of the Lord I will give one legion each to protect them the remainder of their days." I then asked the Lord, "Oh my heavenly father, will we be allowed to be as children some of the time?" The Lord now answered back, "Is not that the way I created you? Would not Belcher have allowed this? It should not your heavenly father's love and care for you more than your earthly father?" Zala and Tolna now spoke, as all in the group were amazed that they were brave enough to speak to the Lord, "Oh heavenly father, we will serve our sister and you in all things you ask for the love of all our hearts."

I was surprised at how fast they learned to talk heavenly talk until I realized they were the masters at manipulating, and not always for questionable issues, parents. The Lord now said to all who were there, "Behold the legions that guard my daughter and Saint Zala and Saint Tolna. Tell all men as I will tell all demons, 'touch not my children.' Blessed is my daughter. Blessed are my Saints. Blessed are the Bucsu. Blessed are the Black Land Tribes for they shall defeat my enemies." We now beheld so many angels that our minds grew faint. The Lord slowly returned as all the angels bowed to him. Next, the colored lights reappeared. We now turned our boats around to return to the shore, which was packed with so many people as all had rushed to see this great event. Angels had before appeared, yet not twelve legions. There had never before been recorded a visitation such as this in the black lands as Oi had marched across them for two long years. Each one changed the way that he or she thought of me from that day forward. Oi now told the people on the shore with tears in his eyes, "Today, you have gained the daughter of the Lord, and I have lost my sister." I think he realized something then, which later I realized.

That was the day the Lord picked me to defeat Rubina. Notwithstanding, a thought such as this would never enter my mind while my greatest hero was still among us, for if the choice was given to me, Oi, or defeating Rubina, I would choose Oi. These issues were far from me now, for the next year I would learn most of my human skills and socialization from Zala and Tolna. Oi at present told the priests, "It is so amazing, yet we can never go too low for the Lord to find and bless us." Zala and Tolna's parents now brought their daughters to Oi, and thanked him for allowing their daughters to be blessed enough to love and serve the daughter of the Lord. It was as if all had lost interest in this wonderful place and wanted to rush back to their homes to share the news about their visit from the Lord.

Then the elder priest said, "Today we have been blessed by the Lord in so many ways. I think it would be wise for us all to allow this wonder world to remain a mystery and instead return to our homes and thank the Lord for the wonderful blessings he has given us. Our times with Oi and the Lord's daughter will not be long; therefore, we should devote ourselves to serve them while they are still with us, and so that we may be better servants to a Lord, we have seen. We all now put down the stones and such that we collected, and began climbing out of this underground heaven.

One of the priests told us, "All the beauty of this place falls short of the beauty of one angel who appeared before us. He then wrote a note telling how we all had seen 50,000 angels here today and that the Lord had spoken to us. We all signed it as we left and gave the elder priest our oath of silence, which is death by torture if broken. This time the door was sealed extra strong so that no one would enter therein again. Zala and Tolna parents walked with us, as Oi asked them, "Will you stay with us until we leave Bucsu?" They then accepted; however, they continued to act as normal parents and allowed their daughters to play with me.

Chapter 04

Tianshire's Ladders And Visions

Oi suggests that we rest in the mouth of the tunnel holding my discovery. He tells the priests that he must pray to ensure we have made the right decision. Oi must be up to something, as he seldom does anything at the spur of the moment, unless the Lord is directing him. He now looks at us and says, "Ok girls, go find some water to clean yourselves, and we will figure out your sleeping arrangements." I then ask him, "What do we have to figure out; I sleep with you, and Zala and Tolna sleep with me?" Oi currently tells me, "When I was your only guardian that was the right way; however, you now have two sisters, and they will tell you, you all must sleep together in your own space." I subsequently asked Oi, "Who will protect us?" Then Zala said, "The Lord will protect us, and of course, all our angels." I looked at Zala as if she was a traitor, for giving Oi a way out of this. I am so confused now, because everything I thought was right is wrong, and I seem to have had more when it was only me. I at present do not have my brother, but I do have been betraying sisters. This may not work out, as I want it to come together.

Oi can tell something is wrong with me and he calls me to take a walk with him. Zala and Tolna tell him they will be okay. Oi tells me, "Tianshire, we must learn to share, as you have heard me talk much about, and we must love our new family, which you selected. You are now sharing yourself and your world by also living in others. This shall create some adjustments, and painful growth. You must do this for it is of your calling." I then told him, "I do not know how to do such a thing. I know myself, and I know you; however, now that which was not." Oi then asked me, "Has not that always been the way with us?" I knew he was correct; it is simply that I do not want to share. I hate the situation I am in, because I have a grown soul in my conscience inside a thirteen-year-old body. This is as being a great thinker who cannot think. I see so many people look at me as if I have all the answers, yet I wonder if I know my name. Everything was so much easier when I was simply a shadow. Oi now asks different around me. I think it was a shock when the Lord declared me as his daughter, yet he declares all women as his daughter. He was simply making a point about the security of my two new friends. My new friends; nevertheless, I have not been that friendly to them since they gave up their families for me. I wonder how they feel now. I need to pull myself together, go with the flow tonight, and then talk with Oi tomorrow if I can get some time with him. The world will have to pause for a few days. Maybe we can get back up on the surface for some time. I think some hot desert sun would brighten up myself-imposed mental confusion. It is so strange to be confused when all I am getting is what I asked to receive. I returned to the area where Zala and Tolna were snuggled beside each other with a loose fur covering them. I walked over to them and asked them what they had been doing. They said hi to me and then told me they were being rested until I returned.

This hit me with a twist. Even though I was acting strange when I departed, they knew I was returning. Therefore, I asked them, "How did you know I would return?" Then Zala told me, "Because sisters always stay together no matter what." I looked at Tolna and asked, "Really?" She told me, "Even if they have to die to return." I then asked them, "Why?" They told me it was because of having the identical blood. I then asked them, "Do we have the same blood?" Tolna told me, "The Lord is the one who makes the blood Tianshire." I then told them, "Well, I guess we have the same blood. How should we sleep tonight?" Zala answers, "That is easy, me on one side and Tolna on the other side, so we can keep you warm." I then questioned, "Why do you want to keep me warm?" Tolna reveals to me, "Because we love you so much." I thought to myself, "Even though I may be losing some things in my life, I am getting some other special things.

Zala then follows by saying, "Why do you think the Lord gave us to you? He knew our hearts. Thus, anything that happens this next year we shall still be together, now get over here and let us get some sleep, so we can pester the big people tomorrow." I then asked her, "How do we pester the great people?" Tolna afterwards says, "Do not worry about it, we will teach you." Maybe I am going to be the one learning so much this next year. I now ask them, "What if I act crazy like tonight?" They subsequently told me, "That is okay, because you have never been taught how to be in a kid's world, so we will teach you; no matter how many tears it takes." I after that, thought to myself, 'no matter how many tears it took," is a concept I want to lock deep in my mind.' This was the key to unite in love, patience, understanding and endurance, plus so many other things. They were not even in the least bit angry or troubled in tonight's events and had suffered none, because they believe this 'blood' thing was the security that would endure all obstacles. I may actually be starting down the road to forming my own thoughts and feelings. My world so far has been, the Lord, my father, Oi are always right, and my mother is very bad and must be stopped. This is a solid foundation and therefore, did not need a lot of thinking as so many people and priests were searching for it. I marvel at how I can debate with priests, yet am lost among thirteen-year olds. I think this is because they want what I have, and I want what the thirteen-year olds wants. As I lay down and they pounce on each side of me and putting our animal fur over us to hold in our warmth, I now feel something else and that is their hearts beating exactly the same rhythm as mine. I wonder how this can be imaginable, nevertheless, it is. Our legs and arms are intermingled in a configuration that cannot be likely. Each body part is positioned in a fashion that brings both comfort and bonding, as if not touching does not exist. Oi constantly tucked me in, and told me stories or things he had done during the day, until I was what he called, 'making a racket.' I could never determine why I always went to sleep first. This is not the case with this 'blood' thing because each goes to sleep when they want to, and for Tolna that was in the middle of a sentence. That was strange yet interesting. I have never been this crowded when I was going to sleep; nonetheless, this feels normal, since they are not heavy. I happen to wake when Oi returns and can feel him smiling at us, and I hear him say, "Thank you Lord." That is when I say the same thing and drift off into my journey for tomorrow. Oi naturally slept between us, and the walkway in our tunnel protecting his little followers.

The next thing I knew our fur was flying, and Tolna and Zala were rushing to their mothers. They each grabbed one of my arms, and I was barely keeping up with them. Tolna then yells, "Mommy brought us some breakfast." I look back at Oi, as the mother says to him, "You too." He jumps in with us, and we start eating away. It is simple things, yet they are prepared by the hands of love. This is delicious. Zala and Tolna act normal while they eat it, picking through it carefully to make sure each thing that is exactly as it should be. Oi and I do not care, and we are flying through our food. Zala later tells me that a kid has to act finically with their food sense the mothers want us to eat so we can use this standard to keep them on their toes. I have eaten many breakfast fruits that I picked from a tree, thus I picked it, so I did not care for the taste, because I did not want to have to go back up and pick some more.

I never ate breakfast with my mother, because I was afraid, I might be eating someone I knew. My father was invariably wonderful about snatching Oi, sometimes Tsarsko, and always me, away first thing on the morning. After we finished eating, Zala's mother asked her how the night went. Zala and Tolna told them not to worry, for they were teaching me everything I needed to know. That is when Tolna's mother said, "That is what I am afraid of." Oi laughed at this, along with the mothers. Zala and Tolna simply carried on as if everything was normal. This caught me by surprise, yet they have taught me enough to know that I should keep quiet. Afterwards when we were alone, as if they could read my mind, they explained that we had to pretend not to know these things so the big people will talk more around us.

We must do this, so we can stay ahead of them. I then thought about how big people acted like this in temple affairs, pretending not to know what they were supposed to do, and thus force the priests continually to repeat their pleas. Adults become children when they find the Lord. I wonder if that is why the Lord wants me to learn how to be as a child. Maybe I should not learn to be as a child, yet I hear a call from deep inside telling me to become like a child and sister to Tolna and Zala. I actually dread not listening to this call of the tempestuous growing inside me, for fear that if I do not, it could become a force, which I do not want to have been growing in me. I approach Oi, and pull at the side of his robe, which is our secret signal that I want to talk with him. He looks down at me, and I ask him, "Brother, may we spend some time on the surface as Tolna told me we are somewhere in the middle of their desert." Oi smiles at me and afterwards confesses, "Tianshire, I am starting to miss the surface also; I will see what the priests can do for us." I next thanked him so much and ran back to my sisters telling them, "It worked, thanks so much. They told me to begin with brother and to explain how I know it would be safe. They additionally told me to thank him and get away looking very happy before he gets a chance to explain the answer could be no." Within the hour, Oi returns and tells us to get ready, because we are going to take a vacation on the surface. Tolna and Zala are so smart, because all they say works. I find myself not even questioning anything they say, because it unfailingly works. When I think a lot about their strategies, I find that many of them; I currently use with the Lord, in that I always begin with his title, constantly disclose to him why, and continually thank him as much as possible. I usually feel foolish informing him why in that I know he is already aware; nevertheless, it gives me peace of mind saying it certifying that he understands me. I will put the thinking to rest and the playing to the forefront a lot. The priests guide us through a windy side tunnel to a special opening with ropes handing down. My sisters fly up the ropes as if they were walking over the ground. Oi and I climb up these ropes with Zala and Tolna coaching us. How strange, Oi and I are placing our lives in their hands through the faith that comes from knowing they can do what we are attempting. As my face meets the sunlight, my eyes quickly close. Although we had only been in the tunnel for a few weeks, so much had happened. I discovered a new world that must remain a secret, and I uncovered a gap in my early life. The heat from the sun soaks into my skin as it is introducing itself to my body. This soft orange light, which is fighting to give my eyes a chance to readjust to this wonderful brightness, will get to them very soon. I ask Zala and Tolna, "Once I open my eyes and see them staring at me, how did your eyes adjust so quickly?" Zala tells me, "We just open them and wait for them to do what they are supposed to do." I like the way take action based on their faith.

They knew their eyes would work on the sun, and thus did not worry about by simply opening them and waiting for their sight to appear. I wished life could be this worry-free, and then it hits me; it can be if I only accept it as facile and behave as if it was. I should precisely do it expecting it to happen.

This is another coin for me to put into my savings. I stand here looking at brown crumbly sands with some faded shrub spread thinly throughout it. They quickly run to a nearby mud puddle, which the priests tell me was formerly a bubbling spring. Tolna and Zala do not worry about what was once, but what is at present, and what they see now is an opportunity for some adventure. They begin by quickly digging a deep hole. Then Tolna drops through the hole, as they both rush to fill their hole. Soon, all that appears is Tolna's head with a titanic smile from ear to ear. Tolna informs me, "Tianshire; you should do this, because it is so much fun." I look at Oi. We both begin digging speedily, and soon I jumped through the hole since it would take too long to hollow out one deep enough for Oi. Shortly, my head is the only part of me that is above the ground. I try to move my body to no avail. Tolna asks me, "Tianshire this is so fun, right?" I think about it for a minute then agree, "Yes; my body is in bondage, yet my mind is free." As long as I rest, I can experience joy. Even though my body is trapped, I know I am, in reality, free. Oi looks at us strangely, and then comments, "You know your bodies' are bound and know how to gain your freedom. You are the wise ones, for so many are bound and do not know they are, foolishly thinking they are free yet are giving up eternity with our Lord." Zala afterwards asks, "Are you talking about Tolna and myself?" Oi subsequently said, "I do not even worry about you two, for the Lord has chosen you and what he chooses he keeps. You could not escape the Lord even if you wanted to do so. Tolna then says, "Why would we want to, for would it not be foolish to betray the one who has done so much kindness." Oi smiled and said, "Your thinking is the sort of thinking, which will guarantee you eternal life. The Lord has nor ever will do harm to any human. He consistently provides a chance for those who are trapped by his enemies to escape, until they choose evil as their god." Zala then says, "Everyone should know that, as when danger comes our way, we unfailingly go with the one who has been kind to us and is strong. I do not think anyone is stronger than the Lord." Oi looks at us and says, "With my three little geniuses my last year to the ministry will be a great one, filled with examples that all can appreciate." I looked at him and asked, "What shall we do after our terminal year?" Oi told me, "We will do as always, and that is the will of the Lord." Tolna then adds, "My life is so simple when I do what I am told or what I know is right. When I do wrong, I take a chance on being punished, yet I never think of the punishment when I am having the temporary joy of being bad. After their joy is gone, the worry takes over and the hope of not being discovered, and shame of being punished."

Oi thenceforth explains that evil will first come as deceivers and create a lust in the hearts of those they wish to take a prisoner. Once you become a part of the deception, the chains begin to solidify their capture, until as the sand is around you; the chains tightly wrap its victim. Now is when the evil begins destroying its victim." Zala then asks, "How do we know when evil is deceiving us?" Oi answers, "Your heart will tell you." Zala now recommended that she and Oi dig out the two of us, so we can play some more fun games. I look around and see dead sand, dying plants and a small mud puddle. How can we have fun with this? Once we are all out, Zala and Tolna rush to the mud puddle and start digging out sand. They start creating sand walls, then some large temples, followed by some rolling hills. It looks so fun that Oi and I both joyfully join them. Soon, we will have roads and a small village around our currently very large temple. What was pestering, agitating, beleaguering, lifeless sand, and a puddle of sand filled undrinkable water, was now a booming village that was filled with energy as each of us is now enjoying our animated people?

Oi is in the temple teaching, as my sisters, and I are fighting some invaders who wish to destroy our small village. I ask them why we are fighting against invaders, and they explain that invaders always destroy what others create. Tolna explains that her parents once lived in Tolna and after invaders destroyed their homes, her parents escaped to Bucsu. They named her after their former home, so that they would never forget the hate and evil of those invaders. I had always wondered if she knew that she was named after another tribe since these people very seldom travel to other tribes. Oi then says, "We may pretend that this place is safe and that the Lord lives in this temple." Zala replies, "I have never heard of such a place." Oi tells her, "The Lord is going to send a leader to us, which shall free all these lands to live as this village we have created shall." Tolna reveals, "My daddy told me you were that leader." Oi then told us once more, "I am not that leader; however, I am the one who is preparing the way for your leader. I tell you that you will see your leader." We all just looked at each other not understanding his words; therefore, we decided to play again. This time our village was enjoying itself. We decided to keep a low profile on the wicked invaders to allow Oi a chance to relax. He never relaxes if sinful, real or fictional, is present. We had so much fun in the sun. However, as in all fun things, the sun went to sleep, and our fun was done. We afterwards returned to the tunnels, as the desert can be quite cold at night and Oi did not want to chance Zala and Tolna's health. He allowed them two hours to experience the desert night and subsequently permit the priests to bed us down inside their tunnel. They warned that the demons would search their deserts for lost or injured people enjoying the easy prey. We were going to take a month to transition Zala and Tolna into our nomadic family. Oi also claimed he wanted some more time with the Lord. The priests showed us to a new side tunnel they had prepared for us. They provided us with some astonishing night wrappings they call 'blankets.' Oi asks the priests, "Where did you get these 'blankets?" The priests tell them, "They were given to our temple by the Widows of Vadessa." Oi asks, "Who are the Widows of Vadessa?" The priests tell him, "They are women who cannot provide for themselves, thus live in our temple as help us to provide for other members who are in need." Oi then comments, "I have never heard about such things as these." The priests hand him a special large bag that straps to his back and showed him how to place all four blankets into these bags. They also gave each of us girls a small bag for our backs, so that we could carry my tablets and inks, plus some feathers. We equally important carried some tools that Zala and Tolna wanted in addition to our bags of feathers that we could put around our necks at night. I thought, 'what a wonderful creation.' They then gave us our dinner and afterwards, we all quickly went to sleep. We were tired because of all the playing today and eagerly looked forward to tomorrow's adventures.

I awoke to find myself falling from a ladder that was in the clouds. How did I get here was a question rolling through my mind? I only saw ladders around the temples in the black land tribes. I saw dark black clouds to each side of the ladder's feet. I could see a strange desert type island below the clouds. Otherwise, should I say through a small opening in the clouds? I saw three of me falling down the ladder, one high with my legs wrapped around a ball and wings as if I were flying away into the open sky. The image of myself in the middle of the ladder revealed me walking up the ladder as if it was flat ground. This image had many chaotic lines scribble all throughout it. My top image had two straight vertical lines, one in front, and one in the back, which extended all the way upwards until the lights overshadowed them. If it were not for this light, the entire image would be covered in darkness. My middle image has four horizontal lines, which extended from one side to the other side, even throughout the darkness.

They formed seven large and two small squares on my right side by crossing over the vertical lines. The two inner horizontal lines anchored me on this ladder. A strange yellow light flowed from the white light, through my body to the unseen surface dropping away and behind this ladder. I could see two fading red flames being sucked into this yellow. The lower vision of myself saw me holding on to the ladder with my wings flapping and my fish body. I cannot see any form of logic in the scribble lines. It was as if a small child was given some black ink and feather and given the freedom to destroy any message in this vision. Chaos ruled everywhere except at the top of the ladder as it reached up to the mysterious sky above the image. The fear or mystery of this vision caused me to wake up as I found my body soaked in sweat. I woke Oi up and told him of my vision. He was curious about every detail. He then prayed for a while and woke up, and began to reveal to me what the Lord had told him, "Tianshire, the Lord has chosen you to continue my work when I am gone. The ladder you saw with sapphire and red steps, the sapphire represents you as friendly, authoritative, peaceful, and trustworthy. The red represents your love, anger, warning, and death. You shall warn your enemies and when they do not do as you have commanded, they shall meet their death. The ladder is a symbol of your interaction between the spiritual and physical worlds, as you move to achieve the mission the Lord has given you. The black chaotic lines represent death, disease, famine, and sorrow, all of which are the results of sin. You work hard to free all from these consequences of sin. Your fish's body represents a body dedicated to the Lord. Your wings will deliver you from the land below to the ladder above the clouds. Your journey will be met by many obstacles and tribulations, yet you will be guided and protected by the Lord, who will prevent you from falling, the horizontal lines and guide you to his throne, the vertical lines. The land below your ladder is a land you will free from darkness, as darkness will not be permitted therein. The yellow light represents how our Lord is warm and friendly. His love shall shine down on all who walk upon New Venus. His love flows through you as the red flames from your anger surrenders to his love.

The yellow that reaches New Venus prepared to heal all the pain, red flames, which are being sucked into the light. Currently Tianshire, you can no longer be my little sister, for you are now the receiver of visions and as such, you are a chosen one. We must work hard in this last year of my ministry to prepare you for your ministry." I now asked Oi, "How do you know that you only have one more year?" Oi told me, "This was revealed to me in a vision." I questioned further, "What will you do after the one year?" Oi then confessed that he did not know, although he did know that the Lord would be with me, as I was purified through darkness. I now complained, "You had me to help in your ministry, whom shall I have?" Oi afterwards told me, "You shall have Zala and Tolna to help you." I next said, "But they must return with their parents." Oi after that told me that they would; however, later they would join me. Oi now said, "Let us rest for the ensuing thirty days, and subsequently finish my work with the black land tribes." The following morning after our breakfast compliments of Tolna's mother, the priests told us they had a special surprise for us this day at the surface. We eagerly rushed back to the surface, as this time the rope that we had to climb offered no resistance. We simply had to wait for Oi who never was too good with physical challenges. Once he arrived on the surface, we could see some sand and dust forming a cloud as it was being scattered. Zala then warns us, "We must get down, because something is coming very fast." Down we go, holding our breaths as we can feel some solid thumping to the ground. Soon the thumping stops and we hear a man ask, "Why are you on the ground?" Zala looks up and says, "So we can hear the horses thumping to the ground." Oi then gets up and says, "Girls, the thumping is finished." Some priests brought us four horses. As they get off the horses, they give the horses the water out of their canteens, go over to our exit hole, and start pulling up the ropes. Attacked to the ropes are buckets of water and some dehydrated grass. The horses drink the water and eat the moisture less grass. I had never seen such wonderful looking horses, for the horses that my mother had were weak. Oi told me that was because she did not give them enough grass, even though so much grass and grain were available, she preferred to watch them suffer. She would have killed them all; however, the farmers needed them to work on their fields, and she saw reduced harvests as decreased taxes and thus ignored them.

Soon her armies rejected them, because they would turn wild when in the black lands and escape, only to return a few months later healthy and ready for the tribes in thanks for their rich grasslands. The priests told us that there was a small oasis about four hours in the sun and that if we left now, we would be there before the sun was overhead. Oi then asked the priests if they thought we would return today, and they told us, "You will be gone for a few days; we have packed some food for you. The oasis has a small village that will also care for you." Oi then asked the priests if they told Zala and Tolna's parents. They agreed to do so, as we all hoped on our horses and proceeded at a normal pace. Oi said we did not want to work them too hard in the sun. None of us complained because of the sun's heat beating down upon us, as we journeyed to the oasis. Soon the sun was over us, and I asked Oi, "What do we do at this moment in time?" "He told me, "We simply keep the sun to our backs now." Tolna then told us, "I have been to the Aconites before. We will be there in about one hour." I then asked her, "Who are the Aconites?" She told me, "They are the people who live on the oasis we are visiting." Oi now asked Tolna, "What are they like?" Tolna reveals to us, "They are smart and kind people. They help those who are kind to them and destroy those who are evil. They can hide and execute ambushes better than any other people we know. They have survived here and defeated every evil thing that has attacked them. They are great lovers of the Lord." About thirty minutes later, we see a group approaching us on the horses. They approach and surround us saying, "The Lord told us that four Saints would arrive today from the direction in which the sun sets. Who are you?" Oi then tells them, "Should not you first ask the Lord, lest you put yourself in danger?" They all begin laughing saying, "How can a young man, and three girls who are still children harm us?" Oi then commanded the horses to fall into a sleep. The horses fell as the twenty men rushed to get off them before being injured. Then one of the men heard a voice inside his head saying, "Behold the four Saints who come to you. Welcome them as you would welcome me." The man jumped up and cried out, "Oh forgive us Saints of the Lord, for the demons have tried so many ways to deceive us."

Oi then yelled out, "Horses, by the name of him who created you awaken." The horses now stood, as all the remaining men began welcoming these chosen from the Lord. Tolna and Zala wasted no time leaping on the horses, as I soon followed. I had learned that they claimed by doing. Oi asked them if the remaining horses could take them backward to their village and they all agreed it could. Then Oi told them, "Since we are going back that way, you may double up with the girls, and whosoever wishes to double up with me is more than welcomed." They insisted that we ride the horses, and that they would guide us back to the village. Soon we were once again en route to the village of the Aconites. Upon arrival, Oi and I was surprised at the size of this oasis. To look ahead in the desert it could not be seen. However, when we approached it, we could see what appeared as mountains of sand. Nothing extraordinary, as our surprise came when we rode up one of these sand hills and was on its top.

The side of these circles of hills was plush green with grazing fields for their livestock and so many fruit trees, plus a nice stream that flowed throughout its bottom forming a large circle, which made an island out of its middle region. Oi asked our hosts how they had created this. They told him that they did not create it, yet only discovered it. Their ancestors also discovered some tunnels, which had some manuscripts that spoke about them as coming from a world on the other side under the stars. This place was a resting place for their empire as they journey throughout the sky. Oi asked them if we could see the tunnel. They told him only after the elders had given their consent, which would not be long as they were riding up the hills now. One of our hosts commented, "This is strange, as our elders never ride out to meet our guests." Oi then said, "We shall soon discover why they are meeting us." Our hosts guided us toward the elders. When we met them, they welcomed us saying, "Our home is your home, oh great prophet Oi, and might perhaps the daughters of the Lord find much joy, as they relax in our humble oasis. Zala now asked, "Can we ride our horses in the streams below?" The elders told her yes and warned, "You should only ride them in the shallow waters where you can watch for holes and sharp rocks that could hurt your horses." Tolna afterwards reassured the elders that they would never want to hurt their horses and next as they were riding away, they asked me if I was joining them. I looked at Oi and he shared, "Tianshire; we are here today for you to play with your sisters, now go play and enjoy." For this reason, I eagerly joined them, as we carefully walked our horses down the hill, stopping for some time while they grazed. I could see how they enjoyed the moister in the grass, which strangely was still covered with moister this late in the day. Our hosts now asked Oi, "Why did not you tell us your name was Oi?" Oi answered them with a question, "Why did you not ask me my name?" They told him, "We wanted you to feel welcomed and not being investigated."

Oi told them, "Hence, I wanted you to relax, so I could see your natural side." The elders then told the hosts, "As often as we have talked about Oi in our temples, you should have known him, yet at least you treated them kindly, so that is the important thing." Afterwards one of our escorts told the elders, "He could make our horses sleep and awaken by his words." Then the elders said, "Oh you are foolish young men, by those deeds who should have known, for we have never spoken about one who could do marvels through our power, save Oi." Oi then told them, "Peace is with you, for no harm was done as I do not seek glory to my name but for glory upon the name of our Lord. I am more interested in the tunnels that were created by the creators of this oasis." The elders told Oi, "There is no evil in those creators, as we have searched their works and words and found nothing except love, kindness, and sharing." Oi then told them, "That I can believe, yet I have seen another underground kingdom in the lands of your tribe and wish to verify if they are the same." Oi then sends some priests to tell me they are going to explore in some secret tunnels. Immediately, we rushed to join him, as we can ride our horses anytime, yet we will never again find an opportunity to explore the unknown. We quickly arrived and released our horses in a nearby fenced area where the priests told us they could graze. We rush to Oi catching him just in time, as he looked shocked to see us. I told him we came to protect him. Oi and the priests all laughed then Oi said, "I welcome your protection, for if I get scared I shall hide behind you." We told him, "Oh, just as you always do." Oi answered, "Precisely." The priests guided us into their beautiful temple, which had nice marble floors and columns with beautiful large paintings upon the walls. I asked them, "Where did you find these floor stones?"

The priests told us that they found them in the tunnels and only had placed the good ones on the temple floors and assembled the columns from the pieces that lay in storage below. Oi later asked, "Since so few people make it here, why did you feel a need to glorify your temple?" The main elder subsequently said, "It is not our temple, but the temple of the Lord; nevertheless, these stones have a special power over the demons as it blinds them when they pass over us. Since we have begun using them, no demon has landed on our site. Any of Rubina's warriors who have tried, we have destroyed, as the stone confuses those who are evil." We lower ourselves down by ropes, a skill we are quickly learning how to master. This tunnel is very much different from the one I discovered. The floors have a smooth finish with solid white rivers to hold them in place. The walls look as if at one time they were finished; however, now they are partially covered by the rock ice that hangs from our ceiling. To my left, I see a large hole with a strange fence made from something that is not wood. I walk over to hit and can see that this fence is stabilized by the floor. As I look at the darkness below, I can only see some of its depth that comes from the strong yellow light shining from above it. Now, as I look around me, I can see some steps in a ladder. I rush over to the ladder, as one priest grabs hold of me saying, "Where are you going Tianshire?" I now see two more lemon lights, one above me, and one down the hallway to my right. I tell him, "I need to see where this yellow light leads to." Oi at present comes over, and asks the priest "Is there any reason why she could not go up the ladder?" One of the elders currently tells us, "We once sent a man to travel up the ladder and see where it went. He climbed for two hours, only seeing darkness and quiet around him with the yellow light out of sight for over one and a half hours; he began to return very slowly. He concentrated on his safety as to what he felt was days until he once again saw the yellow light. Once he was down, he told the elders that he had seen nothing except empty darkness, the darkness of the void. We have seen not climbed up the ladder except to explore the higher floors." I then asked Oi if we could explore the upper floors.

He looked at the elders, and they waved giving me their permission. Oi then said to them, "We probably should tag after these young brave explorers." They all laughed, as that was the sign for the three of us to journey up this ladder. Zala tells me, "Tianshire, you have mastered the art of getting the big people to say yes." I told them, "This was easy since I had to do was ask Oi, as I knew he would ask them, and that they would not say no to him. Nevertheless, this would keep us here a little longer and they in turn would have more time with Oi, as even they knew he could not keep up with the three of us. We walk off onto the first floor, as our right side is so bright that we cannot see. Such a warm light is not from any flames. We cannot determine how it stays very bright for so long. The elders tell us, "These lights are eternal lights, as we can see even the ice rocks avoid them." I look above and see a glowing orange light speckled with yellow. I ask the elders, "Where does that light come from?" They tell me, "We do not know for sure from where it comes, although we have traveled to the hole from which it enters this amazing world. The opening is one the one hundredth floor above us." Oi now adds, "How can that be, for we only lowered ourselves maybe three floors to reach the stone floor?"

The elders then confess, "We know that the logic does not match, for in here there is no sky above us, only a long hard climb to the stars. The people who lived nearby us were so advanced that they evolved into light forms no longer having blood or breath." We suspect that they are now a part of the yellow light. I look around and see a strange-looking deep hallway. The walls are as if they were made from wood, yet my touch discovers it is rock. The roof is, for the most part, smooth except for what looks like stones attached to provide this ceiling with extra support. I am impressed by the line of white lights that are evenly spaced, as if to invite me down this corridor. The pathway is like frozen ice, so smooth; however, it is not cold. I have never witnessed a road such as this before. Zala asks Oi if we can go down this hallway. She is testing her role in our family unit. Oi looks at the elders and asks them, "What is down this tunnel way?" The elders tell him, "This leads to one of their libraries and some very interesting books." Oi then says, "I have searched my entire life for some books to enhance my ministry.

I could in no way pass up a chance like this. Okay girls, we shall go." The elders then asked if they could join us. Oi tells them, "If you are good hosts, then you would join us, as I truly would hope you would do so." They all smiled and down the hallway, we went. I was in the lead as Zala was to my right and Tolna to my left. I do not even think that if one of these large stones hanging above us were to fall would be able to separate us. When we entered this library, the books looked very strange. They had a bright light coming from them, and as we rubbed our hands on the pages, the knowledge they contained entered our minds. The elders asked us what we were doing, and we told them, "We are learning from these books." The chief elder then asked me, "How are you getting the knowledge from the lights?" I told him, "We simply rub our hands over the book, and it enters our minds." They looked at each other and then told Oi, "We have never touched these books when they were opening for fear that they would do us harm. The little girls are very wise." Oi then told them, "When you have seventy legions of angels to protect you, you can take chances." I learned a book that told their long history. They were great people who were cast from their homes, smuggled into some spaceships, and at the appropriate, time took over the ships. They prided themselves in not killing anyone. It was late in their lives, as their children were taking already in control over the ships when they were discovered by the Szombathelyi Empire, who gave them new very fast and strong ships.

The Szombathelyi Empire searched the universe for people who were in need and would save them. Soon, these people were once again zipping through space. They continued to all the original generations had died, and the second generation continued until their children were in control. They told them to continue until the last of the second generation had died. When this happened, they slowed down and settled on a dead planet that was close to the sun. The books tell why they traveled so long. They did this in order to prevent any of their original masters from ever catching them; especially since the Szombathelyian ships, were twice as fast as any of their master's ships were. They had to live underground since they had never lived outside and even so, not on Venus, which was extremely hot reaching 900 degrees Fahrenheit and the air, had too much carbon dioxide, and the atmosphere was so dense that the pressure would have crushed them in seconds. They thus used their ships to drill into the surface and one about eight of what they called miles deep, they began to build their cities. They filled in the surface holes sealing their underground world. Their ships then created the oxygen-rich environment that they needed, which had three times the oxygen that New Venus has, according to their records. They unloaded the ships and sealed them as a security measure. Their religion developed after they received a visitation from the god of the local galaxy. They called him their Lord and their teachings were very much like ours, although they existed the same time, the Old Earth did and thus the Lord told their priests everything about the Old Earth. I will shine that book next. This generation chose Venus as the home of their Empire. They called themselves the Hajdú-Bihar. They never worried about being an empire as the Lord told them that he would permit no other aliens that lived beneath the surface on Venus. The first, second, and third generations died all having enjoyed healthy productive lives. They had a wonderful medical system, which kept diseases out of their world.

The air was completely filtered each time it was recycled, which was usually twice per hour. Clean air, water, and scientifically generated food, which they generated from the stones they had retrieved, guaranteed them long lives. By the time, the fourth generation took control the ships that had brought them, here were now considered a legend. The original generation forgot to create manuals to teach any future generations how to maintain and operate these ships. Of even greater error, they forgot to leave maps of where the ships were hidden, as they were so afraid that uninvited aliens would take their ships. They had all lived good lives, as the maps, I can see reveals that they had drilled over twenty thousand, of their miles, of tunnels. They had also created some large cavities for entertainment. The tunnels were well endowed with side tunnels that led to the family quarters. They also had many temple cavities and libraries drilled. All their people went into the temple, for if one refused, he was placed in one of their tunnel prison cells.

They reported no crimes such as adultery, stealing or killing. One thing that kept the crimes low as the ability of their technology to record everything that they did and report if anything was questionable. Adultery was simply considered a crime in view of the social disorder that it could cause, and simply punished if their spouses pressed the charges, which few did because to press charges immediately divorced them. The law was intended primarily for exposure and shame with the spouses having a right for revenge. The monitoring actually puts a halt on murders and any stealing. Stealing gave very little temptation in that their machines generated any item they needed. Why steal when all that had to be done was ask? One other interesting fact was that anyone might use any machine. Extra machines were placed along the tunnels and at all entertainment areas for public use. They had a solid system established, which worked well for a long time. Notwithstanding, all good things, that are based upon the physical world, run their cycle and meet their ends. When the old Earth was destroyed all the planets within this solar system, as they described, sent large meteors into space. The sun pulled much of it, to include the molten core, into its inferno. As Venus was in its path, some of the meteors struck and bounced off Venus. The loss of a planet so close to the sun also puts the orbit of Venus into chaos, causing it to take some time to find its new orbit. When the meteors hit the dense atmosphere of Venus, they sent a shockwave that shook everything on Venus. This caused tunnel ways to collapse and quakes to shake deep inside the surface opening them. Their breathable air was released through these openings, as also the now approaching 1200 degrees Fahrenheit temperature to begin melting their machines and life-support systems. Within one hour, they existed no more. The Hajdú-Bihar could not produce one survivor, even though small pockets of their civilization. Death greeted them in a cold and unforgiving comprehensive manner. A clean sweep of carbon dioxide and sulfuric acid clouds concealed this.

I have to shake off the sadness of the Hajdú-Bihar and now move on to some more books. I know what happened to them and how they functioned during their golden era. Now, I want to get a feel for what the Lord taught them, as I think, this could help me in my future ministry. I also want to learn all that they taught in their universities. When I would finish a book, Tolna and Zala would in addition read them. They wanted to have the equivalent knowledge as I had. Their books on the Lord covered everything Oi had taught; the only differences were the people in the stories, although they did the duplicate things. We touched the medical books, engineering and architecture, arts, and even some romance. We looked over the romance books because Tolna and Zala unfailingly admired the relationship between their parents. I always wondered why my father sat on a mountain cliff waiting for a mate. The mate relationships must be important when we become adults. Within one day, we had absorbed over one hundred years of knowledge, and this was knowledge that we had been available for all parts of our memory, both long-term and short-term.

Oi touched a few books; however, spent most of his time talking with the priests. I no longer had any fear about leading my ministry or even answering any questions they would ask me. I would not be answering with a thirteen-year-old mind but with one that was fed by ages of knowledge from an advanced civilization. M fresh knowledge about the space disturbed me, as previously I believed New Venus to be flat. They showed me that New Venus was a round rock going around a circle around the sun. I never thought that a New Venus meant that there was one previously. The thought of knowing that our air was filled with oxygen generated by the Hajdú-Bihar's air generators after they had died was special. Their creations during their lives allowed other species to live on the Venus they indirectly helped recreate. We finally left this library and discovered they had left one priest in the corridor to escort us back. I asked him, "Why did no one call for us to return?" He told us, "No adult could ever be forgiven for taking children hungry for knowledge from a library. You were all so deep in your studies." I was now excited, and could not wait to meet Oi again. The priest took us to the first cavity, which was one floor down that we initially entered. When my sisters and I saw Oi, we rushed around him each struggling for a hug. I told Oi I had some good news, and he recommended that we return to the surface and rest first. Therefore, we went up to the surface and the elders guided us to a special home they had prepared for visitors. It was a nice straw house with beds, which had nice large blankets sewn together, which were packed with feathers. I soon found myself sleeping the first night with all my new knowledge, yet if turned out to be not the kind of sleep I expected. This was the night of many visions. My first vision I saw the land in a forest. I could say many strange and friendly shaped. To my upper left, I saw a cross with a light above it that was visible through the brush. The ground in front of me had low small clouds of green. In the center was a head made of rock. He even had a hat that was sculptured although now partially tucked behind the dark-green leaves. He had a bushy striped mustache and beard. His nose, cheeks, and forehead revealed that he was aged, and had been weathered through many troubles. The most pronounced feature was his eyes, for they were wide opened as if he saw something that shocked him. I could guess that he was flesh and become shocked when something turned him into stone. The absolute strangest thing was a little girl staring down at the green clouds. She had her hands, face except for the tip to her nose, hair, and dress covered in green. Her legs were colorless. She also had four wings on her back and a strange white bright cloud on her right side. I equally important saw the outlines of a purple wing to my far right. There also were other items in this vision, which I could not describe.

The little girl saw playing and having so much fun. She reminded me of my fresh sisters and their ability to find something fun to do in any place they were. A strange voice now revealed to me, "Tianshire, what you see here is the cross, as you know, from your unused knowledge and the Lords light which made what you described in this vision visible. The stone man was father wisdom that waits for someone to seek his guidance. The little girl is a daughter into the forest who plays with her green clouds throughout all the trees. The purple wing in front of her was her guardian that ensures she is protected. This vision shows you that the Lord's light shines everywhere, and that wisdom is waiting for you to seek him and use his direction. The little girl reminds you how innocent as the white clouds you saw were the reflection of the Lord's light showing how the Lord helps protect the innocent. "My next vision found me sitting on the clouds. The ones closest to me are a purplish blue as if they were preparing to unleash a powerful thunderstorm. The clouds behind them were a soft, white and yellow. The sky was predominately yellow as it progressed into a warm darkness. The strange thing about this vision was all the bubbles that came from below the clouds, and floated up to the sky climbing out of sight. My knowledge gained from touching the Hajdú-Bihar's books of Earth's history gave me a foundation to recognize the things in these bubbles. No two bubbles were the same. The first bubble divulged a child with his or her father looking up in the sky. They appeared to be pre-historic, as the father had a flaming torch in his left hand.

The ball to their left had three Neanderthal people sitting in the open range with blue bowls extended around them and a single mountaintop under some clouds in their background. The following bubble had a tree covered with white blossoms. The ensuing ball had two hands, palms up holding an apple. This apple was different in that it had a tree growing out of its stem that also had branches with smaller apples growing. The next two balls were the strangest in that one was growing out of the other. They both have been in the same era yet different social classes. The main one had a pilgrim woman with a cycle harvesting her crops with ten children watching her. In the background, were six girls holding hands, and playing in front of their harvested field. The bubble that was being delivered from it had three medieval people, one man, and two women, sitting upon the ground enjoying themselves in a rural meadow. I could see a giant castle in their background, which were many miles behind them. I could make out three more bubbles; however, there were as many ahead of them as they formed a solid column up into the far-off sky. These did not catch my attention now, for it was one giant bubble, which was not in formation, and a part of the horizontal row of bubbles. This bubble is so strange in that it reproduces itself in smaller bubbles repeating this same duplication at least four more times that I can count. The beautiful woman inside was wearing a wonderful highly decorated brown dress. Her hair was curly and very stylish. She was on a tropical island with white lilies blooming the ground. The seawater had rainbow waves flowing inside it. She also had a large thin cigar in her left hand. Horizontal with this giant bubble were three other bubbles. One had a fellow citizen sitting at a table. He had a sad look over his face. He was looking at the large ball in front of him that had death in it carrying his sizeable reaping cycle. The remaining orange bubble had streams of dark orange flowing throughout it. Continuing from the main vertical line of bubbles past the pilgrims, I saw a blue bubble. This bubble and many planets and stars in it. One of the planets had a flat ring spinning around it. The bubble's surface on the inside had rainbow colors flowing in all manners of directions. Another pink bubble was behind it, just sinking low enough for me to see a wonderful futuristic city with beautiful rainbow-colored sky streets. I could see the love following all throughout its insides. The last bubble was yellow and had a golden city inside that was like a mighty space ship with many jet streams to propel it into a deep space.

The voice of these visions now interpreted them for me, "The fourth bubble as the eating of the forbidden fruit from the third bubble. The first two bubbles were the early humans that had wandered the earth. These humans were as animals in that they had no souls. Because they ate the forbidden fruit, death entered into their lives and the misery that goes with it. The beautiful woman is named Babylon, as no one can escape shores once they set foot in it. Her mission was to tempt those who she came into contact. The pilgrim's bubble reveals how the righteous worked hard for their survival, and the medieval bubble shows how humankind became lovers of pleasures. The pink bubble showed how humanity had evolved into advanced cultures. The blue bubble revealed how humanity traveled the universe. The yellow bubble shows how a new city was built in the heavens and now returning by the power of the Lord." I wondered now if these visions were because I had touched so much knowledge. This knowledge; however, did not prepare me for my next vision. Darn, why must I have so many visions? I so wish that every night was not as this one. This next vision disturbed me immensely. I saw a bright white-skinned woman with bushy white hair that had white curls spiraling down to her shoulders. I could see no clothing, although this vision only revealed the top portion of her breasts. She had two rows of white pearls wrapped around her breasts tightly pressing them up. She did not have normal nipples on her breasts. She only had red round rashes in their place. She had red fingernails, eyelids, lips, and ears. She had a tiny blue star and a small golden ring on her left cheek. She had two ram's horns protruding from her head. She had a large white gem on her forehead. She also had seven small patches of black hair projecting from her middle forehead as it drooped down eyes resting against her cheek. Against her item in this vision was the large red fat blood-filled wormlike thing that she was sucking. She next opens her jaw very wide to fit this thing in her mouth.

This blood object, likewise, spilled a large drop of blood that rested on her left breast. Furthermore, this article had a green thorny stem that grows from its end and curved around with its end resting on her little finger nail. The nail of her little finger was longer than the length above her head, as the ones on her other fingers were as long as her nose. The next feature that I was impressed with was her pupil in her eyes. The one on her right eye was green, while her left pupil was bright white. The next feature that caught my eye was the large ear gem that hung from her red ear on her left side. Her head was titled in such a way that I could not see her right ear. The final thing that worried me was her penetrating teasing stare. I was very curious about what the voice would tell me about this vision. After a few minutes, the voice began telling me about this woman saying, "This woman is the great deceiver. Her mission is to deceive and mislead people into becoming slaves to be evil. The red object that she was sucking on was really a heart wrapped with tight black strings, so she can suck all the blood from it before she eats it. The greatest tool that she possesses is the ability to hypnotize with her eyes. Once someone stares at her, she will create movement in her eyes to pull the viewer's eyes into her eyes and afterwards begin locking their eyes, and next she travels into their minds. Once inside she plants her seeds of doubt, emptiness, misery, and her as the option for happiness. Once she obtains their oath and worship of one demon of her choice. After that, she takes her fingernails and cuts out their heart tying it sternly and sticks it into one of the stems of her tree of death. She subsequently sucks all the blood out of their heart, and afterwards eats their heart, killing her victim. Following this, she takes their spirit to the underworld, so they may be punished until they are judged.

We felt it important that you see the temptation of the deceiver who will destroy many people unless you minister hard to them showing them why it is important to avoid her. She can be all things for all people. When she appears, simply call upon the Lord, as she will deliver you." I now rested for what were only a few minutes until my next vision appeared. This one was not as packed as the other ones were. The detail was so sound that I could not reject it was real. It was a woman warrior with a blue sky and green trees behind her. She wore a red robe with a fur short-sleeved fur coat. Her skin was perfect, as it shined with faultlessness. She held a heavy sword parallel to the ground prepared to strike. She had a leather headband that would keep her hair stable when she was ready to strike. Her eyes were a soft brown yet her piercing eyes were locked onto her next attack. She was very beautiful and from the makeup on her eyes and fingernails, she wanted to take full advantage of her looks. I just could not pinpoint anything that would be worth warning in the vision. The voice knocked me into another zone when they revealed this vision to me. I was so amazed that I could not believe if what they said was real or fictional. The voice said, "So, you found no evil in this vision?

We shall tell you why you failed to find evil within this vision. The answer should have been obvious. That image is you, when you are in your battle to free the black land tribes. You shall be known as the greatest military leader ever to come from both Belcher's prison and the black land tribes. Your eyes are filled by the power of your Lord. You will constantly be the most beautiful women ever to be created by the Lord on New Venus." I stopped them and declared, "My father consistently told me that his mother who was called Eve was the most beautiful woman to walk on New Venus." The voice continued, "Eve was not created on New Venus, as the books you read on old Earth should have told you. She was born on Earth and served her on New Venus because of the pleas of Lilith, the Lord of New Venus." I subsequently asked, "Why do you show me these things now?" The voice said, "You only have one more year with Oi, and later you go through your holy and sacred times of trouble, which you will come out stronger and a leader of nations.

Your eyes in this vision revealed to you the power of your determination, for mountains will fall before you. You and your sisters must learn much this last year, for they will rejoin you after your times of trouble for your ministry. Our Lord shall bless you." These visions woke me up, and I spent the rest during the night wide-awake. This was some powerful news for me, as I actually saw myself in my future. That wonderful vision was I. I must ask Tolna and Zala about their face decorations or as the books I touched called this make-up and enlist their help. They know a lot from watching their mother's make themselves beautiful when going out with their fathers. I learned so much tonight. I saw the true face of the deceiver. I saw the evolution of humanity, which when New Venus is destroyed, will be the same as Old Earth. The books I touched contained a wealth of Old Earth during its final days. I can see that if my mother is not stopped, New Venus will be far wickeder than Old Earth. If I stop my mother, then we have a good chance of slowing evil down, for I will warn our people about the deceiver during my ministries.

Somehow, I could feel Tolna and Zala shaking me and waking me up. I thought my night would have no more sleep, yet my body decided different and at this time, I have fallen into a deep sleep. As I was becoming conscious again, I could feel myself completely refreshed, and as I looked at four eyes staring at me, I could see that they were going to host my activities today. Zala and Tolna subsequently asked me, "Where are we going to play today?" I then suggested that we rode our horses today, as I was curious about this oasis and wanted to see if anything here could account for my visions. We afterwards ate lunch with the priests and some of the temple servants. Oi then asked me how things were going. Replying, I told him that we needed to talk after our breakfast. Oi said to me, "I agree sister. When you finish, I will join you in front of this temple." Zala and Tolna looked at me, in which I could see curiosity written all over their faces. I told them, "Do not worry, it will only take a few minutes, and we will go riding and have much fun today, okay sisters."

They then relaxed and began laughing and chattering with excitement. I got the hint that they had worried about me complaining to Oi about them. They now knew that this was one of my bizarre times to talk about uncanny things, as they described this. In a way, I had to agree with how they perceived this. I can feel how the knowledge that I touched has now provided so many answers, even about the most fundamental things. The knowledge described the importance of knowing the basic things, in order to have a stronger foundation to jump for the higher things. After we finished, Zala and Tolna went to get the horses and prepare them for our fun today. I went with Oi, as we sat beneath a tree close to where our horses have been grazing. Oi stared off by saying, "I had some visions last night and that a voice told me that you had the same visions since they were about you." I now told him, "Big brother, I am so scared because I do not know if I can do all the great things that it told me I would be doing." Oi then shared with me, "Sister, do not have fear, for the Lord told me he would never place a burden on you that was too hard. You will be going back to our home and through your suffering; many will turn against our mother in their hearts. They will tell all that you are as was Belcher and that is righteous.

They will not be able to help you, yet when you return to destroy our mother, they will then join you in her hour of the greatest need. You must remember that your times of trouble will give hope and faith in your leadership that will save so many from suffering. Our ministry is based upon the Lord delivering his people from sufferings; therefore, as we represent the Lord, we shall also be willing to suffer for his name's sake. We represent the grace and forgiveness of our Lord, and at times; we can represent his power and wrath. I very much envy you Tianshire, for I dreamed of delivering these people, for my heart shames in knowing that your mother is the one who causes so much misery. Our people follow her deceptions in hope of finding a merciful ending." I then asked, "Oi, how much longer will you be with me?" Oi answered, "I do not know; I hope long enough to serve in your great army of might and power. I have asked the Lord many times, and he simply tells me that I will be rewarded for my ministry and that I must tarry hard to prepare you, as I am the one crying in the wilderness for you. He has given me less than one year to do that; however, with so many following us and our crowds so large, I tell you my sister and the only one in all of New Venus, who shall serve you to my dying breath." I asked him, "Why has the Lord done this to us?"

Oi said, "I think it shows how mighty he truly is and demands more faith from those who follow you. I will not make the mistake our uncle has made recently at our grandfather's death. The Lord selected one of our cousins, and thus our uncle took one-half from Eden into the cold hard wilderness. Our Saint Eve, who has sent letters to our father, hoping someday to see her two favorite grandchildren, told our father that she found so many of their old and women's bodies on her beach. We must remember that our Lord knows all things, and we must trust that his way is the right way for not only ourselves, but also the others who follow him. I trust me more in protecting and serving your ministry, for my pride in you is higher than all the mountains of New Venus." I then told him, "Oi, you must believe that I would so much more prefer to serve in your ministry, notably since I now have two sisters." Oi told me, "I know Tianshire, and I promise you that I shall always strive hard to help make your life better, especially through your times of troubles."

I asked him if he wanted to go riding with us. He nodded his head no. I then said, "Oh, I forgot to tell you I touched a book that had a story from Old Earth, which told how a pronounced leader of a great nation refused to let the Lord's children to return to a land that he had promised them. The Lord gave him many warnings and a plague each time he did not respond to his warning. He eventually lost his great army and made his people suffer so much. This leader stood up to this great king without fear for he trusted in the Lord and did as he said to do. I hope someday to have your astonishing obedience to the Lord's will." Oi afterwards asked, "What do you mean by a book you touched?" I next told him that, "Zala, Tolna, and I had discovered that by touching the pages, its information was permanently engraved upon our minds. I touched so many thousands of pages and have a deep knowledge of so many things." Oi then told me, "Tianshire, I believe I will be spending the next few days in that library. You and your sisters are already showing how great you will be, for do you not know that with knowledge, you will be able to serve our Lord, and his children, so much better. I am even prouder that you did this because of your hunger for knowledge, for I can tell that you will be able to feed his children's minds with great knowledge. I shall see you in four or five days." He quickly got up and ran for the tunnel's opening. The priests rushed to him asking him what was wrong. He told them, "A messenger from our Lord has told me that I should give the Lord sometime in this private tunnel." They then told him, "We will be here if you need any help." Oi told them, "Go and prepare to feed our Lord's children in your temple. Spread the word that my three sisters and I shall begin our ministry again in the Valley of Pétervására twenty-four days henceforth. That will give the ones who were following us time to rejoin us. They rushed to their temple to spread the good word that Oi, Tianshire, and their two sisters whom the Lord had declared Saints would be ministering in the Valley of Pétervására. I then walked over to Tolna and Zala as they were waiting patiently for me. I told them that I appreciated the forbearance that they gave me. They simply responded, "When we are waiting for a sister whom we love very much, there is no forbearance, only faith in that what she has promised will be true." I could see how the touching of the books had also given them so much knowledge. They had a special way of letting this knowledge guide them and applying this as it fit into the steps they were taking. This would help me so much in learning how the generation, which I would be leading into battle, would think and what would motivate them. I feel that the next few days would be good for us, as I had also to live in their hearts. I can now see how important this is, for when I lose Oi and then lose them shortly thereafter, I will have to depend upon the Lord to keep me alive so that I can once again rejoin with them. This does hurt my soul. I have lived my entire life following Oi, and later to be told that he is to follow me, and that we may not always be together. Subsequently to be given two sisters and seventy thousand angels and told that during my tribulation, they would not be with me.

I guess it is better that they not be with me, because the last thing, I would ever want would be for any of them to suffer the wrath of my mother. The love and giant hearts that their mothers gave me in allowing them to join our ministry is so special. I had wondered what it would be like to have a mother filled with love. To have a nice breakfast ready, and clean clothes to join the other children in a classroom was unfailingly too far from my dreams. This is not to say that Oi has not done right by me, for he has worked so hard to make sure I had as much as he could give, and I will always have the best place in my heart for him. If I ever marry, my husband must be exactly as is Oi. Not one difference, so with such a dim hope of finding men better than my father or Oi, I shall most likely never marry. I can probably depend upon Tolna and Zala to tell me all the negative points for being married. At any rate, that is what they told me their mothers did; they tell everyone the bad points of their husbands, as if in a competition to see which one suffers the most. I guess that must be one of the products of love, as we often hear people tell us all the black-hearted things they claim that the Lord has put into their lives. Oi and I know about bad things into our lives, for the Queen of Evil is our mother. We care not about our sufferings. We only care for the glory to the kingdom of our Lord, for each soul we lead to the Lord is another brick to build our city of the Lord. Notwithstanding, today is a day of sisterhood and for my brother to explore where everyone else thinks he has gone. So many people believe that he holds all wisdom, yet he is an ordinary human. He gets sleepy at night, tired during the day, and hungry every day. He hurts when he suffers from an injury. The only difference is that he does not complain of these things, and stays focused upon the work that the Lord has given him to do. Our work today, is for my brother to go where I have been and for me to follow my sisters in our new world of living as one.

I must struggle hard to listen to what they say, because I am discovering that the more they say actually applies to where we are going and how to get there. We begin by riding our horses into the stream we were in the last week. This previous week has changed so much, as we are all three packed libraries of information, yet Zala and Tolna are holding fast to their youth. It is as if they will know that tomorrow will come, and they are ready, thus why not enjoy today. At least one thing I know is that I will indeed enjoy this next week. The water splashing from the stream below us feels so good on my dry skin, as the desert and tunnels have dried them. We ride nice and slow, although we are going against the easy flow and slowly going up this large hill. The sun feels so good soaking into my chilled bones. I feel as if my body is a plant the way it is eating up all this sun. Zala, Tolna, and I are slowly tanning to a nice shade of golden highlight. Zala is so excited about the prospects of how her makeup will blend into this new golden hue. I love the way they find excitement out of the most peculiar things. I really so much want to develop this trait, as I will need it in my times of troubles.

I know that rejoicing while my mother is torturing me while be as heaps of burning ashes upon her head. I rejoice in knowing that the fifty legions of angels with me shall have her demons crawling around me as helpless mendicants. What I am now enjoying is the soft cool wind that seems to be blowing over us. Tolna says that usually areas around water are cooler. She should know, as she is a desert girl, and traveled some in this region. We can see some small fish dashing around in the waters. Zala says the colored ones are minnows or gold fish. Tolna adds that the flat shaped ones are blue gills and not to touch the ones with the fat long whiskers, because that is catfish and daddies have to handle them. I am excited in learning about all these things. I can also see what a person or native of one area knows. My life has been so different from theirs, for Oi and I have been drifters traveling all over this continent and the only two permitted to do so, even though we are from not only Belcher's Prison, but also are the children of their most hated enemy, our mother. I have believed the reason they do not crucify us is that they know we hurt her more by being alive. That is true, for our cries to revenge are louder than theirs are. Moreover, we have the connections to exact our revenge and that is our Lord, who has chosen us, Oi to cry in the wilderness and me to be purified through my mother's fire to return and lead them to the spiritual and physical freedoms. I have longed to belong to one area; nevertheless, I choose to serve my brother and the Lord and travel everywhere to feed his children, or as today being fed by his children. Zala makes it to the top of this high hill first. She screams back to us, "Hurry; this is so amazing." Tolna takes off like an arrow, and follows suit. I wonder what she describes as beautiful, could it be a strange tree or animal. For her, it could be anything. Tolna makes it to the top of this high hill, with me immediately behind her. This is an amazing place, so unexpected. Before us is a large pond with red leaves scattered all over it and green pastures with half of it covered with hay waiting to be collected, as it has been in the other half. It is spotted with a few rows of trees.

Zala tells me they are most likely shading some small streams that flow into this pond. The clouds are now hanging low and look as if a storm may be coming. Tolna tells me not to worry about the clouds, because this area does not get a lot of rain. She further adds that they are most likely collecting moisture, which will be thinly released into the air throughout the desert. If they did not do this, the heat would fry anyone who went outside, even if shaded. We now get a big surprise as a beautiful rainbow, which formed a thick low assemblage of colors that went from one side of the pond to the other side. Zala just gasped as she looked at it and said, "That rainbow is the greatest one I have even seen. It is so close as if it is talking to us. I feel very lucky today, as if the rainbow is telling my sisters how much I love them." Tolna afterwards added, "It is showing us how beautiful our love really is." I next added, "Remember how the books told us that rainbows were a sign of a promise our Lord made for the people who walked upon the Old Earth? I think this one is telling us how the Lord is promising to be with us, until we join him and reminding us of the protection, he has provided us. He may also be telling us our first big test is about to befall us, and that we must remember his promise today." Zala after that adds, "I sure hope you are wrong." I subsequently tell them, "So do I, for this place is so wonderful, yet half the fields have not had their hay collected, and this pond is covered with red leaves as all the trees have green leaves. I wonder where these red leaves come from and why none of the cattle below are not up here eating this thick green grass. We must go to the other side." I started to go to the other side, and my sisters followed me. On the way, I got close to the water, jumped from my horse, and led him to the water, yet he would not drink it. Zala and Tolna did the same thing, and their horses refused to drink the water. They now tell me that this strange. We walk our horses over to the harvested hey. They also refused the hay.

Tolna tells me that this is weird, and at least one of the horses should have gone to the hay. We walk them through this field of hay to the top of a smaller hill that appears to have a view of this entire area. The horses are nervous. Zala says this is a sign that we could be in danger. I yell out, "Okay guardian legions; it is time to get busy." Tolna yells out, "That also goes for Zala's and mine." Zala currently asks us if we do not think it strange that no frogs or insects are around the pond. Tolna answers, "Now that you mention it, this is very peculiar." Our rainbow has now vanished. That is something I think is very strange. I tell my sisters, "It is time for us to get out of here." We all jump on our horses and the three of them, incomprehensibly, lay down and go to a sleep. I first thought they had died, yet I could feel their big hearts still beating. Now I think my sisters, and I could be in real trouble. Nevertheless, I must act calm. I say to them, "Well, looks like we will be camping out here tonight, good thing we brought our blankets." Zala then says, "This will be our first camping trip together." I tell them, "I was hoping that we take advantage of Oi being in the tunnel for four days.

The sky above around us suddenly turned black. It was so dark that we could not see each other. Therefore, we grabbed each other's hand. I fought hard not to appear scared to my sisters. This was the first time we had faced the darkness. I began by saying, "Sisters, let your lights shine so that they can chase this darkness away." I could feel their trembling so I added, "Sisters, do not fear, for our legions of angels shall protect us." Precipitously, four windows appeared before us. The sky now turned to a granite pale purple cracked wall. The window into the middle began to enlarge. The two lower window had two of Satan's stars and a quarter moon with a nighttime view over the land around us. I knew this could not be from the fallen angel Satan, for he was now imprisoned in the bottomless pit, and was not going anywhere. The circle at the top had a shade of light purple sky that blended from the large circle in the middle. It was filled with a full moon, thus had to be from the Old Earth, as New Venus has no moons. Another strange thing about the Old Earth is that the sun rose in the east and sat on the west. On New Venus, it rises in the west and sits on the east.

One nice thing that the books told me was that on Old Venus, a day was 243 days long and a year was 224 days. Our new Venus has a normal day as was on Old earth, except that ours has twenty hours, ten day and ten night and the daytime hours remain the same throughout our year, and our winters are mild. Any ways, the top circle had a dark purple flying dragon. Now the large circle began to take a form. I had a green and blue five-point star with gems at each point. Another huge light purple dragon with two large wings was braced through this star. He had two arms and two legs that looked the same as each had three sharp claws that gripped the star. He had golden scales on his underside. He also had two horns, though I could only see one, he looked so much like the one crossing the moon, and that one had two horns. He had a long scaly tale with an arrowhead at the end. He had a face full of pointed scales and fierce eyes. We could see the pyramids and mountains in his background, so somehow this vision was coming from the deep past. I asked him, "Who are you and why have you taken the light from our sun from us?"

He answered, "I am the flesh eater Várpalotai, and I have taken your light as I will also take your life." I looked at him and said, "That is strange, for I thought your name was looser, and that you came today to beg that we not cast you into your death." We could now feel the ground shaking from his anger, and he jumped from his star and went for me. He grabbed me, and as my blood from his claws began to pour, he lifted me into the sky. I yelled aloud so Zala and Tolna could hear, "Vaperhead; I command that you release me and be taken to your place of punishment." He immediately vanished as I softly dropped upon the ground. We could hear him yelling, "Oh Tianshire, forgive me for I knew not who you were." I commanded that he stops begging so that other fools like him could today meet their deaths. Zala and Tolna began ripping their clothes to make bandages for me. I told them, "Do not worry for the Lord will heal me. We need not to fear evil but instead stand strong against it, for we are stronger than all of them combined."

Tolna said, "Tianshire, I am so scared." Zala began crying, "Tianshire; I do not know if I can be as robust as you." I then told them, "Upon this night, you shall become tough warriors in the kingdom of our Lord." Now before us another strange beast, as one we have never known could exist. His head was so odd. He had two horns, a nose with all the cartilage removed, and a giant mouth that was wide open and facing us. He had a pointed tongue and long space deadly teeth. He had so many men and women in his body. They were trapped inside of him with seven human bodies pressed against his head alone. I could see three sets of female breasts pressing on his skin. He even had people pressing in his arms.

His belly was nothing more than the remains of many people as if they were going into a meat grinder. He had the color of a dark chocolate that I saw in the books I touched. One person in his head has their tongue sticking out, while two others have their mouths open as if they had been screaming. I asked Zala and Tolna if they wanted this one and they both jumped behind me saying, "Oh Tianshire; you are our hero." I can only imagine they never dreamed of being in these situations, or they would not be here now. I told them, "It is our love that will destroy them."

I now looked at this bag of misery and suffering and asked, "What is your name, and have you come here today to meet your death?" He said, "I am called Kiskunfélegyházi and no other has eaten more flesh than I have, and today you shall join the others inside me as I tear your bodies apart slowly as I enjoy so much, the pain and suffering you go will endure." I looked at him and said, "Kiss my leggy Kun hazy, how you dare to threaten me, for today, I shall destroy you? Moreover, I shall restore those whom you have destroyed, and they shall avenge you for the rest of eternity. He then made a dash at Zala, and I jumped between them and said, "You fear me. You cannot defeat me."

He said, "How can three children defeat me, when some of the strongest people of Old Earth could not overpower me?" I said, "They were not from New Venus, nor did they have seventy legions of angels protecting them. They also were not called to destroy the demons of Rubina." He afterwards rebutted with, "I am stronger than all of Rubina's demons." I next said to him, "after that I shall have no trouble defeating you." He subsequently grabbed me and pulled me to his mouth. I laughed at him, while Zala and Tolna were crying. As he put me in his mouth, inside of him, I called out, "By the name of the Lord, I demand that you release all whom you have imprisoned and release me now, so I may lead you to where those you have destroyed my receive their justice." Immediately, he turned red and opened his mouth as I came out, and over two hundred people followed me with new healthy spiritual bodies. I now rose up and commanded, "Kiskunfélegyházi, I command you to suffer in the flames of Hades and all the spirits you have taken their lives from shall rest in the vacant once called Abraham's Bosom. You shall see them come and go before the throne of our God; they shall have many great rewards, and they will judge you every day having received from our Lord a new torture." He currently slowly started descending into the Lake of Fire, which was now at the core of the sun, as Old Earth no longer existed.

We could hear him begging, "Tianshire, please save me and forgive me as your Lord commands." I asked him, "How do you know my name? It is not for me to forgive you; it is for those you destroyed, and the Lord will not allow them to forgive you. Did I beg you when you ate me? No, for once, you ate me; you gave the Lord permission to destroy you. You are lucky that I did not call my guardian legions, for they would have torn you apart, only to put you together and tear you apart again." He answered, while screaming in agony since the Lord was slowly dipping him into his pit, "Your angels told me your name after I ate you. You should have warned me, so that I would not go to this terrible place." I replied, "No; you should have warned the two hundred who now stand with me. I could have had some mercy on you, yet you made my sisters cry, thus for eternity who will be thrown into the Pit with Satan and his fallen demons; however, first you must be tortured for one thousand years. This is only shortened, as they must go to their mansions around our Lord's throne. I now dropped to my knees and told with my Lord saying, "Okay, my pronounced and honorable Lord, drop him into the Abraham's bosom, and I will have some of my angels accompany these great Saints and show them to their temporary sanctuary."

The Lord sent some angels to circle around us and said, "My Saints, today we have freed you from the beast Kiskunfélegyházi who had hidden in the deep cavities of Jupiter. He foolishly came out today, as you shall direct your revenge for the first one thousand years, and afterwards, I will punish him with the other deceivers for eternity. The angels whom you see will make sure you make it to Abraham's bosom and once Kiskunfélegyházi it cast into the everlasting lake of fire in the core of your sun; you will be escorted to your never-ending mansion around my throne. You shall receive your great rewards, for you held fast to my name, knowing that you would be saved, and thus you are saved. Welcome home, great Saints." Zala now spoke saying, "Thank you Lord for saving us, and please make Tolna and me stronger, so we can help protect our sister Tianshire." With this, all the angels raised their weapons and said, "Blessed be the name of our Lord." Tolna now spoke, "Oh these angels are so beautiful and pure white. They have such giant wings, as they extend from the top part of their back and stop at their behinds. Each wing is longer than one and a half of their body's length. They have so many rows of beautiful long white feathers. The females were lined up with the males fighting side by side. The girls have diamond tipped spears. In addition, the males have swords. They all, male and female, have long blond hair. The only thing I do not understand is why they are nude?" I then told her, "These are the mightiest fighting angels who guard the holy of holies in heaven. They do not know the difference between good and evil, as they only know virtuous. They look like special toys; however, they are great warriors." Zala afterwards asks, "What if they want to do something else?" I then told them, "Angels are a different type of creation, and only do that which the Lord created them to do. They no longer can sin, as the Lord upgraded them so as not to lose one-third again to sin." I then looked over at the two hundred Saints before me and declared, "This is a wonderful day for us, as we have brought back such great Saints. I marvel at what you have done, some of you were in that now burning beast for too many years, yet through all these ages; you did not surrender; you did not weaken; you did not lose your faith, as you knew the Lord would save you. As I look into your souls, I see some who came from the old Egyptian kingdom, a few from the old Chinese dynasty, some from the European Middle Ages, and some of the most famous empire of deception and evil, the United States. Oh, I wonder how that beast could capture so many from so many places. They now told me, "He captured us with all manners of deception. He waited until we were alone, and like a flash of light captured us one by one." I now said, "I just cannot thank you enough for standing tall for our Lord, you are proof of the greatness of our kingdom, and shall always be heroes in my heart. I do promise to spend time with you when we all meet in heaven. You are a blessing for our Lord." Then one asked, "Where on Earth are we now, for I would like to see my old hometown?" I afterwards told them, "Do not be alarmed: however, the Old Earth is no more. The Saints all live in a giant city called New Jerusalem, which orbits above the New Earth as the Lord is forming it. We are all on the world called New Venus, which has been overhauled from the Old Venus some of you knew. Kiskunfélegyházi was from another distant part of our universe. He was a master of deception and could evade the Lord for so long. He made his mistake today when he picked up on the daughters of the Lord." Now one of them said, "I knew you girls were something special, especially, by the way, you rested without fear in his mouth. That was when I told the others near me; today, we have the power of the Lord to save us. I thank you for your service to the Lord." I then spoke again, "Today is the best day from my life so far, and I know my sisters also agree. I hope to tell this story many times in my ministry. How many are excited to go to your temporary sanctuary? The Lord's angels will take you to Abraham's bosom first. You will receive visits from many of the great Saints of the ages. Peace will be with you forever." They currently agreed it was time for them to go to their new home. I then said, "Lord's angels, please do the Lord's will now." They now made a complete circle such as a ball with these Saint's inside them and went to Mars, where the Lord had made a new Abraham's bosom.

Now we sit down as the darkness was still around us. Zala said, "I am so proud of you Tianshire; your faith is so strong that evil cannot defeat you. You are truly a great Saint of the Lord." I now said, "Tolna and Zala, at present that you have seen the great power of our Lord and the love he has for his Saints, you also shall someday do great things. It is still dark, so we have some more chances to see the Lord's considerable power tonight." Now, we saw a small light coming at us. I told my sisters, "Get ready sisters, number three is on its way." The image soon filled the sky in front of us, as we could see a large bloodstained mirror with a headless body wearing a blue dinner coat and sitting in a chair in front of the mirror. Against the wall were a white and a green beast with two large green horns and red hair. In front of her was a skinless beast with no stomach, as it had been hollow out. He also had red hair. These two stood on the left-hand side of the headless victim. On the right side, were two beasts, one male dressed in black, and a female dressed in a dirty white.

The female had bloodstained teeth and blood dripping down her face and chest. She also had black eyelids and bloodstained hands. She wore a very short dress and one that shared with others most of her cleavage. She appeared to me to be the bloodthirsty and with an evil matching it. The beast who stood tall behind her wore a black sleeveless top and had many tattoos on his arms. He had a scared face with black eyelids to match the female in front of him, and painted mustache and goatee. His had long black hair and a red band around his head. The most important thing was that he held a nasty ax that was the kind designed for cutting off heads.

The blade was covered with blood. I would think he is the one who does the killing. I then began to talk and Tolna snuggled at my dress and said, "We got this one sister." Tolna called out, "Who are you and why do you come here tonight?" The evil-looking male beast with the ax moved forward and said, "We are the Children of Petrikeresztúr and we have come here tonight to devour you, as my sister wants to eat some little girls tonight. She likes how flexible your legs are and easier for her to chew. Are you ready to die?" Zala now said, "Oh children triker, you have come to the wrong place for tonight you shall die by the power of our Lord."

Now the female with the dirty white dress on said, "Prepare yourself for my feast." Currently both men and the girl in the white dress come at us all at once. The Lord put up an invisible wall that the three of them crashed into hard. The girl with the green dress had not moved, and she now cried out, "Oh little girls, ask your Lord to free me of this curse." The male with the ax now said, "I will free you," and swung his ax cutting off her head. Tolna now screamed, "Go away invisible wall, since we have some more demons for our Lord's Lake of Fire." The man with the red band round his head rushed forward and swung his ax at Zala who remained calm and simply rose her hand. She now said, "Ax, be gone, for you can do no work for our Lord tonight." The ax vanished. The girl with the white dress now crawled across the floor and leaped at us, as would a wild lion. Tolna remained calm and just as the feminine beast went to contact her, she leaped about eight feet through the air and then returned landing on the female beast. She now said, "Your hands shall join your feet so you can no longer walk or crawl."

The female beast said to her, "By what authority do you do this?" Tolna calmly answered, "By the power of the Lord I worship," and the female beast's feet joined her palms. The male beast now jumped at me. I once again rose my hand and said, "You are such a small pest." The Lord shrunk him, making him five inches tall. I walked over to the skinless man and commanded him not to move. I then dropped mini man into the skinless man's stomach, walked over to the headless man, picked up his head, put it on top of his neck, and prayed, "Oh Lord make this victim of evil whole again." He then jumped up and ran over behind Zala, which put a smile on her face, as she stood tall beside Tolna who also displayed a new sense of confidence, and walked over to the female beast who lost her head. Her head back on her and looked into her eyes as I said, "Be made whole again." Now she looked at me and said, "Can you free me from this terrible curse, for they deceived me into becoming one of them?" I looked at her and said, "You have asked that our Lord free you from the chains of evil. You asked the Lord for your freedom rather than commit an evil on us. Thus, the Lord has freed you from this evil and since you have asked for your forgiveness, you are free from evil and shall be given back your body before evil took you as their prisoner."

She then became beautiful again and fell on her knees praising the Lord. I remember seeing her at all my sermons and the remaining of Oi's. I was proud that our Lord could show how when evil repents, he will save them. I now looked at Zala and Tolna and said, "Listen to the voice inside of you and pronounce the punishment on these three demons." Zala said to them, "You shall never again torture and kill for tonight you fought against three Saints, who have been guarding them seventy legions of angels." Tolna then said, "You will be cast into the bottomless pit or the Lake of Fire for eternity. Go now to your pit!" We could hear them crying as they descended into the Lake of Fire. At this time, the saved female dropped upon her knees and cried out to me, "Why has our great Lord blessed me so much, for what work did I do to earn his grace and mercy?" I then said to her, "No one can earn the grace of our Lord. You did the required action, and this was to change from serving evil and desire instead the Lord. He has found great pleasure in your new faith, as evil will no longer deceive you. The mighty angels shall protect you until you rest in peace with the Lord at his throne." Zala and Tolna rushed up to hug her, and she then vanished going to her new home. We could see her sitting in her brand new house and some of her fresh friends talking with her as she shared some fruit with them. Zala said, "Sometimes this work can be so rewarding." I then told her, "Every time we save someone for the Lord is a great time."

I now told them that, "I am so proud of the great work you accomplished in this last battle. You stood tall and confident in your faith. You are currently truly in the Lord's army, and I know shall have no fear of evil, for now you know how easily the Lord's power destroys them. I am so proud that you are my sisters. May our Love bless you forever?" Zala at present said, "I think we will get some more training tonight, for it is still dark." Tolna at the moment said, "This is good, for now our faith and confidence will grow. I do thank the Lord so much for these gifts and hope he allows me to fight on the front lines for his name's sake." Now appearing in front of us was a green eyes female beast. She had spider webs painted on her forehead arms and breasts, which her low-cut dress left mostly exposed. This seems to be a powerful tool for these female beasts to use in deceiving and luring their male prey. She had two large fangs that crossed her red lips. Her hair was sprinkled with gray patches. She had the standard black eyelids. She also had a large earring the hung in its strange design. Her stare was the stare of death and evil. I asked her, "What is your name, and why are you here?"

She smiled and said, "I am called Dorogi, and I have come to play with you." Zala looked at her and said, "Dorogi; we do not want to play with you?" Dorogi then said, "Oh, you are not being nice; I simply want to be your friends." Tolna now said, "Dorogi, I believe you are lying and attempting to deceive us." Dorogi afterwards began to cry as she inched her way to us. Zala next told her, "You are close enough, come no more." Dorogi after that said, "Oh I am so sorry that you all hate me so much and wish to give me your hate." I subsequently told her, "Dorogi, we do not hate you, nor will we give you a chance to deceive us. I will call upon the Lord to test you and make sure you truly want to be our friend." At this time, she leaped at Zala, clutched her arms around her, and went to bite her in the neck and as she bit, her fangs crumbled into powder. Zala simply looked at her and said, "You have not been nice Dorogi. I think you were trying to hurt me." Dorogi later denied this saying, Oh little girl, I was just playing, for I want to make sure you are alert, because there are so many bad boys out there who want to hurt us girls." Tolna then said, "All right Dorogi, we want you to get off your knees and say, "I serve the Lord of all righteousness." Dorogi then said, "Okay, Tolna, guide me to where you wish for me to serve our Lord."

Tolna now walked over to her as Dorogi immediately went to slash Tolna with her fingernails, which turned into sand as she touched Tolna. Tolna jumped back in shock, as I told her, "Tolna, you must be careful, for demons will try to deceive you." Dorogi then looked at me and said, "Oh, little girl, I am not a demon. These spider webs painted on me prove that I am not evil." I afterwards looked at her and said, "Oh Dorogi, how could I have made such a mistake, can you forgive me?" She next said, "If you come here and give me a hug." I after that replied, "Dorogi, my feet hurt from walking too much today, can you come to me?" I subsequently opened my arms as if to offer a hug. She rushed to me and grabbed me, preparing to bite a big chunk of flesh out of my neck. Just as she went to bite me, she turned into stone. I then looked at her and said, "Oh Dorogi, you have been a bad girl, and for your evil, you must be punished." She could say nothing, as she was stone. I later said, "Sisters, let us give her the punishment that the Lord tells us." Tolna then said, "Because you have tried to deceive the chosen of the Lord, you shall be cast into the bottomless pit, and there you shall burn for eternity."

She now pointed her finger at the frail looking stone, lifted her up, and then changed her back into a demon. Zala currently said, "Dorogi, I cast you into the bottomless pit by the name of my Lord." We could hear her scream as the fired began to burn her, and soon she had dropped far enough that we could not hear her voice. Afterwards Zala asks me, "Tianshire; you knew that Dorogi was evil, why did you try to hug her?" I next told her, "Evil will never pass up a chance for a fast victory. This way, I could prove that she was evil, as she failed her third temptation and will be assessed accordingly when she is judged." We all three held our hands now to see what the sky was going to do. We jumped for joy as we saw the dawn arriving and could see the outlines of the trees beginning to reveal themselves. Now a bright red light appeared over us changing to yellow, pink, and shades of purple as it spread throughout the sky. I told my two friends, "I think we made it through this night, and we made it through as heroes. Because of us, two hundred Saints are now receiving their rewards. Dorogi, the Children of Petrikeresztúr less the one that repented, the human eater Kiskunfélegyházi, and the purple demon Várpalotai are no longer available to harm the innocent. These are as giants when compared with the ones that serve Rubina. I can now relax with you two with me, for at present I have great faith in your confidence and ability to channel our Lord's power to save the righteous. One thing that truly impressed me was that with seventy legions of angels available at our command, we instead held fast to our faith in our Lord and stood alone in the face of evil and watched as the Lord protected us." Zala then asked me if we should do something about the curse upon this ground. I told her, "Sister, we need not to do anything; however, if you think something should be done, do it." She now looked out at the fields and said, "Oh Lord; I know not why our horses do not eat this hay, nor drink the water at the pond below us. If it is not aseptic, will you please make it sterile, if it is your will? Either way, I ask that they will be done. Thank you." We now saw the red light pass over the ground and the yellow light shine through the surface of our pond.

The lights faded out as daylight now covered our hill. We saw that all the hay was tied in the bails as the villagers had tied the others. The leaves that floated on the pond now turned green as frogs began jumping in and out of this pond. A nice large bass jumped out of the middle of the pond. It was alive again, and our horses began eating the grass. They are loyal horses, so I simply said to them, "Our faithful friends, we will be sleeping most of the day, so you may feast on the grass on this hill and drink as much of the water that you want. Just do not go far from here and stay close enough that if I call for you, you can come to us." Zala said, "Do you really think they understand?" I said, "I do not know; it just makes me feel better." Tolna now recommends that we get some sleep. We all agree and toss our blankets on the ground below a nearby tree and soon are quickly dead to the world. Nevertheless, my rest was still out of the picture. Before me, it was now nighttime with our trees reflecting the light from the upper right of this vision. On the ground was a man with his head lying upon a rock and blood all over his chest. He was not moving, thus I think he could be dead. He looks like Oi or my father. I cannot make out the details. In the top right, corner is a large bright white light. It has a small bubble behind it and a large thin purple ring then it holds the bright yellow ladder top. Actually, it is more like a series of steps. On the top of the ladder is an angel walking down. On the fourth steps from the ground is an angel with her back to the ground. She is looking up at the angel walking down the steps. The land the last character in this vision is an angel on the first row of steps preparing to journey to the man. I do not see anything dangerous or evil in this vision, except maybe the one who killed the man upon the ground. Nonetheless, he is not in this vision. I now see the two angels who were walking down go over and lift the man from the ground. The angel with her back to the surface remains firm. As the two angels step up on the rungs, the third angel now leads them all the way into the light.

The dead man is currently entering the light still being carried by the two angels. Finally, the yellow stairway merges into the bright light, which now fades away. It is obvious that this man was a Saint being taken into heaven by the Lord's angels. Therefore, the dead man is now receiving his reward from the Lord. That is not the distressing part of this vision. The disturbing part of this vision is that the man looked like either my father or Oi. I could just see enough of his face to know that he was one of the two. I do not know how my father died, so it could be him, or it could be a future vision of Oi dying. I know that he has less than one year remaining. I do not know what will happen to him, except that he will no longer be crying in the wilderness. I just cannot imagine him being alive and not ministering. I know it would break my heart if he were to be killed. I do not like visions that do not tell me what happened. I now fell into my deep sleep. We all woke up in the middle of the afternoon. This only gave us a few hours before nightfall.

Zala recommended that we all go swimming in the pond. Her new confidence amplified her desire for adventure. That is good, because I am tagging after my two new sisters. I have never played with the water before, because if we played with the water in Belcher's prison, we could be killed by all the evil. It was just unheard of, as no one even tempted the demons or the evil raiders. Tolna tells me that we are very lucky to be able to swim, since water is so scarce in the desert that water for pleasure is simply not available. Tolna wants to see if I can swim, thus I save her time and tell her I know nothing about being in the water. Tolna and Zala's eyes light up as they promise to teach me everything. I so much enjoy being unskilled one with them. I can confess to a weakness with no fear of losing their love. The only thing that could cause me to lose their love in this pond would be if I were to drown. I have faith that their tender hearts would not let that happen. They first teach me how to lay upon my back in the water. This is nice, as I stay afloat. They also taught me some different ways to swim, and we had a few races. Then we went exploring under the water, which even at its deepest place was not over our heads. They converted many of the games they played on land, make a few modifications, and turned them into water sports. I would bet that everyone on this large oasis heard us today, and we were cheering each other and laughing from all the fun we were having. I just let go of everything and enjoyed being a small child today. It was fun as the water created a greater sense of freedom. We finally lost all our daylight and went to go back to our tree. Zala recommended we go to another tree in which we all hastily agreed and headed for another tree. I whistled for our horses, and they came running. When they all arrived to me, I gave each one of them a sugar cube that I had been saving in my shirt pocket. I was careful where to lay my shirt when we were swimming, since I did not want any insects to raid it. They each one ate their treat as I could feel their loyalty, so I told them to stay where we could see them; therefore, they would not be in danger.

We all got under our blankets since the desert nights can be cold. They told me about some of the fun things they did in their schools. The way they told it was as if I were there with them. Somehow, everything these girls touch turns out to be fun. The only thing they hated was now that they were thirteen years old; their parents were looking for husbands for them. Bucsu custom is to marry very young. They planned to return after their one year with me and then say good-bye to their parents and move to Tolna's birth town. They would remember her. Any ways, we all drifted off to sleep, and I was now in another ladder vision. This one was different from the others, in that this one had a voice, which told me to climb. I looked up and could see that I was in a room, which had a square hole in the top of it to give a view of the sky. The sky had a bright white light in the lower left corner. I could also see two large worlds. I trust the white light so up to, I go on this ladder, and step out onto the roof. As I look around, I quickly discover that I am in another room. This room has bright white walls, and on one wall, I saw a wooden door and its wooden frame. The peaceful bluish sky opening, which had white clouds passing through. This door had a rope ladder hanging out of it with thin wooden steps. I am curious about what lies ahead, so up to, I go. This is a long climb, yet soon I am looking out the door. It now gets scary, as I walk out on the small platform and see another ladder, which is sturdier than the previous ones, yet passes through the white clouds above me. At least, half of this large cloud is getting dark as if it is forming a storm. This one will be risky, as I cannot see where it goes, or even if it goes, through the clouds. I must remember the part of me that must have faith and seek adventure. Nevertheless, up the ladder I go and go. It did not look as if it would be this high, yet the steps keep going, yet the end continues to evade me. I am soon climbing through the clouds and reach another flat platform. I get off and slowly crawl on it, for I cannot see where it ends, as I know a drop off would see me falling a good-sized distance. Then as the clouds begin to spread out, I see a wonderful sight. Before me is a long row of white steps. It curved widely to the right and then rose into a bright white light. I knew what was in the light, so I walked in the middle of the rows slowly up and up for what I thought was for hours. It amazed me how little these ladders or steps look when I am getting on them. Then once on them the steps appear to multiply forever.

I have no exhaustion of this climb, because I must see through the light. As I get closer, the light is so bright that I begin to lose my eyesight. I now drop to my knees and start crawling up, making sure to stay as close to the middle that I can. Then finally, I reach the top, crawl out onto the surface, and find myself crawling into a room that provides some protection from the bright light. As my eyes begin to see again, in front of me is the Lord. His eyes are the wells of love, and his hair is like wool. I drop to my knees and use some Zala techniques by saying, "Thank you Lord for inviting me here today." I just do not want him to be mad at me for sneaking up these ladders. He answers, "I invited you here today to show you some things, that you may share your visions with our children." I think how special it is for the creator of all people to call his people our children, with me only being thirteen. He then sticks out his hand, and as I touch it, he grabs hold onto my hand strongly and securely as we begin to ascend.

I can see another bright light high above us. We now pass through space towards a giant city. I know there is no air in space from the books I touched, yet I have air in my breathing. We soon arrive at one of this city's twenty-four gates and walk in. All the spirits, who saw him immediately bowed down. He escorted me to his throne and began to tell me why he brought me here. He said, "Tianshire, you shall be the mother of my chosen people." I afterwards asked him, "Are not those who are in the Garden your chosen people?" He next said, "They are my blessed people; the people of the black land tribes will be my chosen people. You shall lead them as they destroy your mother's evil empire. Before that, you will feed them my word so that they will be purified without blemish. You must go through a time of troubles to build your faith. Fear not your death, for I will be with you always. You are the chosen deliverer." I then asked him, "Who was the man the angels carried up the yellow ladder?" He answered, "That was your father." I then asked him, "Why must Oi stop his ministry next year?" The Lord after that said, "His time shall be ended, yet the reason it ends, the Ancient One has not told me. Fear not, Oi will not go through another time of troubles. Do you have the faith to do my will?" I looked at him and said, "Oh great and wonderful Lord; you will shall always be my will and shall be done. I shall strive to serve you with all of my might and my soul. Glory is to your great name." He then brought before me a man, who is my father. I said to him, "Father, is everything okay." He then answered, "I am the luckiest father ever to live on New Venus, for I have two children who have been called by the Lord to serve him. Fear not my daughter, for I will be with you." I went to hug him, yet found it difficult to hug a spirit, as I had nothing to touch. The Lord now said, "Tianshire, it is time for you to return. I shall put you in a sleep and return you to earth. Be not alarmed that your hair is white, for once one has seen the light while still in the flesh, and the hair will remain white for the remainder of your days. This is the sign that you have walked with your Lord."

I then fell into a peaceful sleep only to hear screaming. I sat up, looked around, and saw that the daylight was upon us. I saw Zala and Tolna trembling and hugging each other. I looked at them and asked, "My sisters, why do you tremble?" Zala said, "What has happened to you? Your hair is very bright white, and a glow is flowing from your body." I asked them, "What do you think has happened?" Tolna now said, "You have seen the Lord!" I then looked at them and confirmed this by saying, "Oh, it was so wonderful; he gave me my commission. I also could talk with my father. It was so amazing. He held my hand as we went through the high skies to his great city. They opened one of their gates, and we went inside. There were so many happy and peaceful Saints and angels singing and praising our Lord." Zala currently asked me, "What are your future plans?" I told her, "The same as yesterday, only now I cannot hide from it. I know that I cannot do my great work without your help. Will you help me do our greatest work?" They both came to me and gave me hugs promising to serve the Lord with me. This gave me much satisfaction, for I meant what I had said. To lose them would be as a king losing two of his top Generals. We at present went after our horses and jumped on them. We now rode through this beautiful area and slowly went to where Oi was in the library. I wondered how he would react to this. I knew I would soon find out and gave this burden to the Lord.

Chapter 05

The Road to the Sky

Zala and Tolna behaved towards me as if I was a ghost. I could see the sweat dripping from their faces. They acted as if they were panicked and agitated. I asked them why they were so worried, "Why do you act as if you do not know me?" Zala told me, "We know who you are; however, we do not know who you are!" I told them, "I am me. Tolna then said, "How can you still be you? You look like a spirit now, I do not even know if you have flesh." I extended my hands and asked them to touch them. Zala touched my hand first and said, "I can feel the flesh, yet only see white." Tolna immediately said, "You feel as flesh, yet the books I touched taught me that when one meets the Lord, they shall be as spirits." I then told her, "That is true, if they have been transformed; however, I was not transformed. I shall not keep this white forever, as I once thought, nevertheless, it shall fade. It will never leave the inside of me, thus the demons now will see the spirit of the Lord inside me. This is the spirit from having the Lord being before me and not the spirit of me being before the Lord."

Zala then said, "I thought we had been before the Lord, how is this different?" I told her, "Mine was from being physical in from of the throne, and not just from my spirit, as also yours, being before the throne by his grace." Tolna then said, "I have never heard of one being physically before the Lord while still being alive." I afterwards told them, "I wish you also could have been with me this time." Zala asked me, "Why do you wish that?" I answered, "Because we have a great ministry ahead of us. It shall be you to carry on this ministry when I am gone, as we carry on Oi's ministry when he leaves." Tolna next suggests, "We need to go back to the library and touch some more pages, so that we will also be wise ministers and can help our nation to rebuild itself in accordance with the ages." I after that said, "That is what I like my sisters so much, for you always have so many good ideas. We shall go back to the library; nonetheless, we must stay here until Oi comes for us." Zala asks, "Why must we wait for Oi?" I then told them, "I do not want to scare the Aconites oasis people. I also do not want to chance to hurt Oi's pride in front of others, for I know the deceiver will use this to trip him.

I should be close to normal in a few days." Tolna then says, "Well, I guess we can ride our horses, swim, and have a lot of fun for some more sisterhood memories." That is what I enjoy so much about my sisters, they always find a way to enjoy every situation, and they learn fast no matter what the wind blows our way. Especially worth noting, is the way they very quickly learned how to fight those demons. Words in a book cannot accurately describe their heroism on the front lines. They stood strong, and their enemies fell quickly. They saw me do it, and so they did it. I wish that my ability to learn and implement so efficiently matched theirs and explains why I feel a great need for them on our team. As we now go to get our horses, they come running to us. It is as though they can read our minds. They are so different from us, in that they run to those they serve and love, yet we, seeing their size run from them with fear. Zala tells me that these horses are tamed. They have learned to depend upon humans for their survival. Unlike the wild ones that must live constantly in fear from predators and in search of their food. They serve us for protection from these predators and the convenient availability of their food, all year round. I start petting my horse's head, and he just stands there enjoying it with no fear. It is almost as if he longs for our touches. The thought of me hurting him is buried deep and hidden inside of him. Tolna shows me how to pat them, as they do also enjoy this. We go around our horses and pat them gently. Zala tells me to talk kindly to them, as they will get used to that tone and enjoy it. Then when we yell for them to go faster, they will sense the danger in our voice and run speedier. Since we cannot communicate with words, we have to use voice tone and body gestures to get our intentions known to them. I now go back to his head and smile in his eye. He slowly moves his head to my face and sniffs. Tolna said, "He is learning your smell, so if he cannot see you, he will try to find your scent. We now jump on our horses and start riding around. We soon see a nice small cluster of trees with one large tree in the middle. Zala and Tolna's eyes become revived with life. I can almost perceive what they are thinking; however, I hope I am wrong. Shoot, I was right. They jump from their horses grabbing one of the lower branches from the tallest tree in the middle and yell, "Come on Tianshire." I slowly dismount from my horse and walk over to the tree. They are giving me a nasty look, as if to suggest that I walk faster. I grab hold of the tree, start scooting up, and soon meet them on their branch. I ask them, "Why did you select this tree?" I knew that answer; I just wanted to make sure they knew why. Zala answers, "Because it is the tallest one, and we want to see if we can find where you were when you met the Lord."

I told them, "I had to climb four ladders, each one much higher than this tree and then the Lord had to hold my hand as we went in the forever dark skies above us." Tolna afterwards says, "Well, at least we can see some of the land around us." They then came over to me and Tolna went around me saying, "I will be above you, making sure everything is safe and Zala will be behind you in case you need her help. We will make sure you are okay sister." I next thought about how afraid I was yesterday on the last ladder and after that the curving steps. Nevertheless, I have more fear now, and this time I am with two people I trust, without any doubt in their knowledge of climbing trees. Up the tree, we go, and soon the treetop is getting smaller. I stop to ask Tolna if this can support all of us. She tells me to wait where I am. I stare out at the wonderful scenery. The rolling hills in this small oasis where so beautiful. They have it designed where each section has its privacy. They even have birds that fly around the parameter. It is as if they do not want to travel over the desert. Zala comes up beside me. I tell her, "Please Zala, this tree cannot support all three of us at this elevation." She laughs and says, "Go ahead and go down a few branches, and I will go up and talk to Tolna." She quickly goes up. I stayed where I was in fear watching her go up. I would hate to see them fall, as I need them more than what they do think. Suddenly, I cannot feel any heat from the sun, as an easy cool breeze is starting to blow over us. I hear a strange noise, something like a branch snapping. I look down and see our tree snapping just below me. I need to get to it and hold it while my sisters rush down. I yell, "The tree is snapping, get down now!" I make it to where the branch is snapping and try to hold it together to no avail. The tree snaps and as it does, it pulls me as it drives the branch into my stomach, which knocks the wind out of me. I can see the top of this tree swing down with Zala and Tolna hanging on. This top section is now lodged into the bottom section, and as it does, it flings me lose. Lucky for me, the lesser branches stretch out further than the lower ones. I am flipped out into the air in such a way that it somersaults me back closer to the tree. I crash into the first few branches as I can feel something cracking inside of me. I try to grab at some branches; nevertheless, I do not appear to have control of my hands. The speed that I am descending is so fast I feel like a sword slashing these branches. I keep hitting branches, and now that they are getting thicker; a few of them are bouncing me. Then this last bounce slings me back into the air. This is not pleasant now. At least, I made it a valid way down bouncing off the branches.

That has slowed me down some, so I would have been dropping much faster now. Notwithstanding, I am picking up speed currently as I am trying to glide over to a smaller tree below me. I hit this tree about halfway down it. Its branches are not as hard as the big tree. I am trying to roll where I hit the springy parts of the branches. The ground is coming up fast. I am getting ready to hit it. Bam, ouch, I am having trouble breathing. I think I might have broken every bone in my body. I also feel it strange that I am still conscious. This would be one of those times when I would have preferred to be unconscious and woke up during the final stages of the healing process. I know that death should own me now; then again, I felt the white around my body absorb so much of the impact. It must have done something, because I am no longer white. I would more accurately be dead if I had not been saved by that last little shock absorber. at present all I see is blood and bones piercing out of skin. I think I will get some praying in now, because who knows, this could be the time of troubles; they were predicting. Whatever it is, it is not what I was expecting today to share with me. I can now hear Tolna and Zala screaming as they are running towards me. Oh, this is like heaven to my soul.

I can only praise the Lord for giving me such a wonderful blessing in this situation. I can look at Tolna and Zala and see that they are okay and that is the most important thing for me, because I want my sisters always to be healthy and happy. They rush up to me and start crying about how apologetic they are. I cannot, for any reason feel regretful about what we did, because they are okay. I think their pain would hurt me more than the pain that is now tearing me apart. Their tears falling on me currently hurt worse than the branches that I crashed through painfully. Zala takes her water bag from her saddle and an extra shirt she had in case of rain and begins to clean some of my wounds. There is little that she can do, since I have so many bones spearing out of my skin. I just noticed that I could not see out of my right eye. Tolna is talking, yet I cannot answer her, because by jaw is broken. Darn, I cannot feel my legs. It may take a while to be completely healed. I hope that I can spend some time with Oi; nevertheless, it would kill him not to be able to devote his time to his powerful ministry. I can in no way try to hold him back. I am sure the Lord will talk to him about it. Tolna and Zala both are trying to clean me, when Zala says, "We need to get a doctor or some medicine men to put these bones back together." I now start coughing up blood. Tolna adds, "She will never make it; we need to find someone to save her fast."

Zala stands up, raises her hands to the heavens and begins her petition, "Oh mighty Lord; I am Zala, whom you said was a Saint. We have a great melancholy before us now. Your faithful servant Tianshire is in deep trouble and my die soon, unless you heal her. In exchange, I promise to serve you with her for as long or whenever you want for the remainder of her days." At this point, Tolna stands up and raises her arms saying, "I also promise, oh mighty Lord. Take anything you want from me, just, please do not take my master, when through you, I will serve." Zala currently says, "I believe in your healing powers and have faith in my authority through your name. I now declare that in your name your faithful servant Tianshire shall be healed." Tolna also adds, "We not only believe, but we have your faith in our words." Immediately, a white light descended upon Tianshire. Tolna and Zala stood strong and continued praising the Lord. The light covered me and within a split second, my body was made complete again. The light returned to the sky. Zala looked at me and saw that I was now absolute again. The Lord even cleaned the blood from my clothing. I now felt shame in that I had not thought about the Lord healing me. Tolna and Zala both jumped for joy and thanked the Lord. I now saw how much they truly loved me. The only reason they had me in the tree with them was, so I could have the great fun that they had. I smile at them and say, "Thank you so much for your love and your faith." Zala now asks whether I will forgive them. I ask her, "Why should you be forgiven, for I am the one that fell, so I must not have been learning from you like I should have been. I will try harder the next time." Tolna then confesses, "Oh no, Tianshire, it was us who forgot to teach you how to handle a split. We should have told you to let go, for as long as we were with the tree, we would not get hurt much at all. The next time, we will think about strange things that can happen and prepare accordingly for those contingencies." I now added, "I am so proud about the way my sisters learned and mastered the healing through the Lord." Zala said, "It was easy, "We knew he would do it; therefore, the only this we were truly hoping was that he did it at present." "I then looked at them and said, "Because of your faith, many shall receive their healing. I am so blessed to have you with me. For I can see now, that you will be genuine ministers and healers when we begin our ministry. I thank the Lord so much that I may put my love inside you as real believers and doers of his mighty words." Tolna then added, "We so much want to do whatever we can help your ministry. We promise truly to be able to help you in your ministry for the remainder of your days, which if we keep you out of trees, may be long." The three of us now laughed, as I jumped up and said, "What you say we go to the temple, eat, and then pray at their altar?" We afterwards jumped on our horses and raced to the temple. I let them battle it out, as my horse and I, took our time. When I reached the forest and was under the trees, I heard some noises and turned around to see what made them. I then saw two faces emerging and shouting, "Wait for us Tianshire." Zala and Tolna had stopped their race and were waiting for me. I asked Tolna, "Why did you stop your race?" She said, "I was too far ahead of Zala, plus we have never raced inside the forest because we might hurt the horses. Lastly, we know you are clumsy and thus agreed that it would be better to wait for you while also making sure you were safe." I then answered, "As would true sisters do for each other. I thank you so much, as strangely, I was starting to miss you two also." We now took our time while discussing all the different kinds of trees. They knew everything about these trees. I asked Tolna, "How can you know so much about trees, since you and Zala live inside a tunnel where there are no trees?" Tolna then answered, "I once lived in Tolna, plus I touched the pages of some books about plant life." I now said, "I think we should go back to that library and touch many more books." They agreed; nevertheless, we currently headed for the temple. When we arrived, the Widows of Vadessa quickly guided us to the priest's dining room. They brought us hot food and tea. Then they guided us to a room where they had buckets of water on swivels connected to a rope.

We asked the widows what this place was, and they told us to put our clothes on the bench, handed us some homemade soap, and said, "If you do not get all the dirt off, we will. Tell us when you are ready to be inspected." These old women looked serious, so we agreed, striped, put our clothes on the bench, and pulled our ropes just a little to get ourselves wet. We now rubbed the soap over our complete bodies, except for our faces that we would do last. Sense we could not get our backs; we scrubbed each other's backs. We now rubbed some lightly on our hair; I made sure we were standing where the bucket's water would hit us, soaped our faces, and pulled the rope, which released the cold water on us. We used our hands to rub the soap from our skin. We inspected each other, and then took a towel the widows had left for us and dried ourselves. We started to walk for our clothes when some of the widows came rushing in and inspected us. They had some special carved sticks to clean out our ears. They inspected us and then said, "Okay, you beautiful girls get dressed." We rushed to where we had put our clothes, strangely to discover they had been cleaned, any ways we quickly dressed ourselves. I then asked one of the widows, "How did your clean our clothes so fast?" She explained, "We cleaned them with our special soap and then dried them over our big temple fire place." I afterwards said, "We do very much thank you. We now plan to go to the altar and pray. Would this be okay?" She next told us, "We will show you the way and see if there is something you want?" I after that said, "Oh, we do thank you for your kindness." She then said to me, "Oh no, by all means, it is us who thank you. Your ministry with your brothers has changed the temples in our land to where before they were to the ancient dead gods; we now worship your live God. Your teachings are what enlisted the priests to help the needy with food and clothing. The words you have shared with our people have generated much love and sharing. I worship your Lord every day." By now, most of the widows were standing in a line on both sides of the hallway that directed to the altar area. Tolna now said, "Oh wonderful servant of our Lord, the Lord belongs to you also. If he lives inside of you, you must accept him as your Lord. Rejoice for the Lord is your Lord also." I smiled at Tolna and then said, "My sister who is a Saint has spoken the truth." The widows now said, "We believe you to be the deliverer that Oi speaks about crying in the wilderness saying a great deliverer will come." I asked them, "How do you know of such a thing?"

The widows said, "You are a daughter of the Lord. He has given you two Saints. Who else could deliver us?" I looked at them and said, "You speak the truth; nonetheless, I must go back to my mother's kingdom and suffer through my 'times of trouble' before I return to finishing Oi's great work. Then shall I free the world of my mother's evil." They afterwards rejoiced saying, "We believe that the Lord will deliver us from all evil. He is a mighty and wonderful Lord." I tell them straight away, "You speak the truth, for it shall be the Lord, who will deliver us. Immediately, we proceeded to the altar. Tolna, Zala, and I now began to pray. I was pleasantly surprised at how sincerely my sisters were praying. They had many issues that they wanted help with the Lord. I can see why the Lord made them Saints now. Before, I could not truly understand why; nevertheless, I consider it an act of grace. I now can feel why the Lord has done this. I shall keep them greatly involved in our ministry since I can feel that the Lord wants them to be involved. I have now fallen deep into my prayer, as the Lord reveals to me that Zala and Tolna will be spreading his word throughout the black land's tribes during my times of trouble. He tells me that all will know that they are Saints, for he will tell all the priests, so they can prepare a meeting site for his Saints to deliver his word. I thank the Lord so much, knowing that I love them so much.

We now awake the next day with many stories to tell each other. The widows come rushing to us with some drying clothes they made and begin wiping the sweat from our bodies. They tell us that it is the next day and ask us to go with them to the dining area, so they can feed us. They act like our mothers, and I tell them, "You care for us as if we were your children." One of them at present tells us, "You are the little girls we always wanted as our daughters; notwithstanding, our children are now all married and busy with their lives." I felt so sorry about this and decided to ask Oi about including this in his ministry. I remember touching a commandment in one of the Lord's many books that directed us to, 'honor our parents.' We now followed them down the hallway to the dining area to discover they had made for each of us a nice dress and shorts. Three of the widows gave them to us. Zala then said to them, "We thank you so much for clothing us. Surely, you not only know the laws, but also live them. You shall be blessed. We will strive to keep them clean and not destroy them by playing." Then one of the widows said, "Oh Saint Zala, you can play in these clothes, for at your age it is so important to play and get dirty. We have made some extra sets for you, as they are light and will fit into your back bags easy. Here take the ones that you each want. We thank you very much Saint Zala." I was therefore, pleased by hearing they call my sisters Saints. They are at present, acting so mature. The widows currently wanted to know if we had any fresh news from the Lord. I told them, "We have received many words from our Lord; however, it will take some time for it to return to our conscience. I know that I did not receive any warnings about any bad things." Now, I looked at Zala who confirmed, "Neither, I," as she looked at Tolna, who also agreed, "Nor did I." The widows now smiled and started guiding us to their tables. We ate many excellent things, as these widows were such pleasant cooks, I could now understand why some of the priests were rather fat. I patted my belly and then said, "I am glad you made these dresses loose, for I will have to play extra hard the next few days while waiting for my brother to return. Your food tastes so good I cannot stop eating." They all laughed as one of them told the other widows, "Hurry, we would currently give them their deserts." They at present brought out chocolates, cakes, and pies. Our eyes lit up in shock. I have only seen these treats a few times in the temples and not this wide of a selection. I knew what chocolate is from touching some pages in the cookbooks. I meanwhile realize that none of the other temples of widows. I will ask Oi to mention this in his final ministries. I eat the chocolates and as their fruit inside release a burst in my mouth exploding with rich flavor. I asked them, "How do you create the chocolate?" One of the widows answered saying, "We trade with the Komaromi, who produce an exceptional bean that we grind, much like the unique coffees we serve to the priests and deacons." We decided to eat these treats conservative, telling the widows that we believed the priests had worked hard and deserved some of this. I also told them, "If I eat too much of the treat, I will become addicted and wish to stay here forever." The head widow said to us, "Well in that situation, eat much, for we would love to have you stay there for eternity. We all laughed as I excused ourselves and told them, "We need to do some exploring before my brother returns from the library." We thanked them as we went out the door. Zala went over and hugged one, which put Tolna, and myself to work hugging, as we continued to thank them. When we departed, they started to cry. This time Tolna told them, "Your love for the Lord's people shall bring you great blessings in heaven. We all truly bless you all." I nodded with a smile in agreement as also did Zala.

They then began cheering, and we slid away in the excitement. We jumped on our horses and began to ride around the village. The people all stood still when we passed through, as the men and women took of head coverings. We waved and smiled at them. We saw a priest walking through the tunnel entrance, and I asked him if my brother was still in the tunnel. He answered me, "Tianshire; your brother is still in the tunnel." I looked at him and asked, "How do you know my name?" He answered, "Everyone knows you, for you will be our deliverer." I then asked him, "How do you know this?" He answered, "Who else would the Lord select if not his daughter?" I marveled at his wisdom and answered, "You are very wise, and I tell you that these young children shall see their lands freed before they reach your years." He gave us his blessings, and we moved on out of the town, going the other direction this time. We went one street over, and I could see the steeples of the temple and thereby went to this street, as it appeared to have a park at the end of it, which gave a wonderful view of the temple. I could see the nice walls of stone that surrounded it. It was only three or four stories high except in the middle where the worship area had a giant steeple, which one could look up at least sixteen stories. It also had a very large open area that had huge columns, which rose to at least eight stories, and supported a large roof that sloped up another two stories, and a sizable windowless four-story wooden house with an amazing double art packed sloping roof. I remember one of the priests telling me that is where they live at night in the winter and go for complete solitude for praying. I truly was impressed with the main entrance that led to the pavilion that stretched above the fourth floor. This floor was used for large celebrations and national ceremonies. It had any steps to walk to the fourth floor. The walls of the temple had a fortress design that would be effective for archers. The main entrance had two large gazebos with V-shaped roofs made of wood. The third roof structure also contained a wooden steeple that rose eight stories tall each with an outside walkway and special rooms for the priests. The main walkway had walls that were over two stories high. What was more amazing was that each of the six corners also had giant steeples each as huge as the center one. They told me that with the open pavilion, they could easily have eight large services at the same time. As I looked around, I saw a small group of priests trying to look natural in front of some trees behind me. I rode my horse over to them and said, "Hi."

They looked at me strangely and asked, "How did you know we were here?" I told them, "When you stand in the open, one must merely open their eyes to see. Anyway, I would like to know more about your wonderful temple. Will you tell me more about your temple?" The four of them smiled and immediately swarmed around me and began talking. They told me that this temple was built before the ages by gods who traveled in the skies. At one time, the pavilion had over two hundred statues of them. We have since destroyed them when we all converted to your Lord. I told them, "He is also your Lord." They afterwards said, "Okay, next to your father." I could only thank them and smile because they needed to hold on to something that identified the Lord as being very pleased with them. I then told them, "My father is very pleased with the pronounced faith that you have shown him. Your people will receive many blessings from him as he also blesses the others of great faith. Please tell me more." They then proceeded. "We converted this into a temple for your father. This has been a great blessing for us, as your mother has sent her armies here five times and all five times, we were victorious. This temple has many tunnels and at night, we could send our soldiers out to release their horses and put special poisons in their foods and water. We would also stab and spear many of them. We learned to cripple their legs and to blind them. Rubina's armies would not take them back with them, so after they retreated, we would easily kill them. They never left with more than twenty percent of their armies, as during their retreat, they would be flooded with arrows, some with fire to destroy any supplies, so they would have to return to Belcher's Prison. I told them, "I am so glad that you shared this magnificent news to me. We shall now see some other wonderful sites in this amazing Aconites oasis. As we turned to leaving, our horses vanished. The sky turned blood red, as blood fell from the sky. The priests began to panic as we could hear much screaming throughout the village as all were now running into the temple. Then before us, we saw a giant skull rise from the ground, as the trees and the ground around it turn to burning dust. The flames burned higher than the steeples to the temple. We could see a partial face made of dark black bones with its giant teeth chewing at the ground. Tolna now yelled out, "Who dares defile the land of my Lord?" He shot a giant flame of fire that thankfully just went straight through us doing no harm. He then said, "I am the great Pilisjászfalu, the fire god whom all in this galaxy worship." Zala now said, "Oh you are a weak child, you are in the wrong galaxy."

He then said, "How dare you to call me weak, for my breath can destroy you." Zala said, "In case you have forgotten, your breath can do us no harm. You may blow until you have no more fire, and then we shall destroy you." He now blew hard, as his breath burned all the trees and buildings behind us, yet we just danced around laughing at him. Tolna currently sang, "Poor weak Pilisjászfalu, he is such a fool, for when he blew, the little girls knew, that Pilisjászfalu is a fool." We could now see many of the villagers forming around the parameters of the burning area. I next said, "Pilisjászfalu, we have judged you to be a fool and to be guilty of teasing the chosen ones of our blessed Lord." I after that looked at Tolna, who grabbed hands with Zala and said, "We now command by the name of our Lord, whom you be frozen and that never again shall you make a fire." Immediately, he froze. I then looked at the blood that was everywhere and said, "Oh blessed Lord, take away this blood, for if it not be your blood than we can have no blood at all." In addition, the blood vanished and the skies turned clear again. Zala now looked behind us and saw all the damage and said, "Oh, Lord, please give back the righteous what evil has taken from them." Everything that was destroyed by the fire or Pilisjászfalu was restored as new. I now said, "Oh Lord, will you please give us back the horses that your wonderful servants have entrusted us with." Our three horses at present reappeared.

We could hear the people begin the cheer; however, their cheers stopped abruptly, as the sky once again turned red; notwithstanding, we had no blood this time. Likewise, the crowd behaved differently this time. They stood calm, with their arms raised up praising the Lord. I told Tolna that I would take this one. I asked, "Who are you fools who are cutting into our play time?" They answered with a roar, "We are the sons of Pilisjászfalu, whom you destroyed. We have come for our revenge." They were ugly monsters who stood four stories tall. They were minute differences from them, and I will do my best to describe them. They both had heads that were like killer dogs. They both have giant S-shaped scaly horns coming from their heads. The one on my right had burning flames running through his ram horns as all six horns that extended from his head were as burning coals at their tips. They both had arm muscle at least ten feet wide and most likely a circumference of at least forty feet. The forearms were as flaming coals running through the razor-sharp scales the protruded through them. The one on my right had large pointed scales extending from his kneecaps. They both had very scaly toenails and fingers. These toenail scales were larger than a man was and burning coals ran through them. They both had a fire in their mouths as their groan areas with burning coals packed these large black scales, as all their scales were black. Zala now told them, "You have picked the wrong time to come here for your revenge, for today you shall join your father in the bottomless pit for eternity." They said, "Oh, you three little girls are going to destroy us." I then told them, "The Lord only uses us for the big ones, such as your dad, who like you was also very ugly. Today, the children of our Lord who are now praising him shall destroy you. They at present tried to blow fire upon them; however, the fire would go halfway and afterwards curve back and hit the parts of them that were not burned, causing them great pain. I next asked them, "Why did you fools come here today?" They answered, "Because so many demons have told us how easy it is to kill our prey here and how frightened you humans are." I then looked at them and said, "Do you see any here today who are frightened?" They have now raised their claws, and began to shoot thick beams of fire at the people. Once again, the flames reversed and hit them at their vulnerable parts. Tolna then laughed, "Come on, cannot you do anything to create some fear in us. This is starting to become foolish. They now ran to Tolna and tried to step on her, and as they did they were flipped into a spiraling circled that spun up and dropped hard to the ground.

As they crashed on the ground, Tolna yelled at them, "You almost got my hair dirty, and if you did, that would mean that the widows would make me wash my hair again, and that would have made me mad." The audience began to laugh as they now realized that these were indeed children standing firmer and stronger against demons greater in size than any event ever recorded in their history. I currently looked at them and said, "Do not move," and as I saw that they could not move, I went back to the people who were praising the Lord. I said to them, "Oh Saints of Aconites, the Lord has found great pleasure in your faith and praise. Today, you may command in his name whom he destroys these two demons." New priests emerged from the group and came to me asking, "How can we do this Tianshire? Will you teach us how?" I looked at them and smiled saying, "Simply just practice your command and when you are ready all of you give the command together, and it will be done. While you are preparing, my sisters and I shall take a nap in front of them." We then went a few feet from them, laid down, and quickly went to sleep. The Widows of Vadessa now began to cry out, "Oh, Lord our little babies have been put under a spell by those beasts." The priests quickly yelled out to all the people, "Fear not for they are simply resting so they may play more after we destroy these demons." The people all marveled at the faith and power of these young Saints. After they practiced a while, the priests all gathered to make any last minute arrangements then all returned to their posts. Then in unison, they all commanded, "By the name of the name of our Lord; we command you to the bottomless pit for eternity." Afterwards in front of us appeared four giant angels who bound them. They then hurled them to the sun as we could see two flashes of flames being pulled into the sun. We also heard them both scream out in pain, begging to be released. Their cries soon vanished as they sank into the bottomless pit. I now stood in front of our people as they were celebrating. It is good when people believe without having seen, but when they can use the power of the Lord to save themselves, the words on the pages of the teachings in the temple at present become words of life, and they realize that their Lord is a living Lord, which they can depend. I now raised my hands as they all became quiet. I now told them, "I give great thanks to you for destroying the demons while my sisters and I slept. It was such a wonderful vision to see the power in your words. You have discovered that if you have the faith of one of those grains of sand in the desert that surrounds this city, you can move and destroy mountains.

You must take great honor in how the Lord could do a pronounced work here today because of your faith, and our faith in knowing that you could do it. When people tell stories about today, they shall say that the Saints of Aconites destroyed the Children of Petrikeresztúr who stood taller than four stories. We have been blessed to enjoy existing with you and trusting our lives in your care. I need three priests to come up to us now." When they arrived, I asked them to check if we were clean. They began by saying, "You are the cleanest Saints ever to walk upon New Venus." I then told them, "No, check if our flesh has any dirt that may need to be cleaned." They began to laugh and one of them said, "Oh, I wish I had children like you little angels." They now checked our hair, elbows, kneecaps, and hands. Zala told me, "Daddies actually check harder than mommies when someone is watching them." The priests said, "You are a very wise young lady." They looked at us and said, "You are all clean." I later raised my hands, as the crowd becomes quiet once more. I subsequently said, "The Widows of Vadessa may take comfort, in that our skin is free from dirt as verified by these three wonderful priests." At this, the crowd began to laugh aloud, as we could now hear conversations between them. One group was discussing how we were truly from the Lord because we were not seeking great fame, yet working hard to teach them how to use the amazing power of the Lord. I heard another group saying that we were truly as great as Oi and that all the black land tribes would know about how we were standing tall and certain in front of giant demons, confident enough to sleep in front of them. We were in a deep sleep, as the priests had to come and wake us up by shaking us. The priests now assembled their messengers to go into all the nearby temples and tell them of the great wonders that happened in the temple of the Aconites. Then each of those temples would send out their messengers. The temples had a strong network setup, which allowed them to communicate throughout all of their tribes. I believe this will come in handy when I take them to war against my mother and those who follow her. Suddenly, the Widows of Vadessa came rushing around us. I told them, "Honestly, we are clean." Their leader then said, "We believe you, we just fear that with all the hard work you did today in saving us that you might like some treats; therefore, we would like for you to join us for a fun party." Zala after that says, "Oh right, a party. Yeah!" Tolna then says, "Count me in, our Aconites mothers." Hey, they had me outnumbered two to one, so I said, "Oh yes, some more of that chocolate." They all cheered as we walked among them back to the temple. Then one man yelled, "They could kill demons, but not escape from the Widows of Vadessa." I then yelled back, "Once you have enjoyed their chocolate, you will become their happy slave forever." All who heard this laughed as one priest said, "They give those little girls something that none of us can give, and that is a mommy. All children must be mothered and when they are mothered they are happy." We feasted with the widows this time with a completely new sense of family. They were so kind to us and told us many stories about their lives. There were so many of them, who lived here now, that had become widows at the hands of my mother's wrath. They lived too far from Aconites to seek the shelter of the temple. Many did not know about the temple; nevertheless, the priests made routine visits through this large section of Bucsu. They would receive reports of the victims of Rubina's raids and visit these people, which sometimes found a widow starving to death. They would bring them back to the temple, so they could continue to live. All the widows here told me that Rubina's beasts would also kill all the children by Rubina's orders. They always killed the males, since they could become warriors against them. They never worried about the women, figuring they would either die, or present a burden on the people slowing them down in their escape attempts.

They also depended upon them to spread the terror of their attacks. Rubina hoped this would create panic and relished the thought that the people would be suffering from the fear of her raids. This is one reason why she hated Oi and Tianshire so much; however, strangely she would at no time, allow a raid on one of Oi's sermons, as she commanded that they not at any time be hurt. She never knew until she died, that the Lord had created that desire in her. Nevertheless, she would attack the sermon's attendees when they were returning to their homes and well away from Oi and Tianshire. She told her generals that her children would be punished in private, since she had given birth to them, she did not want any others to see how she was destroying what she had created. Even evil will put its wings over their offspring. Back to the widows, they had recovered after losing all they loved and had. This created a deeper source of pride in what Oi had accomplished so far; the hungry were being fed, and the naked were being clothed. These widows were so involved in their community, as many were also midwives, and they ran a family medical center, where they would give out the herbs for particular illnesses. They also would baby sit when their parents had to be present at special meetings and always for all who attended their worship services.

I was always getting reports from the congregation saying how the widows were now a community service, which they all depended. Another important service they provided was preparing all the food for the Aconites holidays. The temple really depended upon this time for all the Aconites to join, which also included some who were scattered in the local area. This created the family environment in which the Lord of New Venus, Lilith, had stressed in the Garden of Eden. Though they, at no time had been there, Belcher talked a lot about his former home, added to some of the traders who traveled our globe, which told tales of her commands. I often wondered who Lilith was never much involved with us. Oi always told me that the Lord God took over this area as it as Belcher's prison. Therefore, she would not become involved with this land until all the evil was removed, and that was Oi and my responsibility. I could dwell upon this, yet the time to dwell upon it has not arrived. This time, if the stupid demons stopped invading, was set aside for rest and energizing for our next mission. I finally stood up and asked my sisters if they were prepared to work on today's mission. I did not have the heart to ask them if they were ready to play, as that might break the widows' hearts; nevertheless, I had to get away from them. This was the best dose of mommy I had ever had. Their mommy care and love were seeping into parts of me that had been sealed for so long, and as they were opening, I could feel all the emptiness that was inside me. I can only hope that my sisters can help pull me back together. I actually feel very sorry for the widows, in that they worked so hard to care for us; therefore, I had to struggle hard to conceal this new pain. I must try to forget that I was cheated from that, and with the exception of Oi and our younger brother Tsarsko, and our father, we had no love in our family. I do miss Tsarsko so much. I hated so much that we could not bring him along; sadly, he refused our pleas. I know it was from the fear he had that our mother would catch us and kill him as she did our dad. Oi and I both pray daily that he can stay strong enough for me to deliver him. This is also a strange thing, in that Oi prays so sincerely that, "Tianshire may be capable to save Tsarsko." He at no time prays that he might be competent to do this, which is weird. I never ask him, because I believe he knows some things that I do not. He has been my caregiver and has given his heart to me, so I can never question his sincerity, as I have learned to leave sleeping dogs alone.

The Aconites will be faithful people that shall give wicked very much trouble. They do not have both the faith, and the knowing that they can defeat sinful by the name of our Lord. This new confidence is deeply indoctrinated into them. I am truly lucky that the Lord told me to let his children throw the spear of death. Most of our ministries have been concerned about embedding the faith into their souls. They get this faith into their minds, yet they seldom get a chance to live on the front line with only the Lord as their shield. Today the Aconites were thrust onto the front line. I can only imagine what they were thinking when they saw the three of us lying down and sleeping in front of those giant beasts. I can truly believe that what happened today will be told in stories for many ages, as the stories are already being spread throughout the black land tribes. Our days of rest will be fewer now. Tolna and Zala join me currently as we head for the meadows in this large oasis. I joke with my sisters saying, "I think we should stay away from any temples." Zala fires back, "Especially if we are only going to sleep in front of them." We all had to stop our horses because we were laughing too hard. We decided to ride through some semi-open forests, which had many small meadows in them. They also had an overwhelming assortment of flowers that made this area so beautiful.

I wondered if the Garden of Eden was this beautiful. We decided to head back to our favorite pond and swim for a few hours. Just as we arrived, some priests came riding in yelling, "Tianshire, Oi has awakened." I was glad they came now, instead of five minutes henceforth. If they had come later, we would be trapped in the water, as New Venus swimming does not include bathing suits. Our ancestors declared that swimming could be as one with the nature. This also ensured that everything was cleaned and water soaked into all parts of the body, since the hot summers would dry our skin just sky of being painful. Thankfully, we were spared that today, even though the priests gave us the privacy and respect we would have needed. The only thing that was on my mind now was talking with Oi. There were so many things to discuss. We quickly rushed through the tunnel, and met up with Oi on the road to the temple. When we met, I stopped and said, "Welcome back brother." Oi tells me, "I heard you had a lot of excitement over the past few days." I told him, "You do not even know the half of it." Oi responded, "Oh yes I do, for I had priests watching you all the time." Zala after that says, "What are three helpless little girls to do when their big brother abandons them?" Oi next says, "If they are you three, what would you think big brother could do that you cannot do much better?" We all laughed. I subsequently asked Oi, "Big brother and my leader, would you object if the three of us touched some more pages, because the last few days have taught us there is much we do not know?" Oi afterwards answered, "Only on one condition." I asked him, "Oi, what might that be?" Oi answered, "If I have trouble fighting demons you would rescue me." I jumped off my horse, went over to my brother, and gave him a giant hug telling him, "I will stop any arrow for you and die to save you. Call upon me anytime, for I am here to serve you." I could see a small tear come from his eyes. I had never before seen him cry. He told me, "Tianshire, you are the only one that I have." I then told him, "Now you have three who all so deeply love you." He reached out as Zala and Tolna joined our hug. He said to them, "I have heard great things about your ability to destroy demons. I will need you to take care of her after I am gone?" Zala and Tolna told him, "Do not worry, for we could never live without her, and very much want to even be with her during her times of troubles, yet she refuses to allow us to do so." Oi then told them, "Zala and Tolna, I too have asked the Lord to allow you to be with her during her times of troubles. However, the Lord has declared that this road Tianshire must travel alone.

I shall each day continue begging that he reconsiders, and if you truly want to be by her side, you too should beg, in your prayers each day. It is not wrong to keep asking the Lord, as I know you understand how hard it is for a parent to keep saying no." Zala then answered, "Oi, this we shall do, for we have mastered this art before our parents. Maybe we will be lucky in this issue." I then told Oi, "Take my horse and go to the temple. Tell the widows of Vadessa that you are our older brother, and they will give you a love you have not had." Oi then said, "Am I to seek from widows?" I told him, "It is not that kind of love; you will quickly discover you need this love. Trust them, for they only wish to do you a great service on behalf of our Lord. I told Zala and Tolna, "It is time that we spy on big brother, because I know he needs the widows; however, like all boys, they can at times be masters at not doing what we ask." Tolna then added, "How strange, my mother told me the same thing about my daddy when we would spy on him. We stopped spying when one day we saw him creating beautiful new matching jewelry for us. When he gave it to us, we could only cry for feeling guilty. He then asked us, "Why did you girls stop following me around?" We decided to say nothing, although mommy told me later she wanted to hit him for not telling us he knew. According to my mommy, if a man catches a woman doing something, he must tell her immediately. I really do not know if this is fair, but it is women's law and men must obey this if they want their women to stay with them. I then said to Zala, "My lovely sister, we must get there before he is returning." We afterwards began running the shortcut we had discovered and arrived at the temple as Oi was walking inside. He entered the large pavilion where most of the people were congregated. There I saw the widows surrounding him. I knew that even though he is the greatest prophet ever to walk to surface of New Venus, he had no chance of getting free from them. I took my sisters, and we ran back to the tunnel and quickly went down to the steps that led to the library. We were disappointed when we arrived there, for a large stone had been put in front of it. A priest there told us that Oi has forbidden any to go in here. I thought how strange this was; it is that I would have thought he would want others to share this knowledge. Then I thought that this knowledge would indeed be damaging if evil were to access it. The priest stood in front of us and said, "You may not go past this stone, by order of your brother." I told him, "My brother gave us permission." Instantly, Zala and Tolna agreed to say, "This is true, very true!" The priest now added, "I am so sorry; nevertheless, until Oi tells me otherwise you may not enter." I then looked at the priest and said, "Oh, how I regret fighting with those who also share my Lord, yet for this I shall fight and enter herein. Now, you need to think that if four-story demons fall in our hands, how fast will you fall?" He then said, "I am so sorry; however, Oi's commands must be obeyed." I later said, "Because this is Oi's mistake, I will allow you to live again next week. Now go to sleep." At this, the priest fell to the ground in a deep sleep. Tolna asked, "Why did you not kill him for refusing to obey you?" I told her, "Our power is to make the kingdom of our Lord stronger. Killing priests will not make it tougher, but could divide our house. At no time forget, that a house divided within itself will not at any time stand. This was not his fault; it was Oi and my fault. We were so excited and rushed that we forgot. When he awakes, I will ask Oi to apologize and forgive him. For now, we will go through this stone. Follow me and do not stop walking. Through the stone I went, with Tolna following. We waited, yet Zala did not follow us. I told Tolna to wait here and I went back into the stone and found Zala. I grabbed hold of her hand and pulled her through with me. When she was free once more, we asked her what happened.

She confessed to being scared and within an instance, the rock enclosed her leaving her trapped. I then told her, as she was crying, "Do not cry Zala, you will someday run through these rocks as if they were air. Just remember sisters that when you are depending upon your faith to pull you through a special place, you must keep your eyes and mind upon the Lord. I usually sing songs to him, which has worked so far. I like songs rather than prayer, because songs have many versions, so you must concentrate on the song. Make sure that you use a song that you know, either way, if you get stuck, just start another song." Zala then said, "Oh, we are very stupid, how you could want such senseless girls, as your sisters baffle me? You are so much wiser than we are, we will only slow you down and cause guiltless people to suffer." I looked at her and said, "The lone innocent person who would suffer if you two were gone would be me. You must remember that our Lord, who is the wisest Lord evermore to be, chose both of you to be leaders in our great ministries. Neither you nor I chose to be together, as it was our Lord, who decided this, so how could you ever hold me back. Your time has not yet arrived, so for now is our playtime. You are still babes in these things, so take your time. Time to eat your meat and put away the milk of babies will come, and the Lord will make sure you are ready. Even as babies, you have learned healing and to fight demons. I am so proud of your accomplishments. Remember, the Lord has put the knowledge of the ages here for us to receive. Let us go and enjoy this feast." I could see that they were perking up, and I was pleased with this. I can see where some of our situations could depress them quickly. I guess I need to be passionate in how I show them things, as I guess that would additionally be applicable to the sheep whom I will shepherd. I now remember seeing both sheep and horses on old earth, and wonder how they could have also evolved here. The Lord must have furthermore created them here. I will make sure to brush up on the Hajdú-Bihar's and Szombathelyi and see if there is any link, as only common sense would claim that to be the case. As we go into the big room of books, Zala and Tolna ask me to show them the books I touched last time, and they immediately store them in their possession. In exchange, I asked them to show me the books that they had touched.

Zala looked at me and said, "Oh you are the silly girls; you girls; you have to be joking?" I told her, "No my sister, for inside you is something that our Lord desires me to have, so please show me the books both of you touched." I carefully acted very interested in their selections as they shamefully brought them to me. I asked them, "Why do you bring these books to me while looking so depressed?" Tolna said, "Now you will truly think of us as short-lived girls." I told them, "Excuse me; however, are we not all little girls here, so do you not think that I should learn how to behave for my age? Who knows, maybe next time I will have three or four of the widows kissing my cheeks. We all laughed at this one and when we settled down, I reminded them, "You promised to teach me how to be a bubbling social thirteen-year-old. When we begin our ministry, I really want also to reach the adolescents, as they will soon be starting up their generation and that is a seed that we must plant if the Lord's garden continues." Now, their little buts were jumping from shelf to shelf, as if they were monkeys, getting for me each book they had touched, and they delivered them to me with pride. I kissed each on their cheek and again thanked them. They started with pride as they tore into the books that I had touched. This time we were much more specific than last time. I know that the previous time we each spent more time enjoying the material. We now know that just touching will put it in us for enjoyment for the rest of our days. Therefore, our priority this time was to touch being expeditiously as possible.

I was touching two pages at a time, by using both hands. I looked over to tell Zala and Tolna; however, I could see that they already learned this. This is what I really needed to master, and that is to take each situation for what it is and develop it from there. I now try to fill in the missing holes with my versions and assemble it from there, which can produce a hit or miss outcome. I must learn to think as a child, and therefore, fall into fewer holes. You will never catch Tolna or Zala falling into any holes, as they keep their eyes open and head out of the clouds. Remarkably, I finish all their books in just a few hours. I now lay them off to the side, as there is no need to put them back on the shelves as Oi has banned all from ever entering again. I now concentrate on the military, architectural, historical, and theological books. We kept touching pages for four days, as I had to ask the Lord to give us special energy to continue. My sisters did not slow down either, so that told me that they also had gone to the

Lord for additional energy. Somehow, we had made it through about fifteen percent of the books. I knew two things, and that is someday I would return, and that I am going to ask Zala and Tolna to touch all these books when I leave for my times of troubles. This will be an extra touch, which will allow them to keep our fires burning, when the children of Belcher are no longer traveling with them.

We soon hear a strange noise coming down the hallway to our home for the last four days. We all stand strong defying any evil from even thinking of disturbing us. To our great relief, in walked Oi and the sleeping priest. When he entered with that priest, I just turned away and refused to talk to him. How could he set me up like that and not stand by his word. He asked me, "Tianshire, can you explain this priest to me." I told him, "I will write you a letter from the five tribes of the sisters." I now grabbed my sisters and said, "Come with me, my true family." We now walked past Oi who grabbed me and said, "It is time for your spanking." I then yelled at him to let me go. I further told him, "Why don't you teach your people how to break promises?" Oi then said, "Calm down, my little darling. I was only playing with you." I then told my brother, "I am not going to be in a land in which the priests will treat me as a child." He then told me, "Tianshire, I do feel bad about that, and I promise to tell all the priests to spread wide and far that your wishes are my wishes, and if different your updated wishes will override mine, for it is time now that they learn you will be their chosen one. I did confess to this priest that I had approved of your request, as I do in all of your requests." I then said to the priest, "I had mercy on you this time, the next time, warn them, that as I will not allow demons to hurt my ministry, I shall deal harder on those who serve our Lord." The priest afterwards apologized to me saying, "I confess in doing you an injustice, for you have proven so many times that you are our chosen one. If our enemy fears you, then surely so should I. I pray that you can forgive me. If you wish to cast me from your priests, I will accept your punishment." I told him, "I will not cast you to our enemy, as I give you the mission of telling the priests that they may follow me when I return, or go their own way without my protection." The priest told me, "I will send this message out immediately. I thank you for forgiving me." I now told him, "It is not I who forgive; it is our Lord, and he has forgiven you." Oi next asked me, "Can you postpone your trip to the five tribes of the sisters for a little time, at least until I go away?" I looked at him with a strong stare after that answered, "Sure, big brother. It is that this knowledge is essential for my sisters and me, in order to move on when you are gone." Oi then told me, "I understand Tianshire; it is that I am not so used to you taking this much interest in your future." I told him, "Oi, when the demons continue to send their greatest destroyers in this universe, it does not take long to realize that now is the time to fight or die."

Oi next asked me, "By the way, how did you girls make it past that stone?" Zala then told him, "Why would we want to go past it since it was easier just to go through it?" Oi subsequently looked at us and said, "I am quickly learning why the Lord picked you two as Tianshire's and my sisters." That is the first time that it hit us, that Zala and Tolna were his sisters. They rushed to him and hugged him. He then asked them, "Will you call me big brother from this day forward in front of our followers? I will of course announce it many times, because I want all to know that you are truly my sisters as is our common sister Tianshire. We are a small family of four; nevertheless, we shall be bound by the free love in our hearts." They were now crying while hugging Oi. I was proud of my big brother, for he reached inside of them and took their hearts only to return it with our new special family love. Oi now asked the priest, "How long do you think it will take your temple to assemble our sheep in the Valley of Pétervásárai?" He told us, "Maybe four days tops, because they have stayed near so they can rush back to your ministry." Oi then asked him, "How long will it take us to get to the Valley of Pétervásárai?" He said, "We can get you there in two days." Oi after that said, "Next we shall depart in two days. Tianshire, will you take him through the stone door?" I said, "Sure, come on, we need to go, because I still have many books to touch." He then said, "Should not you have said read, rather than touch?" I looked at him and said, "See, even I make mistakes, as, I so often also fall asleep when reading, so it feels as if I am only touching them." The priest then replied, "I know what you mean, it happens to me a lot also." I glanced over at Oi, as he now had a relaxed look on his face. As I got to the stone, I asked the priest, "Are there any special hymns that you know especially well?" Told me there were many. I told him to pick the one he enjoyed the most and to sing it with his entire mind, thinking of nothing else. I then told him to close his eyes. He started to sing, through the large stone we went. We made it to the other side, I told him to open his eyes. He asked me when we were on the other side, "Tianshire, why did you have me sing?" I told him, "When I was with the Lord on his throne I saw so many angels singing. I could feel the joy it brought the Lord and the Ancient One." Quickly I asked, "Who is the Ancient One?" He answered, "He is our God as our Lord connects us with him, for if we were to speak or see if, we would be destroyed." The priest then looked at me, "I am surprised, I was not immediately destroyed for not obeying you and letting you enter the library tunnel."

I then told him, "He could not destroy you, for you stood on the words of Oi. I cannot fault Oi, as that was the longest, we had ever been separated, and we both were out of our minds at our reunion. The Lord has forgotten about it, as have I. I can only hope that you will forget about it and remember that when you stand on the word of our Lord, nothing can hurt you." The priest at present expressed, "It is too hard to believe that you have been so gifted in our Lord, as he would declare in front of all that you are his daughter." I now said to him, "To them that a lot is given, much more is expected. The Lord has declared that I shall destroy my mother who is the queen of evil. A mother who rules evil, and a father who rules the righteous, is a combustible combination to say the least. I am glad that they live on the opposite sides of the roads and that the Lord will help us in that great battle." The priest then asked me, "I notice you always say 'in that great battle.' Will there be only one battle?" I told him, "Every war has one great battle that decides the eventual outcome of the war. I do know that we shall not win that battle and after that she will fall as does the snow during the few chilly months." He then asked me, "How will you know when we have returned to getting you?" I told him, "That is easy, for you will ask the Lord to tell us, and he will tell us." He now declared, "You say this with no doubt that it will happen." I told him, "It will happen, as we will breathe air into our body, it will happen." He now added, "I pray that you will ask the Lord to help me develop a greater faith. I know you are in a hurry, so I will depart currently and do that which you have asked." I then told him, "I thank you for the faith that you have in my work, and I will pray, as will you, that your faith continues to grow. Bless you so much and I do hope to see you again." I now went back through the rock. I felt ashamed about how I had over reacted when I first saw Oi. This is the hard part, the part where I must show my face to him again, bearing all this shame. I can only hope my sisters can teach me how to get through this. I now rush back in and see Oi flying through the books I left on the floor. He is touching both pages at the same time. In excitement, he tells me, "Tianshire, see what my sisters taught me?" I look at him and smile saying, "I am very proud of our older brother. I cannot believe that there are so many books here. I am going to have Zala and Tolna spend much time in this place when I begin my times of trouble." He looked at me and said, "That is a very wise thing Tianshire. I have asked the Lord to allow me more time with you; however, he continues to tell me you will be ready." I then tell him, "I will miss you so much."

Zala and Tolna both add in how much they will also miss him. Zala then additionally adds, "Neither Tolna nor myself have bigger brothers, as you are the only greater brother we shall ever have." I afterwards went over, hugged them, and whispered in their ears, "I need to talk privately with you." They both shook their heads in agreement. We all quietly slipped into the next room of books, and I whispered to them, "I feel so ashamed at the way I went off on Oi tonight. What should I do?" Zala next gives off a sigh of relief saying, "I thought you were going to warn us about being on the extreme with the sister thing with Oi." Tolna after that added, "That is exactly what I thought." I subsequently looked at them strangely and said, "Do not you think that he also needs more sisters and family, as we both have left too much behind?" Zala later said, "We were worried as you had gone off on him, that you might think we were moving in." I then, while crying told them, "My sisters, you did the right thing, and that is to make sure the greatest big brother in which anyone could ever have was still a part of his family. You were consequently mature, as I was so cruel and hateful. I wonder whether he will forgive me." Zala then said, "You must do as I do when I have wronged my parents and that is to ask for his forgiveness. It is ungodly hard; nevertheless, the wonderful rush of joy and happiness that you get afterwards far makes up for it. We will be beside you for support." Tolna then added, "That is one important thing to learn as a child so you will do it as an adult and that is to confess your weaknesses and wrongs." I afterwards asked, "If you are beside me, I will try to do this. If I try to escape, push me from behind, or pull me by my hair. I cannot bear the thought of Oi suffering an extra minute." We then went to Oi as I called out his name. He stopped and looked up at me, which burst me into immediate tears. Oi next asked me, "Tianshire, what is wrong?" I after that told him, "Oi, I am so ashamed of the way I treated you tonight. I cannot forgive myself for being hence cruel to one who has given me such a wonderful life in the light." Oi then told me, "Tianshire, you forget about all your other sisters that I had to live among. They could get just as, if not more, emotional as you were tonight. That is the way of the girls when they transform from little girls to big girls. I have been longing for the day when we would have emotional difficulties as all true love has. If you love me, you will forgive yourself." I told him, "I do love you so much, as I will travel anywhere and do anything you want me to. I pray that you will allow me to continue to serve you." Oi then said, "If my ministry lost you, I would myself go to the five tribes of the sisters.

I pray that you will never leave me." Then Zala said, "Okay brother and sister, it is time to touch the books." Oi now grabbed all three of us and hugged us tight for about one minute. We then all went into the books, after I thanked Zala and Tolna for saving me. They later said, "It always works for our parents, and since you were deprived of that, we were ever so willing to share this knowledge with you. I then asked Oi, "How will we know when to leave?" He told us, "Do not worry about that sisters, the Lord will chase us out." We were grabbing books and touching as many pages as possible. I was so hungry for history and leadership development. I also found some books on controlling and dealing with my emotions. We all were blessed once again with extra energy and soon Oi told us, "It is time for us to go back through the rock as I do not want the rock to be moved again." I then asked Oi, "Why do you not want to share this ocean of knowledge with the black land tribes?" He gave a very straight to the point answer, "Because the Lord told me to do it." I then looked at him and said, "That is the best reason. Thanks for telling me." I then suggested I hold Zala's hand and Oi hold Tolna's hand and both Zala and Tolna sing some hymn that they know extremely well. Like a flash, we all walked through the stones as the priests were waiting for us. When we were all out, I looked back at the wall and said, "Be there no more door, but extra rock behind that no one may ever enter least they have the permission of our Lord."

In addition, there was no door, as only solid rock appeared before it. The priests now asked, "Why do you seal this library?" I looked at them and said, "Because the Lord told us to do it." The priests all agreed that was the best reason. I now looked at Oi and said, "Take pride in yourself older brother, for you have trained us well." Our small family of four laughed at this as the priests guided us to our horses. Then our group, which had over one hundred people in it, all rode off into the desert toward the Valley of Pétervásárai.

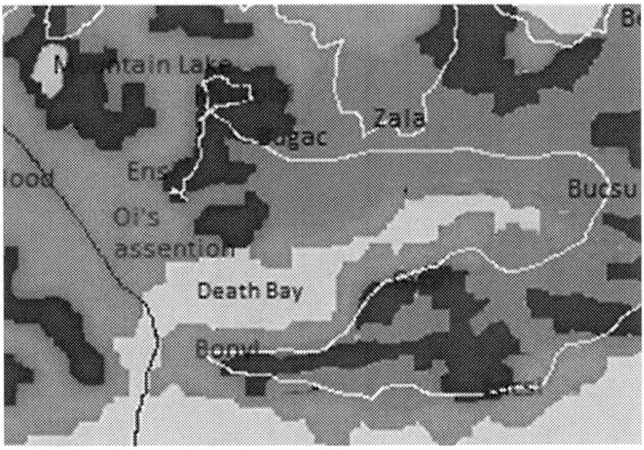

We rode our horses at a steady pace, so as not to harm them in this desert heat. We were backtracking much since the valley was located in the middle of the Bucsu lands, and close enough so that the Zala could also attend. The Bucsu and Zala were as desert brothers. If fact every tribe considered themselves to be the brothers of the Bucsu. The priests finally had us all ride in a single line so that we would not be eating each other's dust. We would eat at night, and yes; the widows fed us all very well. I had to ask some of the priests, "Where do they keep all this food?" One of the priests told me, "I think that they stuff their horses with it."

Then another priest said, "Actually, they have many beans, in which they do their magic with, and it turns out to look like a feast. I can see them preparing the beans for tomorrow, and afterwards when we stop they will do the final preparations, for to do it all in one night would find most of us fast asleep." I next told them, "I almost think that with these wonderful widows, that they may actually be pulling these meals from the air around us." We all laughed and after that began to feast. Our second day was different from the first in that the sky turned black, as a giant storm was approaching. I told Oi, "Oi, every time it got dark on us, we had trouble, and we should bring the people closer where we can protect them." He looked at me and said, "Then we will make it so. You and Tolna warn the left and Zala, and I will warn the right." I was glad that Oi was showing all that Zala, and Tolna were a part of our family. Within about twenty minutes, we had everyone in a formation, and I told Oi, "You stay here; I will get the storm and its demons to pass us by." Oi then said, "Be careful Tianshire, for I cannot lose you." I told him, "Have no fear for the Lord will protect us." Instantly, I rode off to meet the storm, which was now almost upon our formation. I jumped from my horse and yelled out, "By the name of our Lord I command the demons in this storm to be imprisoned in the pit and for the storm to cease." The storm stopped as all could now see angels binding the four legions of demons and taking them to the pits. I asked one of the angels, "Where did these demons come from, and are they in allegiance with my mother?" A centurion among the angels said, "They are among the deceivers who live in the skies. They await a great leader to unite all the deceivers on New Venus and then destroy all who walk on New Venus." I asked the centurion, "What is the difference between a deceiver and a demon?" The centurion answered, "A deceiver may become one as you." I then asked them, "How can we know the difference?" The centurion who said, "Greet each other by saying, 'may the Lord be with you,' for when you say this the Lord will enter, and if it be a deceiver, he will be destroyed and that body shall be given a wandering spirit."

I questioned, "Centurion, what is a wandering spirit?" The Centurion answered, "Do not fear them, for they are Saints from the worlds where there is no god to give them a rest. We only allow the Saints to enter the skies of New Venus." I now looked over at Oi and then noticed all in our group heard this. Our sheep only needed to know that their shepherds were among them, as they would afterwards have no fear. Oi then raised his hands and said to the Bucsu, "We are now learning as much from our enemies that can be possible. I feel that Rubina's powers may not be as great as we once thought. I shall teach all my meetings that we must always greet by saying, 'may the Lord be with you. We shall now continue to the Valley of Pétervásárai. We shall now greet all around us. no one move. At this time, the four of us walked around greeting people and making sure that all were greeting each other. That day, we saw five people, two men, and three women fall to the ground and then as those in their group pulled them up revived. I noticed the people all becoming extremely happy and jolly as if there was no danger. They were staying extra close to each other. I told Oi, "In order to spread them out he and I would have to walk on the ends and we will have Zala follow and Tolna lead."

He looked at us and asked, "Does any object to this?" Zala then asked, "Why must one follow?" I told her, "So that we do not get attacked from behind and if any fall, we can save them." I then handed her a special horn I pulled out of the air and said, "If any fall, or you discover any danger, blow this horn, and we will all respond. Since both of you are responsible for the entire line you will be given horses. Ride in front of us as a wide S. Do you agree my precious Zala and Tolna?" They then asked if they could switch. Oi and I quickly agreed in unison. We did not care; I just want the sheep to see the new shepherds. I can now see how important they will be when I am not here in the black land tribes. We move our herd into the Valley of Pétervásárai where we see more followers that we could have imagined. This will be the greatest meeting yet. I asked one of the priests why so people were here, for this is as if four tribe meetings combined. He told me, "Everyone is waiting for the announcement of the Chosen One." Oi told us, "It is time to announce you Tianshire." I said to him, "I shall obey your will as if it were mine." Oi said, "We shall rest tonight and begin in the morning. You need not to transcribe sermons, as too many are doing that now, I will make sure that they give you copies. Zala and Tolna will be our healing ministers, for we need them among the people so all will know them as being Saints. I shall introduce them during our few remaining meetings." I so dread when he talks about leaving, for even though I can fight demons, I fear losing him much more. It is easy to stand when I know he is there to pick me back up. What will I do when he is gone, and I fall? He makes walking in the Lord's light looks so easy, yet I know it is not that easy. I know I must look strong for the people, yet inside I am as crumbling clay with an iron breastplate hiding my feeble inside. Oi gets to enjoy three sisters tonight. I always wonder whether he will ever get to become a father, for just as our father, I know he would be great. I know; like myself, he misses our Belcher. He is so much like our father, although we have not mastered the skill of working around evil. The Lord made sure that neither, she nor her servants, human or demon, could ever spy upon us. She also tried to get our other brothers and sisters to spy upon us. She cleverly avoided letting our father, Oi, Tsarsko, and myself from knowing what she was up to. I often believe that the only reason we could survive was that she wasted more time hiding from us her mysteries than trying to weaken us. Last night, the Lord gave me a vision showing me that Tsarsko was okay.

The Lord's mighty angels were protecting him. Nevertheless, each day those demons try to destroy him; amazingly, Rubina protects him not allowing the demons to hurt any of her children. That is not to imply we do not get hurt, for she can hurt with more evil than any demon. The oddity is that she will not allow any other to hurt us. Another oddity is that she had difficulty in making any of the siblings in our family to hate or refuse to obey our father. She could manipulate them into doing evil to him, although at any time, he could have ordered them to stop, and they would have stopped. Oi always explained this as our father being hurt by their betrayal, and would never lose the faith he had in his children, as we all know he loved all of us. Oi and I at no time used our father's love against our other siblings. We just would never get him involved. He had too much love in each of us, and we all knew this. Notwithstanding when he died, all his children, good or evil, suffered because of his loss. Sadly, that was the only time we all were united, in spite of Rubina putting on a fake show of suffering his loss. She could never again hide behind his cloak of righteousness after his murder. This is not the day for me to dwell upon this, for I shall have much time to battle these issues later. They have started the singing of the hymns now. It seems like forever since we have been ministering. I wonder how such a few short weeks could feel like another lifetime.

Oi begins by introducing us as follows, "I shall now introduce to you my sister Tianshire, the daughter of our Lord, and my special sisters Saint Tolna and Saint Zala." At this time, we stood in line with him; Zala stands the closest, with Tolna next and me at the end. We felt it important to show that they would now be the center of our family, the part that held us together. I gave Zala a hug and a kiss, as Oi gave Tolna a hug and a kiss. They now went into the congregation looking for those who needed healing. They each touched some crippled servants in the front row. They became healed immediately, and the flock cheered loudly. They then blended into the audience and the only way we knew where they existed was from the local cheers when someone received their healing. This was adding another dimension to our ministry, for we have now been in many places. Oi; nevertheless, would not allow me of the stage. He told me that it was important that the people see me as an integral part of this ministry. Oi now began the meeting, "I welcome the great and honorable saints of the Bucsu in the wonderful Valley of Pétervásárai. The lands of this tribe have brought pronounced learning and many experiences for us during the previous weeks. The Lord has revealed many things to this ministry. The finest revelation is that my greatest love shall be your deliverer, and that is the daughter of our Lord, Tianshire." He then motioned for me to come forward, hugged me, and gave me a big kiss on the cheek. I was starting to wonder if I would still have a cheek with all this kissing; nonetheless, I could live forever with my Oi kissing me on my cheeks. He then walked me back to my seat in the middle of a row of eleven seats. I know had five priests to my left and another five to my right. They had selected tall priests whose long legs supported them in their chairs, yet I had to use my arms to lift my small body up on the stage, as I so proudly wore the dress that the Widows of Vadessa made for me. Oi then began again with fire in his voice, "A few days ago on our journey from your considerable temple to this wonderful valley, Tianshire condemned to the abysmal pit of everlasting fire four legions of demons. The enormous armies of angels whom she commands bound these deceivers and demons and cast them into the bottomless pit. We did not know what a deceiver and a demon was, or that it even made a difference. Tianshire asked one of her centurions if there was a difference. This centurion told us that deceivers might also exist among us as humans. They are a form of evil, misery, and destroyers who walk among us.

We do have a weapon to fight these flesh stealers. At all times, when you greet another person; be it adult or child, you must give the greeting as follows, 'may the Lord be with you.' This salutation will allow the Lord to enter the other person and if a deceiver is there, the Lord will cast this demon into his everlasting lake. I warn you, give this greeting even to your most trusted friend, for the deceivers can appear in any form, and resemble any person. We shall make a small modification and shout this three times today, 'may the Lord be with all who are here." The people did as he said, as Oi told us that one hundred and twenty seven people fell. Oi immediately told his congregation, "Fear not those who have fallen, for our Lord will give them a spirit of a Saint. Let us rejoice on this day, for our tribes have one hundred and twenty seven knew Saints." All rejoiced as our new Saints regained their conscience. Oi began again, "Today you have witnessed the danger that Tianshire discovered for us. I now tell you that she is the chosen one. She shall lead an army from the black lands and defeat Rubina. Within a short time, I shall be taken from the black lands, and Tianshire shall be cast into Belcher's prison. There she will suffer during a time of great troubles for her. Fear not, for you shall have Tolna and Zala to help you with your needs and bring them before our Lord.

You are blessed that the two saints from this tribe shall keep the fire of our Lord alive until Tianshire returns for her ministry. She shall seek any demons or deceivers who live in your black lands, for she will not fight in combat with her back unsecured. I am so pleased that the Lord has selected Tianshire to lead your tribes, for I know firsthand she can fight and fight hard. You have heard many tales about how my three sisters can stand tall and defeat demons. They have done this many times and will do it many more times. We must not forget that they have seventy legions of mighty angels to protect them. They have also been given heavenly titles, for I tell you there is no higher than one given by our Lord. Our Lord has declared Tianshire to be his daughter, and he has declared Tolna and Zala to be Saints. Your tribes are truly blessed." Now a powerful white light came down upon him. The light covered Oi for a few minutes and then disappeared. Oi currently stood in the middle of the stage and as close to the front part of the stage that is possible. The light now vanished and Oi began his message, "Whosoever trusts in the Lord, happy is he. This is the day, which the Lord has made; let us rejoice and be glad in it. Nevertheless, seek ye first the kingdom of God, and his righteousness and all these things shall be added unto you. Be strong and of good courage, fear not, nor be afraid, for the Lord your God, he is that who goes with you; he will not fail you, nor forsake you. Lay up for yourselves treasures in heaven, where neither moth nor rust does corrupt, and where thieves do not break through nor steal; for where your treasure is, there shall your heart be also. I will say of the Lord. He is our refuge and our fortress:

In Him will I trust. Our Lord will instruct you and teach you in the way you should go; He will counsel you and watch over you. Has not he commanded you? Be strong and of good courage; be not afraid, neither be you dismayed; for the Lord thy God is with you wheresoever you go. Be truly glad. There is wonderful joy ahead!" Be content with what you have, for the Lord has said, "At no time will I leave you; never will I forsake you." Therefore, say with confidence, "The Lord is my helper; I will not be afraid. Except you become as little children, you will not enter the Kingdom of Heaven. You have seen the Lord speak unto Tianshire, who is but a child. He will use this child to save you. When you follow our Lord, put away the old things and become reborn in our Lord. If you have faith as a grain of mustard seed, you will say to your mountain, "Move!" It will move, and nothing will be impossible for you!

You have seen Tianshire and our sisters' defeat demon monsters over four stories tall with their faith. They believed it and slept before them, knowing that the Lord would destroy them. Believe and see. Allow the will of the Lord to be manifested through your faith. Blessed is the man who trusts in the Lord and has made the Lord his hope and confidence. Cast your cares upon the Lord, for he cares about you. My soul finds rest in the Lord God alone; our salvation comes from Him. The steadfast love of the Lord at no time ceases; his mercies never end; they are new every morning. Thy word is a lamp for my feet, and a light to my path. The fruit of the spirit is love, joy, and peace. The kingdom of our Lord God is within you. He covers the sky with clouds; he supplies the earth with rain, and makes the grass grow on your hills. Come unto the Lord, you who are weary and overburdened, and he will give you rest. Stand still and consider the wondrous works of God. Beloved, I wish above all things that you may succeed and be in good health, even as your soul prospers. There is no fear in love; for perfect love casts out fear. Love is patient and love is kind, love does not insist on its own way. Love bears all things, believes all things, Hopes all things, and endures all things.

Love never fails. Blessed is the man who trusts in the Lord and has made the Lord his hope and confidence. Moreover, why are you anxious about what to wear? Consider the lilies of the field, how they grow; they toil not; neither do they spin. Even so, I say to you that even Szombathelyi Empire in all their glory was not arrayed like one of these. Peace, I leave with you; my peace I give to you; not as the black lands fail give to do, he will do for you. Let not your heart be troubled, neither let it be afraid. Our Lord God has poured out his love into our hearts. The Lord has come that you may have and enjoy life and have it in abundance, until it overflows. Know you not that you are the temple of the Lord God and that the spirit of God dwells in you. Do to the best of your ability what so ever your hand finds for you to do. With men, it is impossible; however, with God, all things are possible. Remember the Lord your God, for it is He that gives you the power to defeat evil. In the Lord, put your trust. God is with you in all that you do. The Lord will give you peace and quietness. Freely, you have received, and freely you shall give. Glorious, majestic are his deeds, and his righteousness will endure forever. His name shall be called Wonderful Counselor, the Mighty God, the Everlasting Father, and the Prince of Peace. Tell the heavens and earth to celebrate and sing! Command every mountain to join in song!

For the Lord is not the author of confusion, but of peace. Let not the sun goes down upon your wrath. In time of trouble, the Lord shall set you upon a rock. Cast your bread upon the waters, for you will find it after many days. Happy is the man who finds wisdom and understanding for the gain from it is better than gain from silver and profit better than gold. Seek peace, and pursue it. The earth is full of the goodness of the Lord. In addition, be kind one to another, tenderhearted, forgiving one another. Behold he is with you, and will keep you in all places wherever you go. Your Father knows what things you have need of before you ask Him. Now accept, faith, hope, love, these three, but the greatest of this is Love. It is more blessed to give than to receive. Trust in the Lord with all your heart, and lean not on your own understanding. In all your ways acknowledge Him, and He shall direct your paths. It is done unto you, as you believe. Moreover, I am sure; that he who began a good work in you will complete it. I will never fail you or forsake you. A merry heart does well like medicine. Share your happiness with those among you, so that all may have joy. Wait on the Lord, be of good courage, and he shall strengthen your heart. Wait, I say on the Lord. You shall decree a thing; it shall be established unto you, and a light shall shine upon your ways. If you can believe, all things are possible to him who believes. Oh, give thanks unto the Lord, for He is good. For in Him, we live, and move and have our being. Fear you not he who will strengthen you.

Our Lord will help you. He will fill your mouth with laughter and your lips with shouts of joy. Follow the way of love. The Lord will guide you always; he will satisfy your needs in a sun-scorched land. You will be like a spring whose waters never fail. You, O Lord, keep my lamp burning; my God turns my darkness into light. I can do all things through Him who strengthens me. May the Lord continually bless you with heaven's blessings as well as with human joys? Behold, our Lord makes all things new. The Lord is good. His love will endure forever; his faithfulness continues through all generations. Let the name of the Lord be praised both now and forevermore. I delight to do your will, oh Lord, for I know your will for me is supremely good in my present and in my future. I greatly enjoyed your hospitality. I extend to you all the blessings that the Lord can give unto you. Keep your faith strong so that some of the weaker tribes may seek shelter of your wings. I pray all your days give into great joy in the Lord. I must now follow my sisters into your neighbor's land. My final words to you are once again to thank you for loving your neighbors.

We both left the stage and had to wait for three hours for Zala and Tolna to bring their exhausted bodies back. We both just hugged them as I started to massage Tolna's back and neck, Oi did the same for Zala. Three priests came in and told us, "Your little Saints worked so hard for the Lord's children at this night. They are definitely a chip from your block. The Lord was truly wise to take these two daughters from us. We have some special guests for them tonight. In addition, the widows are going to feed you this night. You can take your horses and leave under our courtesy escort until you are received by your Bugac escorts." Oi told them, "We do not really need any escorts." The priest said to him, "It is the neighborly thing to do, for as you are in someone's house, does not the host escort to the door? Should it not be the same for our lands?" I looked at Oi and commented, "He does have a point." Oi smiled and shook his head in agreement. Then the priest added, "We also have been studying the art of human interaction as advanced by Zala and Tolna. This is an art, which works every time. Nevertheless, what I have told you is authentic; hitherto, the true reason we wish to do this is to honor you as the true chosen ones of the Lord. To our great Lord who lives in the dark space so high in our skies has given us love through his greatest prophets.

The priests who escort you will have a special place in all our hopes as our last times with you." I then told the priests, "Both reasons are based upon love and the desire to give into our Lord. Those who travel with us will receive our thanks and love." The priests then said, "Now we must choose the one hundred priests and of course widows for our meals to travel with you." I winked at them and we all laughed as I added, "Best of luck." Currently six of the widows came in and said, "Okay girls; it is time for your baths. Come with us now." Tolna and Zala jumped up, and I jumped in line behind them as one of the widows said, "We must make this fast, so we can get back to prepare your evening meals, okay follow the widows now." We did not say a word but did exactly as they said and were soon out of our tent. Oi just stood there in amazement. His sisters were being cleaned as if by their parents. The widows were not even going to compromise on this, and for that Oi was very pleased. He knew that he also could use come cleaning; however, was not too fond of the widows or priests performing this service on him. He peeked out of his tent and saw us going into a tent that the widows prepared. There was just something so magical about this event. It was as if the instincts of both the widows and sisters knew this is the way of things, somewhat as the natural order of things. The widows cleaned us different this time, since the water was extremely limited. They took off our dresses and shorts then with wet rags each of us had two of them cleaning at the same time. They double-checked under our fingernails, behind our ears, and even for any dirt rings around our neck. They now added some nice smelling oils to our hair as they brushed it and then put our hair into piggy tails. They told us that this was better for when traveling a long distance in the deserts. I asked them, how long we would be traveling in the desert, and they told us, "About one week or so." I knew the last thing I wanted was sweat filled dirty windblown hair to deal with. They now rubbed some special salves over all our skin. I could feel relief as this perfumed odor salve completely revitalized my skin. I could see that Zala and Tolna also enjoyed it. My Lord, this having a caring mother to make us into adorable little girls is heavenly. They replaced our clothes, and then put another fresh smelling oil on them. They next inspected us and then their leader commented, "I cannot remember seeing such pretty little angels." We each rushed to the two that had cleaned us, and started kissing them like there will be no tomorrow. They hugged and kissed us also as we all were about to cry, one of the widows said, "You girls had better get to the rear to Oi before he worries." We then ran backward to Oi. His face showed how surprised he was as he said, "I think someone took my dirty little girls and gave me angels in return."

Some priests who were in there commented, "The widows did their magic on them." Oi then added, "They know how make little girls look as if they are truly loved with the motherly touch. I have so many times wished I could have given that to Tianshire." I told him, "You are our big brother whom we also desperately need." Then some other widows came in and gave each of us a nice plate of food. Their head cook afterwards said to us, "I hope you guys enjoy this." We each took a bite and started bombing them with compliments. Oi gave the best one, "I do not think this is food because it takes too much like love." They each kissed his forehead and departed from us. As we ate, I told Oi, "I will miss these widows so much. I wish we could get this program continued in the other tribes. Hey, I have an idea." I called for the head widows to come back in and for some elders of the temples. I then told the elders, "I have learned in my trips to the Lord's throne, the defeating of demons, the love of the greatest brother ever to exist, coupled with the sisters, which the Lord gave me, there is still one thing missing, that is built into my whole foundation of being."

The elders asked, "What might that be the daughter of the Lord." I looked at them while I was patting my piggy tail and responded, "A daily mother who cares." The elders now asked me, "What would you like our chosen one, maybe some of our strongest warriors?" I told him, "The Lord has forbidden us to marry until your land is free. Anyway, the only men is shall ever love is my father, and older brother." The elder then said, "That is so sad, for we would love to give you a husband to father your children. However, if it is later, I know the Lord will give you three the strongest in all our lands. How can we help you?" I then told them, "We need some of the widows to care for us, and that we can love back, for I am going to fight hard for your widow program to exist in all your lands. They fill a need that is essential if we are to have a strong family unit." The elder looked at the widows who were in our tent and asked, "Would this be something that would interest you?" The head of this group looked at the elder as if he were crazy and said, "There is not a one of us who would not cherish to have little girls to love and help them become precious young ladies." The elder then asked, "Do you know of a fair way to pick six of you?" The head widow said, "We will choose now and have the lucky widows who once again can have little angels to feed and love. They will be here in twenty minutes." I looked at the elder and asked, "I do thank you so much; however, I wonder what made you decide on six?" He afterwards told me, "I could only see a giant six in my head. Then it hit me that since you are trying to sell this program to other tribes you will need some widows to help answer any technical questions." I looked at him and confessed, "You are truly filled with the Lord's spirit. Those who made you an elder were very wise." He then said, "Thank you so much Tianshire. We must excuse ourselves while you finish your dinner." They next departed our tent. Oi after that asked me, "I hope you know what you asked for." I told him, "I have never been surer, nor more selfish in anything before." One of the priests who was currently with us; as we always had the priests among, as was Oi's tradition that while he was with them, they could live with us, spoke to me saying, "Tianshire, what you ask for is merely what you need, as you will be someday long to be a mother also. For now, you need that maternal bond, which you did not even know existed in you before the widows uncovered it." I looked at him and smiled, "So that is what all this crazy stuff inside is doing?" The priest laughed along with me and then added, "Honey; we all go through this, hence welcome to your human side."

I now thought that might be what is happening. My human side is demanding that it receive some of me. I thought playing with Tolna, and Zala would handle this. Now rushing into our tent so fast that the front three hit the ground, and the remaining three landed on them. When we saw this, we just began laughing hence hysterical that many of us began to suffer real pain. These former mothers were so happy and now embarrassed. I decided to have some fun with them and asked, "Which one is my mommy?" They all froze and just looked at me. I subsequently busted out laughing, and later told them, "Come in and relax, for you are our precious gifts from the Lord, whom we will cherish." They currently started to relax, as Tolna, Zala, and myself walked among them kissing their hands and foreheads, as if they were queens. Oi then said, "You are at present a part of our growing family. Soon, I will send to do another mission for the Lord, and Tianshire must return to Belcher's prison to plant the seeds for their downfall. She will return; however, while she is gone, you will still need to care for Saint Zala and Saint Tolna." The widows then looked as if they were paranoid. I now told them again, "Relax, for there will be sometimes days that we do not see you, everything will work, as long as I pray you let us cry on your shoulders eventually. The priests are going to bring our new gowns for us females, and a robe for Oi that will all look the same so all the tribes will know you are a part of our family, and we will fight to save you if we need to do so. Relax for the rest of the evening, do whatever you want, as this is also your home, and get used to your fresh family and remember to thank our Lord for his great blessings." They started slowly cleaning everything and putting our things in order. We just come in and toss it, since a good sermon takes all our energy. That reminded me of one more thing, "Mothers, I also need for you to do one other thing for our people of the black land tribes. The family services that you provide for your fellow people is what I believe essential to help ensure a better family-centered tribe. We shall stress the need to let the widows serve the public as a member of the temple. We will need you to explain to the temples how this system functions and tells them about some of the things you do. Remember, to keep it human and a truthful as possible. This is to save some widows, as is clearly our duty." At this time, we received our surprise. Tolna and Zala's parents come into our tent as Oi welcomed them. Their daughters naturally fell deep into their parents' arms as the tears soaked their clothing. Zala's mother asked me, "How are things going with you Tianshire?"

I asked her if it was okay for me also calling her mother; and both mothers gave their consent, then I looked at Zala and Tolna and they both said, 'oh, absolutely sister.' I afterwards told them, "I do not know if you know this; however, my real mother is very bad." The mothers then told me they understood. Wow, I do have the skills of Zala and Tolna down to an art now. The irony was that Zala and Tolna could not defend their parents. They did not really want to defend their parents against me, as anything I got over on them; they could do the same someday. Then Tolna's mother asked me, "What are your plans for your sisters, you pretty little angel." She was playing with my pigtail. It amazes me how they, as if magnets, attract to my pigtails as if they were metal. I just smile, because the rule is, if you are a little girl, any mommy can enjoy you. Actually, this is a two-way street in that I also enjoy that extra 'mommy only' touch. I subsequently tell them that Oi's ministry shall soon end, as we will speak to the Bugac, Miskoldi and Ensi tribes, and later he will serve the Lord in another position. I shall return to Belcher's prison and try to minister to my fellow prisoners. Rubina will capture me, and I must suffer many things for the Lord. I shall, after three years return to the black land tribes for my ministry, with an emphasis on destroying demons. I do hope to have Zala, Tolna, and the widows with me as we do the final cleaning of the tribes. I shall then prepare the armies and destroy Rubina's Empire. After her complete destruction, I shall be called for another mission for the Lord." The fathers now asked, "Do you or Oi know your new missions?" I told him, "The Lord has not revealed this to us, and if he does not desire to tell us, then we must be patient that his will to be done." The fathers after that said, "That is truly a very wise young lady."

Our time with the Bugac quickly began. We now had our 'uniform gowns and Oi's robes.' We called for a private meeting with the elders concerning the widows, which did not last that long since they already had a similar program hitherto in effect. They promised to expand it. I told Zala to record this in our ministry notes. The following was now twice what it was before we rest. Everyone wanted to see the 'Chosen One.' The widows did so much to make the one-week journey through the desert from the Valley of Pétervásárai to the Foothills of the Radostyán. They were the first official province of the Bugac. Their history was one of the fighting to keep the mountains free. They had actually done a good job, considering three tribes, Bugac, Miskoldi, and Ensi were concentrated in this small mountain range. They only had a short mountain range between them and Death Bay to their south. What even made this worse was that they had rich open green lands around three of their four sides and a wide-open border with Belcher's Prison. These green lands had plenty of small rivers that kept plenty of water in the area.

These rivers were not like most rivers, in that the fresh water came in from the Death Bay as if an irrigation system created by nature. The Bugac was hunters and survived, for the most part, of the game that they harvested. They also had a strong network of forts, which were effective in holding back Rubina's warriors. Except for their fortress strongholds, they were guerrilla style fighters. If they had one foot of grass or an occasional tree, they would strike, and reform before the enemy had a chance counter attack, they would be in their new positions. They have contributed so much to holding Rubina at bay and forcing her to raid along the northern coasts or from the sea. As we began our meetings with the Bugac, it was different this time. Now, Zola, Tolna, and I sat around the meeting table. The widows took out our pigtails and put our hair up as the young women wore them. Our uniform gowns really added a special touch, because it identified as one united group. Many of the elders in the tribes we had visited before were so concerned with my childhood, and all Oi would tell them was, "The Lord has put her with me, so he will take care of all things." This was no longer the issue with the widows bouncing around giving their orders. Zala, Tolna, and I always did what they said, because we knew life without their wings would not be a good flight.

This was evident in our high-level meetings, as we were starting to lay a framework for our war, the widows would come in and wash our hands and give us a small snack. The elders and the priests always commended the widows for their undying devotion to us, and something strange about adults is how they all become happy when little people are getting their hands cleaned. This is as they have a new feeling of victory when seeing us surrender the dirt that we worked so hard to take as our prisoners. Zala, Tolna, and I will continue to take baths and keep our things in order so that we can enjoy preserving them in our lives. Today is the first time we are actually sitting at their round table. Oi calls us in, sets us, and then looks at the tribe's elders and says, "It is time that we let the ones in which the Lord has chosen to create your new nation tells us how they plan or want to do this." They all agreed. I almost have pity on these old men, as three thirteen-year-old girls are responsible. I begin by saying, "I am so glad you have joined us today. I know for some, the logic of discussing this with children does not appear to be reasonable; however, I assure you that the Lord, who is telling me what to do make up with his eternity of years to compensate for my lack of these years." They then say, "Oh, Tianshire does not think that way, for we have heard how you slay demons and how your two small sisters roam between the masses healing people.

Because you have the Lord in you, we would not care if you were like the birds from the sky. I began, "Okay, now we can discuss how I will defeat my mother. I will bring my main invasion force in from the northern seas. During my times of troubles in Belcher's prison, I will finalize who and what I hit first. I plan to use the Miskoldi and Ensi to hold our southern border. I will need you, the Zala, Bucsu, Gyori, and Bonyl to free up the Death Bay. It is simple; Rubina cannot have the use of this Bay, since it allows her to strike at will insides us, and I tell you, no warrior can fight if his enemy has an arrow in him and is free to move that knife at will. The Death Bay battles will be two-fold, stage one will have five tribes destroying all her land fortifications, and any ships that we can seize. I do not want to destroy the ships, unless we have no choice, as these ships can come in handy when our new nation builds its navy and worldwide markets. Stage 2, you, and the Zala will protect our capture ships and hold the northern seacoast of Death Bay. At the time, the Bonyl, Gyori, and Encsi will put all Rubina's remaining forces off their peninsula striking her naval positions along the southern ocean first." Oi then looked at me and smiled. He now said to the elders, "Gentlemen, does this sound like a plan?" They were looking at their maps and confessed, "No doubt about it; this will work.

Tianshire was wise to think about our nation after the war and our future trading, which will be essential if our new nation is able to support its people. Perfect. They looked at me and said, "Tianshire; you have our armies and command thereof." I then continued, "Because the Lord appointed so late in Oi's ministry, I will need for you to distribute this plan to the other tribes, as I will ask the Miskoldi and Ensi to help you, plus the widows are preparing letters for the other tribes that I will be sending out. We will not invade until I begin our attacks. Nevertheless, any invasion from Rubina must be destroyed. You have done much better in this area recently. You are planting bait and then drawing them into your solid ambushes are now vital. Remember; always let one go back blind. Make sure to release him at least two hundred miles from where you ambushed them. Rubina knows where she sent the raiders, however, by releasing the lone survivor at another point would let her know we now fight tactfully and skillfully. Furthermore, please steal as many of their horses as possible. Take them to Becske, have them taken across the small strait, and release them in the western green lands of the Labarians. When we launch our great invasion, we will have these horses available.

We will also need many horses when we plant our grains on the green lands. We must ensure that our grain reserves are enough to last for at least four years, as I know Rubina will stop all our imports through her blockades." The elders now motioned for a chance to speak. I told them, "Please bless me with your ideas and inputs!" One elder than commented, "How might a child such as you present military campaigns and tactics for more advanced than ever before known on New Venus?" I told him, "I have almost memorized all the great armed campaigns in the histories of the Szombathelyi Empire and Hajdú-Bihar. They were truly among the greatest in our universe. One thing that they were serious about it was making sure to raid only for a purpose, and just when you might easily project a victory. When they raid, we must be able to determine how far letting them advance before we ambush. Deeper ambushes work extremely well, as we have a better chance to capture those who are trying to escape. When I go back to Belcher's prison, before any battle except ambushes, you will mark a white flag in an area away from the fighting. These will be sanctuary areas. Any Rubina soldier who surrenders before or during the battle will be spared. The elders now started rumbling. I looked at them and said, "You must remember that Rubina's citizens suffer much worse than do you. I will prove this to you. I also plan to send messages back to you to prevent any surprises. Now, I need to do some other things before Oi starts speaking, thus we will be able to talk at our meals and informally during our travels. I want to spend some time in my family; I will see you at our sermon." I now went back to our area as the widows hurriedly spruced us up, so we would look very beautiful for our work tonight. Most of our widows were so far talking with priests and temple elders. Zala and Tolna were already using the Lord's power in their healing ministries. I asked one priest to send that to our staging area as we were preparing to begin the meeting. They were soon with us, and Oi lead us on their stage. The elders motioned for the congregation, the largest we had ever spoken before, to be quiet. Oi then walked up to the stages absolute front and began to speak, "This is a blessed day for us, as our Bugac meeting has the greatest attendance for one of our meetings to date. I know now that this ministry shall be the ministry that is giving birth to your independence. You shall not only be made free; you will be given a new life and fresh prosperity. Though little may not know this, I am proud to tell you the name of your deliverer. Tianshire, my younger sister, and greatest love have been chosen by our Lord.

Our Lord has also expanded our family with Saint Zala and Saint Tolna that will serve with me in my final days and serve with Tianshire during her ministries and war. We have also been blessed to have six Widows of Vadessa given to our care by your neighbors, the Bucsu. I tell you, our Lord has told me that he shall begin punishing those who do not help the widows. He will give plagues to those villages that allow the widows to starve and die. Most of these women are mothers, and I curse all who are in a family who cast out their widows. Any who loves the Lord had to know that this was wrong. The Bucsu had discovered a way in which this valuable human resource can contribute back to your tribe. I do not want to hear about a tribe not carrying out this program. I love the six who are helping us as my mother, feeling a part of me that I had forbidden ever to live again. If you think, I am being harsh on this; I warn you that Tianshire is the one who persuaded me of the importance of these widows in our lives. It is now time for your chosen one to speak, 'Please come up here my love." I was so surprised that he called me his love. I mean there shall never be any question that our love is deeper than the deepest ocean and higher than the highest mountain, cemented by our Lord.

That put a big smile on my face as I gave him a great hug. I then began, "Let him who thinks me to be a child not forget that the Lord, who speaks inside me is older than the ages. The Lord has commanded me to deliver you from the evil of Rubina. He told me that I might lead the sinless black land's tribes to their freedom. I tell you, that before I can lead you, I must suffer what the Lord has called my 'times of troubles.' As Oi told you, the Widows of Vadessa are as my mothers. I tell you that everyone you see who is starving is my brother or sister. When I return, I will destroy anyone who let my brothers or sisters go hungry. I can hear one-man thinking, 'how will she know," and I tell you that Rubina's demons will tell me. All demons are your accusers. Our ministry now has more chosen of the Lord to include Saint Zala and Saint Tolna, who are the blessed ones in which the Lord has charged with healing. They shall at present, go through our audience seeking those to heal. I trust that you will do your best to unite them with those who need healing. Now, back to the demons, I am reminded that on our way to our meeting in the Valley of Pétervásárai I was introduced to four legions of demons, who are currently all in the bottomless pit. One of my centurion angels told me that these were both deceivers and demons or destroyers. As deceivers they can walk between you are normal people and deceive you into the chains of sin.

We only have one defense against these deceivers who can take the form of anyone they wish. The Lord has commanded that we all greet one another as follow, 'may the Lord be with you.' When we give one another this greeting, the Lord has promised to destroy any deceiver who hears this. So now, let us all yell out three times, "May the Lord be with you." Oi counted 83 deceivers being chained in the bottomless pit. Once again, the Lord allowed us to view this process. Each deceiver was bound and cast into the pit in vivid detail. Oi now said, "Behold, we are today the light, and the darkness comes after us, I tell you, do as Zala, Tolna and Tianshire did and fill yourself completely in the faith of our Lord, and you also will be able to sleep before the greatest of demons, knowing that your Lord is greater than any force of evil. Today, before you, your Lord has kept his promise that when you say, 'may the Lord be with you,' he will save you from the deceivers. I want also to remind you that the Lord sometimes sends his angels in the flesh to see whether they will be fed or clothed. It would have been better for one who allows the flesh of the Lord's angels to starve to have never been born. I cannot minister to you now, as the Lord has not given me the words to share with you." I turned around and motioned for Oi to return. He again began to talk saying, "The Lord has told me that my days of the ministry in these lands are now few. The Lord has also told me that he has found great pleasure in the three tribes that share this mountain. I know that so many depend on your battle skills to survive in this area. Do not think that your Chosen One will teach all how to fight. She can, if you want to continue to be victimized when she does. Therefore, I ask you to share your military fighting skills with the other tribes, so Tianshire can bring more of your son's home when she returns." Then one woman cried out, "Will she not take our daughters with her?" Oi afterwards said, "I have not actually asked the Lord who question. I do know that he is sending my father's daughter into the war." My brother got a big laugh from the crowd with that answer. He was now getting them loose, as I think, I may have hit too sedulously, as well fast after him. We might be pushing also hard for his end is near, and the mystery of it is driving us insane. Oi now looked at them and let go. "Blessed are those whose ways are blameless, who walk according to the law of the Lord. Blessed are those who keep the Lord's laws and seek him with all their heart. His laws are for your long and prosperous life. Blessed are all who fear the Lord, who walk in obedience to him.

You can rest assured that Tianshire, and I fear the Lord. Moreover, since he has called us to give you his word, we fear how his wrath would be so much greater. Blessed are those who find wisdom, those who gain understanding, now then my children, listen to me; blessed are those who keep the Lord's ways. As we expect your parents to each you, you must also teach your children. Blessed are the poor in spirit, for theirs is the kingdom of heaven. Blessed are those who mourn, for they will be comforted. Blessed are the meek, for they will inherit the earth. Blessed are those who hunger and thirst for righteousness, for they will be filled. Blessed are the merciful, for they will be shown mercy. Blessed is the pure in heart, for they will see God. Blessed are the peacemakers, for they will be called children of God. Blessed are those who are persecuted because of righteousness, for theirs is the kingdom of heaven. Blessed are you when people insult you, persecute you, and falsely say all kinds of evil against you because of our Lord. Notwithstanding, blessed are your eyes because they see, and your ears because they hear. Blessed are you who are poor, for yours is the kingdom of God. Blessed are you who hunger now, for you will be satisfied. Blessed are you currently who weep, for you will laugh. Blessed are you when people hate you, when they exclude you, insult you, and reject your name as evil, because of our Lord.

Blessed rather are those who hear the word of our Lord and obey it. I want to thank all the tribes for the way you have treated Tianshire and myself. I especially want to thank the parents of Zala and Tolna for giving their daughters to us. By them giving, the tribes received two blessed Saints, who shall be with you many years. Goodnight, the honorable Bugac tribe." Oi and I, with our six widows rushed into the temple, where we had many meetings scheduled. The priests would ask for judgments on many civil actions. We always tried to go soft, unless we felt a social lesson had to be learned. Most of our judgments were standing at present; I think it is more than they want to some additional attention now. They wanted to talk some more military with me; however, I told them, "There is no need to hammer the nails when we do not yet have the wood. Why would one plant seeds when they have yet to obtain the land?" I asked the widows if they could find a place for all of us girls to relax some. Actually, I want one of them to hold me when I sleep. I want to know how that feels, before I end up being beaten in front of my mother. The only thing that had us on the edge was that we would have to go over the mountains to reach the Miskoldi who lived in the middle of one of the trickiest ranges.

We could make it to it, which was not the problem, because the priests were going to guide us, since they routinely make this journey. They recommended we would begin tomorrow after they feed us. I am not comfortable with the way Tolna, and Zala's parents are controlling them. They know what we need in order to keep them in our family. This is a hard position to be in; I mean they should just stay away, as this ministry ends soon. I grab a few of the widows and ask them what should I do? They just tell me, "You have a hard decision, do you stand strong, or do you give in?" I should clear something up in my notes about the widows. They are not old hunchbacked cripples. The oldest one who is with us is thirty-seven. We have one widow who are twenty-one. The tribes marry off between thirteen and fourteen. The raiders are also sending small groups to slip around and kill stragglers. We as well have many hazards and other raiders from around New Venus that take away the lives of the innocent. We have been constantly giving new exceptions, which say that if a woman is widowed she may remarry. I will talk to Oi about saying this on stage; therefore, it will be included in his teachings. I guess that is why I believe so hard against leaving these girls to starve, or some villages kill them while burying their husband. We have successfully put an end to that custom.

I now have two of the widows out looking for my sisters. They return about one hour later with the whole gang. I send two of my widows out to hold the parents off and to send them back to wherever they are staying. Zala and Tolna came rushing into me as all bees bopped. I ask them to sit down and to decide, this ministry or their parents. I tell you now; they are not going to disturb me during my ending times with Oi. Surprisingly, my little angel hearts told me, "The only thing that can separate us, besides the Lord, is death." We told our parents repeatedly that this meeting was not for reunions, and that we belong to another family now. They even talked about going ahead to Ensi, so they could take us home. Tolna tells us, "I told my mother that I would never again be their child, for I was now married to our Lord. I shall serve and love only our Lord. I am old enough to marry, and if I marry, my husband can take me as he pleases. I cannot live a life as such, especially now that I have fallen in love with our vulnerable widows. They are only powerless because our old laws made them helpless. Zala and I shall free them if we must fight in every town. We belong forever to you Tianshire; we belong to you, to do as you wish." I then asked them, "Can I love you with all my heart?" They looked at each other and said, "Yep." I then asked them, "How can you break so easily with your parents?" Zala reports, "Tianshire, it is our freedom that we seek?"

A couple of the young widows told me, "This is the way of the black land tribes. The custom was to build stronger future generations." I then said to Zala, "You looked so happy with your parents." Tolna answered on her behalf, "Tianshire, if we do not we will get whipped, and I mean whipped." I then asked, "What is to stop them from just taking you and afterwards beating you later?" Zala said, "Nothing, but your mercy on us." I looked at her and said, "It is not mercy on you; it is love on you." I then started chasing them trying to kiss them. Oh, that was so much fun, and especially as our widows were keeping everything's safe for us. We next sat back down as Tolna said, "See, Tianshire, we will be hurt after you leave." I after that looked at the widows and asked them if they still were willing to care for my sisters while I was gone. They all enthusiastically agreed to do so, even with tears of happiness rolling from their eyes. One of them looked at us and said, "Why do you little girls like us, do not we stifle your fun?" I told them, "You do the opposite, because when people see you around us, they know we will mind you, so they give us no mind."

They felt about it and then started laughing, as one said, "We wondered why you were obeying us, and you are the slickest little girls we have ever known." Subsequently, one of the other widows commented, "Pardon me; they are true and legally adolescent ladies, and I might add, very beautiful young ladies." I then asked them to sit down so we could talk. I started by saying, "We have decided that we do not need any widows around here, because that has a connotation of death." They have now dropped their heads, as I continued, "What we each need instead are two mothers each. Do you know where we could find six mothers?" Their heads and hands popped up. I continued, "We do not want to be young ladies, as evidenced by Zala and Tolna declaring separation forever from their parents. We do not intend to become married, unless the Lord makes us. Therefore, we want to stay your little girls for as long as possible." The mommies now commented, "We can see the logic in that. Who will know that we are to be your mommies?" Tolna said, "Hopefully, first my mother." Next, Zala said, "Then my mother." later one of our mommies said, "That is rather harsh, is it not?" Tolna said, "No mommy, they knew we had cast out demons, and that we had conducted the healing ministries, yet they come here to take us away from others who need the Lord's blessing.

They made a promise; they broke, and then we broke it. You are my mommies." I then told our mommies, "My sisters will be forever dedicated to this family." Afterwards one of the mommies said, "What family will we be dedicated to?" At that time Oi walked in with two high priests and said, "This one, and do not try to get out of it." I after that said to Oi, "Tonight, we adopted them as our mommies, and we promise to do whatever they tell us." One of the priests next said, "We must get the widow program started, and we will call them subsequently, 'Bugac saved mothers.'" I looked at them and said, "That is a wonderful title that perfectly describes what we want to do." I later asked Oi in front of the priests, "Will you declare to these priests that our mommies shall stay with us or this ministry all the days of their lives, unless the Lord grants an exception?" One of the priests now said, "It would be wiser, to leave out the Lord granting an exception, as that leaves an avenue open for abuse and misuse. Believe me, if the Lord grants an exception, we will all honor that immediately." Oi then thought about it and asked, "Why about Zala and Tolna's mothers?" Tolna said, "Our mothers tried to take us from this ministry that they promised to allow us to stay in until you begin your new work. Therefore, they broke the agreement, and we decided to break it also.

We want to continue working for the Lord until Tianshire returns. We will postpone any marriages until after our nation is independent of Rubina, for it would be foolish to stop this great work when there are still so many who need the Lord. Furthermore, we need for the Priests to declare the temple for us; thereby, our mothers may not come and steel us." Oi looked upon the priests and asked them, "Is such a thing possible?" The priests told him, "It is not only promising, but legal, and with their parents hovering over them here, I would say it is probable." Oi then asked the priests, "Would you prepare for me whatever documents would be needed to take them for your temple, and also take their mommies; these are the nine most important people into my life. Please tell all and remind me to declare it in your temple for the morning. Will you also collect their parents, and have they sent back to Bucsu telling them that the Bugac high temple has taken them? I do not want any chance that we will see them again, as the last thing, we need now is trouble. I want also to thank the guides who brought us here yesterday. I know what I saw former times were wonderful; I can only tremble at what we will see on our trip to the Miskoldi lands." The priests now said, "We need to leave you so you and your nine loves can get some sleep." Oi told the priests, "They are my loves and precious headaches.

Once again, please make it so my sisters can keep their mommies." The four head priests and one scribe now departed. It was good that they had the scribe with them, because he had written this in the high priest's records. Now it was history and law. At this time, Zala, Tolna and myself lined up in a line and said, "Mommies; you may at present pick your babies, two for each of us." They slowly made their selections and then asked, "How are we going to work the sleeping arrangements, or just leave them the same?" I later said, "The two mommies sleep with their baby in between them." Oi afterwards told us girls, "Make sure you be good for your mommies because they have shown a great love for you." I next said to Oi, "We promised them always to obey everything they tell us if they were our mommies." Oi then said, "I am so proud of you girls, you know that love comes with responsibilities and that hearts can be broken too easy." Since they are now mothers, we need to know their names, "Mothers, please introduce yourselves to your daughters." They introduced themselves in order by telling us their names, "Heves, Domony, Dömsöd, Esztergomi, Sellyei, Siklósi." Zala then comments, "Wow, they have good names. We got lucky."

Our mothers now said, "Who would like to hear a nice bed time story?" We all three shouted for joy, as Oi said, "Is it in order if I can eavesdrop on this?" The moms just told him, 'All right, child." I know Oi liked that as some parts of himself were opening. Maybe that has something to do with the reason why his ministry ends. We shall soon discover the reason. Meanwhile, each of us, 'young women' snuggled up with our mommies, and all quickly fell during the night.

This night, I once again received a vision. Naturally, I was on a mountain range with only large tree. When I approached the tree, it changed into a man and woman holding each other. The male held the female rest one hand rested on her behind and his right hand firmly holding her left shoulder blade. She had both of her hands holding his head with his nose pressing against her forehead. Their legs appeared as like people, except they had no feet. Their legs blended into a bountiful array of the roots. They both had large roots going out of their backs. The male had two smaller routes growing out of his bed. They had no leaves, for it appeared to be winter. I awoke sweating, as immediately Sellyei, Siklósi began to wipe me dry, and Oi came over to ask me what happened to my dream. Oi after that said, "This dream is very important; I will ask the Lord to explain it to me." Sellyei next told us, "I can read parts of the dream. Let me help you?" We agreed and she began, "You saw two tall people who were holding each other firm. They had no hair, which means as monks they have been called out to be separate. When you saw the large roots that were holding them firm, you did not count them. If you count them, the number will be six. They are your new mothers, for in this family we came last, hence would be closer to the ground.

If you look again, you will see that the male's feet were together, and his roots ran behind this vision, which may be difficult for you to determine. Her body is one, and then she divides into two legs each leg having three roots. Her feet are closer to you, as three roots enter each leg. Look again and you see. She has a long strong tree branch that once it is past the roots, splits into two. The male has three branched from his back, one lengthy and large that itself has a branch that extends a short distance. The male is Oi, and the female is Tianshire. Each of you will have strong powerful ministries. Tianshire's messages, even though now is sturdy will split, very soon, into two, one branch Zala and one branch Tolna. As each back tells their story only from their view, you shall see some repeat. The large branch from Oi's back is his great ministry. The branch that extends far out on the branch is Tianshire's ministry, which will be reborn in the future, using much of the teaching from her main branch, Oi. The two smaller branches that extend from Oi's back only to the distance where Tianshire's branch begins are the ministries from Zala and Tolna. The hug shows how united your independent ministries are. Oi's time shall soon end. Oi looked at me and said, "Sellyei speaks the truth."

I looked at her and said, "I now remember the dream, and you have seen and know the mystery of my dream." I then reached up for her to carry me back to our blanket. Siklósi also joined us; hence, I reaffirmed my love for them. Likewise, back to sleep, we went. As morning arrived, we all enjoyed our morning meal in the temple. The mothers began packing our things as the temple gave us some new horses. The valleys or passes that lead to the Miskoldi were accessible. The priests had been very good about getting them the things they needed. Today, before we began the ten-day journey, not so much for distance, but for all the zigzagging through the passes. Oi revised our travel itinerary adding in four extra days by change where we camped and adding four more camps. I thought that was so kind of my big brother. In the black lands, they would never allow nine women, all marrying age, to travel with one young man, who was not married. There was only one exception, and that was my brother. The Lord's speaking from the sky helped a lot. Now, today all the females, including me, had to agree to be the property to the temple. The high priests had agreed release us to Oi, and once Oi was gone, under the new laws we could have our freedom, which meant that no one, not even parents or extended family members could lay claim to us.

There were a few parts of the ceremony and inspections that we were not impressed with; however, it united us with our fresh mommies, so we did not care. The scribes stayed up all night preparing extra copies; therefore, more messengers could get to more temples, as they would be required to verify the new temple copied it correctly. Ordinary, something like this would only be recorded in the local temple. Since all knew that when I returned we would be traveling all the black land's tribes, everyone felt it best to play it safe and record them all throughout the nation. They were also distributing copies of the new laws concerning widows. After we all surrendered and became the property to the temple, we began the ceremonies something like becoming married in the temple. There were many customs that their traditions kept, which did not contradict what we were teaching; hence, we had no issues with it. It helped keep the families together, and that was our big emphasis. The ceremonies and legal work took up most of the day, so our mommies took us to a private room in the temple and started tickling the living daylight out of us. We laughed so hard that we could only cry. Our mommies then laid out some clean evening gowns they had for us. I started to wonder where they were getting these nice clothes.

Then Dömsöd told me that the mothers who came into the meetings were giving them to us. Daytime they dressed us as travelers making sure we were safe and injury free. Our dinners were a different story. They dressed us to the nines. We were their showcases, the new hope in their lives. Zala, Tolna, and I agreed to obey them to the T, and never shame them. They were giving all they could give to make our lives better. As mommies, we already knew that this was a road that only death would evermore separate us. No matter what situation we were ever in, they would be there to protect us as best they could. I truly believe they could easily defeat any man who tried to hurt us. You can see it in their eyes. Oi agreed that the evenings would be family time for his girls. He only had two more messages, so those nights; family time would be the entire next day. That worked well for him, as the days after his messages were using packed with administration. We often wonder how our ministry is so big, and why so many followed us. I sometimes think that some of the appeal is our mother, the great ruler of evil. Some have told me this gives them reassurance that if the Lord can use those who are from evil for his mighty kingdom than he not only has the power, but he controls everything. That appeal got us started, and our works added with powerful blessings kept us going.

Our moms have made us look beautiful. Anyone who sees us will know that a woman spent much time preparing us. They tell us, "Please, do not get filthy." We tell them that we will try hard to fight against the temptations that grubby things attack little people rendering them helpless. We now wait for them to get ready. Zala is the first, quickly followed us Tolna and I, to ask a mother if they need some help. They give us small jobs and exaggerated praise, which keep us excited and feeling proud. These are not just ordinary people we are helping; they are our mothers, and that makes it so much more glorious and fulfilling.

They also check one another and if one is missing something, that thing comes her way. Sisters who are sharing and caring, as a way of life, are making an impression on the three of us that will be passed on to our children, if we are so blessed, someday. As we leave our special room, the priests gave us, the priests line up on both sides of the hallways, standing straight with one hand holding their hat with strong stern faces. As we go to walk down the steps, two priests would grab our arms and carefully escort us down the steps. We intently gave the impression as honorable women, thus handled as such. The temple is really drumming this event up, which I guess they know that Oi, and I will go, yet the promise is that I come back as the Chosen One.

They have placed Oi and me as being straight from the Lord. The Lord speaking from the sky welcoming my sisters into the family may have contributed to that belief. They also know that we took two little girls and six 'cast-out women' they did not want and turned our unit into a beautiful family full of love. I did not realize it, until now, I can now believe he saw the need to build a spiritual family as an example of how families can live together in love. Tolna, Zala, and I work hard to give our mommies the respect they deserve. Children honoring their parents bring joy to the Lord, also children who belong to the Lord giving love and respect to widows is really opening the doors to some old tribal customs to end, because Oi, and I am living this righteous way. We are not doing anything heroic; instead, we make each other complete and thus stronger. I am so proud at the way the Oi is fighting so hard for this. He has their attention, so I think for our next two times I am going to do the reverse psychology, as one of the pages, I touched called it, and praise them. My mothers are so beautiful for the way they are anchored among us, is whether to protect us from every possible conceivable danger. Finally, I say to one of them, "Esztergomi, you mothers must let the Lord help a little in protecting us." She looks at me seriously and says, "Okay; we will try." We all just laugh; they insanely have our welfare too high among their priorities. Their love is the kind of love that I would want to spread in my ministries. Perhaps now that I have seen it, and I have felt it, perchance a seed from inside me will breed it.

The tone for our last few tribe homilies was different. Oi knew that the ending of our great work was near, thus he wanted us to enjoy the people more during these endmost visits. We had such a large following that he felt it important to the people to see him with 'his women headaches' as he would sometimes call us. He told us now that we had to beware those accusers and deceitful teachers would work hard to destroy us for their personal gain and profit. He also warned that deceivers would pretend, or many times appear with defects and diseases for these false prophets. That would be the focus on his words to the Miskoldi. He wanted us to spend a few days in these mountain ridges alone, so we packed our supplies and our gang of twelve went into some nearby mountains. He invited two of the elders of Miskoldi to join us, for he said it was important that the Miskoldi witnessed what we were doing, to prevent against claims of secretly worshiping demons. As we sat around our fireplace in the early afternoon huddled in our extra furs Oi told us, "My sisters and my mothers, the Lord has ordained unto you to carry on my work.

Each of you will suffer many hardships; however, you must know that the Lord will be at your side during these times. He will deliver you from all your tribulations, as the deliverance will bring glory to his kingdom. If any of you wish to be liberated from this hard journey, you may be unrestrained now with our Lord's blessings. He then had us close our eyes and not to touch anyone. He got up and walked around with the two priests making the sounds of many getting up and leaving. None of his nine faithful even flinched. The priests looked at Oi and gave their thumbs up, which for the Miskoldi meant agreement. Oi now said, "My dedicated family, will you currently open your eyes? As each one opened, they immediately looked at those to their sides. Oi then laughed saying, I blindfolded you, yet using your eyes you could still here, and holding fast to the voice inside of you, did not betray your convictions." Oi added, "You have passed a great hurdle, for many times in our walks with the Lord; many will not travel with you. You have listened to your voice inside you when it told you to stay, even though you believed that many had left. You stayed. This is the sign of a great leader, having no fear when the ones who love you, travel a different road.

I am proud of each of you. You are strong servants of the Lord. I want you to know what things shall happen. Soon, Tianshire shall be betrayed and sold into slavery in Belcher's prison. Five years shall pass. The Lord will tell you where to meet her. She shall then share hers, and your ministry and messages from the Lord with the black land tribes. Serve with her if you are called. Her harangues shall be packed with fire and energy, with a flood of the Lord so deep, that not even the tallest man escape. Then she shall travel to the Labarians and assemble the greatest army that New Venus has ever witnessed. I shall tell you a great secret, 'once her foot touches Belcher's prison; she will be crowned the queen of the prison that only a few years earlier cast her as a beaten dog onto the brush to burn as garbage. The Lord shall afterwards punish those who were against her in all these lands. I now ask the mothers that at least three of them stay until Tianshire returns and then at least one to ride with her during her great teachings. Not one shall ride with her during the wars, for women and sisters are taken as booty from the loser and at last resort by invaders. You are all created woman first and then recreated as the Lord's servant. If any fall in love, you may choose that last and bear for your husband many children. Those who stay with Tianshire may receive great warriors as your husbands."

Oi now stopped and looked at the two priests and their scribe, which arrived while we were making our camp. Oi currently said to the priests, "The Lord has commanded that upon Tianshire's great victory that they be given faith and strong husbands, if they so desire. Any of them who chose not to marry a human shall be considered married to the Lord. Woe unto any who harm the Lord's brides." Oi at present looked up to the sky and spoke again, "I can see Tianshire's victory marches as so many welcome her back their new free from all evil land. I wave now at Tianshire, yet see cannot see me, for the Lord tells me to be patient, for she shall soon join us. I rejoice before the Lord as so many angels continue to celebrate singing, 'Tianshire has defeated the evil of Belcher's prison by believing in the 'word' of the Lord." Oi at present lowered his head, which currently had a glow flowing from it, opened his eyes, and said to me, "Tianshire, congratulations on your victory." He now fell upon the ground in a deep sleep in three days. When the priest's scribe had finished recording Oi's vision, only one priest remained as the others rushed to their temple to send more scribes. The priest who was with me told me, "The new scribes will be here very soon." I asked him, "How can that be true?" The priest said, "We have many scribes and priests waiting at a small temple one hour from here by horseback." I asked him, "Why would you do that?"

The priest said, "Before me are two prophets and two saints with their mothers, who are also the mothers of a daughter of the Lord. We fear that such a collection of the Lord's greatest chosen can never again be received. All in the black land's tribes hunger for every word and deed that the Lord shares with you." I told him, "Thanks for helping us share the words and deeds of our Lord." We now moved Oi closer to the fire and wrapped him with some additional furs that the scribe had left for us. The new priests soon arrived with many supplementary supplies, to include their mountain tents. I welcomed each priest. As I shook their hands, they would faint. I then stopped and complained, "These priests are at present with my brother. I must stop currently so that I may keep some with me." I could see the scribes recording this. I figure someday it will be a part of their great tails. What happened next did qualify! We sat around Oi, and wrapped up the three new priests who had also fainted. Zala commented on how beautiful the mountains were. Most of these had sharp points that no one could travel. We could see that gigantic mountain range that divided Miskoldi and Bugac. They stood so high that clouds refused to cross them. I marvel at how we could maze through the limited passes to make it here. It looks as if the surface was pushed together by the creator's hands.

The dirt must have washed away in the rains, leaving only the naked pressured rocks behind. It feels like they are screaming for us to leave, and that we are not welcomed here. No ridge before me has an area large enough to build a house. I can now understand the importance of these priests guiding us. These resemble each other so much, that I cannot determine my location. If the priests were to leave me, I would need the Lord to lift me out to the grasslands. The priests call this the land of the Gods. The previous gods forbid any to walk through these mountains, warning that none would return. No one ever returned. The raiders from Belcher's prison could pass through. They left markers, so they would know for future raids. When the Miskoldi found the Lord, from the early teaching from Belcher, they began using these paths. I tremble as I see these mountains fighting the sky for the heavens. One of the priests yells out, "I think that cloud in going to make it over the Miskoldi Mountains. We all set back and watch in suspense as the priests are rooting for the cloud. Then one priest says," Tianshire, please help us root." I afterwards said, "Oh Lord, for sport will you bring a giant white cloud over the mountains I am looking at."

We then heard a loud thunder as the white cloud grew large enough to cover the entire visible Miskoldi Mountain ridge. It at present grew to the heavens as it slowly covered the Miskoldi Mountains, as would an avalanche. The priests now fell on the ground begging me to ask the Lord to spare us. I told them, "Fear not, but enjoy for this is a gift from our Lord for sport." Now the center of this sky dominating cloud formed a face that looked like a joker for children's games. This face like cloud was heading for us, as it did not follow the other clouds. A short time later, all in front of us was white, as the head now has positioned itself directly above us. The head currently begins to drop on us. The priests are crying and begging for their salvation. Zala, Tolna, and the mothers are playing a game laughing and rejoicing. I finally tell them, "Rejoice children of the Lord, for he now comes to visit you. Do you not know the face of our father, the Ancient One? I now called everyone to form beside me and for all to wrap heavy clothes around their eyes, as I told them, "Today we are blessed, for the Lord God or Ancient One shall speak unto us. You cannot look on him, for to do so would make you blind, as you will not receive your eternal eyes until you live with our Lord." The white cloud now covered all of us, then a room opened and two spirits stood before me. The main spirits spoke, "It is timed for you to wake up Oi and the priests, all who have protected your eyes, remove your protection so you can see.

We have been sent for the Ancient One. Then all were blindfolded to include Zala and Tolna. A voice inside me told me to wake up Oi, thus I went to Oi, with my knees on the ground and took hold of his hand. I now spoke, "Oi and the priests who followed you; it is time for you to awaken. Oi, I want the first words that you hear that me declaring my allegiance and eternal love for you. You are my teacher and all I shall ever do is for you and the Lord." Oi and the priests awoke, and I kissed each of Oi's cheeks and lifted him up, so he stood tall in front of me, then he lifted me. The voice in me was telling me, "Tianshire, many are declaring for you while others declare for Oi, which would result in Civil wars in which many will shed blood. Today, you have declared yourself unto Oi and bowed on your knees declaring your eternal love. All here have seen it, thus now we speak it." I looked and saw two spirits; therefore, I asked, "I am called Tianshire, how are you called?" The senior spirit said, "I am called Enoch." That was the first time I met Enoch, who later in the heavens took me under his wings, and we flew in the upper heavens.

The other spirit said, "I am called Aman, your grandfather. I have longed to see the children of my son. Remember, always standing with all your angels will be me, soon Oi, and your father." I now began to cry. Aman asked me, "Why do you cry Tianshire?" I then said, "Because you will say soon Oi will be with you. I want to keep me with me forever." Aman then said, "Fear not Tianshire, you will be with both Oi, Belcher, and the entire Lord's Saints. Your time on New Venus is but a drop of water in all the oceans of all the worlds. Now is the time for you to continue your work for our Lord." Then the one who was called Enoch came over and wiped my tears from my eyes. I asked, "How can a spirit of light wipe away my tears?" Enoch said to all who were there, "Many angels have taken on flesh to test the people of the five tribes of the sisters and the black land tribes. The black land tribes have always given food to these angels, some giving even their last food, and their clothing." Enoch now looked upon the priests and said, "The Ancient One has found great pleasure in the black land's tribes. He shall deliver you through Tianshire from evil. As we now speak, I tell you that the greatest one ever to come from New Venus is but a six-year-old girl walking among you. The black land tribes shall become a land flowing with milk and honey. All will know that you are blessed people.

You must remember that Oi, and Tianshire is as one with the Lord. Those who follow Tianshire also follow Oi, and those who follow Oi, likewise, follow Tianshire. The Lord gives them to same messages. He only chose Tianshire to deliver you from Rubina to show how mighty he is, that with him, a woman can receive victory. Blessed is Oi, for he may help Tianshire from the throne of our Lord." Enoch now called my sisters, our mothers, and myself to join him for a short time. We disappeared into the clouds. Aman stayed with Oi, and spoke with the priests reiterating over their great deeds. Enoch now repeated to us our missions as Oi already revealed to us. He gave each of us a blessing. I was so happy that he knew the names of our mothers. When he touched them, I could see a gift entering their bodies. This was their first spiritual encounter with the throne. They felt themselves to be worthless disposable servants; notwithstanding, he told them, "You are the mothers of Tianshire, Zala and Tolna. The Lord thanks you for this great deed. As Tianshire is a daughter of the Lord, you mothers of a daughter of the Lord and shall be blessed as such." Enoch looked at me with unhappy eyes. I asked him, "Why do you look at me with sad eyes?" He told me, "I wished to bring you back to the throne today; however, the Lord has declared that you must tarry here a while longer, to save his children. I will be your servant when you come before the throne." I asked him, "Do they have servants in heaven?" Enoch declared, "Only by our free will, for we all serve the Lord and help other special Saints. You shall be a Queen in our heavens and join Lablonta and Eve. You and Oi will select the fourth and last Queen of the Heavens." I enunciated back to Enoch, "I so much want to meet Lablonta." Enoch asked, "How do you know of Lablonta?" I then told him that, "She was in the books of the Szombathelyi Empire." In parting he said, "The Lord blesses those who seek knowledge as did Zala, Tolna and yourselves. You shall have great joy when you see the treasures that the Lord has laid up for you in the heavens." That was when I decided to do as Oi when I began my ministry and that was to report to a temple of a tribe, unclothed and unfed. If they fed me and gave me clothing, they would be blessed. Those who laughed at my shame, I would curse them with a plague and move onto another temple. Oi has never had to curse a temple, although since he is with his sisters and mothers, he enters clothed. The power of sisters in this issue was quickly approved by the Lord when Oi requested an exception.

The clouds now lifted, and we all sat in wonder. I told Oi, "I never expected to meet the Lord on a barren mountaintop." He then told me, "Tianshire, constantly expect the Lord, for he is always at your side." I gave him a kiss on the cheek and slowly retreated to my sisters. In my mind, I thought, 'my statement was only a figure of speech, yet Oi turned it into a message as if I knew the Lord not.' The voice currently spoke back, "He must do so, as all his words are recorded." I at present understood and asked my sisters if they wanted to play. Our mothers asked us, "Should you play so soon after the Lord has visited us?" I looked around, saw many scribes looking at me, and said, "The key point is after, and the answer is yes, for the Lord is always with me and not a mystery. When I rejoice so does he, if my joy is from the love, the Lord has given me. A happy righteous child brings great joy to the Lord's ears." The scribes were writing extremely swift. I was glad that they were putting that in our writings. I remember how our father always talked of his days as a child in the Garden of Eden, how he would play, and have so much fun with the animals. Those were the days when beasts and humanity enjoyed peace with one another. Aman and Eve would tell those wonderful stories, and teach them games to play. Eve always told him that the sound of children playing in laughter in righteousness brought joy to the Lord's ears. Unfortunately, the Lord never received that joy from the children of Belcher's prison.

We, therefore, played with our mothers. Our mothers knew many fun games and things to play. They once had children, with the dream of enjoying their grandchildren, only to be cast out as a burden. How could people be so heartless? How did we make it this far without knowing? I think that is one reason the Oi is spreading the time between his last visions. He wants to learn more about what happens in these tribes. You will seldom hear the wrong about a tribe from that tribe. Nevertheless, they will share with you the questionable activities of their neighbor tribes. We now had to start returning to the temple, for Oi feared that the great multitude that followed us would suffer. We slowly returned, as the scribes had their replacements with us, so that all these events could be recorded and sent to the other tribes. The priests and scribes who were in the cloud with us became, known as 'one who was in the Lord's cloud, as the Lord spoke to Oi, Tianshire, and all who were of his family.' They were good priests and scribes. I asked them before their replacements came for them, "Who chose when you would be with us?" They said, "An elder of our temple said he felt it in his heart." I then said, "As I have told you, "The Lord dwells with all his children."

Each priest and scribe who was leaving kissed Tolna, Zala, all the mothers and my hand, then hugged Oi afterwards in tears departed. One of our new priests said, "Surely, the love of the Lord is here!" I then looked upon the priest as said, "The Lord loves all the righteous and shall give them their reward with eternal life at his throne." Now one of the priests asked, "Tianshire, will the Lord take us to his throne, as we are not from Aman and Eve?" Oi came over and held my hand, as he motioned for Zala, Tolna, and our mothers to join us with their hands. He then looked at me. I looked at him, and he motioned for me to answer this question. I looked to the priest and asked him, "What do you see when you look upon us?" The priests and scribes all debated and finally said, "Tianshire, what should we see?" My thoughts now revealed an amazement for the wisdom of these servants of the Lord. I smiled at him and said, "You should see your brothers and sisters in the Lord's family. The Lord always 'adopts' children from other lords who confess him as their Lord. You all show rejoice beside me in the Lord's throne as equals having been born from Aman and Eve." They all now rejoiced as Oi, and I asked each other, "How did such an important issue escape our messages?"

I told my brother, "The Lord decides the food that we feed unto his children. He added this food today, as I will not be the only one to hurt from losing my brother." He quickly rushed to hug me, and a priest gave him a cloth to wipe my tears. A priest currently commented, "Tianshire loves her brother very much." Oi then responded, "The sister I hold in my arms at present I have loved no other more. I tell you that she has cried before the Lord because of how your people have suffered." Each priest and scribe now sat down and cried. Our mommies quickly took Zala and Tolna away, not fearing that my sisters would cry, but that they would cry. Sometimes I wonder how adults have kept such great secrets from their children. We now returned to the meeting place as the giant white cloud followed us. As we entered the great valley that was our meeting place, manna appeared from the heavens as money priests came running out of the temple yelling for all to claim their winter clothing that just appeared. I then asked Oi if he thought we should also give to them fish. He told me, "No, let us save that for my final sermon." I looked at him and laughed, "You know I shall always love you." He then told me, "As I shall love you for eternity." I think the Lord kept putting these messages in our minds so that many scribes would record it and thereby reduce a chance of civil wars.

I thought to myself, 'how can one kill another by the name of the same Lord?' This must be a mystery, which I must wait to understand when I become an adult. We waited for our following to eat, and from the manna they were eating gave evidence that they were truly hungry. The priests passed out the new winter clothing, which had pants, heavy coat, gloves, head garments, and thick fur boots. Once they gave these items to the one who was to receive them, the garments immediately tailored to their bodies perfectly. I could hear one woman say, "Surely the Lord loves his children." She then noticed that I heard her and fell upon her knees begging forgiveness. Tolna and Zala lifted her up while I gave her a kiss upon the cheek. I feared that she would not hear my words, for she panicked so much. I then asked her, "Woman, why do you have so much fear?" She told me, "You heard me speaking of the Lord." I told her, "I heard you confess about the Lord's love toward his children. You should not fear ones of the Lord from being angry over such a great testimony, yet you should look around you to make sure our enemy is not seeking his revenge. I then stood out in the open while holding this woman's hand saying, "This woman has confessed the love the Lord has for his children.

I tell you now, that our Lord loves all who serve him. I ask you that if the Lord feeds the game that you need to survive, would he not feed you, his children. As the Lord covers the beasts, so they may survive the freezing winters, would he not feed you. I ask you that if you feed your children, would not the Lord also feed his children. Do not your children ask you to give them the things they need? Can you not know that if the Lord created you that he would not know your needs? As you care about your children, will you not let the Lord care over his children? I tell you that you do not have because you do not ask. I declare that the righteous among us are the children of our Lord. He is not my Lord, for can I control he who created all things? I tell you, he is our Lord." I now looked on the woman and said, "Woman, go to kiss my sisters and mothers." The Lord did a wonderful job at amplifying my voice so that all heard. I now wanted to slip back behind Oi so that the people would remember that Oi was to feed their spirits tonight. Notwithstanding, I rushed to Oi, jumped while he grabbed him, and we hugged, receiving an ovation henceforth apparently our followers. I knew not to get excited about this for even I knew that they would soon forget us when we were no longer with them.

Oi now took us into the temple to pray before his meeting. The elders of this temple also joined us. We were to pray in silence, as Oi told the elders, "Those who pray so man can hear them receive their reward from man, yet those who pray only to the Lord receive their reward from the Lord." We prayed for a while, and as we stood up, the elders and my mothers' rushed to me, once again, I was soaking wet. The elders gave my mothers' wiping garments, as they dug through our bags to give me another garment. They then took me to another room, and dried me while also putting on my dry clothing. They quickly returned, me to

Oi, as we now prepared for his meeting. We formed at the stage, as Oi wanted his sisters and mothers in the first row behind him, and the elders filled in the second row. Oi began, "Will all here today repeats this phrase four times, each time turning so that all around you hear this, 'may the Lord be with you.' And we saw two hundred and seventy two deceivers be bound by angels and cast into a lake of burning fire." I wondered why Oi had changed it from three times to four times, as a small voice said to me, "As the deceiver looks for ways to avoid detection, we must think of new methods to trap them." I now realized this is very much correspondingly a spiritual war, and my comment about the woman about fearing our enemy hearing us, was not that far-off target. As Oi begins to speak again, "I have great news for you, although I suspect all know this by now, I must say it once for our records. The Lord your God has chosen Tianshire to deliver you from all evil, only the evil from Rubina, but also I repeat, "from all evil."

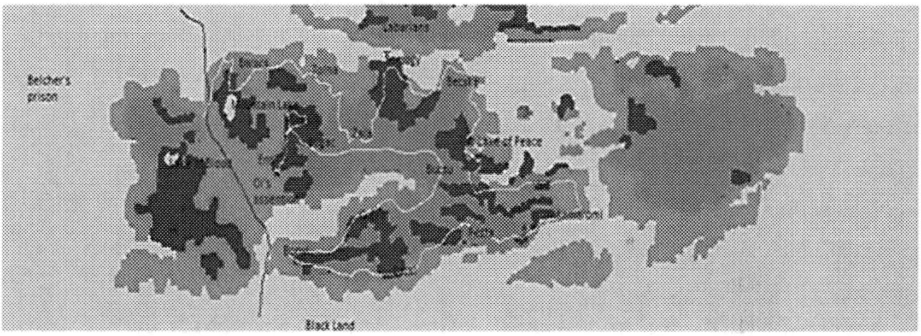

I know this to be true for, as Tianshire has walked in the Lord's throne, so did I only a few days ago. The Lord showed me her victories, as she prepared a great army from the shores of the Labarians where no evil shall he allow to witness. He has also told me I have only one more meeting for the Ensi, and that I shall no longer walk on New Venus. Tianshire shall go back to our father's prison to prepare her way for her second entry, which she shall then win the independence of the black land's tribes. Upon her return from Belcher's prison, she shall travel through all your tribes once again to feed you with our Lord's words. Let all be warned, that those who curse her shall be also cursing the Lord, and shall die a terrible death before being cast into the lake of fire until the great judgment. Remember while she is gone to care and protect my sisters and mothers. They are holy people. I have not come here today to warn or find faults in your ways. I can see that those who are in the foreground with me today are truly the righteous of the Lord. Remember what the Lord said through the mouth of Tianshire, "You have not because you ask not." All things that you receive are received through your faith. If you receive not, then make your faith stronger. I tell you that all deeds you have heard of my sisters, and mother was not done by them, but done through their great faith. Today for your message from our Lord, we shall talk about the road to your victory. Remember no temptation has seized you except what is common to man. Our Lord God is faithful; he will not let you be tempted beyond what you can bear. However, when you are tempted, he will also provide a way out so that you can stand under it. We have told you these things, so that in the Lord, you may have peace. In New Venus, you will have trouble. Nevertheless, take heart! The Lord shall overcome all who walk upon New Venus.

Think not that the wicked prospers even to their death; for it is then they shall pay greatly for their evil. It would have been better for them that they lived not. Therefore, put on the full armor of our Lord God, hence that when the day of evil comes, you may be able to stand your ground, and after you have done everything, then shall our Lord stand with you. Consider it pure joy, my family, whenever you face trials of many kinds, because you know that the testing of your faith develops perseverance. Perseverance must finish its work so that you may be mature and complete, not lacking anything. Blessed is the man who perseveres under trial, because, when he has stood the test, he will receive the eternal life that our Lord God has promised to those who love him. When tempted, no one should say, 'the Lord is tempting me.' Our Lord God cannot be tempted by evil, nor does he tempt anyone; nonetheless, each one is tempted when, by his own evil desire, he is dragged away and enticed. Then, after desire has conceived, it gives birth to sin; and sin, when it is full-grown, gives birth to death. I have told the tribes this previously; however, it must be told many times. Be strong in the Lord, and in his mighty power. From the Lord comes deliverance. This blessing may be on your people, for everyone born of our Lord overcomes this world. This is the victory, which has overcome the world, even our faith. If our Lord is for us, who, then can be against us? Do not be afraid of Rubina's demons and raiders; our Lord has given them into your hand. Not one of them will be able to withstand you. Your horse is made ready for the day of battle, but the victory rests with the Lord. I tell you that today we should begin celebrating our victory. I shall once more speak to you from the lower mountains of the Ensi, so keep your winter clothing that the Lord has given you. Tianshire has asked me to give to you more food. Therefore, I ask oh Lord, will you give unto us fire and game that we may eat thereof." Instantly, each family received a fire for each four people. This fire came from the ground and made no black or white smoke. On each fire was a large pan filled with fresh animal flesh, ready to eat. The Lord also gave them cups filled with wine and plates that they may each eat the meat before them. The Lord refilled the pans with meat again, so that all who were there did feast greatly. Not all received the same meat, as each person received the meat they enjoyed the most. The people from the tribes had learned to go many days without food and then feast until the life once again returned to their starving flesh. Oi now told these people, "Keep your plates but leave the pans for the poor to collect. The Lord will feed you hot food from these plates, as you will have no need to cook your future meals.

As the birds from the sky eat, so shall you. Zala, Tolna and our mothers shall now walk among you for the healing ministry of our Lord. Tianshire will walk among you to shake your hands. I shall now meet with the elders and priests from the temple. Enjoy the fires, as they will help keep you warm, even if you stay here tonight to rest. The Lord had given sufficient space between the fires as his servants moved towards the fires. This was the first time I walked among the people. It was so special to shake hands with the men and hug the women. I was pleased to see so many young strong men. I asked each one, "Will you serve in my army during the great war?" Every one of them shouted yes with inordinate enthusiasm." I then thanked them and their parents if they were beside them. All said, "I shall serve you to my death." I said to them, "Remember to serve our Lord first." The joy that came across their parent's face to have witnessed me asking their son or sons to fight in my army was overwhelming. I thought to myself, 'do they realize that my army shall go to war.' I nowadays, wonder if anyone thinks about war. Even I am currently excited at the end; however, I must endure it as that is my destiny. That might explain their excitement to be a part of this war, and it would be a part of their destiny. Our following is staying with us.

This must explain why the Lord gave them refilling plates. Zala, Tolna, our mothers, and I spend five days with our following. I can see battered aged people who now for the first time have faith since they have seen their hope. The way they hold their babies with the penetrating stares, a stare that says, 'this baby is all I have, yet I am willing to return it to the Lord.' I wonder what kind of lives they have had to live. The saddest part is that my mother is responsible for this. This is my shame, as it is also Oi's shame.

These people are very forgiving. They do not blame Oi and me for our mother's deeds that have destroyed so much of their lives, yet instead hold onto us for their hope of a better tomorrow. I envy them for their patience, which is a weakness in myself that must be purged. I can see where a lack of my ability to control my temper could hurt so many people. Staying with Oi has done so much to keep me in control; notwithstanding, when he is gone, I fear my anger may grow stronger than my control. I can tell that by bodies, many of these people have suffered the ill effects of eating good food. These refilling plates may be feeding them the best meals they have eaten in their lives. Nevertheless, they departed from what was keeping them alive to follow Oi, living in freezing weather to be a part of our calling. The men have been collecting rocks, which suddenly are readily available, and building a rock wall around the borders of their group. It cuts the wind down and keeps the men busy. The family groups are now merging with other groups and especially the children forming new friendships. I walk around, see little huddles of children, and visit with them. They have such innocent looks upon their faces, and pleasantly the only thing that they understand me is that I am a good person. These produces such an overwhelming joy, as someone would not know us by our works, but by our kindness. They can feel our goodness and accept it. Our mothers are so much enjoying this, as they also work well with the mature women. Since I am only thirteen, I shy away from the older women, as I try not to humble them. Some naturally corner that me, and for those, I work hard to show my respect, especially as they bring their sons to petition for their enlistment in my army. I can feel their sons as they look at me. They do not see a thirteen-year-old; instead, they see a twenty-one-year old leading them. I respect that they see me in the future. Many of the scribe's records vary across the age, in which I led the war, as some do not include the times of my trouble, and others include varying periods during my year's back in Belcher's prison, citing that I was not in the black land tribes; on the contrary, It was with the dead. The same is with my name, as some scribes recorded it as Tianshir while others correctly recorded me as Tianshire. With, or without the E, it is still me.

Even I never desired to rehash those years, except in this manuscript for the ages. How old they debate I was, does not bother me, for I know the years I walked or crawled on New Venus. There are so many other greater things to be concerned about, such as I free the people, how I will feed them. Then build a nation, which can provide what it needs for its people. I now see two little boys wrapped together sleeping against a wall. I call on a priest who comes rushing. I ask him, "Why do they not have warm blankets and have they eaten?" He guides me to the little boys, as the smallest one is refreshing my memories of Tsarsko and one of our other brothers, as they would often sleep together, especially on the cold nights. The priests wake the boys as I ask them, "My little brothers, where are your parents?" The older boy tells us, "They were killed by the evil raiders." I tell him, "What would you say if I told you my mother was their leader?" The little boy then said, "I would not care for I love you too much." I motioned for a priest to help wipe my tears from my face. I saw many of the women who were now formed around us as they also were crying. The young lad now asked me, "I am so sorry; I did not mean to make you cry." I reached over and slowly ran my hand through his hair saying, "Oh son; you did not make me cry from sorrow but cry for joy, as you have reminded me why I must lead this nation to its independence." Subsequently, many around us began clapping and praising the Lord. I asked the boy if he and his brothers have eaten. He told me, "No, but please do not concern yourself with us, but help those here who are better than us."

I then stood tall, looked him in the face, and yelled out, "There is not one among us, not even me, am better than you, or the lowest person in this nation. Our Lord created us equal and as such loves us alike. Your Lord whom you serve is the same Lord, whom I serve. We are equal to my brothers." The Lord now gave me two plates that I gave the boys. You may eat the food from these plates until our temple finds you two special witnesses of our Lord a fresh family and home. I reached inside my coat and pulled out new furs for them to wear, including gloves, hats, boots, pants, under furs and a big winter coat for each. I then pulled out a large fur blanket for them. The boy asked me, "Oh kind woman, how do you have so many things under your coat?" I looked at him and said, "My son; it was your faith that put them under my jacket." I looked to the priest and said, "This child does not even know my name, for he only listens to the voices that cry inside his heart that tells him I am from the empire of righteousness. Will you and some male volunteers give him shelter in your temple, as this evening before sleep; I will bring Oi, my sisters, and our mothers, to bless him." I now looked upon the people here and asked, "How can this be? The Lord gave you clothing and food, could you not ask the Lord also to give to these boys. I warn you that the hungry have no laws and can easily be made slaves of the deceivers and create havens for the evil. We must work to help the kingdom of our Lord and not to increase the kingdom of our evil adversaries." As I scanned the group, I saw one small female child alone, and I asked her to come to me. She shyly worked her way to me, and I asked her, "Little girl, where are your parents? She told me, "They are at home. I left my home to see your sermon." I asked her, "Why would you do such a thing?" She looked at me as if in shock and boldly perked up and said with a loud voice, "Because I love the Lord, and want to learn from the Lord's greatest teachers." I told her, "Well, young lady that is indeed a very good reason. Have you eaten today?" She told me, "Yes, our Lord has given me more to eat than I need; therefore, I gave most of it to the little hungry children."

I motioned for her to come before me, and I said to the large group had now formed around us, "I tell you that these are the love and faith the Lord cherishes greater than all others, that coming from a child such is this girl. If you have the faith and love as a child you shall walk a long journey with the Lord." I currently placed my hand on her shoulder, and my body froze as lightning bolts jolted through my body. My body then became free again as I currently knew what the Lord was telling me. I asked the young girl, "What is your name?" She told me it was Boudica. I afterwards called for all to listen, "Scribes record this, "I tell you today that this child named Boudica, shall be a Saint far greater than Oi or myself." I next gave her a soft hug and whispered into her ear, "Boudica, will you walk with me until Oi no longer walks upon New Venus?" She looked at me and said, "Did you ever think that you could have prevented me from following you?" I said, "Oh no, Boudica, I asked if you would walk with me, not follow me." Boudica after that said, "I will do whatever you ask of me." I subsequently reached out and softly gripped her hand and said, "Stay with me my special friend." I then saw some scribes and asked them, "Did you record what I said about this child?"

They told me they had absolutely heard this and afterwards carried on as normal. I then said to Boudica, "Having ears they do not hear, for it is their foolishness to think that one will not come who is finer and Oi or myself." Boudica next asked me, "Why would I want to be greater than you?" I then told her, "By finer, I mean you will do greater work for our Lord than any other who has ever lived on the Lord's worlds. I tell you now to think on such things, as tomorrow will come, yet for at present enjoy being a child." Boudica subsequently asked me, "If I am to be such a great leader for our Lord, later why do I currently know of this?" I told her, "The Lord reveals these things when he wants us to know. There still are many missing gaps in my future, which the Lord has yet to reveal to me. I tell you to have no fear for he is with you." The evening darkness was now approaching as many families and groups had at present bedded down for the night. I told Boudica that we could now assemble my sisters, mothers, and Oi and visit the two boys I have been staying at the temple. I was getting cold thereby I knew our flock was also getting cold and thus raised my hands while looked at the fires so the flames would give more heat. Boudica asked me, "How did you do that?" I told her, "Boudica, it was the Lord using my faith that did this." She smiled as if she understood this, and I believe she did. Remember, Boudica that the Lord truly cares about his children. We all met inside the temple's altar area where we prayed while waiting for our family members. I arrived first and took Boudica to the altar where we prayed. I can clearly see a glow over her body, a glow that is coming from inside. I can believe that this jewel is very special, and I thank the Lord, whom he has allowed my eyes to see her. Soon, Oi enters and kneels beside me and asks, "Who is our new friend?" I tell him, "She is called Boudica, and it would please me if you shook her hand, as I know she is a great follower of you." Oi, never denying my request, reaches over and shakes her hand. I see his eyes glow and his body lightly twitched. He asks me again, "Who did you say she was, "She is called Boudica, and she shall be greater in the kingdom of our Lord than both, you and I." Oi now looks at poor little Boudica, who is shell shocked by meeting her greatest hero, and says, "That is exactly what the Lord has told me."

I tell Oi, "The Lord has truly blessed us by allowing us to see the one who will save the righteous when we no longer walk through this world." Oi then asked, "How did you find her?" I afterwards looked at him and laughed, "She found us, even leaving her home to do so. I want to keep her with us until you are no more in this world. I want her to see as many great things from our Lord as she can with her physical eyes, as I can clearly see that her faith has already seen." Oi then agreed, "Yes, we must do all we can to help her. I will have the scribes record my requests to her parents to forgive her as blame us for her desire to serve our Lord." I next kissed him on the check and while crying, "How will I make it without you?" After that little Boudica subsequently said as clear as if she was seeing it, "Do not worry Tianshire, I will take care of you." Oi and I later hugged her as we each kissed her checks. Tolna and Zala brought our mothers to this altar and asked, "Who is that little fellow who is stealing all our love?" Boudica then stood up apologizing, "I am sorry; I did not know I was stealing." Tolna next said, "I think we will forgive you if we also get some of that loving." Oi and I stepped back as they all smothered that child. The mothers naturally tickled her as the joyous sound of a child's laughter filled the temple. The elders now rushed in and asked if everything was okay. I told them, "Oh yes, for we were giving back to the Lord some love he has given us." They pretended to understand and I pretended to believe them, as I did not want to repeat this message again. Now some priests entered and asked, "Are you ready to see your two boys?" Oi then looked at me and said, "My, you were very busy today." I afterwards asked them, "Will you please join me in seeing some special little boys I met today?" The mothers then quickly answered, "Of course we will, at present you lead the way and do not go slow." One of the scribes currently asked, "Oi, are you certain the Lord did not give you angels instead of these ten women?" Oi looked at him serious and said, "You know; I truly am not confident, yet the work these women do for the Kingdom of our Lord I sometime think is greater than what angels could do." We all now surrounded him, and I told the scribes, "He is ours at present, for a short while." We now followed the priest to the boys' room. While we were departing the elders another scribe said, "See, not even the greatest prophet of the Lord can defeat ten females."

Then an elder said, "Who would want to defeat that much love given by our Lord?" We now entered the little boy's rooms where I saw their plates beside their beds.

I could see the look of peace before their faces as they now slept upon a bed, had food in their bellies, and faith in their hearts. I then told Oi their story. The mothers were now busy washing everyone's eyes. I asked Oi, as the priests and at present elders looked on, "How can this be? Where did our ministry fail? Will you get official authorization to keep these boys in the house of our Lord, as we have sinned by leaving them naked and hungry? I also need for you to get our Lord's servants her working on finding them a home." I then looked at the elders as Oi quickly got behind me and put his hands on my shoulders. I think that Oi feared that I was going to get very angry and lose my temper. Instead, I looked at them, and the four scribes who were recording this and warned, "Woe unto he who takes children from the Lord's house that the Lord placed therein. Blessed are the parents who take these boys as their sons, for as they care for the Lord's sons, he will care for them as they stand before his father." All of a sudden, all the elders looked at Oi and asked, "Our Lord has a father?" Oi then told them, "I reveal to you a great mystery, and that is our Lord has a father, the Ancient One, yet in the beginning our Lord was with his father, and his father was with him for they are one.

At the end of time, we shall all stand before the Father as the angels read the books of all our works. The Father will say about his son, "How do you judge this created spirit. If the son says righteous, his Father will take him or her. If the son says evil, the Father will punish him. The Father and Son are one. It hurts my heart that I must soon depart from New Venus, for so many more things I could have shared. I do promise you that when my sister Tianshire and the small child named Boudica teach you about the Lord; I will also be there with them." Then one of the priests said, "This is truly a blessed room, for the Lord has revealed to us, a great mystery, and the next two Prophets, who will feed us his word." Remarkably, as I walked over to kiss our boys on their cheek, Boudica walked to the other side of the boys, so she could, at the same time, kiss their other cheek. She was as a carbon copy in which one of the elders said, "Tianshire and Boudica serve as one with the Lord. Those boys are so lucky to have been blessed by these two future sibyls." Boudica and I gave these boys their blessings as Tolna and Zala looked on in amazement and excitement. We all drug ourselves back to our chambers, and poor little Boudica had to stand in line with my sisters and I for our nightly cleaning. Our mothers did a wonderful job, as they afterwards put on our nighttime garments. I was surprised that they had clothing already prepared for Boudica, and I had to ask them, "How did you make her clothing so fast, as I was prepared to give her mine?

Then Heves answered, "A vision put the knowledge in our minds, and these came from our hands." I afterwards looked at Boudica and said, "See; you belong with us." Zala wanted to sleep beside me tonight and Tolna wanted to sleep beside Boudica, and the mothers sleep two to each of our sides, and one above and one below; thereby, no one could make it to us, without first going past them. They were afraid that Boudica would feel uncomfortable around so many new faces. The sisters wanted to get close to them and make them feel like a part of our family. Poor Oi had to sleep against the wall alone. He always told us, "This is a small sacrifice to make for being very close to so much beauty." We would smile and thank him for his kind words. Boudica followed me the next day, Tolna the second day, Zala the third day and Oi the last day we were with the Miskoldi. Boudica noticed that anytime a mother asked us to do something, we all did it without question. She asked me one night while we were walking together, "Why do you all obey the widows without question?" I told her, "They were widows to the black land tribes; however, the Lord gave them and their love to us as mothers. We know that the Lord cares for us through them, for that is their ministry. We are commanded to love and honor our parents. If we do not love and honor the mothers, the Lord has given us; he will take them from us. We can, under no circumstances, lose them for my life would be so empty without them, as they fill the part of me that is to love my mother, as evil took my real mother thereby I can never love her. As I look at each of them, I can feel myself being in their wombs. I am so blessed that our Lord loved me so much to give me so many mothers. They are the greatest in our group." Boudica then looked at me, with her childish, grin, and said, "That is what I thought." This reminds me of the way I used to answer Oi. I thereby bent over and kissed her cheek saying, "I love you princess" exactly as Oi would do for me. Boudica's disadvantage is that

I learned these tricks late, and she has learned them young. Either way, I view it as a treat coming from a daughter whom I may never have. Now is beginning the road to my times of troubles, for we currently guide our gigantic flock to our final pasture. This path is the easiest in these mountains. We also see much more destruction, as Rubina's warriors have frequently raided this path. They have not even entered their southern borders with us in a few months, as we can as well see many raiders under large stones and burned, appearing to have met the hand of our Lord. As we walked by Boudica, and I pointed our fingers at the decaying bodies thus burning them.

Tolna and Zala were very overjoyed, as they saw me, and repeat me at work. They understood the difference in our relationships, since Boudica would be receiving the torch from me for her run. Tolna and Zala were here to help me with our torch. As I would someday receive my torch from Oi, it was important that Boudica be confidentially involved with Oi, and my relationship for she would see Oi pass the torch from me that I would pass to her, and she would pass to another as the cycle of the same seasons continued to run in their circle. The mountains are not far from rolling hills here, with a few towers to spot the horizon. The weather broke for the good as many had wrapped their winter garments in their sleeping fur blankets and carried them on their backs. The refilling plates helped keep us together as a group, as the hunting parties no longer had to be launched. The gigantic following we had with us turned out to be a midget against a giant as we went to approach the Ensi temple of their elders. Oi and I fell upon our knees when we first saw what we now thought had to be more people than were alive on New Venus. I asked Oi, "How can we care for such a gargantuan multitude?" He looked at me and said, "We cannot, but the Lord can." Boudica then added, "Exactly what I was thinking."

This was the laughing medicine that we needed as we both laughed. Oi then said, "The greatest problems can be solved easiest by the youngest." Boudica smiled as we both hugged her and we both grabbed a hand so that all could see, she was part of, and equal to us. I asked Oi, "Can we get some refillable plates and fur blankets for them?" Oi said, "The Lord is filling the temple's storage rooms with them now." Then a delegation of high elders came on horseback to meet us. They gave us their greetings and asked us, "Who is this lovely child you have with you?" Oi looked at them and said, "Behold Boudica, who shall someday be your Queen. She shall be greater in heavens than Tianshire, and myself combined." The scribes did not write these words, it was time for both Oi, and I to become angry. Oi asked, "Why do you not write my words, do you wish that I go to another tribe?" I then said, "Woe unto him that rejects a Queen chosen by our Lord, for on judgment day, he will not allow them to the kingdom that she will be ruling. It would be so much better if such a person were never to be born. I tell you that those who respect and love her now, will be respected and loved by our Lord." At this time, Oi got down on one side of her, I fell to the other side, and we both kissed her confessing our love. The elders now begged, as the scribes were writing with both hands now, "You reveal so many great things that we become confused." I then told them, "Fear not for soon the Lord will take Oi from us, and he shall send me to my father's prison, and you will have five years to become masters of Oi's teachings." The elders afterwards asked, "Is this a punishment to us?" I looked at them and Boudica spoke saying, "It is not a punishment, for these things were decided before New Venus was born. Oi returns as his reward and so he can help all in New Venus as only those in the heavens can do. Tianshire must be sacrificed to evil so that she can accuse them before the Lord and receive his authority to destroy the evil that has cursed us since Rubina first set foot on our mainland. She sacrifices herself so you may not suffer from evil." We all now looked at her as Oi said, and I repeated thereafter, "That is what I thought." Oi and I looked at each other, as we knew without question; we were in the midst of a great servant of our Lord. Now Oi and I wrestled over who could hug Boudica when she said, "Children, there is plenty of me for both of you." Therefore, Oi hugged her first as I massaged her legs. Oi then released her to me as I held and hugged her with tears rolling down my face. Oi lightly combed her hair like a brush that Siklósi handed him. Our mothers can now predict what we need with so much accuracy.

This day witnessed the scribes releasing their first reports of Boudica; the future great Queen sent from the Heavens. We now worked our way into the temple when I asked the priests, "Have our children been clothed and fed?" They looked at me and asked, "How can we fed and cloth so many?" I said, "Their clothing and plates that they shall not be hungry and cups that they shall not thirst are in your storage rooms."

They all rushed to different storage rooms only to find all of them packed. I then asked if we could put priests at each entrance door to hand out these supplies before dark. Everyone, to include the elders, and the new widows who was now a part of this temple, worked hard at giving out the supplies, as Oi and his girls mingled among the people to find those who needed healing and other miracles for their lives. We also carried our refilling bags to cloth and fed those who were not able to make it to the temple doors. We could see what evil had done to the people who not only lived close to the borders with Belcher's prison, but also were surrounded by so much green land with their hills being easily accessible. Rubina equally important had a straight shot from Death Bay to them. This enabled her to make her northern armies active in the misery and torture of these people.

It actually took us two days to get the food and clothing to these people, and that was with the help of so many in our congregation. Initially, the priests were worried about accountability until they saw me handing out armfuls to people. They asked me, "Do you not worry about these people taking more than they need?" I told them, "No, I worry more about one who needs these things and not receiving it, as that person could accuse me at the great judgment." Within minutes, priests were handing them out by the armfuls, only to discover the storage rooms were furthermore packed. The priests now said, "If the Lord is even so giving these to us, then we need to continue giving these to his children." Oi asked the Elders if they knew about a place where the followers and the temple's multitudes could join. They knew about a place that they had prepared, which they called the Valley of Mezokovácsházi. This valley was a half-day's walk. We would start tomorrow morning, as it would take a complete day and maybe longer. We were telling the people our plans, so we could prepare for the move. Oi and his girls all walked among the people to the Valley. We were extremely surprised at how the people knew so much about our messages. This group was very special in that they were so relaxed and kind with us. They addressed each of us by name, to include Boudica.

All among us traveled down to the valley. Once again, Oi wanted us on the stage behind him. This was his last message, and the deceivers were too eager for when Oi had all say to each corner, 'may the Lord be with you,' the sky became dark. Afterwards, some small lights began to appear.

Soon, we could see the angels rounding up the deceivers, the number that was so great; I could not begin to count. After one hour a powerful angel comes down, took Boudica's and my hands, standing between us, and spoke saying, "This is the great final battle of the deceivers. They are no more upon New Venus. We could hear the deceivers screaming as the mighty angels bound them, and cast them in a giant lake of fire, which this time melted all the snow in this area.

Soon the sky became bright again, shining a luminous white from the angels who formed a dome over our meeting. Oi would not, for no reason once more see the skies of New Venus while still living. The dome of angels would never depart him, as the Lord had taken him in possession not to let him go. We all stayed with him on the stage, since we did not want to go a long way from him nor did he want to go far from us. I could see to sweat dripping from his face. I had never realized about the internal torment that he was also suffering. The one who is leaving is equally important departing from everything ever recorded in their days. Oi shared his last words with the black land's tribes declaring, "I have extreme joy in having beside me your last two great prophets, Tianshire, who shall begin her teaching and fighting in the not too far-off future, and then Boudica shall rebuild the new free Black Land's tribes. We have seen here today the importance that evil has placed on this meeting, since so many of the deceivers fell into the pits trying to destroy our Lord's people. No one nearby today should fear, for the Lord will be with you until you reach your home. I shall soon be no more, for it is only a matter of days. I do tell you that Tianshire shall return for five years and after her victory giving you independence, Boudica will build for you a great nation. Honor my mothers, which are now with me on this stage. Always remember that our Lord selected them to care for Tianshire, Zala, Tolna, Boudica, and myself. I am so proud at my girls, as they worked hard sharing the Lord's blessings, allowing all who are here now to have whole bodies again. Tianshire tells me that many mothers have offered their willing strong sons to be in your liberation army. I still give thanks to our Lord for showing me her victory ride. I thank all the temples who worked hard to care for our sheep in the pastures that I walked.

You now have many manuscripts from our scribes so that any who wish to learn about the love and mystery of our Lord shall it be revealed unto them. Many have wondered about our recent message concerning a great judgment. I tell all who are here now that every good deed you have done will be revealed to the Lord. Every great thing you done in darkness shall be known to our Lord in the light. Every time you walked past a hungry person, that person shall accuse you before the Lord. Every evil deed you committed in the dark you will once again do this in front of the Lord in the light. I have heard people complain, "This is too hard of a road." I ask you, how can this be difficult? Loving those who are around you should make your heart joyous, for as the Lord loves you abundantly, it is demanding that you give some of that love to his other children. Some find it easy to receive, but arduous to give. It is better to give than to receive. He who receives too much becomes a slave of his property and walks away from our Lord. The poorest person that loves and obeys our Lord is richer than kings who hate and disobey our Lord." He then waives me to his side and says, "As I depart, Tianshire and Boudica shall come back and rebuild." We both waived for Boudica to come up and stand between us. Oi now said, "Goodbye, we now bless you all." Once again, that giant cloud we met in the mountains fell down upon our stage. It rested upon us for a few minutes and then rose once more until we could see it no more. I looked around our group and quickly discovered Oi was not here. I know he always liked to join the priests and elders after his meetings. Strangely, the elders and priests were still in their seats. As I continued to look, a voice spoke in my head, the voice of Oi saying, "Tianshire, fear not, for I am with our Lord. Stay strong, do as our Love wishes, and we shall someday be rejoined in the heavens." I fell on my face in the center of the stage crying aloud, "My brother is gone; he is no more with me."

Chapter 06

The Sting of death

The pain that was flooding my body now with my brother gone just would not stop and acted as a virus spreading all over my body. I foolishly thought, I was tough enough to handle this and could be a study leader for little stunned Boudica. I am what I am and now that is lost and alone. I have nine of my adopted family members taking me away from the stage to a chamber in the temple. The congregation cannot believe what they see. The news spreads like wildfire all through their gigantic group. 'Oi is gone, for the Lord has taken him," was their mantra. I placed my hands as hard that were possible around my ears hoping to drown their intonation. These were like the demons stabbing my heart, for they had won. Zala now takes charge of me along with Tolna. The mommies are restoring Boudica from the shock she had when watching me. I lost my mother, most of my brothers, all my sisters, then my father and now Oi, who taught me just about everything I know and was with me every day of my life. He was my crutch. I just cannot understand why he had to be taken away from me. I did everything the Lord wanted me to do; therefore, why this punishment. There just will never be a man such as Oi again. As night comes, I see in my corner all my mothers, sisters, and Boudica. They each are positioned in such a way to touch me. I can see the maneuvering that they have positioned their bodies, which is depriving them of much comfort; nevertheless, they all have smiles across their faces. The next day, which I ask Tolna, "How can you continue your life after the loss of Oi?" Tolna says, "I am so thankful to the Lord, whom he enabled Oi to escape death. He was, and was still blessed. The wonder of being so loved by the Lord, whom the heavens would take him, is beyond my comprehension. You need to rejoice that the Lord gave you nine family girls to continue loving you as we did very much even with Oi." I said okay, since they did not know how I felt; I did not, nor should I waste my time explaining it to them. That is like begging someone not to watch you suffer or even worse, for him or her to tell you that you truly have no suffering. I just need to get away from them. As I am crunched in my corner, little Boudica comes over to me and starts kissing my tear-stained cheeks. I motion lightly trying to force her away, as would anyone when a loving dog is licking your face. This kid does not budge and easily stratagems around my lazy movements, because the one thing I can never do is to strike or hurt Boudica. I peek over at her face as tears are flowing down her cheeks. I ask her, "My Boudica, why do you cry?" She answers, "Because you cry from all your pain." It now hits me. Boudica is inside me.

She knows the pain I have inside me. I now reach over to pull her into my arms and whisper in her ear, "Boudica, what should I do?" She answers, "Keep doing what the Lord wants you to do." She hit the nail on its head. I then asked, "Tell me, what you would do?" Boudica looked me square in the eyes and afterwards those little hands rested on my cheeks as she answered, "I would do what I have done, and now that you have released much of your grief, I will stay with you while doing everything you request, I will also work to get you back on your feet. Tianshire, you must remember your time of troubles is at hand." Then a chill came down my back, and fear flooded my soul, as I fell down on my knees and started begging the Lord, "Oh Lord, you know my heart and love for you, why must you forsake me now and have me suffer that, which I have unshackled your people? I beg that you do not cast me among the evil of my mother's empire, as a lamb before its slaughter. Take me to be with you, as you did my brother. Why must I suffer as punishment for being righteous?" Then little Boudica whom was in my lap cried out to the Lord, "Oh great master, take me instead, so that my love for your servant Tianshire will not suffer in her. As I will suffer either way, let me suffer to spare her from this inordinate curse." I then believed and said, "Oh Lord, take me instead of Boudica. She needs time to study our teachings and prepare to do great works in your name." I now grabbed a hold of this little sister whom, I never had and told her, "Your safety and protection are more important to me than mine is." I told Boudica that it time to go to a mountaintop old day away so that the Lord will give us our duties." The priests told me, as we were preparing to visit with our Lord, the mountaintop was called Yurenev. In the times before the Garden, their ancestors fought an evil army, and it was on this peak that Yurenev could see where they were and how to stop them. After many months of hard fighting, his armies saved their homelands. It is today a special place for the Ensi. They seldom would allow anyone to go there; however, for this occasion, they gave our gang of girls' unlimited access. I then asked them if we could be there alone, especially no scribes. I added, "We may have no scribes, as neither mine nor Boudica's time has come. We must wait for my brother's spirit to give us the Lord's will." Then an elder said to me, "It is good that you learn to travel your new road. I tell you that all people say, 'you did great things in helping Oi's ministry.' I do not think he could have made it without you and the other women in your group that he loved so much. You are a true and loyal person. Oi was so lucky to have you." I then looked at him and said, "I thank you so much for your kind words, and want to reassure you that I was lucky to have Oi, as I know what he gave me will help me survive my times of troubles." We now started our walk to Yurenev. The priests were good about giving us our space; nevertheless, they refused to let us walk unprotected through these mountains. They had us ensconced on all angles. This gave us some reprieve, by knowing that others would help protect us. The elders said, "While in our lands, we cannot afford the loss of so many chosen by the Lord." I now could only wonder about being chosen by the Lord, or was I a toy that he had to share with our enemies. I am having difficulty in understand why our lives are as they happen. I saw so many people with so many defects in their body's and wondered, why is he blind and the woman whom can barely breathe or that child who cannot walk? Who decided what happens to each of us? We all must bear a burden on the long road that we walk. I also get confused about why we are where we are, in that whoever decided that this person would live in one nation and not the others. I then realize that most of these mysteries, I do not truly want to know their secrets. I even though I do not know the complete answer for why I must have my time of troubles, although Oi tried to sugarcoat it when telling me, if the Lord tells me, I must do it for his kingdom, next who am I to argue.

We are lucky that the refilling plates are still producing our meals. It was impossible not to talk to my family during this walk. They proved how much they cared about me, for I honestly think that if you were to stay in that corner, they would have stayed with me. In a strong way, I pray that they handle my departure better than I handled Oi's. Our mothers are letting Zala, Tolna and myself walk freely; nonetheless, they have their wings over little Boudica. They are extremely happy that we have a child so young with us. I know that they have painful memories about how hard they worked to protect and care for their children, only to be cast away into a life of shame and misery. I can be proud of all the reports I have seen where so many temples have adopted the widows in their areas and their community helping arms. In addition, their strong will to produce income for their temples has relieved the temples of any financial burdens associated with providing for their widows. The black land's tribes were slowly healing from the wounds inflicted by Rubina. Her raids were not producing the booty she wanted, so she now raided other parts of New Venus. Having been a raiding Flexster, she knew her way into our world. We were getting reports from those we traded with that the Garden was no more and that Dawedu was worshiping a new god. The lands that feared the Lord, was dwindling. The northern lands also complained that Lilith had vanished, and the throne was too preoccupied to give it any attention. As I think about it, I ask myself, can these issues change my times of troubles; therefore, I slowly rule them out and decide to worry about our continent. We are now climbing up a streamed to the top of this towering peak. It strangely has a dark-brown tree at the base of the final peak, which is only about 30 feet from its highest point. We are now forming a small circle on the tiny base of this top. We are lucky today because the sky is clear, and we can see greater distance. I can see the desert in my east where our sun, will descend tonight. To my west, I can see so much green land only knowing our borders by the stone walls that Rubina built to keep people in her empire. Recently, the tribes have planted soldiers against the walls, where they can kill the small raiding teams as they try to compromise the walls. They have also been able to hide in the tall grass and ambush them as they pass. Rubina's soldiers make too much noise when their marching boots hit the ground. This allows the hidden soldiers to determine where they are coming from, with an estimate telling how many fighters their party has. To the South of where we are, I can see Death Bay. It looks so peaceful up here, even though I can see a few killing ships floating on it. It looks so peaceful up here, even though I can see a few killing ships floating on it.

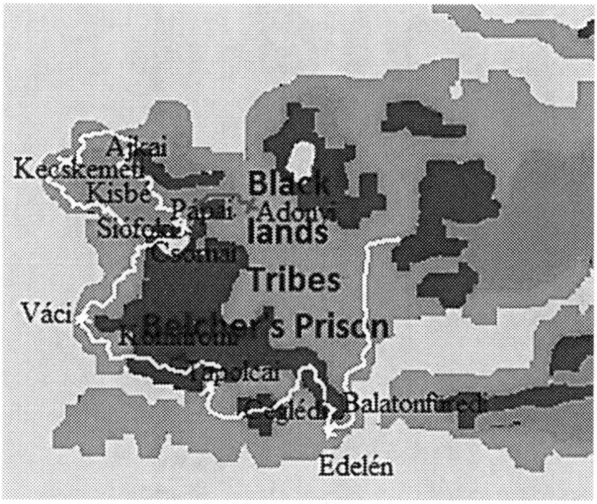

Tianshire's Times of Troubles

In my Northeast, I can see Mountain Lake in the Mountains that the Baracs occupy leaving much of their seacoast and green lands barren, except for ambushes. I can now hear a voice inside me telling me to enter Belcher's prison through the southern green lands between the sea and mountains. The green lands in Belcher's prison had many trees that yielded it too difficult to determine how many people lived there. We knew that many families had been split by the border, as the border was for Rubina's gain even though it split many clans. I was now searching my mind to see if I could capture one thing that might be good in my old land, and only one name kept appearing, Tsarsko. Tsarsko was my last hope of having a family member in that terrifying prison. The short nighttime hours are at hand, as I look down at a special tree. Then, without notice, the sky opens up with mighty swirling clouds. The sky is very dark, so much so that I cannot see in the tree. Now the large circle opens up a hole in the heavens, as I see three powerful beams filled with light give luminosity to the overcast ground. I can see a blazing fire in the part of this hole that is the closet to the ground. The fire rushes through the tree, yet I do not smell the smoke from a fire that burns. The ground between the tree and me is not burning with enlarging holes. The beauty of this vision causes not one of us to panic with any type of fear. As I gaze downhill, at the fire burning over the ground, I see a man walking inside the largest beam. The ground below him had no fire. That ground is shiny blue, as if water or the sky was flowing through it. Now I rub my eyes as if they are betraying me, for I see a white man with his robe on walking towards the tree. I run up, as something is holding onto my dress, not missing one-step. I, or we, want to see what this spirit or man is doing. I look down beside me to verify who was holding onto my dress, and it was the only small girl I could think of and that is little Boudica. Sure enough, she is here beside me. I ask her, "Boudica, you know that when you hold on to me like this, especially when we do not know for sure if danger is present, I cannot guarantee your safety. I hate having you where I do not know for sure you are protected. When you are with us, you know we all work hard to keep you safe because we all love you, as if you were a part of each of us." She apologizes; nevertheless, we know she will do it again. We have that special bond that requires us to be together. I will confess, when I am going somewhere, I eagerly wait for her to catch up with me. I can remember Oi walking slow enough that I could catch up with him. Something about having a young dedicated admirer cherishing our attention excites us to no end. As I am checking Boudica over to make sure she is not hurt and with my dress rub the light dirt on her face, the man comes toward us. Boudica alerts me, and as I turn around, he is already inside us. We both look at him, and since I am still on my knees from touching up my little girl, Boudica whispers in my ear, "Tianshire; this is Oi." I now turned around and saw it was Oi, without skin and bones. I now gave my special jester, which Boudica would jump up for me to hold her. I turned sideways enabling Boudica, likewise, to examine our situation. Oi came up to us and asked, "Do you know who I am?" I looked at him and said, "You are my brother Oi who left me. What happened to your body, since I thought you took it with you?" Oi then said, "My eternal body grew from inside me, and I shed my flesh, considering that I can no longer use it. You know that I told you I would not leave you. That is why I am here today, to see my two most favorite girls in all New Venus." That melted the ice between us as

Boudica worked her way free of me and went to run to Oi. Oi motioned for her to stop and said, "Boudica, no one may touch me for their safety." I then called Boudica back giving her a great hug and kisses on her cheeks and afterwards said, "My daughter, you must let me check things out first, okay my little girl." She agreed; therefore, while still holding her hand, I once again stood up. I now looked at Oi and asked, "What happened in the Valley of Mezokovácsházi?" He told me, "As I had told you so many times, I would walk our world no more. I could not figure out how I was to die, and surprisingly discovered that I was not to die. I felt so guilty when I saw you crying in my absence; nevertheless, I could not control this since it was the will of our Lord.

I will be speaking to you much in your heart and sometimes in spirit while you endure your times of troubles. Remember, you will live and once again be whole. When you suffer to the point that death could be a possibility, we will rebuild you. The reason you must suffer and shed blood on this land is for the sins of our mother. This will do great work in releasing the hold the demons have upon this land and force them out in the open where we can destroy them, for they will no longer have a claim over the righteous, who will slowly begin to break free. Only the blood from one of Rubina's daughters, who must be righteous, can break this curse. Your blood in the land will destroy the evil our mother has done. Be strong and remember these things will also pass." This totally has thrown me off tract. At least, I now know why it must be me and that this is a spiritual war. Oi currently tells me, "Your path has been given unto you, and its days have a number. The sooner you start, the earlier you can rejoin your loves and begin your great ministry." I then asked him, "Do not forget, or forsake me my brother." Boudica currently waved as Oi once again went into the light. I now started back up the hill holding Boudica with my tight hug. She asked me, "Tianshire, will you let me go with you, so that I can tend to your injuries?"

I told her, "Boudica, you must stay here. If you were to be captured, it could destroy the future of this nation. You cannot risk that. You must be a good girl and stay back here preparing my ministry. We arrived at our campfire to see all our family sitting quietly around the fire. Then our mommies came after us, crying, while screaming at the same time. Our mommies scolded us, rightfully, afterwards for rushing to a stranger.

They told us, "Young ladies and especially little girls do not rush up to strangers; they hide from them. Everyone expects females to protect themselves first, as we seldom pose threats. I told Boudica, "Honey, never do what I did today, grab hold of a mommy and put your magic on them, so they will make sure you are safe. They then asked me, "Who was that white person?" I told them, "It was Oi who was telling me that my time is at hand." We were currently sitting at our fireplace preparing to talk as a family. I told them, "The time of my troubles is now, and I must leave you and go into the dungeon of my mother's prison. You have your missions. I especially ask that at least two of our mothers watch after little Boudica. I will be gone for five years. You will find me in the Adonyi lands in their largest village. I ask Tolna and Zala to help our future chosen Queen, selected by our Lord.

She will be a blessing to you. If any worry about not finding a husband, you are putting yourself through great heartache for no reason. When I free this land, the Lord will give the husbands to each one that wants to marry, except for Boudica, who as Queen can take who she wants. I hope that most of you return with me, as my ministry shall begin. Tolna and Zala, you have great knowledge. Please keep the fires burning for our Lord." I now asked the mothers, "Please care for my precious sisters and our cherished child. The Lord will continue to be with you for your healing ministries. We must have as many people freed from the suffering caused by Rubina inasmuch possible. I thank you for those who will be working so hard for the kingdom of our Lord and please take care of this rambunctious little fellow." We now gave each, our hugs as Tolna asked me, "How should we call ourselves?" I told my sisters Zala and Tolna to say they were the 'sisters of Oi and Tianshire,' for the mothers say they are the 'mothers of Oi and Tianshire',' and that Boudica was the 'Queen sent from the Lord.' The Lord gave me an official manuscript with Oi, Boudica and my signatures. I would give this to the scribes as I went down this mountain on the border. I gave each one of my loves a big hug and wiped away their tears. I asked them, "Who cries now for someone leaving?" I currently started down the mountains into the green lands. Dömsöd said, "We did not clean, sleep with, and feed Oi as we did you. A mother cries when her daughter leaves as a father cries when his son leaves." Esztergomi asked, "Tianshire, will you stay here tonight? I told my girls, "I must cross the border at night, for try during the day would be impossible." Everyone's one said good-bye to me, and I slowly walked down to the priests and scribes. I gave a few of the elders the manuscript the Lord had just given us, and asked them, "Please honor the women Oi, and I have left behind. The Lord needs them for our people, so they can stay strong until my return. When I return I will need them. I can only pray that your love for the Lord will guide you to help them. They are chosen from the Lord, as also are all who love the Lord in the black land's tribe." I could see a glow come over their faces, as I know they never before considered themselves chosen. At least, they were not chosen to do what I must do, for, in reality, it was my mother, who chose this for me. They asked whom I was talking with at the burning tree, and why Boudica was in such a dangerous place. I told them, "We were talking to our brother, Oi, as the Lord wanted to ensure I knew why it was I who had to go through these troubles.

He also worried about our girls and if I asked for the temples to help them. You will see that this manuscript is written on a documenting surface that we do not yet have on New Venus." They looked at it again and confessed to seeing the difference. I told them it was now time for me to enter my mother's empire. They asked me, which way I was going to go in, and I told them, "Oi said to enter through Balatonalmádi." They then told me to be careful because they prefer to hide and wait until their victims are too far to escape and next ambush them. I then asked them, "Where did they learn that from?" After smiling, I started the one-week walk to the Balatonalmádi. When out of sight of the priests, I removed my dress and tore it into one-foot strips. I tied one across my breasts and another around my waist. I then tied one more vertical with my genital area running it into my waistband in the front and the back. I now took the remaining part of my dress and wrapped it around my waist. This can be used as a blanket at night and for bandages if I am dripping blood, which is great for trappers. I now crawled up beside a small stream and dipped my hand it the water rubbing the water on me as I throw dirt on top of it. My mothers would be furious currently; then again, I am the one with white tannish skin and a need to look like the dirt if I am spotted. Oi had taught me how to eat from the land, as we did much while growing up, because we never trusted the food, Rubina was preparing. I must avoid catching game, because I can in no way make a fire. There should be many night holes in this area. If I find one, I will sleep in it tonight. I found an apple tree, so that will give me some energy, and of course take the sting from the hunger in my belly. Belcher, my father, never talked much about mountains and green lands, as he always lived in the brown lands or deserts. He found one remote single hill mountain. It rose slowly from the desert; conversely, it had a very steep rock cliff on the ocean side. He knew that the ocean winds would blow ships past this shore. Belcher could see them long before they could see him. Even when they call him, all they saw from the sea was a gigantic cliff that no one ever tried to climb. Belcher could work his way back to the desert and there disappear. He also could stay in one of the countless caves that spotted the backside of the mountain. He always told us that these caves did not feel like caves made from nature. The areas were perfect for living and multiple escape routes. We always ignored him; on the other hand, now that I know about the Szombathelyi Empire and the Empire of the Hajdú-Bihar, I can see where they would have built some protection areas around the ocean shores. Our desert and hill top land was called Kisbe, and that is where we are from Belcher stayed. Many other nations and planets flooded people into this mainland.

I know that the Lord gives many a chance to leave and go to other worlds with transportation provided by Mempire, and those who did not go were destroyed. Notwithstanding, other worlds starting planting people on New Venus, and these people were warned from their deities to be good. The trouble had been that the children of Eve have caused all the problems, Dawedu to the North, and Rubina in the South. Rubina was not a daughter of Eve, yet she married my father, which grafted her into the Garden family. Rubina, who was a Flexster and the Flexsters were from the five sisters who lived in the Garden with Eve. The Flexsters attracted all the bad people and the most of their earlier evils were against people from other lands. It was after they felt invincible that they turned on the sisters' tribes. I slide into a hole that I found. It has much brush growing in it. Luckily, I have found no thorns. I will find out tomorrow if any poisonous vegetation, like poison veleno. That will give you painful blisters from head to foot. Once I was settled in and almost to sleep, I heard some sneaky footprints.

Passing by me were two raiders, and they were preparing to do some snooping around in the black land's tribe. I freeze and one of them walks by me, yet when his foot starts to drop in the hole, he swings around, plants it back on the ground and naturally walks away, not even looking forward to seeing what he avoided. I would had been a duster if he had looked backward anyway they are gone now. I am glad that I was down for the remainder of the night, or I could have walked into them. I hear some more footprints immediately; these are careless and moving faster. Here comes a mid-size bear, which is moving fast. He is not concerned about me, because my tracks were superseded by one of the raiders. This bear is moving fast, so he is getting ready for his kill. Just a few minutes later, I hear two screams. I wonder how he could get both. I decided it might be best for me to find a good sturdy branch, and next cut out a point of my knife. I was more concerned about the raiders in this area and forgot we have some hungry beasts. I am going to continue soaking the dirt into my skin to keep my scent down. I will mash some wild berries over me to control my scent, which the raiders are also good at discovering.

I will have to walk slowly at night, and I am going to walk on some of the paths. Carefully, and listening all around me. When dawn comes, I will start looking for a big tree, climb up, and find a branch to sleep. Now that a have a trimmed branch for fighting off animals and maybe raiders, which do not have a bow and arrow, I should not be as vulnerable. Ouch, oh I am hurting. What has happened to my foot? I look down, and two inches pointed thorn stick out the bottom of my foot. These thorns grow on special thick bushes and there are two branches wrapped into a circle and tied to stay in place. They were tucked along the road with loose sticks to help camouflage them. This is my first bloodshed in my father's prison. That stupid thorn puts a long gash in the bottom of my foot, because my foot bone blocked it, compelled it to go sideways, rather than straight in my foot. If I had known about these sneaky items of war, I would had been watching closely. I should have stayed in the hole until morning. I found a thin rock and with some of my dress torn into another strip tied the rock to the bottom of my foot. At least, this way, when I step down I have something to support this big gash. Now is the time to find a sizable tree and climb up it. I can see a big tree on the other side of the nearby field. Yours truly will crawl across the field then when I get close to go up. As I crawl closer, I can see that it is a cherry tree, which is great.

I can eat the cherries while I am recovering for a few days. I must stay off the ground. Upon arrival up I go, having to use both arms with only one leg to support me. Somehow, I make it up the tree as far as I can go. I reach around me and start collecting some cherries. When I collect them, I immediately eat them. The leaves on this tree will help fight the sunlight and make my sleeping much easier. I usually only stay asleep for a few hours, then slowly eat some cherries, while listening and watching for any activity. I take the rock off the bottom of my foot and tie the bandage on a nearby branch so that my blood soaks into the tree may be helping my mission. The constant stinging of this wound is hammering me senseless. Without my feet, I am in big trouble early. I have noticed a large number of raiders snooping around. I can bet that they got hold of a temple worker and through their tortures obtained information about me. It cannot be good to have a massive manhunt for me and still be a one-day walk to the border. My luck runs out after five days. My foot is better; however, I will have to walk on my toes for one leg. I was sleeping on a branch when I felt something on me. When I looked, it was a snake. I rolled on the branch while shaking myself, and the snake broke free; nevertheless, so did I.

I fell down straight on another branch shaking the branch hard when I heard a crack and saw the birds flocking away. Snake hit the ground. I worked my way back to the trunk and then lowered myself one more branch and rotated around to the other side of the tree. Suddenly, the split branch begins to drop some more. I hear a man screaming below me, as the snake puts a big bite into him. Their leader yells out as he looks up the tree, "No snake broke that branch; I can see we will have to cut this tree down." This does not faze me, if the cut down this tree, the branches will cushion the fall, and as I am halfway up to its truck, I should have enough time to crawl out to the grass fields. I will hold as tight as possible, until that stupid arrow got my leg, and down I go, straight for the ground. Then, just as I am to hit the ground, some raiders catch me. These raiders look different, as they have gone up now to finish removing the branch that I broke. These men have teeth that are somewhat normal and not the long fangs I always heard they had. Their skin wrappings, although showing many wears, do not have blood stains. They ask me, "Whom are you?" I smile and pretend that the pain from the arrow in my leg is hurting too much, which is not to say it is not nauseating with pain.

They begin to examine me, and one says, "She does not have whipped marks, thus she must be from the black land's tribe." I ponder now, do I confess to being among the enemy that kills them on day-to-day or do I say the daughter to their Queen? The last one could be a double edge sword, in that if they are steadfast to my mother, they will take me to her, and that would be the end of me honestly fast. If they are not loyal to her, afterwards they will kill me for revenge. They give me a broken branch to stick in my mouth, subsequently as one holds me down the other two carefully take out the arrow. I am lucky that this arrow has no razor blade head. That tells me they must not be raiders. They are now rubbing some leaves on the incision and next after covering it, wrap it with the remains of my dress. Then two of them left me on the back of the third one motioning for me to hold his neck. They place me into the position, they want me, and while one is holding me, the other places my arms around their comrade's neck. I get the message; they want to carry me piggyback. I can only wonder why. One of the other ones is taking the leaves with my blood on them and running toward our stream. I can see that if he puts them in the stream, they will spread out away from us. The three of them now carry me off to somewhere. I can feel no danger in the man whom is holding me, so in an attempt to build up some favorable points with them; I rest my head on his shoulder.

They stop and rotate me among themselves, as I think growing into a big girl may have put some weight on me. This next night, they find some small brush and lay me down behind it. They seem not to worry about their footprints, as I guess no one can see them tonight. They leave one to watch me, while the other two are rummaging the nearby area. I point to my injured leg showing it to my guard. Therefore, I motion for him to go away. He looks at my leg and me and then goes to join our local exploration attempts. I just fall back on the ground to rest, for I know Belcher's prison is not far. I look up at the night sky and see a bright star above us. It hits me that if this star is for me, then everyone in the world knows where I am. I now close my eyes and ask the Lord, "Lord, why is that star who is so bright above me?" Then I hear a voice in my head say, "Because you are the chosen one, therefore, the demon spirits are warned not to touch you; your suffering is to be from the humans only. The demons will work hard to keep the people away from you, so your suffering will be less and most likely cause disappointment in the heavens." I guess this will have to be the deal. Now, one of the men takes off the wrapping on my leg and soaks another rag he had made from my dwindling dress. They take their knife, I pierced a small cut into the wound, both leg and foot.

They now rub a new root they found in the incisions once they drained them. They place two new kinds of leaves on my wounds and wrap them again. I had been with these people one complete day now and no one has talked. Knowing we speak the same language, I ask them, "What are you going to do with me?" One looks at me and says, "We must get you to our small village and our medicine man because your leg is showing some infection. The roots we have put on your wound should help drain it. If you are found to be from Rubina, you will die." I then told them, "The only thing I am guilty of is getting lost from my friends, especially while not listening to them." They hand me some nuts and berries they had found, and we ate together. They were getting relaxed with me, which was not advantageous to me, as I was not going anywhere. They carried me again the next day as one of them told me he was getting close to his village in the Balatonalmádi. Because that is where I was going, I asked them, "Will you take me to Balatonalmádi?" According to Oi's spirit, we had a few loyal friends who lived there. They agreed to do so, since I had to be judged. When we arrived at their village, some elders came out to great us. One of them yelled out, "This is Tianshire, daughter of Rubina. She has come here today so she can tell her mother evil things about us. Tie her upside down on the beating rope." In my mind, I hear, click, click, and pain here you come. Upside down, oh how I hate being upside down as the blood is rushing to my head. Now, another man says, "We must spare her, for she had been in the black land's tribes as a Saint for Belcher's God." They all loved Belcher's God, as this was free from Rubina. The elder looked me over and said, "What Saint covers themselves in dirt awaiting in ambush to kill us. I remember a man telling me that Tianshire was dead. This woman is here to kill and destroy. Remove her wrappings." Next, a couple of young men came over to me and unwrapped my wrappings. I could not resist, because I was upside down and my injured leg would hurt when I moved. Nevertheless, if I fight to keep two men from striping me, then they will only send more who were being angrier. Where are my friends? They must fear this mob. Now the elder says, "Bring all the men here, so we can show this killer what we do to women who come to deceive and destroy us." This was emotionally the lowest point I had ever been. I was continuously with Oi or my father, and they always made sure I was treated like a young woman. When we were joined by our mothers, they enforced strict courtesies be rendered to us.

I presently hang here as a cow would before being butchered. It is bad enough when they all look at me, yet when the girls laugh at me, I think how stupid they are, because they have nothing different than me, thus when those boys are looking at me, they are actually looking at all of us. The men in this place must have lived sheltered lives as act as if they have never seen it before. Then a man yells, "Take your look at it before we beat it." He is practicing with that ungodly whip by slashing the tree. Now, I am thinking that whip is going to hurt worse than the loss of any dignity. Then the first one hit me across my face lashing also around my head. I think one million demons are sticking needles in me now. That is the first lash that I have received in my life. Next, another cutting lashes across my pain filled face. Why does not he save time and slash me with a knife instead? He waits so long between my lashes swinging his whip in circles. He should take pride in making me look like a monster. I will have to hide my face everywhere I go. Then he unleashes another lash across my breasts, followed by one across my legs. I hear another man say, "Remember, do not strike her womb least she be with a child." "The monster snaps another lash across my legs, this time about three inches higher. He now yells, "Take it down; it is not evil."

I think, 'how can this be a test for evil; they remove my clothing, gawk at me like perverts, destroy my appearance buy literally cutting me alive, then simply declare, let her live for she is innocent.' I can almost understand why my mother kills so many of them for sport. As my body, crashes into the ground and with all my blood that is spread everywhere. I now cannot even verify if I have enough blood to function. Four teenagers, two boys, and two girls wrap me inside a bearskin rug of some kind and slowly take me into the woods behind this beating place. They start putting some sort of lotion on my cuts and ploddingly clean of the blood, yet best of all they give me a root to chew on. Something in the root is dulling my pain. The pain is so strange in that once it hits you; it tries stay. It is always unwelcome and is currently my number-one enemy.

I notice that the boys and girls are paired off as couples and working diligently with me. I can sense the girls watching the boys when they are working on my breast lash, motioning for them to work on the legs. They defuse my lower area by cleaning it and wrapping a rag to conceal it. They have a shirt laying on the grass nearby, which they will most likely put on me afterwards. I subsequently ask the girls, "Are those your boyfriends?" Then they tell me, "No, they are our lovers.

We have tried to get the elders to marry us; however, they refuse to let any of our generations marry and have children. They claim that too many have died and that the future has no hope." I then asked, "Why are you helping me?" They all said, "Because it was wrong how they punished you. My uncle told him that you slept with your head on his shoulder most of the way. An evil person would have searched hard to find a way to escape. They even left you unguarded at your campsite, and you stayed, as when they came back you were asleep. Just know that he who brought you back is very angry. I am so glad they stopped at five; they usually stop at twenty for females. Each time he hit you, no one cheered. Everyone looked so angry. We could feel the anxiety while he stops and all rush to see if you were okay. Look around us; you are a hero now with us." I then said, "Thanks for your kindness and faith in my righteousness. I tell you that as of this day, you are both married, and I will bless your wombs with many children who will grow old with you." Next, a man comes rushing up to me and yells, "It is she; this is she, the one I saw a few days ago in the Valley of Mezokovácsházi. She is chosen by the Lord to free all from the grips of Rubina. How could you have done these horrible shameful things and then whip a prophet from the God of Belcher?

What will we do now? You should not have shamed her and made her flesh unholy. I just thank the God of Belcher that she only got five lashes." The people now rushed over and carried me to one of their caves. My two couples stayed close to me as if to control what happened to me. Then one of the elders ordered them to leave, and I yelled back, "If they leave, later so must I. Come here my four friends and help me." The elder yelled back, "Why do they get you, oh great prophet?" I looked backward and said, "When I was naked, they gave me clothes, when I had pain they cared for me, when no other wanted me, they wanted me and prayed for their forgiveness. When they were single I married them." The elder then said, "How can you marry them when we have forbidden it?" I pointed up to the sky, and a bolt of lightning hit this man burning him to his death instantaneously. I then asked, "Let him who has cause with me over this marriage tell me now, or forever hold their peace." They all rejoiced and gave their congratulations. History had been made here today, as the town's scribes recorded my last phrase to put it in all weddings on New Venus, which soon it was with a few modifications changing, 'let him who has cause with me to let him who has cause with this marriage.' The parents of these fresh couples came up and told their children how proud they were of them.

The children then asked their parents if they could take me to the pass where their lands ended. The parents granted permission. They now got me up and put the dress on me. It was short and loose, so I think climbing trees will not be too cumbersome. As we walk slowly, I am trying to decide if I have any part that does not hurt. It appears that one hurt can jump into many other hurts, which forgetting about the logic of this because everything hurts. My right leg has taken four blows, one from the thorn, one from the arrow, and two from the whip that got both legs in the fleshy part where they could cut deeper. I am barely walking. The kids, although they are my age, are troubleshooting with my bandages, trying to find the one that both protect me and allow me to run. I will be a funny site trying to run. The girls also did one more thing nice for me, which was to make a wrapping that covered my eyes and whip marks on my face. I have one massive cut on my forehead just above my eyes. It is enough to cause me pain when I blink my eyes. The other lash was halfway up my nose. I truly feel that he had to be going for my eyes and when he missed the top one, he decided to make sure my face was disfigured so that all could see this lash. Now I would be known as a bandit.

This was better than having everyone stare at me in disgust or plagued. They went with me for about one hour, and as we were going up, a hill stopped at the top and told me they could go no farther. I asked them why and they told me it was the border for their tribes and if one was caught passing it, many people would die from Rubina's raiders. I remember hearing about this law as this gave Rubina the power to control the areas, because even in fear of their lives they would not pass those borders. I told them I could not make it on my own, and understood why they would not go on, thus in desperation I asked them if they stayed with me for a couple of weeks until the swelling, and infection goes down. They all agreed enthusiastically so I asked for their names, which were girls first then boys, 'Dúzs, Pécsi, Ajkai, and Ebergoc.' They spoiled me, by making a comfortable place for me to rest on their furs. They checked and reapplied their whip salves each morning and night. The girls would work my legs for around one hour each day. They were afraid that all this laying around would hurt my legs and that the cuts had to be carefully attended to so that I could walk and run again. Actually, I did not do that much running except for playing with Zala and Tolna. The only way that I am going to do it now is by using my head, which so far has not worked that well.

Dúzs and Pécsi stay with me nursing me non-stop while Ajkai and Ebergoc do all the food gathering, hunting, and protection. They are going to make good couples. They sleep apart from me at night. I have an idea what they are doing, because most new couples go at it heavy in the beginning of their marriages. Dúzs and Pécsi come to me in the mornings, both with their hair and clothing all put into the perfect order, as they have double-checked each other, then gives me some food, and starts working on my bandages. They are somewhat clumsy, so I ask them if everything is okay. They stutter that they have no problems. I feel for them, because they did something that was the greatest thing in their lives so far, yet now comes the shame and shyness. I let them off the hook, "Dúzs and Pécsi, why do you look strange today? Have you enjoyed your first few nights with your husbands? Fear not and have no shame, as you have done nothing wrong or and followed the same road your mother has traveled." They relaxed a little now, so I told them, "Are you two going to get alone and compare your adventures?" They asked me if that were okay. I told them to go up the tree over there, and if I need you; I will whistle, now go, and talk the things that wives talk about."

They rushed off like two children; however, those walks will end when they give birth to their first child. My recovery took longer than we expected; nevertheless, I am ready to move on, a little slower than I hoped, yet I am still alive and have fond memories of my new friends. I am now officially in Balatonalmádi whatever that if good for. Dúzs and

Pécsi told me much about the people who live here. They do not sleep aboveground and only in their caves. They try to keep their sons whom Rubina is demanding her high percentage. Therefore, Rubina comes in and takes twice her quota kills every elder she finds. The last few years, their quota had been waiting at the border. This forces Rubina to accept this, although she wants to kill every here, she needs people to be here in the event of a raid from the black land's tribes. I can see a wide road that goes from the sea up into the mountains. As I am sitting here trying to figure a good way to follow this road and not get . . .

Why do I have such a terrible headache, a bump on my head, and tied and stretched in the weird wooden machine? One hour later, this ugly thing whose face reminds me of a mouse, wearing a yellow ragged cap, two long strings coming out of the front part of his nose staring at me through his minute blue eyes, locks onto me, which produces fear. His face is scared and has tiny lesions with his hair behind are floppy ears and mouth hanging open with his tongue sticking out as he moves toward me. I wonder what this ogre is going to do to me. He looks me over sneezing all over me. My mothers got angry with us when we would sneeze on each other. They claimed that would spread sickness. I am horrified at the thought that something from this reject would touch me. He pulls down on his lever, and now I can feel these ropes pulling my legs and arms in opposite directions. He pulls it again and can feel my muscles tightening up and my bones working to separate. He afterwards laughs and says, "I will keep you like this until I get ready for my dinner." He then picks up a log and strikes me with both hands of the log straight in my belly where one of the lash marks were. He then walks to the other side of me, and strikes my other leg with that painful log he is striking me. He gives a hideous laugh and while crying I asked him, "Why do you do this to me?" He laughs while laying down his log and says, "It is so fun." He then picks up a thin nail with a sharp razor like top. He walks over to me, and starts sticking it in me repeating it. With myself being stretched like this, each injection hurts twice as hard. When will this evil demon stop? Just then, I hear a pounding noise as I see him try to make it to the lever, yet his attacker strikes him in the back of his head and then continues to strike him. I cry out, "My hero, can you release this lever." As the lever is being released, I can still hear the solid hits on the torturer. I am trying to open my eyes; nevertheless, I cannot control my eyelids. I feel a familiar touch massaging my face and slowly my eyes return vision to me. I feel a soft kiss on my right cheek, and I know whom these are. I now see Dúzs and Ajkai, and I ask them, "Why are you here?" Dúzs tells me that some raiders caught the four of them, "We fought hard; nonetheless, they got Pécsi with an arrow through her head and Ebergoc a spear in his back. When Ebergoc fell, they rushed us from behind, while leaving their front unguarded. We went over the rocks and ran like crazy to the cave of the bears and afterwards backtracked to the nearby stream and jumped on it until we recognized your hill and next came looking for you, only to find you lying in front of a man letting him play with you." I was still in too much pain to talk, so I just leaned forward and kissed her cheek. I could not pull back so I rested my head on her shoulder. Then Pécsi came behind me and lifted me up, and Dúzs got up to stabilize my right side. Dúzs after that told us we must get out of here fast in case this pervert's friends come looking for him. He tells us, "We will go to that stream and swim along the banks until we make it to Edelén."

The swimming or mostly walking in the water was good for me. It kept a lot of pressure off my joints, which had taken a beating. I am confident that with some rest for about one month, I will be able to use them again; unfortunately, I will not be capable to use them in my aging years. I can only hope that if I make it out of here, the war is not long hence they will not have to carry my crippled body around to our battle sites. The stream is now moving out into an endless wide meadow. We cannot take a chance on being spotted and must stay in the high grass. We can see a small patch of trees ahead. Usually they are following a stream. Pécsi recommends we follow the stream, yet from a safe distance. Then at night, he can sneak over to the Creek and get the water we need. I marvel at how high the grass is. Dúzs then tells me, "That is what happens when all the sons are taken to Rubina's navy, and the others work making her ships around the Bay of Tapolcai. Before enlisting them to build her ships, Rubina went to their closest of kin and recorded the addresses and names. If the builder would escape, her police immediately would go back and kill of their next of kin, two per day. They would take them to the center of that area, in front of the residents took their swords, and cut off their heads. Few escaped and the ones that did surrendered within a few days only to live in shame and misery for the rest of their days for causing the deaths of their loved ones. Naturally, with few men, the woman migrated to other tribes and delivered babies for the men of those other provinces. As the grass kept getting higher predators, found it easy to kill their prey. With their prey, not reproducing to keep their dwindled population the predators some found themselves starving. The Edelén live along the seas on their southern peninsula.

Rubina, knowing she has crippled this land to a point of total collapse only collects a reasonable amount for their tax. She plans to build Prisoner of War (POW) camps on this uninhabited green land so when she destroys the black land's tribes, she can keep her demon's food supply available. The Edelén had suffered the wrath of Rubina doing things that most thought to be beyond sane. She would have the children gathered, and then her soldiers cut off their heads. She would eat the children in front of the parents. The Edelén never recorded or even talk about these brain-twisting horrors. I now hear something and turn around to see, when I trip on something. The next thing I know we are surrounded. I look over at Dúzs and Pécsi to see them evilly staring at me with a long sharp knife in one hand and a rope in the other. All the men on the horses around us have a whip in one hand. I look at Dúzs and ask her, "Why; I thought you loved me, and we were soul friends, yet now you look at me with hate in your eyes." Dúzs then told me, "Tianshire, I have hated you and your family my whole life and vowed revenge against Rubina. When we kill you, it will only be a small justice for us; nevertheless, it will be a victory, for when we hear your cry; we will know they are coming from Rubina's daughter." I afterwards ask her, "Why must I pay for my mother's sins?" Dúzs then said, "Because her blood runs in you." She currently rushed to me and tripped on a rock; therefore, as I had moved her knife went deep into one of the warrior's horses, which went crazy. He spooked the other horses, which were now throwing the soldiers everywhere. One landed on Dúzs and the other on Pécsi's head. He died instantly. I ran to the side of a startled horse, grabbed one of the matrimonial ropes, and jumped on his back with my belly on his back, so I could reach over and get the other bridal string. I then, used then-new adrenaline to bounce up in the saddle and prepare to run. Dúzs also jumped on a horse and chased me through the grass. I have no idea where I could be.

With only small trees spotting the fields that, surround the village in the lower meadow on the other side of the valley's floor. I see a heavy forest about one mile to my left. It runs all the way down and up to the blinding white thick clouds. I slowly walk over to the forest line when I drop fast to the ground. I hear something walking toward me. I do not know which way to move, left or right. What I will do is roll adjusting my position, as it gets closer. Soon I see a horse; with no rider, walking passed me. This has to be one of the soldier's horses, resembling the one I lost. I start to move to it when something hits me in my head again. Down I go, only to wake up the few minutes later with my feet tied with a rope that Dúzs is holding. My head and shoulders are dragging along the ground. At least, this is a grassland so only my dress is being soiled. She stops and ties me to a tree leaving me back exposed. I start at her again, "Dúzs, how can you blame me, for as my mother was killing I was in the black land's tribes healing and saving? Does that sound like a bad person to you? You know that I poured my heart and my love out to you. Why would you want to kill someone who has loved you? I am the one that you cared for, and tried to make feel better. Why must you punish me? Am I my mother's keeper?"

She now took her small whip, and lashed me on my back another time saying, "I told you that Rubina's blood ran in your veins, and all this hallowed ground cries for your blood." She whipped me again. The pain has returned for his glory. This last lash swung around the back and hit the rope holding my hands cutting it. I am now rubbing it again the bark. I am rubbing it back and forth to generate heat. She hits me again on my back. These lashes sting a lot but do not cut into my skin. This last lash splits the rope holding my hands. I keep them frozen so she will not know. Yikes, Dúzs is walking toward me; fortunately, for me, she stops and begins talking, "Tianshire; I have great news for your dinner tonight. The mayor of the village over there has invited you for dinner tonight." I then ask her, "Why does he want me for dinner?" Dúzs tells me, "He thinks your muscles are toned, both arms and legs pretty much fat-free." I ask her, "Dúzs, what does tone muscles have to do with their dinner?" Dúzs then replies with a smile, "Tianshire, I do not think you understand because you are the village's dinner tonight. My job is to tenderize your flesh with this tenderizing whip. The swelling hold some of the delicious juices in." That is when I thought, "Oh crap, I am the dinner. That is not good at all." She swung the lash again across my upper back. She forgot that she was closer to the tree and that allowed the end of the whip to zip around the tree where I could grab it; I pulled the rope as hard as I could and smashed her head into the tree. She went down; nevertheless, she was still conscious. I asked her, "Dúzs, if I let you live will you promise not to kill me." Dúzs then told me, "Tianshire, I will hunt all over your father's prison to kill you." I told her, "I love you too much to kill you." I then reached my face down and kissed her cheek. She afterwards reached her arms up hugging me and said into my ear, "Tianshire, do you know how hard it is to kill someone you love?" I said, "No Dúzs, nor do I ever want to find out. I have to tie you up, can you help me?" She said sure and stood up to the tree and told me to walk the whip around in when it was in the front, she made one of her special knots. This was so strange, "Enemies working together. When she finished I went over to her cheek and kissed her again. I saw tears starting to fall down her face. Therefore, I told her, "I love you, and I need to borrow your bow and arrows." She told me, "Sure Tianshire, take whatever you want. What is mine is yours." I knew that I had to go, yet for this few minutes I sat on the ground in front of Dúzs and cried. As I hobbled down the valley into the forest, I could feel the importance of getting out of here.

Thus far, the Balatonalmádi and Edelén proved to be dangerous. I do not want to call them wicked, because I need to look at what they have been through first. I cannot shake off my mind what Dúzs just told me. When one suffers so hard and painfully long, any strike that has any form of relationship to the source must be considered bad. I am going to pay for the sins of someone I have always hated. It just cannot be any other way. I know that Dúzs loves me; however, war is war and a strike against me is a strike against their enemy. I am going to Ceglédi, which is a Kingdom that has been stronger than the others that surround it. They have always stood strong against my mother, who avoids them because they know many magic words that hurt her demons. The Ceglédi had also blocked out all people from entering their lands. Therefore, when I go there I must keep a low profile. Shrew, an arrow just went by. It had a knife carved tip and not the razor tipped ones I got from Dúzs. I stop just for a second hiding behind a tree and look back to see Dúzs following me. How did she get loose so fast? I should have known that a whip would not be the first choice to tie someone up. Oh well, I do not care, because I would not want her tied up too long, and then be placed in possible danger.

I see something disturbing behind Dúzs and that is a mountain Lion. He rushes and leaps upon her, clawing and biting, ripping parts of her body into the ground. I load an arrow and with the skills, my daddy put in me, let my first arrow go. It lands in the Lion's neck, and this is where my father told me to get that second shot off fast, because that beast is mad now. I get an additional shot off and another hit in the jaw area. It enters his jaw and then cuts its way to the base of his neck, immediately paralyzing him. I see three men come out of the bushes, rush to the Lion with their knives turn him over, and stab his heart. I now start to move toward the Lion, and another man jumps out of the bush in front of me yelling for me to go away. I point to the Lion, then make a circle through the air that encompasses all them, and motion for them to take it off. As I move closer, the three of them, stand up and point their bows with an arrow loaded at me. I stop, take of Dúzs's bow and arrow, then put it on the ground; next put my hands up afterwards continue walking to them. When I get there I look at Dúzs's body, and what a mess. The Lion ripped half her chest open. He must have dug in deep when he clawed into her and with his ripping motion, destroyed her inside. Strangely, her face is still okay and clean. I fall down beside her face and start petting her hair and kissing her check while trying to hold my tears back, "My Dúzs, why did you fight your heart? Why did fight someone else's war? Why could you not see that I was innocent of your charge?"

I think what made Dúzs special to me was her being my first friend in Belcher's prison. I can just think about these three men think me to be crazy for crying over someone who was trying to kill me. Dúzs could have shot me many times, as she was such a perfect shot. I think that if it had come down to the wire, she would have found a way to lose gracefully. I am just so disappointed that she believed someone had to die because I lived. The four men come back with shovels and one of them lifts me up from Dúzs, as I begin crying louder. He holds me in his arms and pets my hair. My 'mothers' told me that when a man pets a child's head, it means they have children at home. He keeps telling me it will be okay. The four of them dig a three-foot deep hole and lay Dúzs's body in it and then start filling the hole. I walk across the dirt packing it in. They lay some stones on her grave, and after that, I go to lie on top of her grave as the men all turn to take the tiger away. Then they all return and tell me, "Child you must go with us." I ask them, "Why?" They tell me,

"Your friend's brothers will be here soon, and they will revenge you. We will take you to our village for your judgment."

I then asked, "Why must I be judged?" They told me, "It is the law of our land, which if you are judged as good, you may live in our lands." I asked, "What lands do we go to?" They told me, "We go to Ceglédi because you have so many injuries that much time will be needed to heal you." I then said, "Okay" and started to follow them. We went up the hill, and at the top, they had a large almost empty wagon. I asked them, "What happened to the Lion?" They pointed down, for they had wrapped him in fur and put him in a special storage container under the wagon. Then two of them lifted me up to the back openings while a third one said, "Go ahead, and go in there, young woman." Thus, I did as they said to do. As I stepped in, I could see so many furs all laid out; accordingly, I stopped to look back at them, and they just motioned to me that it was okay. Then they made the motion of head on pillows to tell me it was all right to sleep. Moreover, to sleep, I went fast, with no worries, for the way I figured it, if these men wanted me, they could have killed me and tossed me in the same grave as Dúzs. After all, I was doing nothing to defend myself. Then one man looked back at me, missed up the furs some, and told me, "Trying to hide you better." We seemed to move steady for the next few days, while on the third day, a large gang came riding up beside us and asked the people if they had seen a little girl. My men made a joke about this;

"Shame, shame on you,
Little girls you ***no*** do"

This had been a famous saying throughout our provinces that were developed when first civilizing the alien tribes. These search groups would all leave in both anger and shame when my boys would sing this riddle. After all, it is rather strange to be riding around looking for a little girl. Then my life got dangerous again when these warriors started offering rewards. I told the men in this group, "They will never pay a reward, but kill any who tries to collect it." They agreed; nevertheless, told me, 'Honey, you stay down and hidden. We know how they deal; unfortunately, not all people know this. We will take the green land route that goes over the little mountain and comes up into Ceglédi on the seacoast side. Old people, such as us, usually travel this route if trouble is brewing elsewhere. This took longer; nevertheless, I can now see the Statues of Egerbocs. Belcher had always told me about these; nevertheless, Rubina would not let him stay out that long with the children. The legend was that a band of thieves who escaped from their prison to hide her. Their master told them to surrender, or they would die.

They failed to surrender so they all were turned into rocks for eternity. There are almost one hundred statues here, many of the elegant beautiful women in their formal evening gowns and ravishing hairstyles. There is a race of some kinds of small angels scattered throughout them, many of these angels being children. It is hard to deny the theory that these statues represent the children who died. There is also one in which a strong-looking woman is walking with authority as she is tossing off her robe. I remember my father talking about how Lilith believed her nudity proved she had no shame. My first experience with nudity in public did not work out so well because I was tied upside down while the little kids were allowed to come up to me and play with me, laughing about how ugly it was. It may be unsightly; nevertheless, it was not to be shared in that situation, and it was the ugliness to reveal it. The woman looks like the type if anyone said her body was ugly she would destroy them worse than that Lion did Dúzs. I can tell from the different sculptures that these men prided themselves on how they cared for their woman. This is such a beautiful place so peaceful, and not a worry in the air, for all such worries were frozen in time a long time ago. Until . . . where did all these raiders come from?

These are absolutely Rubina's raiders, because they have the smell of death on them. One comes up to me and hits me in my face knocking me to the ground, where I stay. A man might have pride to force him back up; nevertheless, I am not a man. Now two raiders come from behind me and then chain my neck while raising the chain over a tree branch, lifting me up so my feet are not on the ground. The chains are wrapped loose enough so as not to choke me. Another creep comes over and hit me in my stomach. I think the big boys are playing tonight. I ask them, "Which province are you from? They tell me, "We are from Siófoki, yet stationed in Csornai." I then said, "Yes, my mother always said she sent the ones who acted like girls to Csornai." Now three came over and started bashing me until their boss came in and said, "Stop it you idiots; Rubina wants to beat the life out of this traitor." That really could make a kid feel secure, when your mother wants to have all the fun destroying me. Welcome home to you as well. They now bring before me, as blood is dripping down my dress, the four caring men whom, I am within their wagon. They tie them up and start beating them. They ask no questions nor give any answers. They just keep beating. They then ask me, "Did these men help you?" I turn my face away. A guard takes his sword, with a fast slash, cuts off the first man's head, then brings the head to me, and rubs the blood over my face.

He repeats the process with the second man. They then ask me again, "Did these two men help you?" I ask them, "What will you do to them if I say they did?" The killers afterwards said, "Then we would punish them." I next said, "I know these men not." The killers now rub my whole head with the blood of these four wonderful men and after that placed their heads in front of me. I then heard the laugh I hate above all other laughs as Rubina came to me laughing. She said, "Tianshire, I thought your Lord did not allow lying? Even so, to come on my holy ground, lie before our true gods, and expect to go unpunished. I will not let one bad child destroy the good reputation of my other children. You, give me your knife. The raider looks shocked then hurriedly pulls out the knife and drops it in front of her. He rushes over, picks it up, and hands it to her. Rubina tells him, "Do not move, you reject." She subsequently takes the knife and cuts his throat as he drops toward the ground in death. Rubina next tells the guards to hold my mouth open and pull out my tongue. One slice and I see my tongue in her hand. She says, "I liar does not need a tongue." This has introduced a level of pain that I have never even dreamed possible. I immediately go into shock. I guess some of her doctors tied the stub of my tongue together to stop the internal bleeding. They tell me that my blood was gushing everywhere, as traders were selling clothes with my blood on them to sell throughout Rubina's Empire. If only they knew the purpose of my blood and the help, they were doing for the Lord. Rubina commanded that I not be fed, yet somehow late at night some food makes its way into my cell. Tonight I am determined to find out who is doing this, because, if my mother discovers this, she will kill them. The hand slowly moves a bottom cell wall block and starts to slide out a bowl. I always leave the previous bowl next to the wall so whoever can take it back hence Rubina does not find it. As the hand goes to collect the old bowl, I grab it and pull saying nothing, since I cannot talk, then the other hand puts out a necklace and when I see the necklace, I release his hand immediately and gently touch it. This is the hand to the only possible blood relative I may have, and that is Tsarsko. Rubina now had my clothing removed, as it would be years before I would once again be clothed. She had me tied to her whipping wall and lashed me twenty-five times. Her style was to beat excessively first later discuss her command. She next demanded that all my hair from my head be cut off. There was nothing of beauty or pride for me anymore.

She then had two of her raider's hold me up and said in front of all, "Today, you shall worship me, for I am the true god. Fall to your knees, beg me for forgiveness, and curse your god. I quickly pulled both raiders in as they hit each other's head. Then I grabbed one of their swords and began chasing Rubina, who ran like a scared dog. The other guards quickly got me. Now Rubina once again got brave in front of her disenchanted audience and yelled out, "Tianshire; you will beg me for permission to worship me, for each day you do not; you shall watch a child be beaten to death. His or her death will be your will. Their blood is on your hands." My days and nights have now been long and cold, as insects roamed my cell considering it their sanctuary. The raiders then chained my legs and walked me to the killing field. Rubina would have five children marched off the field. She then had the guards remove a money pouch they put on me in my cell. They would take one coin from it and give it to a woman who would give it to Rubina, who would announce the name of one child that was to be tied against the beating wall beside me. Each whack splashed blood on me. Those poor children as they cried out begging me to save them. Each day was horrible as the people were now becoming angry with me. They could not understand my reluctance, after all my brothers and sisters worship my mother, as did the entire Empire. I cannot get these little faces as their bodies were being ripped by a razor whip begging me to save them. I can never sleep again during the hours of darkness, because throughout the night, I hear them begging to be saved, and suffer their blood splashing on my face. I knew my mother was evil, yet I never knew that evil could be this wicked. She mastered the ultimate tortures. She knows that I can be beaten nonstop forever and not give in, yet too precious innocent children suffer so bad in front of me, believing it is I who am doing this to them while they beg to be saved. I hate my life, and I never want to live another day. If she unties me, I would find some way to kill myself. This pain is too great. Why would the Lord put me through something this terrible? He knows how I can never pass a baby without kissing it nor a little child without hugging it. I have tried every way to cope with this, and I cannot cope with it. The blood of these children is on me. I am killing these children. Tomorrow I will worship Rubina, for if I must worship demons to save the innocent than that shall I do. How can I be worshiping righteousness while killing children? I only want the Lord to erase me from eternity, make it, as I was never born, for these scars will never heal.

I did not ask for this, nor did I want it. I thought that I was doing righteousness. Instead, I am killing babies. I worked so hard to clothe the naked, yet I now have no clothing. Each day, I see people look after my body as if it was the bed of a plague. No one will ever think of me as a human again, scared from my head to foot, no tongue, no hair, and the blood of so many children off my hands. I beg whoever has my soul to crumble it and cast it into a fire where the demons are being punished, for the innocent blood on my hands makes my guilt much greater. I now fell into a great sleep and beheld Oi who asked me, "Tianshire, what are you doing?" I told him, "I am preparing to jump into the lake of fire for the demons who are extremely wicked." He asked me, "Why Tianshire?" I told him, "For in my refusal to worship my mother and curse the Lord, I have killed so many innocent children. I have felt their blood drip from my skin. I have looked into their painful eyes and watched them give up their barely beginning lives. I have heard them beg me for their lives that they may not die. I turned my back on them and denied them their lives. I worked hard to clothe the naked, yet now all feast upon my shame, and laugh at my great ugliness. Even as I am naked, they turn their faces away not wanting to sin as I am. I beg that my existence end. It must end.

Then the most wonderful, pronounced peace came over me, and I screamed, "Go away oh great peace, for my Lord has abandoned me, he leaves me naked among the heathen; he puts my hands upon the blood of innocent children." Next Oi said, "The Lord wants you to name a new place he has created here in heaven." I then said, "Is it the pit for she who is evil?" The Lord said, "No, it is a place for she who is blessed."

I afterwards said, "Then that place I am not worthy to defile with my touch." Then I heard some children playing. I pressed my hands against my ears and screamed, "My curse has returned to punish me." Oi then said, "Those do not look like curses to me." I rushed behind him as my entire body was nothing but tremors and quakes, I looked over, and I saw so many children, who looked familiar. As I walked among the children, they all began to say together, "Thank you Tianshire for saving us." Everyone one of their faces matched a face in my mind. They were here playing and so happily. Oi subsequently told me, "Tianshire, they had no pain, for when the whips began, we brought them hither, and the deceivers entered their bodies. I later asked Oi, "Do you think the Lord will forgive me?" Oi then said, "No, for the innocent cannot be forgiven." I told Oi, "I became weak and lost my faith." Oi then said, "No Tianshire, your righteousness demanded justice, as it was entitled. I should have told you earlier. We are so proud of you. Are you ready to return?" I asked Oi, "Will you see if Rubina can get some sort of punishment for this, so she will stop it? I fear that all who are faithful will fall if this continues." Oi then said, "We will have some surprises tomorrow." When I woke up again in my cell, I could hold onto the hope that the last 18 months would now take a new course. The next day, we went through the same process once more; however, this time when the raiders when to beat the child the chips turned into snakes and whipped around biting them in their necks. They then began moving quickly to Rubina, who was now screaming and running back to her palace. The snakes continued killing raiders that all, if fact all who were on the killing field. The snakes did not touch the children or their parents. I looked at the little boy and smiled with my mouth closed. Today, I actually saved one child. Rubina's foolishness is the key that would be her downfall. She cannot accept defeat. The next day, she lined up all five children against the beating wall and ordered their execution. Once again, the whips turned into the deadly snakes; however, this time they appeared beside each exit. As she tried to escape, they would bite her many times. She had to have her demons save her. Rubina decided it was, time to play another game.

Rubina had all the children's heads that she had executed placed on wagons with a big sign that read, "Tianshire, the baby killer!" She then had her raiders put into my head a partial metal helmet that covered the top and the side with my head down to my ears. Rubina was afraid that any flying objects might hit my skull and instantaneously kill me; conversely, any objects hitting my body would not kill me yet would cause me great pain. She would have the wagons filled with the little heads spaced against the street in front of her. Rubina next had her raiders pull me into the open area in front of her. She would now shout, "Here is the one who killed all these children, the leader of the black land's tribes, the great deceiver Tianshire." Rubina afterwards had ten children brought forward with their hands tied to one another. She subsequently would yell out, "Tianshire, for before me, your God and worship me as do all in my Empire, or we will have the blood of another child upon her hands, ten children in twenty minutes." I would stand straight, looking instead to the people, as each child begged aloud for me to save them, and each one ended their lives with a large pain filled scream. Now is when the real pain started. The raiders would not take the little heads, toss them into the wagon, and drive a large post into the ground. Next, she had my neck tied at the post and then my hands behind the post followed by my feet. Rubina afterwards had the people line up in rows in front of me. Women were allowed no closer than thirty feet and men no closer than fifty feet. They received rocks as she told them, "You may stone this baby killer for revenge of her killing these children. Then the stones would begin the strike me, as I had no defense. My body was turning into an exhibition for bruises, as my skin no longer represented a race. It merely was an exhibition of pain. She tied me to the back against a wagon filled with the newest children's heads and made me walk from town to town with this display. She regretted having to increase the stoning distance as my bruises were now approaching the destruction of my internal organs. Rubina sets up my stoning events in Siófoki, Pápai, Kisbe, Kecskeméti, Ajkai and Csornai. She would take me to a killed twice each month and then return me to her dungeon to await the next event. My brothers and sisters who were still alive were permitted to visit with me. They all acted so differently toward me now. It was different as before I was the little one who was Oi's shadow.

They could never get that close to me, as Belcher and Oi would swiftly take me with them. They seldom called, me by my name, as they called me their shadow. I remember how hard my sisters would keep me in my bed at night, although each night I would escape while they were put into a deep sleep. A few of my sisters who visited with me showed me the scars from where our mother beats them for falling asleep when they were supposed to be guarding me. Finally, they gotten wise and would lie to our mother by saying I stayed in my bed the entire night. I was at no time able to know any of them, as Oi told me they were dangerous and had to be avoided. I now question why we were so busy saving our neighbors while we never tried to save our family. None of my siblings looked well, as most told me; they also were in prison. Our mother could care for no other person and actually hated most people. One of my sisters told me that our mother kept her children in prison, so none of the people could harm them. My brothers claimed that they were kept in prison so the demons could not hurt them. The truth lies somewhere between these two versions. It is so strange to all us grown us now. I thought they would come here to beat me or push me around as they did when we were but children.

They looked upon me now in many ways. One-way was the look of sorrow in seeing how badly I had been beaten and stoned. I now represented what would be if they tried to escape. The other way they looked at me was the road to their freedom. I left and survived in the black land's tribes. I was foolish to return. Some of my siblings were rejoiced in that they finally could meet with me. I was their lost sibling. I also represented something else for them, and that was my father. I had chosen to follow my father, and even though Rubina made it miserable about doing so, I have stood tall like our father did. He was the only thing that she feared. That explains why she did everything behind his back. We could never understand why she was two people, courteous and warm when our father was present and evil when he was not. It took her years and the absence of Oi for her to get brave enough to authorize the killing of Belcher. My siblings told me she had been so much worse since our father's death. Another shocking bit of news was that only one of my sisters had taken the oath of allegiance to our mother, and as of yet, no brothers. She had killed a couple of our brothers, the ones who looked like our father to pressure them into swearing their allegiance. This in turn united my remaining siblings forever to bequeath their allegiance.

I then told them, "I tell you a great secret and that is Rubina's years are less than six and that those who refuse to accept and those who show to be false their allegiance shall be saved." They asked, "Who will save us?" I then told them, "I shall return with my armies and free all from Rubina's curse who desire to be free." They again asked, "How can you save us?" I told them, "I cannot save you; however, our father's God shall save you in your faith. Spread throughout this land the good news." I cannot remember such softer wonderful lips kissing my bruised cheeks as those from my siblings. As their lips touched my cheek, I could feel the sadness and emptiness inside them. The Lord gave me something unique to tell each one, thereby creating the appearance as if I knew all things about them. I told my first sister who kissed me, "In your new home, you will not be awakened at night by the cries of mothers who have lost their children." She had nightmares about this memory from her high school days. She asked me, "How did you know my greatest shame?" I told her, "That is not a shame but the pump to a deep well of love. Your faith will defeat this monster inside you." The Lord and I did this to each of my siblings, as each finished, they would go to the other side of my prison cell to pray, as they saw our father do many times. When I finished, I went to each one and told them, "The Lord has found favor with you, be strong for someday he will come to save you." I looked at all them praying with rivers of tears flowing down their scared faces. I now looked at my beat up bruised body and could say only one thing to the Lord, and that was a loud, 'Thank you so much." This is a serious thank you, in that I can see no pain that would be too much, for seeing my siblings accepting our Lord. I received a special visit with Tsarsko, who stayed after the others left. He wanted to know all about Oi and me. He also told me of messages Oi had sent back for him. I asked them how our mother treated him after Oi, and I had departed. He told me that she ignored him believing that if he wanted to go, he would have gone. Any ways, only a few of our siblings knew of his part-time relationship with our father, and they kept it a secret. When our mother had our father killed, it also killed any loyalty from all, save one, of her siblings. I now saw how lucky Oi, and I was in that we at least had our father. My other siblings only had our mother, which is the same as having nothing. I never saw them again until I return. They now gave me a reason to return. My siblings indeed spread the word about 'the wonderful future for those who are loyal to Tianshire." Rubina tied me to her whipping posts to watch her eat dinner with her demons. The ritual was always the same. One man and one woman, beaten to death, completely roasted, then the choicest parts for

Rubina, such as arms and legs and male genitals. All she devoured the remaining parts guest demons. Nothing was remaining, as they even finished Rubina's leftovers. This was such a sickening sight, a vision that forever sealed my hate for her in my mind and gave me so much more ammunition to fight giving her my allegiance. Strangely, I started to feel additional kindness from my guards. They no longer put me up against the wall and hit me with their fists.

They also stopped throwing me across my cell. No more did they push me to the floor and stomp me with their feet. I was also having mysterious bags of food through the air holes in my cell's front door. Even though they were not openly kind to me, they made no extra efforts to hurt me or give me any additional grief. A few of the guards would now talk to me. One guard told me the reason my mother was allowing the citizens to stone me was to instill a deeper fear of revolt. The fear now was that if she could do this to Belcher's chosen daughter, then she would do much worse to them. Rubina had been building her navy and armies built to staggering numbers. She was taking people from remote lands and bringing them to her Empire. Here she would have her demons give

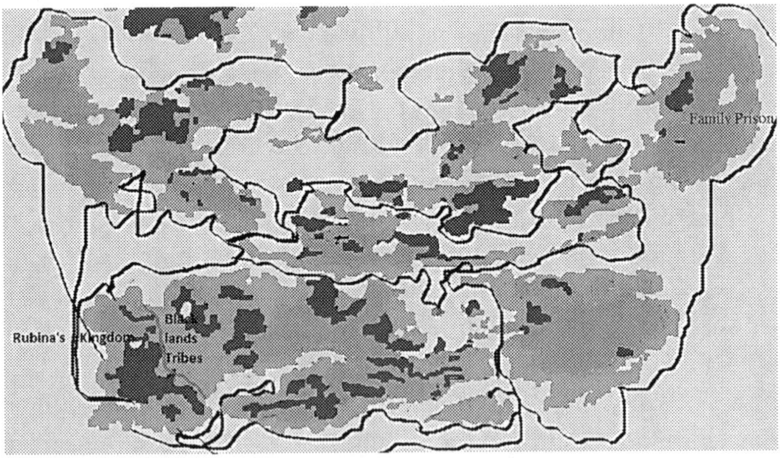

Rubina's Slave Raids

their terror demonstrations, which seemed to instill an unquestionable allegiance. That was the greatest capture of slaves ever yet recorded on

New Venus. She also took at least one family member for each man she took and placed him or her on the Family Prison Island. She used some torture on them to motivate them to write strong letters begging their family member to give his allegiance to Rubina. She now had the largest army ever assembled on New Venus and would parade them in her naval fleets around the shores of the Black land tribes. She would release small children in these ports is such a way they thought their escape was successful. These children had been told in secret that Tianshire was dead and that the Lord was now blessing Belcher's prison. Rubina also launched some terrifying raids along their border moving her armies to secure new fortifications in the black land's tribes. Rubina also had my only unconverted sister, the one that looks much like me, to lead these raids. They would bring the captives before her, and she would order their execution. The guards would secretly release these people claiming that 'Tianshire was too wicked a leader." This spreads both fear and hatred of Tianshire throughout the black land's tribes. Zala, Tolna, Boudica, and the mothers were declared deceivers and forced to hide in the secret tunnels of the Bugac for fear of losing their lives. Rubina now thought she had the tide coming her way, for when the black land's tribes began losing faith in the Lord; she would easily be able to destroy them. However, this tide was slow to develop, even though fertile seeds had been planted; nevertheless, weeds were currently growing in her garden. The wave was changing. I had now been beaten and tortured in front of the people too many times, and the people were currently becoming disenchanted with this method. My refusal to surrender had many questioning if my Lord was of that much value. They knew Rubina was no great value, so why would also her own daughter refuse to give her allegiance, unless there was a greater Lord. They knew my Lord was true, as he was also Belcher's Lord, and their alien ancestors had warned of such a Lord.

When the reports began to surface from my siblings, many decided to hold on for the new nation that would govern them. Rubina now was horrified when she took me into villages to be publicly tortured. The crowds stop coming, and those who did come refused to cheer. Instead, they declared their allegiance to me. Even I knew that was not a wise thing to do because Rubina immediately had them beat to death. I asked the guards, "Why are these people so foolish?" They told me, "This is the only way that they might be free." Rubina stopped taking me out of my cell leaving me alone currently for almost six months. My flesh was slowly beginning to heal, and small shells to my finger and toenails were now forming again. Rubina had each one removed because she feared I was not in pain one night. I did not really smile that much as I did not need teeth without possessing a tongue. The Lord allowed me to talk to certain guards and my siblings through some sort of mind talk. What I would think, would come into their minds, so I had to control my thoughts so as not to bring any additional shame upon my bruised unclothed body. I wondered if I ever again would be clothed, not so much to hide my gifts from the Lord, but the terrifying scares and bruised from so much torture for so long. The scars had now grown over themselves rendering it difficult for the new lashes to cut. This took any joy from Rubina watching me be beaten, so she stopped beating me.

One night I received a shocking surprise while sitting in my corner crying. My prison door flew open as ten guards came in. At first, I rejoiced, because ten guards meant execution, and for the first time in so long I would not be in total pain, only fearing new pain. Then the guard who always talked with me came to my side with a robe and lifted my arms to slide it through my arms. Two other guards picked me up, as a few females with them pulled down the robe to cover my body. Then the guard said to me, "I am sorry Tianshire; we have not come to execute you." I now broke down into tears again, as this was such a painful loss of hope. My dream of being free from this endless pain was currently itself dead. All I can think about is the constant cries and begs for mercy everywhere that I go. This Empire is nothing more than a bed for the wails of pain, misery, and suffering. I have seen no rock that forms the roads in any city that is not covered by bloodstains. The roads in the rural areas are spotted in too many places with bloodstains. I find it very hard to believe that this much horror in one being or demon personification could be responsible for so much death and trepidation. I even now feel great shame in how I so wrongly judged so many in the hellhole. At first, I hated them so much for stoning me, yet how could I blame them, as I also hated myself so much for the children, I surrendered to Rubina. Hate helps cover up pain. Hate will not drown the pain, but instead feed it to new levels of authority. One of the guards is shaking me now as I come back to responsiveness. My skin feels something all over it. If the women were not present I would be foolish alarmed, yet what woman, with no tongue or teeth, scared mutilated face and body would ever be alarmed at the presence of men, except that they cause me pain from their stampede to escape from me. The guard, who is my friend is called Égerszög, and comes from the Váci along the seashore. Égerszög has some somewhat magical power over me, as it could because; only he talked to me for so many years in this cage, save the one visit from my siblings. I ask him, through my mind talk with him, "Why have you come to me this night?" He then says, "Tianshire, we have come to take you to your freedom and nurse you back to your health." I afterwards asked him, "Why are so many here?" Égerszög answered, "Tianshire; your mother will kill all us if you are not here." I thought for a minute and asked, "What about your families, may they also join us?" Égerszög gave me that smile, which for some months was the only evidence.

I had that not all people were hateful monster and replied, "Would that be okay with you?" I proclaimed, "Égerszög, too much blood has been spilled for me; I can have no more blood upon my hands." Égerszög then said, "Oh my precious Tianshire, their blood would be on our hands, not yours, for we are the ones who wish to free you." I avowed, "Égerszög, I beg that you let me bring them with us." His face lights with a giant smile as he turns around and says to the other guards, "She wants us to bring our families." They all raise their hands waving them; considering this is a prison, and the walls have ears that back to Rubina, is a wise move. They are all happy now. I think it is sad that they have lived a life that demands a high price for any reward. I ask Égerszög, "Why were you willing to lose all your families to save me?" Égerszög, "We could no longer handle the pain of seeing you suffer. We all deserve to suffer as we could have all escaped if only we had been brave like you. Not one of us has ever witnessed one prisoner suffer as you have, as all would have died years ago. We currently believe that your suffering must have a reason. So many people now ask us each day to tell you how much you are loved. We have never known any other, except for your father, who was loved so much."

I then said, "Thank you Égerszög, for if it was not for you, I would be ignorant of the things about this land. We need to go; do you have the keys to the cages?" He motioned, and the other guards rushed him the keys. I then told Égerszög, "We must open all the cages, so that history will say, 'when Tianshire became liberated, she set free the prisoners who were her neighbors, accordingly the command, love your neighbor, was obeyed.'" The guards went now and unlocked the doors telling the prisoners to wait one hour and go out the back door that would be open. They currently took me to a house on the outer side of this city where the families and horses were waiting. I counted among them eight children, thereby asked Égerszög, "Why are there only eight children?" The mister joker man told me, "Because we have to spend our nights with you." Even I had to place my hand over my mouth and laugh, which strangely sounded normal. I am so lucky we do not need teeth and a tongue to laugh. I went to each of the children to hug them and pat their hair. They were so scared of me. Their mothers told them that it was okay, they were safe. All the children believed me to be the monster that killed children. Égerszög led us into the desert lands to a stream that flowed from the great mountain. We stopped here for a few minutes so the horses could drink some water.

Égerszög now took me to a spot beside some trees and told me, "I once saw you playing with your father from this tree." I looked around the tree again, and the memory came to me as I told him, "I remember Oi was afraid you were spying for our mother, but I told him, you looked like a wonderful boy, and we were safe. I hit the nail on the dead perfectly." Égerszög smiled and we now moved out into the windy part of the desert to travel. This path was harder; nonetheless, the winds would erase all our tracks. We had been traveling north to the smaller mountains, which was famous for easier paths into the green lands of the black land's tribes we stayed northwards along the wind path slowly moving deeper into the wind path to make it appear, we were heading to a trading post in the small mountains. Once we were in far enough where all our tracks were invisible, we then went due east. I asked Égerszög why we were going east, and he told me that his father once took him to a cave just into the green lands that was like many roads inside. I thought to myself, "Oh it must be from the Szombathelyi Empire."

Égerszög asked me, "What is the Szombathelyi Empire?" I told him, "The question is, "What was the Szombathelyi Empire, have no fear their places are safe. You will enjoy those tunnels." Égerszög then asked, "How do you know of these tunnels?" I told him, "We found them when we were teaching in the deserts of the Bugac tribes." He then said, "Okay, I am going to ride back with the families now, can you lead the way?" I told him, "I cannot, but the Lord can." As he merged back into our group, something hit me in my mind. For the first time, I had really felt naked, and it was good. Having someone see inside us exposes our true nakedness. Égerszög could look at me and know my mind. Somehow, the five years without clothing did not seem naked years, as I had my mind clothed. That is not to say how wonderful the robe feels that the women put on me. I was also surprised at how much food they had brought with us. We all ate good meals that kept us full and energetic. We were lucky enough to find some small patches of dried grass along our journey to allow our horses to eat. They cleaned up all the vegetation along our route, as the first couple of days were a struggle for them. They could not run so Égerszög guided us back to a stream in the big mountains. Rubina seldom went into the desert here, and thus ravished the green lands on the other side. We finished spending one week nearby to rebuild the health in our horses. We tied some long grass together and spread them out on each horse, behind our saddles and off, we went again. Soon we made it to our caves, and Égerszög guided us all in.

Once they put the children and me in, the guards went back out to lay a new set of tracks. When they finished that, work began to recover our entrance, which proved to be a wise thing to do. Three days later, a raiding group passed by our area and followed the false path. Raiding parties travel in a parallel formation to elicit fear in their victims. The disadvantage to this formation is that once they are in an area, they destroy any tracks previously made. An advantage for those who are being attacked is that they know it is not an invasion to occupy the lands, but to destroy and rape. They can determine how many are in the death gang. Raiders always raid in a one-way formation a large circle; therefore, they can be expected to swing around, and kill from behind. This created a great advantage for the black land's tribes to ambush on the rebound. This was important in that the raiding parties had to return to the black land's tribes destroyed with no booty. This did not give the tribes the long-term relief they needed because Rubina now sent into war armies that were like shooting arrows. They came to kill and destroy then return. So many of these armies were raiding now that a shadow of hopelessness was covered so much of the black land's tribes currently, as Rubina could strike from anywhere the bordered the sea. My sister lived on the battlefields now, as she was always in command with a raiding force, claiming to be Tianshire's revenge. She was an important nail that was being used to seal the black land's destruction, through challenging their faith in the Lord. Oi was gone and Tianshire, who all knew returned to her father's prison, was now invading them with great armies, rather than delivering them. A land with its hope destroyed, loses its faith and spirit. My mother was the master at destroying people long and slow. She only had me to show as a failure, and now all her children, except for one, whose luck finally ran out on the battlefield. Rubina had to be greedy and careless in demanding that her daughter be continuously visible on the front lines of her battles. When my sister went down, the soldiers quickly took her body into hiding so the tribes would not think she had died. This, however, did not stop the stories as many who saw this rushed behind the front to tell the news, "Tianshire is dead." This at least gave the tribes the hope that the Lord was not on the enemy's side. The guards and their families all worked hard to help me recover as best. I fumbled around in the tunnels, and then ran into a network layout that I thought similar. I soon found some small holes to wiggle in and found an excellent open cavern. The guards always had some people with me, for my protection and care.

This was a girl's walk, in which only two mothers and two female children went with me. These had stronger stomachs and could handle my hideous appearance. I then turned on some of the lights and climbed back up the steps to the entrance. Here I tossed a rock through the hole. Then one of the mothers came into the small hole and saw me. I waived my hands with excitement and gave my thumbs up. The mother then went back out and sent the other mother to the rear to get the gang, while taking one of the remaining children to sit on the top of the steps and talk with the little girl who had to wait in the tunnel for the group to arrive. When everyone was in place I showed them, speaking through Égerszög how to use the food processors and the bed warmers and showed them how to use the clothing generators. I also searched through their medical logs on how to repair destroyed skin. Unfortunately, they had not made it completely through this procedure, however, had many salves and other medicines to help me some, so at least soon I would have some white, although scared, spots on my body. It now appears that I will forever have to live in this cave. The days of being told how beautiful I was, were never to be any more. Nevertheless, some of the mothers went crazy for the cosmetic generators.

They learned how to scan the catalogues of the items this machine could create. I can only think that the women of the Szombathelyi Empire created this machine so that any woman on any world from any point in their evolution could generate. The children loved this machine as soon they were painted and playing with their new toys as if they were in a different world, which in theory is not far from the truth. I could feel some parts of me that had tones of pain holding doors closed start open just a little as those children spread their happiness and joy throughout our entire cavern. I noticed many of the other adults watching them and laughing. I tried to laugh yet the monsters who recently decided to spend eternity with me pulled my laughs back inside me. Maybe someday; nevertheless, I know I must see happiness and love slowly to melt the glaciers of pain frozen inside me. I noticed many of the women applying their cosmetics with their backs to me, with their applicator partner keeping a close eye on me. This made me feel sad, as I knew they were doing this so as not to hurt me and for guilt in them looking beautiful when in the presence of an angel. A strange thought now ran across my mind, and that was, 'where have my fifty legions been?' I figured that they have forever abandoned me, and if they ever were to return, I would fire them, unless they had a very good reason they left me to suffer as the demons they cast into the bottomless pit.

I can compare this as physical pain and spiritual pain is different. Our flesh was not designed to take the beating that I took and for everyone else would have stopped, yet I lived only to learn my sister was killing my people in my name. I saw so many people healed, yet not me. My five years of the prophetic times of trouble would be over in three months. Last week, if someone told me that I would be with my guards in a Szombathelyi Empire tunnel facing the black lands, I would curse them for giving false hope. I can now actually envision the ending of my troubles, yet I can never see my ministry, or having an army to revenge Rubina. I cannot even foresee what could happen in these next three months to change this feeling. Two of the mothers bring some cosmetics over to me, and they ask me if I wanted to try some cosmetics. I shake my head yes, because I know they want to share something special with me. Next, their children arrive and one of the little girls spills a bottle of the blue skin coat on my leg. I look down at it and then look again. It has been so many years since I have been able to look at a part of my body without terrifying shame. The child begins to cry, as her mother says to her, "It is okay." The mother looks at me and says, "We are so sorry." I smiled and winked at them. The children now rushed to clean it, and I motioned for them not to. For the first time, I had hoped of hiding my scars and bruises. Now, all I would have to do is keep my mouth shut, which having so many of my young years in the ministry would not be an easy chore. The following week, the mothers and wives all joined and generated a bucket of tone skin paint and took me to a part of our room where they had hung a curtain. They had that look that escape was futile, as the mothers had mastered this with their children. These girls were serious. They got me behind the curtain and took off my robe. As I stood before them naked again, I did not feel that much shame in that they were also women, and they had me here because they wanted to do something good for me. Somehow, I felt like I did when my 'mothers' would line me up for a bath. These women now divided my body into sections and started painting me, using the care that only mothers, and sister's use. They finally did my face, adding eye, lip, and cheek make-ups. I felt very good about the way that they looked at me with so much excitement. I smiled and winked at them repeatedly, and then one of them said, "We had better put her clothes on or all our men will want her tonight." I just looked at them and waved my head to say no.

They put a beautiful evening gown, a nice stylish hat, wonderful high heels, on me. They handed me a mirror in which I did not need, as the little girls who now invaded over us looked at me with big smiles. The smiles of children never lie. As I looked over this new creation, I gave my mirror to one of the children and started hugging these wonderful sisters. They all left our secret room except for two. I could not figure out what they were up to; however, I knew they were up to something. One of the women returned and gave the ones with me a signal, and they began to bring me out. They had all their husbands sitting on chairs in a row, and brought me out for them to see. I actually think these husbands thought it was their birthdays, for they all jumped and ran over to me struggling to get me in their arms. The wives looked on cheering. These husbands must have thought they were in heaven because I was completely dressed to the nines. Where else could they hold a woman looking like I did that night from their wives cheering them. The wives next started bumping in for some hugs. They were teasing their husbands, 'now this is the way the woman wants to be hugged.' The only thing, I can say is that they were right, because they knew how to hug; however, if one of those husbands had hugged me like that, they would put that poor boy into the ground never to return.

I knew only one thing, and that was how good it felt to be in someone's arms again. The sad part is that this is, pretend and my new family loved me so much to give me this special treat. I knew that this false dream would end. I would wake up tomorrow and see the destroyed skin that covered my body. I knew that to heal my skin needed air, and this paint would take that air from my skin. Anyway, if an emergency, I could go out for a short period. I can only hope that no one invades this cave. All the mothers agreed the next morning that I could cover my face with special lotions. They would make some special medical lotions that would both help my skin to heal, and create a beautiful appearance. My hair was not cut off some time now. No one cuts it when Rubina stopped dragging me out for her public chastisements coupled with castigations. These mothers were serious about not compromising my recovery, as we all could see. All the females, to include the children pitched in as this turned to the girls' part during the day, in which no boys were allowed, which brought great pride and pleasure to the little girls. This gang was so different from the black land's tribes. These people were serious about change and were willing to share everything to find a better life.

We all still sleep in this large entrance cavity. I have shown them in other rooms; however, they look at these rooms as not being them. Every one of them has worked so hard to melt these glaciers in me. I had to ask Égerszög one day, "Why are you all so kind to me, for would it not be so much better for you if I were dead?" He swung at me with a hard blow, which I could avoid barely. I felt his knuckles scarcely hit the tip of my nose. He now looked at me with hate in his eyes. I asked him, "Égerszög, if you want to kill me tell me, and I will not avoid my life-giving death at your hands." He told me, "Tianshire I did not try to hit you out of hate, but out of love, for I just do not know how to convince you how much we all love you, only the way you are and selfishly want to keep you like you are." At this point, everyone was around us telling me how much he or she loved me. The children grabbed my scared bruised deformed legs and cried on them sputtering, "Tianshire we love you, please do not leave us, promise . . . promise." At this, tear flowed from my eyes as I petted their hair and said aloud, "Promise only to leave if the Lord calls me." The children looked at their parents who shook their heads yes, which meant they had their promise. I thought in my mind, "I am so lucky to have the love of so many wonderful people." I now received a jolt in shock that took away my power to stand up, because every one of them answered back, "No Tianshire, we are the lucky ones." They did not move their mouths. They all could hear me talk currently. Now this was going to be marvelous, for what did I have to hide from them, except for maybe a few of the children; they all saw my nakedness, and Égerszög has known my mind since we was here. I so much want to be naked on the inside with these wonderful people. The inside is the greatest place to be without shame and have no secrets. It is also a good place to have the Lord, as I often hope; he will take me back to his kingdom. Life really changed so much for us now, especially in that no one feared touching me anymore, particularly the children when these little people discovered I knew how to create some far-out toys and games. I remembered the pages I scanned on raising children while in the Bugac tunnels. Those were the days when I foolishly thought someday children would flow from my womb. Unfortunately, the world outside is not as in here. Ordinarily, I would feel sadness keeping people with me under these conditions; however, where can they go? Rubina will beat them to death, and the black land's tribes would kill them as invaders. The rule was to kill all who crossed their border, if possible. That is why Rubina was launching her raids from the oceans, which she controlled without question.

Time flew by so fast now that I did not even catch that my five years of troubles were over. I healed some, yet for this much skin destruction it will take a long time for the Szombathelyi Empire's formulas to take effect. I now asked the Lord what he wanted me to do. He told me, "Tianshire, rest for your times of troubles shall soon end." I looked around our room now, as they all looked at me terrified and finally, Ózdi, my beloved of the wives, ask me; 'Oh great one, who were you talking with?" I looked at her and said, "Ózdi; I was speaking to the Lord of Belcher." Then I could feel a great relief come to the preceding stiff bodies. I asked, "Why were you all so frightened?" Ózdi told me, "We thought you might be talking with one of Rubina's demons." I looked at them and laughed saying, "Oh, do not worry for I will have a short talk with each of them when my angels cast them into the lake of fire for eternity." They all clapped as the children rushed up to hug my legs again. The actions of children never lie, as I wonder what my children would have looked like. At least, the Lord has allowed me to receive the love of these children to demand much of my time. I confess, when they call for me, I go. They proved repeatedly that if I do not go to them, they would come to me and take me to where they want me to go.

What the heck, I also confess that I enjoy every minute of their time. They now jump into my lap and grab my hands or any part of me; they can grip and pull. They do not care about my hideous appearance, all though thank the Lord the wives keep my face covered with their special lotions and salves. I just cannot believe how comfortable I am with these children, their honesty and truthfully speaking their minds is so wonderful. If they tell me, they are mad; they expect me to figure out why. I usually am able to do so, as they give me ample clues. Our life is very wonderful here, packed with love, sharing and caring. I can feel some of the scars in my heart now healing. I so hope we do not end this for a long time. That foolish hope is now facing its first major challenge. One of the guards come rushing into our cavern asking help to roll our inside rock, we made to cover the entrance. He came rushing in warning that someone had entered the cave. They pushed the rock over our entrance and used loose dirt to ensure a solid seal. We all formed in our emergency huddle as I lowered the lights and turned on the noise concealers. I then was surprised when a wife scooted up to me from each side as two children sat on my legs. I would have thought that this much pressure on my body would be painful and extremely uncomfortable; however, the opposite was true. The group had faith that if something were to happen, I would protect them. I did not know how to tell them that if I had legs that could run away from me; I would have been long gone. We patiently wait while our tunnel noise trackers pick up the invaders walking toward us. Then the walking stopped. We were now frozen, which really did not matter as our noise concealers were operating. Even I am frozen, for if I were not, I still would not be able to move. I have a frozen woman on each side of me and four, yes four, children frozen on me. We now hear our rock moving. It moves steadily for a short distance and then rolls over the side on the steps crashing onto our cavern's floor. Even now, I wonder how someone without torches, as I smell no burned oils, can go into our cave and zigzag through all our tunnels. To end up in front of our little dent in the wall, which looks like all the other dents, and crawls up our cramped crawl space and have enough power to move such a great sealed rock with ease just does not add together. Something is abnormally weird here. For some strange reason, I am not afraid and wiggle for the other parts of my 'body' to release me. I now walk up the steps to the stranger who is standing at the top of the steps. The guards try to pull me back yet I tell them in our mind talk, "Do not fear, it will be okay my great friends."

That helps some, yet they are right behind me. They tell me, "We have put too much love in you to risk losing you." I tell them, "I understand, just be imperturbable before we fight our invaders." I am now about eight steps from the top and getting ready to push the rock that turns on our lights. I push the rock, and the lights shine strong. We all look up and see only one invader. The guards now turn around and go down the steps. One of the lights along the wall is blinding me; therefore, I cannot see our invader. I am puzzled as to why all the guards, who only a few minutes were willing to die, just turned around and left me here all alone. Now I see another terrible sight as our children are running up the steps. I must be prepared to fight now to save these brave young warriors. I ponder what sort of parents would force their children to fight in their behalf. All eight of them are rushing up these steps, the first three land on me, while the other ones go straight to the invader. I try to scream, yet quickly stop, as the sound is hideous. I hear the little girls asking the invader, "Do you want to play?" My Lord, this is not the way to fight off invaders. I subsequently hear a voice that is locked somewhere deep in my mind say, "Okay." Now three little girls, all about the same age go down the steps over me.

That must be a universal custom of children, if it looks like a mommy, do not worry. The remaining children help me to get up and once up I felt an itch on my right hand. I reach over and rub my hand over the itch. Then one of the little girl's screams, "Tianshire, your hand is fixed at the top." I look down and see my hand is healed where I rubbed it. I started to think to myself, "Who is the only person that would have so much faith that just by passing me? I would begin to heal." My mind gave me a name whom I searched so hard to find a face to match it. The face is stuck somewhere beyond my comprehension. I have a name, so I will ask this new little girl in our group through one of the wives if she understands a person who is called Boudica. Ózdi asks the little girl, "Do you know a little girl named Boudica?" Boudica looks over at me and answers, "Tianshire, do you not remember your daughter?" Wow, what a surprise, I have a daughter. What was I doing in the black lands when I had a daughter? How could I have been so terrible? I fall on my knees with tears flowing from my eyes and open my arms saying, "Please forgive me my daughter." Boudica instantaneously jumps into my arms, without any competition from the other eight children. I guess since I am her mother, that gives her special privileges. I was sitting here wondering if a child would ever come from my womb, and in my arms now is a child who came from my womb, many years ago." Oh, if only I could find Boudica to give me a healing from our Lord, then I could truly enjoy this daughter. I now speak to Ózdi asking her to speak to this child once more, "Do you know where we could find the one who is named Boudica?" Boudica looks at me and says, "I know where she is, and if you close your eyes, I will put her in your arms kissing your checks. I closed my eyes and she said, "Count to one very fast." In the excitement, my foolishness took over my mind as I spoke out, "one." I froze as I could hear the excitement from my family. I could have sworn that I said one. Ózdi tells me in mind talk, "I guess you do not need mind talk any longer." I then shouted out, "Praise the Lord and my daughter." Boudica looked at me and started kissing my cheeks repeatedly as she had done so many times before. I knew those lips had touched me many times. She then said, "Mommy let's wipe that yucky stuff off your face." The four little girls rushed to get some water, soap, and towels and returned. These kids knew all about getting their faces washed. Ózdi now asked me, "Tianshire, are you sure?" I answered, "Ózdi, if this child came from my womb, how I can refuse her, for I am not me to her, I am her mother?" The mothers all shook their heads in agreement, and the little girls started cleaning my face. They soon stopped and yelled for their mommies saying, "Look mommy, look." Ózdi rushed in ahead of them and told me, "Tianshire; your face is new." I could feel my skin, discovering how soft it was now. When feeling the inside my mouth with my tongue, something that it was doing so much now, I noticed something strange. I opened my mouth and Ózdi yelled out to me, "Tianshire; you have teeth again." I ran my tongue against the top of these new teeth and verified that I had all my teeth. Ózdi was kissing my face everywhere, forcing me to say, "Ózdi; you have to slow down or your husband will be jealous of me." Her husband spoke out saying, "Fear not Tianshire for if I must lose her; I could only pray that it is to you." My daughter came up to me and asked in excitement, "Do I have two mommies now?" We looked at her, and each gave her a kiss on her cheeks telling her, "Sorry; you have only one mommy." The little girl then puts her arms around me giving me that familiar hug and said, "At least I got the one I love with all my heart." I afterwards looked at her and showed her my arms and legs and said, "Honey, mommy has been beaten too many times to remember my old life. Please tell me your name." Boudica answered, "Mommy I have told you my name many times tonight, yet having ears you did not hear me." I then showed her my scared partial ears and told her, "Honey, your mommy cannot hear like she could before, so please tell me your name. If you do, I will let you sleep with me tonight." She answers and looks to me, "You would let me sleep with you anyway, because you never could deny me that right." I shake my head yes and kiss her cheeks saying, "Pretty please." Boudica answers, "Okay, you said the magic words, "I am your daughter who is called Boudica, and the Lord has sent me to you that I may ask you if you are ready for your healing?" I then hugged her and said, "I now remember the greatest name upon my heart being Boudica." I subsequently looked up and said, "Lord I accept the healing from you if it be your will." Then in an instant, I was completely made new. My hair ran all the way down my back and was shiny gold. I tried to stand up; however, the mothers rolled on top of me crying tears of joy. Ózdi told me, "If ever a person was worthy of a healing from the heavens, it is you, the mother of Boudica." The name Tianshire was never spoken by any in this group again, for their custom was to call a mother the mother for her child or children. I asked Ózdi, "What if a mother has many children?"

She looked at me and answered seriously and truthfully, "Such a situation is never to be found in your father's prison." I was even once more shocked by not knowing this after five terrifying years living in Rubina's kingdom that her evil had reached deep into her population, sparing no one. We now heard a strong voice that echoed all through our cavern, "Tianshire; your times of troubles are no more. It is time for you to save your sheep, for they are lost without their shepherd." I tried to think yet shamefully could not even remember my sheep. I wonder which fields they are hiding.

Chapter 07

Restitution of Tianshire's Empire

The time that we give for our sleep returned. I went into the area designated for me to sleep and started laying out my furs as I normally do. I think someone watching me; however, I pretend like all things were normal. Then I cannot take it anymore and say, "Come on over here so I can check your ears?" Afterwards as if in a flash my daughter is on my lap and says, "I was worried that you forgot me." I answered, "Now, you know that would be impossible." I put her down along the wall and scooted in beside her thereby allowing her head to rest on my shoulders. Our tired bodies quickly go to the Land of rest. This land is not peaceful for me tonight as a man keeps asking me, "Tianshire, where are your sheep?" I look over the hills and in the valleys and can find no sheep. I ride to the man who stands with his back to me, and I ask him, "Sir, where are these sheep you keep asking me?" He then tells me, "You must go into the land of the Adonyi where you will meet your shepherds and tell them to find your sheep." I thenceforward ask him, "Why should I look for sheep who escape from me?" The man explains, "You know that without you, your sheep are lost. Would you have it that the wolves destroy them?" Afterwards, I said, "I shall go to Adonyi so that my sheep do not perish. Can you tell me if I may bring my daughter with me?" The man then said, as he lifted his large sword, "Fear not Tianshire, I shall be with you and all among you will be protected." I, nevertheless, felt someone pressing up against my side. I awoke to see it was my daughter.

After asking if she was awake, I questioned, "Do you know where a place called Adonyi is?" Boudica answered, "Yes; it is in the green lands where the sheep are spread out, because so many were lost in Rubina's raids." I never really knew what Rubina's raiders ate on their raids, nor did I ever want to know. Boudica then said, "Sometimes the shepherds go there to find their sheep." I next told her, "Tomorrow we shall journey there." Boudica asked, "Will our new friends join us?" I smiled at her and said, "We shall ask them." I enjoy so much the way that whatever I have belonged to my daughter also. This is the way I always want our relationship. After we all had finished our morning meal, I call our group together. I told them, "I must go to Adonyi to gather some sheep. You may join us if you want." Égerszög now spoke, "Oh, Tianshire; the people in Adonyi hate us and will gather an army to kill us, even our children." Boudica after that said, "Fear not, for the Lord will protect you." Ózdi subsequently asked, "Tianshire, do you really want us to be with you?" I looked at them and said, "Oh yes, for you are my family and no other have ever loved me as you do. It is time now that I repay that great faith, by taking you out of the hell you saved me." Égerszög asked, "How can you hide us with these clothes?" I then said, "I will ask your wives to prepare robes for you, and Boudica will tell you the safest styles. I know that when those who kill see your wives they will marvel saying, 'surely these men are to have such beautiful wives and children."

Just when I was to say wives, I saw some little hands moving around and knew that I had to add them. I had her powder keg for their decision making, for if they refused to go, they were saying their wives could not create good clothing, and would therefore be treated accordingly. The women rushed to produce the new robes for their families. Boudica found some drawing paper from the hosting Empires aged inventory and drew some key emblems that were popular among the tribes. She chose to put three, as one would add an emblem for each tribe, they lived in.

To have three meant they traveled much, so could be expected to be on the border's green lands and to dress not so much the standard. I then bragged, "My daughter knows many things." Afterwards I saw the other children and added, "I hope she does not know how to catch me like you guys do." I started to run down the tunnel to the play area as Boudica was with our other ten children, and they were all screaming, "We will get you; you cannot escape, you must surrender." Our cavern was once again filled with joyful laughter. I naturally had to let them catch me and when they did, they offered me chances to escape, then when I did not take them, the toys and games came out, thereafter all I could hear repeatedly was, "Boudica, look at this!" I could hear her laughter blend in with the other children with so much rhythm. My daughter was very trustful and willing to share. Their world was so simple, they rejoiced in having a new friend as Boudica celebrated the same event.

This instinctively gave me great pride. She was having so much fun. An eerie feeling inside me was telling me that she and I had childhoods without this sort of companionship. This innocent child was trying to heal a pain that was growing inside her. I wondered now; what kind of mother was I that my child would be so mistreated. I understood why my childhood was empty from the feelings I gained from my siblings. Inside my mind are so many things fighting once again to live in my conscience. What can I do to invite them back? How much longer will they hide from me? I now wonder what I did to anger them so much. I have my flesh back; therefore, I once again own a shame to hide. Painfully, my mind does not know who it is, who is the 'my' is inside me that refuses to join me again. I do understand that the sheep I search for have something to do with that hidden person inside me. That evening, I take the children, and we prepare the evening meals for our families because the mothers worked so hard on our gowns today. There is excitement back in our group as a new adventure is before us, and that to hide from it would be wrong. Ózdi then says to me, "We will create for your family their robes tonight." Boudica looks at her and says, "Aunt Ózdi, we must wear what the Lord has given us. I am so sorry." Ózdi reaches over and kisses her head and replies, "I understand my niece." I later whispered into her ear, "Where did you learn of the aunt part?" She whispers back in my ear, "Mommy, from my friends," afterwards plasters my face with her slobbery, yet wonderful, kisses.

Ózdi then laughs saying, "Somebody's mommy is getting a whole bunch of loving' now." I then laughed and hugged my daughter saying, "How was I capable to survive without this little heart to love me?" Boudica looked at me and seriously, answers, "You were not able." I told her, "Daughter, never teach me how, okay." We now prepare some evening snacks and formulate our story circle as the guards tell us some funnier stories. We are lucky that they have removed the sad things from them. The men collected all our horses, as we gave a hefty bag from the cave machine's grain generator hooked on the front of each saddle. I was at first puzzled that such these advanced people would have machines for horse grain, yet after reviewing some of their culture discovered that the recreation of riding horses was created not long after the horses met humanity. I marvel how Rubina had, according to one tale demanded the executing a demon for eating one of her horses. She threatened to end their link with this world if ever again a horse were eaten. As a result, her kingdom has more horses than people who might ride them. We now get in our formation, as Boudica leads the way. She tells us that I must go second, with the wives equal on each side and the remaining children in the third row and the men in the last row. Égerszög asks Boudica, "How do you know these things and how do we know they will work?" Boudica says, "You know one by the deeds they have done. I have come from the black land's tribes and will return as I have come."

Égerszög then asked, "Will you tell me the reason for this formation?" Boudica tells us, "I am known as the next Great Queen and those who follow me understand the future. My reputation was damaged relentlessly; thereby we shall place all our beautiful women at her sides. This will remind them of the Love Tianshire gave them. The children behind these women show they are mothers, the givers of life. Our men are our protection, and because we are a family, we ride in peace. If we were the invaders, the men would ride in front." Égerszög then replied, "For such a small girl, you have great wisdom." Ózdi next chuckles, "What else would we expect from the womb of Tianshire?" I stood here confused not understanding how my daughter was so wise in the things of the world; nonetheless, she came straight to our cavern, moving the rock like it were the air. Can she really be my daughter? I would reason some answers would be forthcoming in the black land's tribes. We start our ride into grasslands of the plains of Adonyi. We launched our ride and in one-hour were on the borders. The borders were easy to discover, in that it was now a path the width of two men in the bones. We crossed the bones with horror and fear into our hearts. Boudica then stopped and said, "Fear not my family, these bones are to keep me out and you in."

I just do not know how much longer I can take having this prophet talking, as each voice from her creates additional fear that she is not my daughter, and that I burden I cannot carry. I do not believe her to be a deceiver, and I know that she has claimed me to be her mother. What child would show much love to one she claimed to be her mother if it were not true? She worked hard to be my daughter first and conceal her name. She did not deny her name, she confessed each time accordingly as not to lie to me. I feel something deep in my hidden self that says this child is from me, and any fool can see that she loves me so much. The pride I have now as she rides very strong and brave in our lead; however, each time we dismount, she rushes to grab one of my legs. I cannot understand how someone so great can rush to be so low before me. She could never get too low for me, for my arms pull her up, so she can rest on my waist. I now understand the purpose of a woman's design. Boudica's legs rest so perfect on my waist, and her little legs lock encircling my leg. We can see many skulls laying around in the grass. I am surprised that these skulls were not used for the border paths. Rubina's raiders did not enjoy taking back their dead, as Rubina would see their loss.

Instead, they would return in a loose formation and when the lead made it safely past Rubina, they would fall on the rear and pass again, hiding the number of loses. We all agreed on a place to spend the night. The children were so excited seeing rabbits jumping around. Most of the small game no longer survived in Belcher's prison because the people had eaten them to ward off starvation. Our horses enjoyed the fresh green grass that grew taller than they did. Boudica made up the fur for us to sleep on. She put it off in the side, as we would have some privacy. I lay down and she begins to rub my neck, exactly where it has become tight. Her little fingers pulsate through my muscles completely relaxing my body. My mind is driving me insane, how does this 'life' know the keys to me? I ask her once more, "Boudica, who are you?" She answers, "I am the one who loves you more than any other," and then jumps on me. The thump from her body crashing into mine feels heavenly. She jumped on me with no fear and a sense of right. She is telling me she has that right. My arms automatically wrap her into position. Now her innocent head rests on my shoulder falling to sleep instantly. The little fellow was tired, and she came to the place she wanted to rest and that was with me. I try to determine if there is any significance in her laying on me, except to avoid the ground.

Subsequently, I understand that she is not only protecting me but also assuring that I do not escape from her. My angelic daughter regaining a mother she lost for five years, entering a forbidden territory to get her mother back. Life feels so good now, when I get my breath from that last thump. Who ever heard of one being fruition over a thump? I guess only a thing that a mother would enjoy. As I now slowly fall asleep, I can feel something about this land, as I have slept on this nation's ground many times. I wish my preceding life would be revealed to me. It seems wrong to remember so many pain and suffering, yet not know why. I could sense that even my siblings knew much about me. We finish our morning activities, and the children are lined up for their cleaning, including Boudica. I collect the soap; water can, towels, and scrub the little gift from head to toe. She is without question obedient, thankful, and exceedingly submissive. Ózdi, who is motherless, is with me, helping me as much as possible. Ózdi tells me, "If ever I had a daughter, I would want one like this. A child knows their parents, and this child knows her mother. Boudica, you are so good for your mother, allowing her to stand strong among the other mothers." Boudica said to her, "I have spent the last five years each night crying to my father whom my mother returns." Ózdi then asks, "You know your father."

Boudica said, "My father is the Lord, for I have no father in this world. The Lord adopted me, as he also did my mother, into his family." I, sensing an opening here, ask her, "Boudica, why do we go back to the black land's tribes?" Boudica looked at us and said, "Mommy; you are the Queen of the black land's tribes." Égerszög then asked, "If she is the Queen, why have I heard so many reports of her being hated so much?" Boudica said, "They might need some reminding; nonetheless, we have the reminder on our side. I tell you all, that my mommy shall be the only Queen of her father's prison and the black land's tribes. Égerszög continued his questioning, "I heard they already have a Queen, do you know her?" Boudica answers, "They do have a Queen, who has refused the throne because the Lord will let them only have one Queen. Yes, I do know her." I then asked her, "Honey, who is the Queen they want?" Boudica answered, "Mommy; they want me; however, you need not to worry for the Lord said it is your time, not mine. We must obey the Lord, who is also your heavenly father. In addition, today you must ride in my lap on your horse to the lead. I only led yesterday, if raiders would attack you."

We became situated on our horse as another strange memory comes to me. It is not a memory of a specific event, but a memory of a lacking. I remember that while young I had few friends.

I now see a little girl whose name was Tvář Lásky playing with me. I see me crying and missing her after we separated. I ask my daughter, "Do you have friends to play with?" She answers, "Oh yes mommy, nevertheless; you always find the best ones for me, like the ten who ride with us. Whenever you do not find me friends to play with, your six mothers find them for me, or they do as you did in the cavern and play with me. Ózdi while choking asks for clarification, "Boudica, did you say your mommy has six mommies?" Boudica answers back quickly saying, "Oh yes their names are Heves, Domony, Dömsöd, Esztergomi, Sellyei, Siklósi, and they are also my grandmas. Equally important, they love us very much." Looks in my starry eyes and asks, "Are you okay Tianshire?" I look at her with a smile and answer, "Oh yes, Ózdi; I can see all my mothers, and they are so wonderful. Boudica and I are playing with them. Boudica is really my daughter. As I walk across the room they hand her to me, and we hug and kiss." I had a colossal glow over my face.

Even though these visions were partial and only verified what Boudica had told me, I will never have any doubt that without Boudica during this period, I would have perished. Her love pumped too much power over my soul, destroying the scars driven so deep by Rubina. I got my first taste of tribees, a new slang term for those who lived in the black lands, today.

We were riding along and suddenly smoke began to fill the sky as the wind blew the smoke toward us. As the smoke went to hit us, Boudica turned around and said, "Go away!" The smoke afterwards retreated to its source.

Boudica then asked me, "Mommy, why did not you tell the smoke to go away?" I told her, "I forgot honey; you need to teach mommy everything once more." "She afterwards told me, "Do not worry mommy, soon you will know all things again, until then I will take care of you." Accordingly, I informed her, "Well; I cannot think of any better hands to be in. Do you know what that smoke was all about?" She answered, "Yes, some bad people; you will see them soon. They will had not hurt us now." As she had told me, we soon passed an area that was burned and there were about 30 people lying on the ground dead. As we passed through this opening, another gang poured through the opening and began to throw rocks. Two tall, the height of two men, angels appeared and tossed the rocks back killing half of them. The angels then told those who still lived, "Return to your temples and tell them your Queens will soon arrive. Make unadulterated the Lord's house or you shall welcome his wrath."

Boudica disclosed to us, "Soon we will arrive at a small village. We shall rest there for three days. They are our friends." Then two hills ahead we saw a small village inside a series of wooden walls. As we approached the front gates, they began to open. Then two columns of men appeared with flowers in their hands. As we rode past them, they threw the flowers on the ground before us. Once we were all in, they closed the gates behind us, and I guess the leader of this post came out to welcome us. His words were, "Welcome daughters of our Lord and Queens of this Land. We will care for you for three days when the Lord wants you to continue to reclaim your thrones. A few children now came out and asked our children, "You want to play with us?" Boudica and our children were gone in a flash as they sound of laughing, with a few boo boos filled this village. Many adults right away appeared inviting my family to different functions. All departed except for Ózdi and Égerszög that now stood by my sides. The leader asked if there was anything he could do for them, and they told him, "We are okay, we still at our Queen's side." The man now identified himself as a priest and asked us to join him for a midday meal. As we prepared to enter, I felt a tug on my leg and a little head locked to my waist.

I looked at our host and asked him, "Do we have room for another guest?" He looks at me and says, "There always room for Boudica." I look at him and ask, "Does everyone know Boudica?" The priest then answers, "All who know her know you." I afterwards said, "Yet I do not know me." I know a word that would bring many memories, and that is Oi. When I heard this word, my mind exploded. Fragments of me were totally separated and next, as if by a magnet, all united again. This was quite a sensation like diminishing into dust subsequently reemerging reunified. I can see myself following a bigger brother; I see us doing everything together. My siblings talked to me about this brother, as being his shadow. I feel years of visions flooding my mind. Most of my life was centered on this brother. Whatever he was representing; it included me. He was preparing me for something. That something must be why I am here currently. I ask the priest, "A voice told me I would find my sheep and that many are lost now since their shepherd is gone. Do you know who the shepherd is and who my sheep are? He looked at Boudica, who shook her little head yes, and said, "Tianshire; I am one of your sheep, and you are my shepherd who has returned. Tell me how I may serve you and your Lord." I looked at him and said, "I hope you forgive me; Rubina beat my mind from me, and the Lord is feeding it again slowly.

If not for the new flesh he gave me, I would still be in hiding with great shame." The priest said, "Oh, fear not, my shepherd, when the time is for you the Lord will give you back your wonderful mind. Your reward now is to love and enjoy your child, the Queen daughter." Boudica then jumped from her chair and landing perfectly into my lap. She does this just as a mountain lion does when he is climbing the ledges on a cliff. It may be strange how these insignificant things marvel me so; however, when one is beaten whacking low and then more until the body is nothing more than a bag of pain, little things such as this gain exceptionally much more value. Back to Boudica she wraps her arms around me and kisses my cheeks saying, "And to my mother, the Queen Mother." I later learned this verification was all the priests needed. They were now sending scribes to all the temples to spread the good news, "Tianshire has returned, and Boudica has verified her." The problem with my return was that it represented the power of a Queen and the inheritance of all the authority Oi had earned. On my departure, the unification of the temples dissolved while local false prophets seized the temples, took the power over the temple, and used it for personal gain. My return represented their dethroning; therefore, they worked hard to defame my mission and me.

My sister's raids with so many armies claiming to be me was all they needed to put the fear back into the people and build their allegiance against me. The priests told me so many things my sister had done and her lack of fear for death. She would fight ahead of her armies in the streets with only a few raiders at her sides. She fought, for the most part, with a whip; lashing out at all, she could see. She apparently had no desire to kill, just to hurt, as she wanted her victims scared, and alive to report her wicked deeds. She was successful at this for a few years, hitting towns along all the seashores of the tribes. She evens, has local artists paint her, and left behind paintings of her beating black lander's, which her artists painted when she was on her ship. It was a well-orchestrated campaign until she hit the wrong town. This time, having spotted her fleet coming to attack them, set up ambushes in the houses. The assembled no force to fight head-on in the battlefield practices at that time. The generals refused to take their armies into the town fearing an ambush. Your sister, Nógrád, feared that Rubina would be angry at the extended time between the raids; thereby, she took a few raiders, and marched through the streets having her raiders pull people out of the houses and beat them in public. In anger, Nógrád had these people executed after she beat them.

She warned that if all came out on the street that she would let those she beat live. Still no resistance, hence she became less concerned for her safety and had all her escorts in the houses searching for people. She stood in the middle of the street and yelled out, "I am Tianshire, the sister of Hoi. I have come to avenge you for casting me into my father's prison. You will all suffer." She continued with her threats, and then unexpectedly three arrows from three directions struck the head and one in her heart. When she went down, her raiders detected that she no longer was yelling her threats and rushed out to see what had happened. They saw her dead in the street and therefore, unable to know where the arrows came from because no one witnessed it, rushed her body back to the ship. The army then surrounded the town and shot arrows with fire through the town burning the houses. The soldiers watched the streets and killed any who tried to escape the fire. They had to contain this story. Nevertheless, in the time it took to confiscate Nógrád's body back to the lead ship and organize the fire attack, a small group of witnesses rode horseback to the nearest temple to tell that Tianshire was dead.

The raiding force then went back to sea; however, five raiders, who were captured slaves from the islands, jumped overboard, swam to the black land's shores, and afterwards found a temple to verify that Tianshire was dead. This brought great joy to the tribes knowing that Tianshire's wrath was finished. They also received reports that all the other sisters refused to continue her raids. I sat back in my seat shocked that Rubina could still cause me much pain, even without her bloody whips. Ózdi patted me on my head and told me, "Do not fear Tianshire; our husbands will protect you. Even though, you only know them as prison guards, they were royal prison guards and were recruited from the best of the armies. We will take care of you." The priest currently added, "Do not fear Tianshire, for you were appointed by the Lord, and you will receive it." I now went into a chamber they had prepared for Boudica and me, and fell upon the floor in a deep sleep. My mind was reprocessing my life, which, for the most part, was centered on my brother Oi. He fits with all parts of my life as I also see Boudica with us on many occasions; however, in our ending parts of the ministries. That is something that I can understand, for a ministry is not a place for a little girl; thus, I must have kept her with somebody until close to the end. I must have been miserable without the little headache. I can also see the six mothers doing many things with us, and they joined us later in our travels. Another important part of me is still missing. I will wait patiently, because I am slowly forming the vision of what I must do. I am so disappointed in how much we did, for the things to have turned this way. I now must rest and enjoy what I have; Oooooh, and the little monster whom, I have just landed on me. Breath, where did you go?" I can feel no pain, because my little partner is slobbering all over my face. I now wrap my arms around her and say, "I was so sad, because I thought you left me." Boudica next answers, "Mommy, you are such a silly girl." I asked her, "Will you help tell me some things to help my memory?" Boudica asks, "I know you now about uncle Oi; nevertheless, I have not heard you talk about aunt Zala and aunt Tolna. Do not worry; I will take you to your family. Two powerful faces now appear before my mind, the faces of Zala and Tolna. They were the missing links, the sisters whom, I played with. So many fun things and we also worked hard in our ministry. I imagine currently that it must have been unyielding to leave them following me. I now believe that when I see them, I will be able to stand on my feet. It is now almost time for us to leave. The priests come rushing in, telling us that a giant raiding attack army is passing our way. They ask me, "How can we fight?" They discussed this among themselves and told me, "We will not fight, but all go to our tunnels and hide until they leave. The raiders usually do not destroy anything if no people are living here. Their mission is terror in people." We all then go through the tunnels. The priests tell me that they will go with me to the next station because too many raiders are now roaming this land and pushing the borders back to the three mountains and controlling most of the green lands along the northern seashore. Many of the tribes lost territory. Rubina's current control of Death Bay gives her the threat of pushing to Tabil and separating the tribes. The control of so much northern green land allows her to place raiding armies close to the Battlefront as resupply them with ease. The tribes now fight day-and-night guerrilla style. We cannot fight openly, as her armies are too strong. I look at the map and ask him, "Are we still in her Empire?" The priest answers, "Yes, we were waiting for your return." I looked at Boudica and said, "Do you know how far you went into Rubina's cage to get me?" In return, "I did not care; I mother returned and the Lord told me to go get you, and I went to get you." I patted my hip and instantaneously

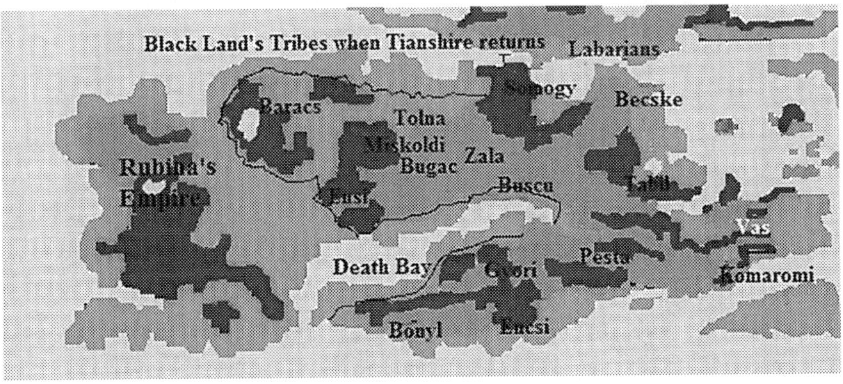

my sidekick was aboard and off, we walked to get our horses. I established our formation outside and away we went to what was left of the dwindling black lands.

We follow a creek bed up a series of rolling hills, each roll perfect for ambushes. The hills are not like the mountains, with its deep valleys and towering peaks that one can see for miles. These have lower grass, as wild herd animals can graze, enjoying the ease in finding hiding places. The hilltops appear all to be the same height, as I get over the top of one, I can only see on the top of the next one. I am consequently, confused about why the black lands lost this territory. The hills offer few ridges to the top and can only be traveled by negotiating the smaller individual ridges or a streambed if available. We now travel along a long high ridge, which the priests say is dangerous, yet will get us to the next station sooner. As we stroll along, a scribe comes up to warning that a scout for one of the raiding armies has spotted us. Boudica then starts laughing saying, "This is good, now mommy can work on her faith commands." I look at her and say, "What, honey?" Boudica explains, "Mommy, you have to stand up and with your hand lift, this army in the sky and when they are high, drop them over there." I look at her and say, "Honey; mommy cannot do that." She looks at me and says, "Will you do it if I gave you a big kiss?" I respond, "Oh honey; I would do anything for a Boudica kiss, but I cannot do that honey." She looked at me and said, "Yes you can, and if you do not we will die." Ózdi then asked, "If we are going to die, do I get a Boudica kiss?"

Boudica looked at her and said, "We are not going to die, because my mommy will save us." The ground around us was trembling, and the thump of the horses drummed throughout this entire area. The priests came up and stood between our families. One priest said aloud, "Thank you oh great Lord for giving us back our shepherd Tianshire that she might punish the wicked in her name. I could feel both anticipation and desperation in the air around me. I saw my little girl standing in front of me, with not one ounce of fear in her heart. She believed her mommy could do this; therefore, she was waiting for the horses to go into the sky and drop. I felt my feet go lame, yet I did not fall. I fell asleep, yet I was still awake. This is not a good time for everything to stop working. I am blind, for my eyes have stopped working. Then a bright light grows big in front of me. Currently thousands of angels begin to appear. The light stops and says, "Tianshire, your power from heaven is now returning to you. If you tell a star to sink into the sea, it will sink into the sea. You shall destroy a wicked army that has persecution my sheep at this hour. I walk with you once again. My legs stood again; I was awake again, and my eyes could see. I scooted Boudica over walked out in front of our group facing the army.

Boudica was now shouting, "Yeah, my mommies going to get them now." She motioned to the children to follow her as she said, "We can see them splash over here." The army was forthwith only a few hundred feet from us now. They began to shoot their arrows. I moved my palm up, and the arrows went over pass us. I have now placed my palm up to stop them and yelled out, "Today you all shall die, save two. You have entered the Lord's lands and committed evil. I am Tianshire, and I have returned to my sheep. I then pointed my finger up, and the army went to the sky as a snake. When they were high enough, I released them, and they fell toward the ground splashing as Boudica predicted. All were dead, except two that I had back from the sky. I pulled them to me, and told them, "Tell all who invade my lands that the Lord will destroy them. Tell all who wish to serve the Lord, and to be spared from this curse; they may cross this border. Tell my mother that I shall make the blood in her land turn to green poison. Shed no more blood. Now go." The two generals turned around and rode straight to the border. I picked generals because I knew the armies would believe them and that Rubina would order them back when they would refuse to obey her. This would plant the seeds for generals to refuse to march their armies.

This place was named, 'Dalen af Blod' or Valley of Blood. I now saw something move on the next ridge over. They were a group of locals that were trying to get away from this great raiding army. They came riding to me with a white flag, which the tribes used when meeting one another as a sign of peace. The priests came up to me and said, "Welcome home our Queen. This is a great day, for the Lord walks with Tianshire once more." The group that arrived was part of a local guerrilla fighting force. When they arrived, they got off their horses, threw down their hats, weapons, and their leader walked up to the priest beside me then asked, "Who is this angel?" The priests told them, "Behold your Queen Tianshire. She has returned with the power of our Lord." They all gave the courtesy that should be given to a Queen. The priests then asked the men if they told the tribes that the power of the Lord has returned in our Queen Tianshire. They grabbed their hats and as they were jumping off their horses to leave, the priests rushed up to them and told them not to forget their weapons. Their leader looked on the priests and said, "We do not need weapons because we once again have our Queen Tianshire." They then vanished quickly into the rolling hills.

The head priest now sent half the priests with some scribes to the next village and temple to spread the great news about the Queen, who has returned. Égerszög now came to me and said, "Oh; mighty Queen shall you promise not to forget us." As I went to speak Boudica said, "We will never forget the great mercy that you had on us. We will consistently take care of those we shall always love so much." I looked at him and said, "My baby speaks the truth, thereby you have not only one Queen promises you her loyalty, but two Queens. The Lord has told me that you will be blessed for the days of your lives." Égerszög then confessed to me, "I loved you so much when you were in that prison. Did you know that?" I looked at him and said, "I felt so much shame in needing your love too exceedingly, for I wondered how a man could want to have so much shame to hold his love. Égerszög, I did dream that we had a great love. Talking with you was all I had that was not filled with pain and misery, although the misery of knowing that I could never have your love cut deep inside me; however, I could not let that dream die." Ózdi then came to me and said, "You can have my husband anytime you want while you also take me." I looked at her, laughed, and said, "Why would I want him, when I could have you?" Égerszög then grabbed us both and swinging us around in a circle said, "Why should I take one when I can have two?" He could tickle us with his thumb while swinging us around; thereby, causing us to laugh so hard that it hurt. When he stopped all three of us dropped to the ground victims of our spinning heads, yet we were all still laughing so hard.

After a few minutes, we heard clapping and cheering only to see that all who were with us was enjoying our uncontrolled play. Then Boudica sticks her face in mine, and as we are spinning she asks, "Mommy, do I have another mommy and daddy now?" Our family and priests began to laugh at this with us. Little Boudica was working hard to get something from this adult play. Then Égerszög and Ózdi grabbed her, while they were kissing, she told her, "Boudica, we will always be a mommy and daddy for you, anytime you want us. We hope you know how much we love you." Boudica looks at them and then answers, "I know," afterwards jumps up to tell the other children the good news. I sometimes wonder what I am going to do with this child. We all agree to move a few hilltops over to avoid the smell of all the dead bodies around us. The priests shake their heads saying, "We never saw armies that big previously." I cheerfully said to them, "Wait until you see the army that I will invade with." Then the priest replies, "I know every strong young man wants to serve in your army."

We now went to the great plain that retained the currently empty temple of Adonyi. I did not really remember this temple, except passing it on my departure. That night, while preparing to sleep, I asked my somnolent daughter why we were going to Adonyi. She told me, "Oh mommy, we have the greatest surprise for you there." Then her little eyes drifted off into dreamland. The next day, we were on our way early, as the smell of death was starting to make our stomachs sick. Around noon, Boudica tells me that we shall be there soon. Next, I can see the battered steeples to this temple. As I look out halfway between us is a row of women in white dresses walking toward us. My little scammer, Boudica now tells me, "Mommy, you should ride out and make sure those poor girls are okay, I truly hope the priests had not been bad again." I hand Boudica to Ózdi and rush out to meet these women. As I approach them, I start to hear screaming and crying, in voice tones that I have known before. I hope they are okay, because for what I can see they look helpless. They are all now laying down the ground. I jump from my horse and rush to them saying, "My fair ladies, how can I help you?" Then one grabs my leg, and I fall on the three in the middle. Now the five on the parameters jump on our huddle.

I now hear my name being screamed non-stop and feel their faces kissing me. This is insane. These women are hysterical. One of them lefts her face enough to let some sunshine, and I recognize this face, yet cannot put a name on it until she says, "We have missed you so much Tianshire." I now yell from the top of my lungs, "Zala" and start shaking in eminently excitement. Égerszög, now says to me, "I hope you are okay Tianshire, for I do not know what to do." Tolna looked at him and says, "She will not be okay when we get done loving her for a long time," and she starts her famous tickling. I now yell, "Someone chain these women to me and forbid them ever to leave me again." Égerszög then says, "Tianshire, if you are okay I am going back." I yell out, "Égerszög, do not leave me." Then the mothers start teasing, "Someone has a man." Then Esztergomi says, "Okay, girls we need to let Tianshire introduce us to this strong man." Zala next complains, "We thought you were suffering." I after that say, "Zala, do not you think that would make you suffer." Tolna then says, "Only if someone were to try to take him away from me." Sellyei now asks, "Tianshire, is he yours?" I tell them, "Well girls, he is when his wife lets me have him." They all moan in disappointment as Tolna complains, "Darn Tianshire, I was going to ask you if I could borrow him." Then Heves says, "Tianshire, I do not think you are to be messing around with married men, or you will get into trouble."

Zala then says, "I am in trouble." I afterwards say, "My true love, Égerszög will you come to meet my mothers and crazy sisters." Égerszög then starts laughing, "Tianshire, you had me scared to death as did your family. I thought that they were going to kill you." Tolna says, "Only if she were to try to escape." Égerszög next laughs and says, "Oh, I understand that." Tolna after that says, "However, I will not try to escape." I then say, "Hello Ózdi and Boudica." They both say hello as Boudica jumps on me also. Tolna subsequently says, "So, you found your mommy." I later said, "Just in time my family, in the nick of time." Tolna later asks, "Who is Ózdi?" I afterwards say, "Oh she is my greatest friend and my lover's husband." Tolna face turns red as she looks at Ózdi and says, "Honest, we were just teasing." Sellyei now says, "You girls need to clean up your mouths in front of Boudica." Boudica looks at her and says, "Sellyei, I already know everything they know." We all begin to laugh as I tell her, "Baby, there are a couple of things we are keeping a secret until later." Boudica now says, "Somebody tells me please, please, oh please." I look over at Sellyei and say, "Sellyei, why do not you tell her?"

Her face turns red as she says, "Tianshire, please do not make me spank you the first day that you are back along with Boudica." Boudica gets quiet and sits on my lap. Ózdi currently laughs, "Oh right, someone finally to make Tianshire mind. Now, I hope you will stop pestering my husband." Égerszög then laughs and says, "I sure hope she does not stop pestering me." Zala and Tolna start to release their childlike moans of envy. Sellyei afterwards says, "I can see that we may have to drag this group to the priest's altar and do some serious praying for this gang. She then walks over to Boudica and myself, subsequently starts kissing us. Now I can stay here and kiss my angels while the rest of you get some cleaning. Everyone starts yelling boos. Tolna then asks, "How many friends did our Queen bring to retreat with her?" Boudica answered, "Mommy brought about 20 for her and ten for me." I immediately hugged Boudica crying on her saying, "I could never forget my life saving daughter could I." The mothers and sisters gave each an uneasy look. All our gangs were here now, accordingly; I asked the priests, "What do we do currently?" He said, "We have prepared chambers for you and your large family. We will relax for a couple of days to give you a change to reunite with your sisters and mothers." As we entered our chambers, I noticed many separate rooms.

I then called the priests and asked them if they had a large classroom or something similar so that we could all sleep together. He told me there were some; however, they were not clean. I told him, "We will clean them; if you had eaten as much dirt as I have in the last half within a decade, then you would know I am no stranger to dirt." Anyway, I was going to ask the Lord if I could cheat, in which he allowed me, so we instantly had a new beautiful clean large room that we may sleep. A few scribes asked if they could also join us, and I told them, "This is our father's house, and all his children are welcome." The scribe looked at me and said, "Oh, if you only knew how long I have been yearned-for such as words of authority from the Lord's chosen." I then told him, "It also gives me great joy to speak them once again." I was so satisfied how my two lives were merging here. Zala and Tolna were big hits with the wives and fell in love with Ózdi, which I could understand because there is some hidden magic that draws us to her. It is so amazing how she finds the greatest joy in the minutest things. My mothers are also blending in with the children's mothers, as surprisingly there is not that wide of an age gap. The one thing I do know is that every child will meet my 'mothers' tonight and that the guard's wives will never again worry about childcare.

They will instead worry about ever seeing their children awake, because these widows can totally tucker out any child. They have all mingled absolutely, with Ózdi in the lead with my two sisters. It is so clear that she is a great gift. The one I so completely trust is Égerszög, as he could have easily raped me many times, yet never touched me in that way. Even though I was so ugly, many of the guards would place bags over our faces and do their evil. A few times, I was not lucky enough to have Égerszög close to protect me, or was in public. Several who tried to stop our being raped in public was punished terribly, so most just walked on by as if nothing were happening, so we had a greater chance of rescue by not making a noise, with the hope that our knight in shiny armor would not get caught. On the nights that Égerszög was my guard, no one touched me. He was senior guard and could reassign what he called troublemakers to the nasty areas. I can honestly say that even if had taken what by law was his; I could never have faulted him because he did treat me as if he thought something was inside me, and that I was not an animal. I have cried in Ózdi's arms many nights, telling her how great that her husband has been in my life. She also cries when I tell her about his kindness, such as extra food and protection.

She is so proud of him, and I know someday the Lord will bless her womb many times. She is my example of having and willing to share. If she has if, she will give it to someone she thinks needs it more. She has begged me to take and marry her husband. I told her, "I can only be given in marriage by the Lord, and he loves you too much to take such a great gift from you." I have an exceptional group here, the royal guards, and their families, which received special privileges for their positions. They gave it up for a hideous monster who would be a burden and curse on them for the remainder of their lives. They not only put their lives in danger, but the lives of their families who also gave up everything. I have six widows here, even though they are wonderful people were scheduled to be what I have declared as sinfully executed. Zala and Tolna had everything and gave it up for their love for me. I now lie here remembering all the things they taught and gave me. Moreover, little Boudica, if she is or is not my daughter, I care not if that is what she wants she has it from me. She made it deep into Rubina's expanding Empire straight with me and saved us. I lay here with a face drenched in little-girl slobber the happiest woman in this world. This room is about love and even better; it is about love for me and for me to love.

To have love and not a place to put it is hell, as I discovered during my times of troubles. As we awake the next day, I receive some disturbing news. A council with the tribes has come out to tell me I may not enter my nation. They want to ask the Lord about me. I asked them, "Where is this council from?" They tell me, "They are from the Becske tribe." I then ask, "Do they speak for all the tribes?" The council tells me, "No other tribe will talk to you?" I then asked, "How long before they answer?" They said, "The council will try hard to study your case in the next few weeks." I then told them, "No man may take away from me what the Lord has given me. My people now chose darkness over my light. So be it. I will give you three days to return to Becske, and then I shall take away all light from my tribes. You will have no sunlight, nor will your candles burn until a council from each tribe returns here with the head of their high priest. Do not try to deceive me, for the Lord will tell me if you bring lies. Those who bring me lies shall die by fire. When I have the unquestionable allegiance from my tribes, you may have daylight again. The tribes proved to be stubborn in giving their response, some waiting for two months.

Those now lost, this year's harvest, and grass stopped growing as the herd animals now flooded toward the lights of the converted tribes, Rubina's Empire, and Death Bay. We were still in conquered lands where I held the herds close to the boarded. I instead, could spend much time with my new family, looking at them; you would think they had grown up as one. They turned into mud in the mixture of water and dirt. They were mixed so strongly I could never foresee them being apart again. I was particularly impressed by the way my sisters and mothers taught my family Oi and my teachings. My family was so hungry to learn these things as my mothers and sisters were eager to teach them. Naturally, little Boudica had the children assembled as she also taught them. This gave me time with my priests, as those who followed me now would be my priests and scribes. They were bringing me the heads and oaths of allegiance from the tribes as they arrived with the high priest's head. Once the Lord told me this was the true head, we turned the light back on for that tribe. The first tribe to convert was the Bugac. I was so glad they had converted, as they had been my favorite with the adventures in their tunnels were among the highlights of my previous life. I now only can recognize any existence through the memories that came forward. I had enough memories to give me a foundation in my new life.

The Ensi converted next, which was good in that I could now move into my nation and begin my work. It was, time to begin my work as I assembled my new family, for no more would I label them as a sister or mother, but all as my new family. I can only that my Lord for giving me such strong and time-tested people. Although those who I brought from the prison may not have been friends that long, with Égerszög being the longest, they were tested. This risked being beaten, shamed and tortured for the remainder of their days and to watch their children destroyed. They took an immense risk, for someone who was pronounced the greatest threat to Rubina's Empire. This went against everything they had been brainwashed. The loyalty of their wives also to bring the children is astonishing. I can never forget how hard they cared for me when my appearance was that of rotting flesh on crumbling bones. I know that they had to wonder why they had to lose everything for someone so close to death. I must get back my country, so I can place these trusted people in the leadership positions to inhibit such chaos and ruin to destroy my land again. We had to enter Ensi from the mountains because the animal herds were flooding the green lands. Just as I was preparing to enter Ensi, we received another head, and that was of the Baracs. The Lord verified it and their lights returned along with the herds, which came from the west and north for that who was grazing along the ocean.

I now entered Ensi, seeing a great army before me. I band of priests came up to welcome me. They yelled out, "This is a great day, for our Queen has returned." I saw all the soldiers cheering. I asked the priest, "Why do you bring an army here today?" The priests answered, "Oh Great Queen, for there is still much darkness in this land. You are our first Queen and shall be protected always." I then said, "That will be good since it does not keep the Lord's sheep from the Lord's shepherd." The priests afterwards replied, "We have also given our soldiers extra food and clothing, so that not one who appear before you are hungry or naked." I told them, "This is good that you furthermore care for your brothers and sisters. Where do I meet my sheep?" The priests then said, "Where you left them, in the Valley of Mezokovácsházi. They await your arrival." I told the priest, "At least there will not be as many, this time." The priests looked at me and laughed saying, "You may be surprised oh Great Queen." When we arrived, I was indeed surprised as was also my family. Boudica rode on my lap ever since we entered the tribal lands. When I would dismount, she would jump into my arms and then grab my hand when her feet hit the ground.

I was pleased that she did this because, for some reason, I felt safer with her at my side. Whoever would meet us always looked at her first, and then they would shift to me. She was the verifier. The wives wisely made her a smaller version of any garment that I wore; it was like a little me on my side. We were now getting close to the mountaintop that overlooked the Valley of Mezokovácsházi. This visit was in the springtime with all its blooming spring flowers and birds singing through the air. When I made it to the top and looked down, I was consequently surprised, as before I was a crowd much larger than the crowds was we had left behind. I asked the priests, “How can this be, for I thought so many hated me for the deeds of my sister?” The priests answered, “Those who asked the Lord received the truth, and those who are here today belong to the Lord.” I then looked up to the Lord and cried out, “Lord, please feed our children.” Instantly, the refilling plates were now floating among these people. I heard considerable cheers coming from the people as they looked up and saw Boudica and me. My family was now standing on this peak and showing great relief. Égerszög told me, “I do believe their Queen has returned.” I said, “Égerszög, they would have no Queen if not for you. My family, my sheep want to meet their shepherd. Let us go down to them.” We rode down the path and went to pass the temple in the valley. The priests escorted us to the stage.

I have requested that my family all be on the stage with me; we had no need to be among the people, for if they had troubles, it was because they had not asked the Lord. I had given them water, if they did not drink it, they would suffer, not me. The crowd began chanting, “Queen Tianshire,” repeatedly. We now walked off the stage, and I rose my hands and lowered them. They all quickly became quiet, as my three-year rebuilding has begun.

I began by saying, “I am Queen Tianshire, and I have returned the kingdom my Lord has given me. I have come to feed and claim those who are in the light. Those who remain in the dark shall fall to my wrath. I am your Queen, who has survived the deepest depths of evil, for if evil could not destroy me, how can those who live in darkness. I shall only save the tribes, who are in the light, those in the dark I shall feed to Rubina’s demons. The deceivers came, and some of my children laid down their shields surrendering to them. Those who followed Oi teachings stayed strong in the lights and are now to receive a future home in my kingdom. I left being a servant of the Lord and returned as a Queen chosen by our Lord. I am accordingly pleased that so many of you have become victorious over the dark.

Remember, my people that hatred stirs up dissension, but love covers over all wrongs. Work with me to remove the hatred in these lands and once again let love flow in our rivers and love to warm the tops of our mountains.”

I discovered large parts of my teachings to be the teachings of Oi. The priests had the people meet in the area in which they had met when Oi was speaking to them. This mission also included visiting many temples. So many temples knew Boudica. I told my family, "I think maybe my daughter knows all in the land, or leastwise, they know her." This time, I could not allow the great followings to stream after us; considering, I wanted to set foot in as many temples as possible and rebuild our priest network that would be the skeleton of my new body in this land. My family and I traveled by horseback this time, as the Ensi gave us enough powerful white horses for each of us, thereby we could travel quickly. We now traveled to the Baracs, where on our entry; another army escorted us to the main temple. I complained to the Lord about the armies; however, the heavens felt it wise to start showing me leading armies. On arriving at the temple, a group met me who had the head of the Tolna high priest. I had them put the head-on a table, and called out to the Lord, whom he can test it.

The Lord took it, which meant it was the head of their deceiver. The lights come on throughout Tolna, which naturally brought a smile to my Tolna. The Tolna ministry complained that so much of their animal herds were in Baracs' lands. I then told them, "Those who saw the light first receive the bounty from those were delayed in seeing my truth. How can you, you, until now, accused me as being false now ask me to give what my children have to you? I tell you all, 'I am Queen Tianshire, a Queen of war and not the helper of Oi.' You should rejoice in that you may still have a harvest before the winter months arrive. How can you stand brave before me and demand, when you crawl before Rubina as weaklings losing your lands to her weak armies? You lay before her as begging dogs, yet I stood before her holding fast to my Lord. I did not deny my Lord as you have denied my Lord. I tell you another thing, "I shall never lead an army to fight the evil of Rubina's Empire when my land also is a bed for evil. Cast evil from your beds, least it drags you to the pits." I emphasized to this group the urging to, "Speak to all about the Lord that they may choose the Lord, as I tell you a day shall arrive when merely those who serve the Lord will drink the water from my land. I left my people strong in the Lord, and they fell to only a few weak servants.

I will not share my nation with those who serve the dark. You have made high priests out of the deceivers. You ask me, how we could know they were deceivers. I tell you when they told you to curse the Lord and his prophets you should run in the mountains or deserts warning all that a deceiver had stolen your temple. I noticed something special beginning now as we went to each temple and that is Boudica was meeting with the young children. I thought this was so good, considering that she will have a long foundation with her people, by also being a hero in their childhood. My first two large meetings got around soon as all the remaining tribes, except for one that being the Vas, had submitted their high priest's head, and light were on once more in those lands. The animal herds left Death Bay and ran around the tip along the seashores of the Bonyl and Ensci. A few more months went by without the Vas converting, so I issued the final warning to them. "Oh Vas you land of fools; you desire so much to live in the dark, yet do you not know that even Rubina's Empire lives for the day. They shall now see the light as they invade you in your darkness. Those who wish to live must escape to a temple in another tribe and accept once more, the Lord. My revenge on Vas will be such that I will allow no human to live and any who stands on these lands in 30 days shall be destroyed."

It did not take long for the demons to give this news to Rubina, who shifted her navy packed with armies to raid Vas. She expected an easy victory; however, did not heed to the warning that all who remained on the land after 30 days were to be destroyed. Her armies raided throughout Vas killing all they saw. They killed all the priests who had remained. Those who have escaped were given safe passage to the borders. To ensure that all receive the warning, the Lord sent thousands of angels who knocked on all the doors, walked all the streets telling everyone that their end was near, and it was now time to seek salvation in another tribe's temple. Rubina landed eight fighting armies in Vas to destroy all they could. They tried to destroy the temples; however, they could not do so, as the Lord would not let them. The raiders are greedy and if they cannot get one thing, they will rush to another thing and try their luck there. After 30 days, all were destroyed who were from Vas; however, when the 30th day arrived, Rubina still had eight armies spread throughout Vas. She was afraid the when the lights came back that the black land's tribes would try to reclaim her land, and she wanted this land because it gave her a foothold on the eastern shores that she had craved all her life.

On the 30th day, all her eight armies that still stood in Vas were destroyed. When the naval commanders saw this, they rushed their fleets back to Rubina's Palace to tell her the bad news. She now recalled all her raiding armies and fleets and decided once more to capture more slaves. This time around, these islands prepared defenses and could fight to keep their people. Rubina sound learned that she was losing more than she was gaining, thus recalled her fleets and used her armies to regain civil control. When we arrived in Tolna, Tolna wanted to show us where her family had previously lived. She was surprised when we arrived, in that the people had placed a large statue of her there, as a show of their love for her. I could feel the warmth that she felt flowing through her body. I asked her why she did not come here during my five years of absence. She told me these things had changed slowly once I departed. Many of the rich were angry about Oi's teachings against the rich not feeding the poor. They began starving the poor by taking work away from them among many other evil things. The temples fought hard against these aristocrats. The aristocrats created armies to take control over the temples. They also came to put us in a prison.

The Bugac came to take us back to the tunnels. It was here that Boudica learned how to track you and when you entered one of the tunnels' extensions, she went after you. Meanwhile, the high priests were taken out then beaten in public as deceivers of the masses and accused of altering the teachings of Oi. The new head priests came out and retold the altered stories, which included false reports of great sex sin among the whores of Oi. That was when your loyal Bugac came to our rescue. The times were bad, as many missions were sent into Rubina's Empire to find you. When they discovered you were in the royal prison, in which no one has ever escaped, all returned and gave up. The masses are now returning and you can rest ensured that those who speak badly of you would meet the wrath of your subjects. We rode from town to town, for I felt it important to touch each person's hand whom I could. My family also enjoyed the interaction among the people. I can witness how each village we go, we are hearing more people call for them by name. They always give special attention to those who call for them by name. This fosters a hope for an ear to the Queen. As we travel through the wavy hills, a group dressed in black surrounds us and with knives, demand we go with them. I ask Zala, "Who are these thieves?" She tells me, "They are the 'Riddarens av självständighet' or Knights of Independence." I ask her, "What do they want independence from?"

Tolna answers, 'From you, my Queen." Then one of them goes to hit me and misses as his hand goes through me. I later look at him and say, "Go into the pit!" We can see and hear him sink in the pit as his screams echo chills into his comrade's bones. I next look at them and say, "If any touch a member of my group, they also shall be cast into the pit." I after that looked to the leader and asked, "What did you plan to do unto us?" He subsequently jumped from his horse and bowed toward the ground, as did all in his minuscule band and said, "My leader sent me to bring you to him." I later sent Zala to tell my army, we were going to take a short private pilgrimage, and that we would return. I told this Riddarens av självständighet, "Take me to your leader!" He then said, "I take you only if it is your will, my Queen." I told him, "It is my will, and those among you who stay loyal to me shall escape the pit." I then asked for permission to tell his men this good news. Soon his men were cheering as they rode their horse past me, raising their sword high and said, "I serve you, oh mighty Queen." They then mingled beside my family. I asked their leader, "Why do they ride beside my family?" He then told me, "Oh, my Queen, to protect your family."

I smiled, winked at him, and then said, "Let us go to your previous leader." He raised his sword afterwards rode in front of me with his sword across his heart as a sign of allegiance. I called him back to me and asked, "Why do you and those in your group ride with your swords over your hearts?" He said, "Oh Great Queen we do this as our sign of respect for our Queen." I asked him, "Does your leader respect his Queen?" He answered back, "Oh no, my Queen; he would wish you dead." I next said to him, "Would not it be wise if you rode as if we were your prisoners?" He looked confused subsequently replied, "Yes, my Queen. He after that rode back to tell his gang to look like you will be guiding prisoners." We later arrived at a small camp in front of a cave. They guided us into the cave and then told everyone to bow on the ground. I refused to tell him, "I am a Queen appointed by our Lord, and I shall never bow except to my Lord." Their leader now came across the room with approximately 50 of his bandits and went to stand in front of me. Two of his guards yelled at me to bow before my new leader and as such swung their whips at me. I immediately sent the whips back to strike them in their faces, and afterwards had the whips make a noose round their necks, afterwards having the whips to lift them to the roof of this cave cavity where they were hanged. I then looked at my family and raised my hands for them to raise saying, "Your Queen desires you to stand." The leader now yelled, "We have no Queen."

I looked at him and said, "When I was imprisoned by Rubina, she removed my tongue, so I could not speak. Your tongue is now in your belly." He motioned for another to take his place, and he ran from the cavity. As he was running I yelled, "Crawl, you dog." His legs and arms have now been those of a dog, and he crawled like a dog. I looked about the room and said, "Those who will serve their Queen may give their allegiance to me and go outside." The allegiance pledge was that they would come before me, giving me their sword and say, "I shall obey you my Queen." I would return their sword to them. Slightly, over one-half of them remained, dedicated to their folly. I looked at them and said, "As a dog returns to its vomit, so shall a fool in his folly. Be gone, for the Lord shall judge and punish you." Instantaneously, they were gone. We now walked out to greet our followers who were all on the ground trembling. I asked them, "Why are you on the ground trembling?" They cried out, "So you will not also punish us." I looked at them and began laughing saying, "You serve the Lord currently; thereby we are on the same team. For now, you are blessed. Rejoice, for the days of those who follow me will be many." All in our group looked puzzled, as Zala then spoke asking, "What about those who follow you in the great war?" I looked at her and said, "Zala; some mysteries are only known by our Lord, yet I will say that whosoever has faith in our Lord, their days shall be many."

It was now apparent to my former sisters and mothers whom their little Tianshire that has returned is a Queen. They now asked me if I wanted to play some games we used to play. I looked at them and said, "I am so sorry about my family, yet when I was a child, I did the things of children; however, now that I am a Queen, I must do the things as a Queen." Boudica looked at me and asked, "Then must I also to the things as a Queen?" I grabbed her up and started swinging her saying, "Children are the great exception so that into the future, we may send our love. Boudica, when your time comes to be a Queen, then you shall act as a

Queen. I warn you that your days as a child are few, so enjoy them well." The family looked at one another wondering why Boudica's days, as a child would be few. All held their peace not wanting to know the true answer for fear that this knowledge would bring, once again, grief to their hearts. We now rode to my next meeting with the masses. The masses were somewhat controllable currently, as many were amassing around their local villages and temples.

As we returned to my army, the Riddarens av självständighet asked me, "Oh Queen, what shall we do now, for we have no mission?" I asked them, "Would you like to join my army?" They all agreed, "Oh Queen, which would be nice." I then added, "And you may keep your uniforms if you wish, for I like my citizens to see that from evil can come Saints, as I came from the prisons of Rubina to be your Queen." I called up my army commanders and said to them, "I found some Riddarens av självständighet, which have pledged to serve their Queen. I wish for them to be a part of my army. Furthermore, ensure that my soldiers know that we are on the identical team with the same mission. These men will help us to avoid any dangers from their previous comrades." The commanders raised their swords and said, "As the Queen has commanded, it will be done." I could see the people jump back in fear when one of my Riddarens av självständighet rode by them, and then in shock as they kept on riding. The people marveled that even some of the Riddarens av självständighet have chosen to serve their Queen. We now rode into our next meeting, and as I was riding in some priests rushed up beside me and asked, "Oh Queen, we have some mighty news for you. Will you please stop and talk with us?"

I looked at them and said, "You are the ones who feed my flocks, of course I will always talk with my shepherds. If it were not for so many of you, like before these sheep fell." The priest came to me and said, "All the of the black land's tribes have light now. Vas refused and Rubina destroyed all who lived there, then foolishly disobeyed the commandment to depart on the 30th day, and lost eight great armies in Vas. This is our greatest defeat over Rubina." I told him, "This was no defeat over Rubina, for she destroyed a complete tribe. I tell you that a day will come when many more armies that eight will fall to my armies." The priests all looked surprised and yet also very happy because for the first time I spoke of leading many armies against Rubina. They announced the conditions in Vas, and the crowds cheered, for never before had they known of eight armies being defeated on their soil. I then walked out on stage and raised my arms as the refilling plates and cups started floating through the air around them. I was tired of people suffering to see me or be with me; therefore, the Lord allowed me to feed them. I began speaking to them about Love and Oi's teachings and cursed those who called my sisters and mothers Oi's whores. I now warned them that soon the Lord's spirit would move throughout the black land's tribes, and destroy those that served evil.

I told them no evil would ever live again in my kingdom. I also told them that the time to save the lost, as in Vas, was over. It is now time for me to save my people. Never can one say unto me, "I have suffered from the hand of evil more than you." I have suffered from the hand of the wicked more than any other has, and was freed by the love of the pure of heart. I came from the land from the evil to save the children of the Lord, and I tell you they shall be saved." The night arrived in which all the lost who lived in the black land's tribes were destroyed. We remained in the mountains of Somogy while the nation buried the dead. This was taking longer as many tribes were still burying the dead from Vas. This would be okay, since I wanted a few months to enjoy my family. Ózdi, Zala, and Tolna have been looking somewhat depressed lately. I know that I must take them under my wings, as they should fly closest to me, especially considering how they have bonded so close to my little girl. That night, Boudica asked me to take a walk with her alone. I agreed and off into the woods we went. The army commanders were shocked and prepared to rush and defend their next two Queens. Zala held them back saying, "Do you honestly think that if Rubina could not kill her that any in a land of the righteous could fare better? Now relax, your Queens will return.

Sometimes a mother and her daughter must be alone so her mother can give to her only the things that a mother can give." They then sat down in unrest. Égerszög came over, sat with the commanders, and said to them, "Even if I had ten armies, I would fear attacking our Queen. Here, drink some of this as we celebrate our Queen's return." Soon all the former guards were among the army commanders drinking and telling stories. One of the commanders asked a guard, "Where did you get this perfect whiskey?" Égerszög told them, "Our Queen gave it to us." Then the commanders all cried out, "Oh what a Great Queen that we have." The remaining women came and asked the commanders, "Can we also share this with the soldiers, for it would please the Queen very much?" The commanders then said, "If it pleases the Queen, give them all you want to give whereas you may greatly please our Queen." Meanwhile, Boudica pulled me to a rock ledge where we sat down. She began by saying, "Queen, you know I love you with all my heart do not you?" I put my arm around her and asked, "Since when did you call me Queen and not your mother?" Boudica then said, "That is what I must talk to you about? I have deceived my Queen. I therein must be punished with my death.

You are not my true mother. If you command me, then I will jump from this ledge and to the death I deserve." I looked at her and said, "Would you give me a kiss and big hug before you left me?" Boudica replied, "If my Queen so desires it, I will do whatever she commands." She afterwards wrapped those little arms around me and this time those slobbery kisses were flowing with her tears." I then asked her, "If I commanded you to be my daughter, would you obey my command?" She began crying aloud saying, "I would obey that command and be the happiest daughter that you will ever have." I then told her, "I command it, Boudica my daughter. Did you think that the Lord had not told me about the gift he gave me when he gave me, you? Boudica, we are both cursed in that we will bear no children. You must also adopt you a daughter someday, and then you will understand how easy it is to love such a wonderful gift from our Lord." Boudica now asked me, "Why did not you tell me you knew?" I told her, "It was thus fun, and I needed you so much that I could not face losing you or giving you to another." She later said in her wonderful 'smarty pants' fashion, "Same here." I subsequently asked her, "Tell me your story, my daughter." She said, "I saw you with Oi in the Tolna lands, where my parent's lived. I was at your ministry when some evil raiders came and killed them.

When I returned, I had nothing. I thereby decided to follow your ministry and became close to the Lord. He sent an angel one night to ask me if I served the Lord. I absolutely agreed and so put my entire self into his service. He afterwards told me one day to go to meet with you and

Oi, and that he had a great mission for me. I was so happy with you all, until Oi left, and then you went into Rubina's Empire. Then the bad men tried to hurt us, so we hid in the caves that Tolna and Zala told me you loved so much. They even took me to your secret library where I touch the pages for three complete years. Then Tolna and Zala forced me out telling me that they also needed, my love. They are so very special. Then my greatest day came when the Lord guided me through the tunnels to where you were. I at no time once touched the surface; nevertheless, I could never get enough of your praise." I told her, "You will stay with me now always, even when I go to the great war as soon after the great war, the Lord will call me home." Boudica then cried, "This is so unfair, because I waited for you too long." I told her, "I will still be in your dreams, and vision's little guy so do not think you will get away with not washing behind those ears. You will have all who are in our family to be with you, and Zala and Tolna will serve you as your mothers, for they are my sisters.

Now every time I yell for my daughter, you shall come to me, and when you yell for your mother, I shall come to you. Do we have a deal?" Boudica told me, "We do; nevertheless, I need for you tell your sisters and mothers that I told you the truth." I told her, "That I can do, if you ride on my hip." The little person was on her mother's hip immediately as the sweet sound of those slobbers began to flow from my cheek coupled with 'I love you' by the dozens. We were laughing and singing so loud that Égerszög and some of the guards rushed out to make sure I was not drunk. I told them, "I am drinking the wine, which will not make one intoxicated nor will it make one sober." They turned, and say to one another, "What can one drink that will not let them be sober or drunk?" Then one of the guards said, "I do not know; however, I will ask her to give us some bottles of it; you can rest guaranteed." When I arrived, the guards had already assembled their places among the army. Boudica and I were so surprised when we saw my complete army singing and dancing, although my family was enjoying it, especially the mothers, Zala, Tolna, and the wives of the guards. I asked Égerszög, "Do the wives' dance with your permission?" He answered, "Oh course they do my Queen, as we have the greatest wives ever, and if we cannot trust them, after that how can we have them?" Boudica subsequently says, "Wow, I want to have a husband like that someday." Égerszög then laughed and said, "So do our wives.

Your family decided to share the strong drink you gave us with the ones who sacrifice so much to serve with us." I then said, "Égerszög, I am very glad that Ózdi approved sharing you with me. I would be a lost Queen without your special insight into the ways of men." Then Boudica asked him, "Will my family stay with me when I am Queen?" Égerszög later answered, "Oh Queen's daughter Boudica; Ózdi would crucify any who tried to abandon you." Boudica afterwards said, "Guess I should be extra good to my other mother!" Égerszög then answered, "I know she would enjoy nothing more." As Boudica departed Égerszög afterwards asked, "Tianshire, there may be something that you need to understand Boudica." I looked at him and told me, "What can humanity tell me that the Lord would not tell me?" Early the next morning, I walked among my soldiers, as those who jumped; I told them to lay back down. Then a few of the commanders came rushing to me crying out, "Forgive us oh mighty Queen." I subsequently motioned for the commander to be quiet, and consequently said to him, "It is I who should be forgiven, for I never knew you would like the strong drink I made for my family.

From now on, all will share as much as you see fit, for man cannot work each day without a special hope. My army deserves the best exceptional strong drink that shall ever be made on New Venus. I honestly do not understand the ways of man, for the only two I knew was my father Belcher and my prophet brother Oi. Égerszög has promised to help me, so please feel free to share your hearts with my guards. I wish that all would know that these guards saved my life, for if not for them, I would still be chained into the grips of pain from the claws of Rubina. I follow their guidance without question, for they are my eyes to the men who serve me as their Queen." Then I heard a soldier say, "Wow, we have the greatest Queen, who not even dreams could create." I looked at the commander and laughed saying, "I think I may be on the right track now." The commander asked me, "Do you not fear your safety if we are drunk?" I looked at him and said, "No one or thing of this world can defeat my Lord nor take from me what he has given." The commander then looked again at me and said, "My Queen that I do believe." I now looked over at my family and saw Boudica talking to them. She was acting very strange as many of the mothers were pointing their hands at her. I immediately ran over to them and asked, "What is going on here?" The mothers lined up in a row and told me, "Boudica, has something she needs to tell you."

I looked at Boudica and asked, "Is there something you need to tell me?" Boudica answered, "No mommy." Then Dömsöd said to me, "Boudica is not your daughter." I looked at them and said, "That is the same thing that she told me; however, as my reward from the Lord, he has given me this daughter and nothing upon this world can take from me what the Lord has given me.

Do you not think that if the Lord did not want Boudica as my daughter our love could be this great? I tell that Boudica is my daughter and cursed is anyone who denies this." The skies then grew dark, and a wind comes down as I lifted my hands and the sun became bright once more. I afterwards said to my family, "Does anyone need any more clarification?" I then pointed at my hip and little Boudica locked hold of me tight, and tucked her head beginning to cry. Zala, Tolna, and Ózdi grouped around us kissing Boudica's head saying, "We all love you honey and are so proud that you told your mother the truth. You are a special little person." I afterwards told those thanks, walked over to my family, and told those thanks for caring. I subsequently confessed, "This gift from the Lord I cannot give back. I tell you another great mystery, in that someday I shall bow before her and call her Queen in front of the Lord's throne. This is truly the greatest gift that a woman without a child could ever receive, a child with the wisdom of the Ancient One and the faith to move all the stars in the skies." Then I heard a light snore beside my ear, as Tolna and Zala reached over to carry her. Ózdi after that said to me, 'You are stuck with me again." I told her, "No my love, we are all stuck with my little dream tonight, call your husband to join you with us." As Ózdi and I followed Tolna and her gang, I told Ózdi, "Ózdi, today I have found a new mission for Égerszög and that is to help me to do fair by the men who serve me." Ózdi then answered, "Égerszög surely knows the ways of men, and he will do you great justice." I told her thanks for sharing him with our kingdom.

We traveled throughout all the tribes and all the villages, as over three years had quickly passed by us. I then summoned some of the high priests for a secret mission. I asked them to find some old widows and have them meet on two boats I would have been waiting for them in a small port called Lenti in the tribe of Becske. The Lord will guide the ships to where he wants them to go. They asked me, "Why does the Lord want this?" I told them, "That he has also kept a mystery from me, it could be a test to see how we obey, yet I truly do not know and am foolish for guessing." I shall now take my family and settle them in the land of Vas. I took them to the rich valleys on the northeastern plains and gave to them, much land. I put them behind a small mountain that was closest to the eastern shore. I placed their giant ranches alongside the North Central desert in Vas. We discovered another ancient tunnel that ran along the mountain bay on the northern coast.

Here, we built for them many ships so that they could trade the bountiful harvests the Lord would give unto them. I gave to them many cattle and horses, for theirs would be easy to identify, as they all were white. The Lord gave them all nice homes and all the things they needed, to include refillable plates until the first harvest was finished. We also built a large temple, the largest in all the tribes for here Tolna and Zala would share the Lord's words to his servants. This temple was built on the desert plateau on top of the small mountain range below their ranches. Many roads were built to gain access to this temple, for I wanted to make sure that the Lord's word would still be strong for when Boudica was to take her throne, which her time was quickly coming. I wrongfully did not remind her anymore, for I wanted our days before the war to be glorious. Finally, I disbanded my army. I told the commander that any could travel back to their home tribes with a refillable plate until they made it to their home. Following that, I told the commanders that if any wanted to stay here, the Lord would give them a house and land with a planted garden and many-colored herd animals. We would also be inviting women, especially widows as possible brides. They would also receive a refillable plate. I now took Boudica and traveled to the tribe of the Somogy.

Soon after we left, two strangers rushed on us screaming and yelling, "How can you, a Queen of the Lord departs without your two Saints?" I looked back and two very angry young women quickly caught up with us. I asked them, "Tolna and Zala, why are you here?" They answered, "We are that right as chosen Saints of our Lord." I next looked at them and said, "My boss has told me the error in my judgment, will you forgive me and ride with me?" Tolna after that reached over to give me a kiss while Zala snuck one from Boudica. Tolna said to me, "This time oh Queen, but next time here by the will of our Lord. He made us Saints to serve with you, and that we shall do." I felt a tuck in my back and lowered my head when a little head appeared and said, "Mommy, they have check with our boss first, okay?" Then Boudica rips out, "Yes, mommy okay; you are getting to be a handful for me." We all began to laugh as I stopped and said, "That little fellow gets me every time," and after that continued to laugh. We took our time to Somogy and when the villages seen us ride through all knew what was on the road ahead. The time had come as they lined the roads saying, "May our Lord Save our Great Queen."

Chapter 08

Great War Against the Wicked Empire

The honorable manuscripts of Oi told: "Then she shall travel to the Labarians and assemble the greatest army that New Venus has ever witnessed. I shall tell you a great secret, 'once her foot touches Belcher's prison; she will be crowned the Queen of the prison that only a few years earlier cast her as a beaten dog onto the brush to burn as garbage." I knew my time had arrived, and that I must face head on the evil, which bitterly chipped at the bones of my soul for so many years. I recognized that this must not be done only for the tribes, but also for the tormented in Rubina's Empire that dreamed of freedom now. They were being tormented beyond imagination since I was gone and the demons had returned, especially after I had beheaded the puppets they established as the head priests and then the terrible defeat that they suffered in Vas and on the day of cleaning. We had some extra time in the port of Lenti in the tribe of Becske. A priest could smuggle us into a local leader's home. The area was now flooding with people actually to pray with me and wish me a great victory.

I could understand that they wanted to be a part of this, and I will give them a good speech when I go to the Labarians to prepare our inordinate army. Even I was currently confused as to why I would need a great army, as I could lift one of Rubina's army high in the sky and drop them. I know that the Lord likes patience and obedience and for what he is giving, the tribes and all New Venus now that Rubina's warships were raiding this small world. Her goal was to surpass the terror of the Flexsters, and she was on her way to accomplishing this, to the terror of the world. That would soon end, as I intended to defeat all her militaries and police forces. The blood will come later, for now I must enlighten my group concerning our mission. Zala, Tolna, Boudica, and I sat down to a private evening meal. The host has done much to honor us, and has told me he never waists any food, always giving the remaining to the poor. I thank him for doing this, as even the poor need, some luxurious food sometimes. He told me that guilt always filled his heart when he enjoyed his wealth. I told him, "It is not what you have that will destroy you, it is how you received it and keep it that will abolish you. I tell you that if you share, you will have to spare. That is the law of the ages, and the way of things." He thanked me and departed. Zala asked me, "My Queen, what did that mean?"

I said, "Zala, if one abuses others to gain their riches, then they shall have a high debt in heaven. If they are to be paid, afterwards yes, they need to work, yet not worked to death. If they die, then at the throne, they will accuse their killer. In addition, if one hides his wealth and sins to keep it, he shall lose that wealth. If you can give up what you have, then you can have it. Never let your gains or wealth own you for when you are judged, those things will not be, and you will therefore stand before the Lord with great shame and no defense to save you." I still remember my growing years with Oi, and I would travel with no food or money. We would at times for many days without food, yet we enjoyed the freedom it also gave us. Even though we struggled hard for our food, we still enjoyed our nights of prayer. I enjoy owning no things as it gives me the freedom to ride throughout this land. I did not come to have things; I came to save the world from my mother. Each night as I rest, I see a vision, in which I am standing on a cloud and Boudica, and her friends are playing in the blue skies that surround me. I see other mothers also playing with the children. Above us is a bright light that shines on us. I look down on

New Venus and see my people surrounded with all manners of grazing animals, and it brings joy to my heart." Tolna then asked, "Why do you speak about being in the heavens so much?"

I told her, "Because those visions bring me the greatest joy." Tolna then asked, "Did you have those visions during your times of trouble?" I revealed to her, "I had no visions of the heavens during my times of trouble. This was a test of my faith and strength, to have such visions would have altered my ability to survive." Zala now asked, "Did you break down at any time?" I told them, "There was one time I broke down and Oi gave me proof that my suffering from this was not needed." Boudica then asked, "What was it mother?" I divulged to them, "I thought the innocent children who Rubina was killing were my fault as they would beg me for their lives, only to have their blood shower me. Oi showed me where they were taking these spirits before the pain of death and bringing them to the heavens. This brought me joy and gave me the power to carry on, for I had no desire to win if so many others had to lose for my stubbornness. I now hung onto the manuscripts that I had memorized about Oi's teachings. These were inside me and could not be moved. It is what I inside you, which will save you during times of trouble. You must strive to put much inside you, for if you do not make your mind full of the word, the troubles you face may defeat you."

Boudica then told me, "Mommy, you were worried about the babies, which are a good thing; you did great as I am still so proud of you. Can you tell us what things shall pass on us?" I can tell you what will happen with us. I can see us riding on four horses throughout the tribes celebrating our great victory. Always, when we are observed, you three, shall be with me. I can never be seen alone. My ride with you will be short, as we will be traveling to the high cliff, which my father always dreamed of climbing. I next see Boudica coroneted as Queen. Her reign is short, as the heavens will call my little baby for a great mission, which naturally, my daughter excels. I now see Zala and Tolna reigning as joint Queens or Queen Sisters. This is why you must work hard on these Armies, so that all will know your great military minds and if ever you need to go to war, they will be ready for you. When we are training our Armies, you will never look to me for approval. Whatever you say has been approved by me on this day. You stand tall with the confidence of knowing great power is in your voice, for I know the Lord will once again show wonders through your works. If any look to me for approval to what you have commanded, I will point to you and turn away. This they will know is to be done with all my confidence. We will reinforce this in front of our Armies.

I shall bow before each of you, and you shall pat me on my head and place your hand on my face as I shall kiss it." Zala and Tolna refused ever to do this and would prefer to die evermore to see me humbled in public." I told them, "You must do this, for if you do not let me serve you in front of all. How can they believe the great love and faith I have in you? I give, and you receive so that I can receive my greatest gift, and that is my love may live among the tribes when I am no longer walking through this world." Boudica now began crying, "Why must you do this to me, because I know how Rubina punished you so badly that I can never think of you serving another. You paid the price mommy." I told her, "Boudica, as we are humble to the Lord then us, as his servants must be humble before his creation. I am humble before you to give my Lord thanks for sharing with me his pronounced creations of love." Tolna then asked, "How can we thank the Lord for giving us the Great Queen as our sister?" I looked at her with my arms open and said, "Come on women, if you only knew how much thanks I have for each minute I have with you. You are more important to me than my life." The last two years have seen Boudica grow practically one foot. She is a strong looking and almost as tall as I am. She still has a deep love for our relationship.

Her knowledge is so advanced; she can quote every word from Oi's manuscript, and that was not included in the Szombathelyi Empire's libraries. Then she touched so many pages, for actually over three years, going into great depth on so many subjects. She will rebuild our current black land's tribes and my father's prison into a continent free over any seeds from the Flexsters. I feel sad that she will have one hurt, the hurt that puts you against the wall and dares you ever to put yourself into another. That hurt will be because of my absence. I know that she should have been forced to keep the widows as her mommies, yet she was so hungry to be a part of Oi's vision and legacy, that she gave me the most important thing in my short life. That was of course a daughter. I know that Tolna, Zala, and Ózdi will care for her intimately resealing, the bond of daughter and mother. My big girl, even though 15 years old, will ride on the horse with me, in front of me during training and behind me during any hostile situations. I do not completely understand why I must leave so soon after the war, yet I know there must be a good reason. Tolna and Zala will rule the longest as I can see my guards and their families doing many great works for them. Égerszög will be beside them running the new Armies.

A prison guard illegally giving food to the most despised beast ever to be imprisoned, and then talk all his comrades into joining him and risk the lives of their families taking this disfigured bag of beaten bones into the forbidden lands where they could easily have become prisoners. I remember how they began to relax when Rubina's army rode into the sky and dropped to their deaths, as not even their horses lived. The miracles the Boudica did in repairing me still left this in confusion, because Rubina's demons did wonders in front of the people, and having a 13-year-old girl to rescue them kept their eyes open at night. I often wonder why life could not be like it was when I was a young child and Oi or my father would carry me to the pond or special place where they would play with me. Our mother never said anything against what Belcher wanted to do and which children he would take. She would wait until he went off to pray and then get even. We told our father a couple of times, as bruises are hard to hide when we were playing. We knew never to lie to our father, or his Lord would punish us. We would warn Rubina and then take us for a couple of weeks somewhere. Rubina liked keeping our father around, where she could keep an eye on him and his Lord. I remember when I first looked at my mended body and now being able, I would have no terror to show any who looked at it, only to discover that I will never have a husband, nor will Boudica.

We have finished our secret walks; all cut short by someone discovering us. The priests have arrived now, and I prepare to speak with them. I tell them, "My work on rebuilding the tribes into a land with brings favor to the Lord has now finished. Evil has been driven from our remaining lands. We now must consider that while Rubina lives in this world, peace will never be. My brother Oi told you long ago that I would be the one who leads your Armies into our great war. That day has come. We shall lead your great Armies as Queen Sister Zala, Queen Sister Tolna and

Queen Daughter Boudica shall be at my side. We now go into the lands of the Labarians and wait for our soldiers to come to us so that we may prepare. I ask you to send messages on all who live among the tribes to the Labarians. Give to me all the men; old, and young, who wish to fight in this war." The priests now celebrated, for their days of dreams were at hand. She took her women and went into the land of the Labarians. The priests from many of the local temples sent for their widows whom they might help care for the soldiers who were to come. Tianshire asked the Lord to make a giant tent for them and her a tent beside them.

I explained to all that we could construct no buildings on Labarian land. The Lord now constructed all the military trainee tents, temples, classrooms, dining halls, and recreational areas. As we explored the nearby hills, we looked down on the giant valley where we would train and live. It was as a sea of tents, too many to count. Tolna asked, "Why do many tents?" I told her, "The greatest army ever to come from the tribes or Rubina shall train here." Boudica then asked a very wise collection, "Why do we need an army so large?" I told her, "Daughter, this size is to remove fear from the soldiers and build confidence and power in their bodies." Tolna then told her, "It is to provide an opportunity for Zala and me to find strong husbands." Boudica asked, "Really," while looking at me. I just shrugged my shoulders and then told her, "Who knows? It would be a good time." Boudica then asked, "What about me?" I told her, "Boudica, I will share you with no one; you need only to tell the priests to look for you, and they will find you one if that is your desire." Boudica then told me, "I agree, because I am not sharing you either, or will I share myself with another." I next gave her a pat on the back, and we all continued our sightseeing. We were surprised to see so many large towns spread out in the central lands.

They dedicated much to have their seashores showing not life since Rubina's slave raids. When we returned, I selected a nice high hill where I could look out on the sea. It was here the Lord gave me thousands of flags for our new nation. It was solid red with a white cross, centered on both sides. It had five stars who ran parallel along the top. The first star was the largest. The five stars stood for the leaders the Lord had selected, namely Oi, Boudica, Tolna, Zala, and myself. Four of the five were here now, which adds some strength to the five stars, considering no one would ever question Oi as the first star. One large flag was before me, then a pole started rising from the ground, and this flag attached itself to the pole as it continued to rise at least three hundred feet into the air. It was so big and high that many could see it throughout Somogy and Becske. The first ship arrived with some soldiers and supplies. We rode to the shore and greeted them. I then asked the ship's captain to take our new flags back to the temples. We led these soldiers, which were, for the most part, commanders, to our introduction or receiving area in our camp. We had a tall flag here also, yet only tall enough to be seen throughout the camp. I told these soldiers to count the stars in the flag. They told me there were five. I then told them, "Four of those five are before you now. You are the fortunate ones, for you will be the only army to fight for four of the stars."

I could see their backs start to become conventional again and a new completeness to their pride. I know much more about the thinking of men, thanks to Égerszög. We must consider their pride; and not run over them as women thirsting for power or crazy, such as my mother. I told my girls, we must always look beautiful with our makeup and nice washed white gowns on our clean horses. We must control our anger in public. These men are here to fight a war for us, as many could lose their lives. Even though all men need the spiritual reason to fight, such as saving their nation and freedoms, it also does not hurt to give them something beautiful to fight for in their hearts. I now could understand the perfection in our bodies. I understood the suffering and sacrifices Boudica had made, yet she now was a very beautiful young woman. Zala and Tolna come from successful families, and I later learned that when I went to Rubina's Empire (Belcher's prison) they came to help care for the mothers and then in the tunnels of Bugac. I felt good about that, because it gave them a chance to finish their childhood. Boudica kept sneaking out and living in the temples, which delighted the priests but terrified Zala and Tolna, as they had also adopted her as their daughter.

The warmth in her face has such a way to weaken any woman and create a longing to be her mother. I was constantly surprised at the enthusiasm Boudica created in Ózdi and Égerszög. Égerszög fell into the role as the agreed father from all four of us, Tolna, Zala, Ózdi, and myself. We always stepped back and let Égerszög speak to her. When he talked, we did not. We struggled hard to show him the utmost respect, as we also did around all men, who deserved. We wanted to develop in her the respect for men, and with pride, we report that she developed very well in this area. One night, Boudica asked me why she had to give respect to all men. She understood the priests and Égerszög, but not the others. I told her that, "The man is the one who traditionally leads the family. He provides for his family. Since not all women are good, then we must realize that not all men are pleasant. Nevertheless, those who are decent deserve our respect to foster their pride. We were created to glorify men with our beauty. That is one reason why the Lord gave us such beauty. We make the babies in a special part of our belly and provide the love and guidance for our children by sharing the love we receive from the man the Lord bonded us with, and enforce his guidance among our children. And this is the way of things." My young woman has never questioned what I tell her and accept it as truth.

I know that she is very wise, so I try to tell her the truth as best I can explain it. The little tiger and assembled a water wagon with barrels of water that the soldiers would refill for her from a nice river that flowed beside our training camp. She would make her routes each day giving the soldiers water. I will give her credit, because she did know the soldiers in our camp, as she would talk with them while they drank their water. She would boast about their progress and listen to their tales about the heroic things they were doing, and she told them how thankful that she was for their great deeds. Zala, Tolna, and I stuck, close with the commanders except for our Friday night parties. The Lord had given me refillable barrels, which produced different types of wine, beer, and whiskeys. These barrels were placed throughout the camp so that all could have access to them, without standing in long lines. During the remaining six days of the week, the barrels were dry; however, on Fridays, they would flow again. Zala, Tolna and myself spoke with some local 'large towns' and invited the young single women to join my soldiers for these Friday night parties. I guaranteed their safety, as my angels protected them. A few soldiers pressed their luck as my angels immediately seized them saving these young women from any harm.

My punishment was simple; I sent them back to the tribes with the mark of a large S on their forehead, which meant sinner. A few begged to stay and in these situations I let the commanders decide if they could stay and the punishment. The punishment could not be in sight of my tent, as I told my commanders, "I have come to take blood from Rubina, not the tribes. Furthermore, make sure you pray in the temple to see if your punishment is just. The punishment must allow the soldier to fight and still be able to train. Any punishment, which permanently renders the soldier disabled, is not permitted. I want to have all disabilities caused from the battlefield, as our new nation will care for them. We must keep as many of our people strong as possible, so we can build a mighty nation." I saw what torture does as a punishment and how it punishes the executor when they fail to get the response they desire. Some give the desired response early as a lie, never intending to honor their word. The dangerous thing is that they always seek revenge. I see no reason to create people who will be looming to ambush me. Moreover, I do not want to create a hate for women by judging and punishing opening. They know to expect punishment from their commander. This keeps the power in the leader.

Returning to the Friday parties, I was proud how many of the men treated these women with courtesy and respect, even with a river of strong drink available. On Monday, mornings, I would outline our training objectives for the week. Our first Monday morning, I had our soldiers count the number of the stars. I then introduced three of the stars, Boudica the Queen Daughter, Tolna the Queen Sister and Zala the Queen Sister. I now had them to lift their gowns about one foot, knelt before each, and kissed their legs. When I was finished, I motioned that they lower their gowns and told my soldiers, "As you have seen me humbled before these great stars, you also must obey them, serving to their death if called to do so." This now reinforced Zala and Tolna, as they would ride among the training and among the family tents, as many soldiers brought their families. The wives made uniforms, battle front tents, boots, and would bring in the material the soldiers needed by wagons. I had the army make large swords, head and chest shields, and other miscellaneous battlefield items. Then one day, many ships packed with women and old men came ashore. I went down to meet them. They were skilled archers, who at one time made up the complete fighting force of the black lands. They begged me to let them fight in my great army.

I told them to wait while I went to a nearby tree and ask the Lord. The news was not good; however, I had to tell them why the Lord said to send them home. They must make a new generation that they may eat from a land flowing with milk and honey. They then complained to me, "How can we make babies when you have taken all our men?" I told them not to fear for they would have men to be fathers for their children, who will raise them in a land of love and peace. The old men asked, "What will you have us to do oh mighty Queen." Subsequently, Zala came riding down to me, and I asked her to have the commanders send down horses for these men. She looked at me in disbelief, for in our camp, we had almost 100,000 young strong fighting men, trained for two hard years. She did as I asked her and soon commanders brought down horses for the old men. I told them, "Wait and you shall ride back with me. I also told the single women archers that if they wanted husbands to go to my Queen's tent, and we would make them so that the fires of lust would burn in my soldiers. My army was now prepared, as I could see it was time for my destiny to unfold on New Venus. I took the old men up and told them to ride around the camp and to stay strong. Those who finished the ride were to return to our receiving area. As these men rode throughout the camp as so many laughed at them, calling them fools and other abuses.

They all returned and waited for me. Boudica, Tolna, and Zala quickly transformed our one thousand new woman so that they could enjoy our Friday night party. These women were currently dressed in light blue evening gowns. I now called up my ten division commanders and told them, "I give each of you 100 wonderful women who tonight they may be married, if they so desire. All my priests will be riding among you tonight and perform the ceremonies as requested. These new wives have special blue tents that have the fronts open. The wives may pick from any tent that still has its front open. The local women who visit tonight might also become brides and live in our wives' tents; thereafter, become citizens in our nation. The party went exceptional this Friday as all women were married, both the archers and locals. Monday morning, I had the Armies make some 200-pound spears, the same number as the aged men I had accepted. I had the old men wait in the widows' tent. I called my giant army together on our drill field and said to them, "So that all will know that the Lord God shall save us, all young men go back and take unto them wives and marry and multiply. Your children shall be raised in a land of love." The commanders now rushed up to me and asked, "How can you fight your war without Armies?" I told them that the Lord would deliver us.

I then complained as to why I had wasted two years of their lives. I told them, "I have not wasted two years of your lives. A new nation must have a tough trained fighting force available. Even though, the Lord takes me shortly after this war, my daughter and sisters will need a strong army to help them defend our nation. A new nation will not last without an available army. I hope you can understand this." They bowed and told me, "We understand and wish you the best in the war you are now to fight." I also sent the widows back. We waited for three days for all the soldiers to make it home. The Lord then took back the tents and restored all the land to the condition it was when we arrived. I now told these old men to lift their 200-pound swords. The first try they failed. I commanded them to try once more. This time the swords were lighter than feathers, and they slung them up with ease. I told them that they must, always be touching the sword and that their shoulder counted as a touch because I knew them to have at least one arm up would cause unjustified hardship. As we prepared to board our two ships, a saw a fleet of Rubina's war ships sailing toward us. I could count at least fifty. She had finally discovered where my army was; however, she did not know where it is now.

I raised my hands, and the ships rose with my hands. I felt bad because I knew many innocent men were on these ships. The Lord lifted the innocent out of the ships and afterwards crashed this fleet deep into the sea so that no one on board could live. The Lord then sent the innocent back to their homelands. This made me feel good, in that once again we gave her a giant defeat. She now had lost about one-third of her fleet. She would have to recall many of her invading ships to protect her shores. She then became so outraged at this second setback that she launched all her demons onto the black lands. However, she once again was met with a serious defeating blow. Meanwhile, our ship landed on the shore of Somogy. Once I walked out onto the shore to meet my people cheering, I fell into a deep sleep. A great fear came over my people. While in this deep sleep, I felt my spirit go to visit Oi. He told me about his great pride in my work and that the time for my destiny was at hand. He invited me to dine with him, although he sat in his chair meditating. An angel came over to sit beside me. He handed me an aged scroll and told me to eat it. I asked him what I was eating. Now many angels appeared. He told me that I had eaten the 'Word' and was the first living person ever to be given the 'Word.' I then told him, "I have all the teachings of Oi in my mind, is that not enough knowledge?"

The angels now all laughed as another giant angel came before me and said, "Tianshire, you do not understand. This 'Word' is not knowledge; it is a great power, and when you speak this 'Word', all demons shall be destroyed." You are to take your Queens and old men back to the Labarian lands and travel down the coast to the strait at the northernmost tip on the previous green lands of the Tolna and Baracs or Fonó Peninsula. It is here when you ride across the forty-mile sea and meet all Rubina's demons and Armies. You shall rest nearby for two months as the rebels in Rubina's Empire destroy all remaining evil, except for Rubina, which the Lord has saved for you. You shall ride to her palace, take her, and burn her with fire. You will receive a map dividing her Empire among your brothers and sisters, as they shall also fall under your crown. You shall take them to their new homes and declare them as governors. After this, you will return and declare our Boudica as Queen and afterwards go to the high mountains of Miskoldi or Pásztói Peak, where you will walk up a cliff that no one has ever climbed into a cave along that wall. Once in the cave, you shall join Oi and live among the Lord's throne." I now asked, "Why must I return so fast after our victory?"

The angel said, "Because you have the 'Word' in you, and the risk is too high that evil would steal it from you." I then said, "Okay that I understand, and I also want to thank the Lord for making my brothers and sisters governors. I know that they shall do a great job." The angel then said, "So does the Lord, we wish you considerable success as your destiny now unfolds before you." At this time, I began to awaken. I now stood up and said to the people, "I have received my mission from the Lord, and I tell you that your new nation shall soon be. I must return with my army up to the coast of the Labarians. All who go to the mountains between Mountain Lake and Somogy shall see the greatest battle in our history. We now returned to the shores of the Labarians and started riding down the coast. Many watched us travel from the mountains at Somogy and laughed saying, "How can she win with only old men who carry spears heavier than they are?" Then one priest said to them, "That they carry swords heavier than they are, tells us that their victory is nigh. I made sure that we rode, close enough to the score to be visible; however, at times we had to move inland from too many bodies washed up on the beaches. We finally arrived at our crossover point in the middle of summer. I was flabbergasted, for how can we walk over forty miles of the sea.

It was here where I got another surprise as the Lord gave me my fighting suit, which was nothing. I grew so fond of clothing again and now to be bare, in front of old men at that. At least let me be around young men so that I could watch them burn as I shared my shame. I ask the Lord, "Why?" He told me, "To show that you are pure with no sin. Without clothing did you come from Rubina; therefore, your purity will cast her into the sea. Many saw you naked, as Rubina shamed you before her Empire. Now, you came back in power and show them that in purity, there is no shame and that purity always defeats evil." I then said, "I shall be as you want me to be." As I thought about it while looking at my beautiful white gown lying on the ground, I realized that my body was destroyed long ago, and my body held my spirit for this mission was created when I prepared to return to the tribes. Moreover, many saw me whipped so many times, and the blood poured from my wounds. They shall now see a perfect body without blemish. This would also motivate me to finish faster. The most embarrassing part, even worse than the old men, would be riding with Boudica holding me with Tolna and Zala on my sides. With all the times, we bathed together in the streams and ponds, the nudity were not the issue; it was where the nudity would be. I pulled myself and walked out, going through the old men, to my Queen family.

The old men pretended as if everything was normal. If only I could read their minds, they are probably saying, 'this woman is crazy.' I am glad no one is reading minds today. I now go up to my girls and ask them if we are ready to go. Tolna and Zala shake their heads yes, and jump up on their horses. Boudica looks at me and says, "Mommy, you forgot to get dressed." I told her, "Honey, this is the way I am to fight." Boudica next says, "Okay, me too." She afterwards starts to strip as I yell for her to stop. Zala and Tolna now ask, "Do you want us to join you also Tianshire?" I tell them all, "You may fight in your gowns." Then Tolna surprises me by saying, "Tianshire; you are truly a loyal and courageous leader." It after that hit me how I would have to stay brave to do this. I really do not think that my enemies as they are dying will be laughing at me. I then say to my small group, "It is time we invade Fonó Peninsula. Follow me." I rode into the sea and for the first eight or nine steps from my horse, the water splashed. Then we were lifted, and the sea turned to stone. I looked behind me, and my soldiers were walking single file behind my Queens. We were all in the water. They truly trusted, this lunatic that is leading them. We were at least 30 miles in when I saw the sky get dark in front of me.

Tolna asked, "Are we to have a storm today?" I then said, "Well if we do, I will not have to worry about getting my gown wet, anyway my family; those are not storm clouds. Those are clouds packed with demons." I stopped and turned around, while looking at everyone I said, "Fear not, we shall be victorious as the greatest battle ever to be fought on our homeland is to begin soon." I now could see ahead as the sea was stone to the shore, yet water behind us. We could only move ahead. I then saw five great Armies moving toward us. We could feel their horses rattle through the stone below us. When the first one got within one mile of us, and the last one was maybe three miles ahead of us, the sea below them turned into water and they all fell into the sea, as it turned to rock again over them. Nothing, which was with these five Armies, survived. We could hear the horns blowing in celebration from Pásztói Peak. I knew that soon the people would begin reclaiming their former homes in the green lands. Those who had settled there from the Empire were now preparing for a mass exodus. Tolna asked me, "Why do the demons not fight with us?" I told them, "They cannot leave the shores." I had them wait for me now, as I traveled the last quarter mile alone. When I reached the shore, I got off my horse, and the demons went to attack me.

I spoke the 'Word',' and every demon on this continent vanished. I now could see Rubina's ships throughout New Venus and especially in Death Bay. I spoke saying, "I command every ship of Rubina's be destroyed and all who serve in her fleet that are guilty to vanish and those who are innocent to return to their homelands." I then asked the Lord about the five Armies that attacked me in the sea. He told me that the innocents there also were returned to their

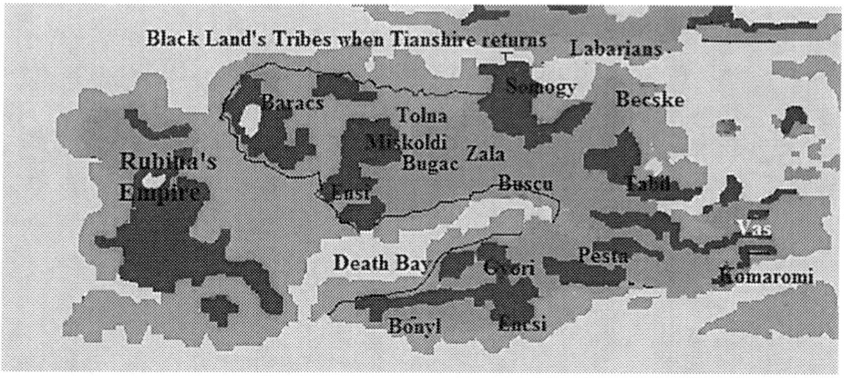

homes as well. I returned to my army and told them, "We must now destroy Rubina and set up the new governors. I told my aged men to drive their arrows into the ground here so that all would remember this great battle. We now rode toward the old borders as all the occupying people stood along our road and cheered. This was a good feeling, for they were my native people and had suffered, as had I. We waved at them with our palms as a sign of peace. With no demons to oppress, her people Rubina had lost control of her Empire as rebellion broke out and the people killed the corrupt officials who had made them suffer so much. Fires burned in every village as the evil met their death. I also restored many of Rubina's warships as cargo ships and left them hidden out in the sea. These ships would return the slaves who wanted to go home. Boudica would need peaceful relations with her neighboring islands.

The crowds continued to cheer us, now all waved white rags; therefore, so did we. That was also special; we had a celebration language, a way that the people who had suffered this much could furthermore share in this victory. Tianshire has returned in victory. I was soon joined by all my brothers and sisters. They were all very happy this time, as they could visit with me not having to rub all the salves and lotions, they had brought with them. Tolna and Zala were so amazed by the resemblance I had with all my sisters. I never noticed it that much when I was in prison, for

I believe the not being yelled at, and the feeling of the lotions and salves coupled with the dark and cold rock walls distorted my perceptions. We continued to ride west and then started riding southwest and follow the desert that I played in as a child. This is the only desert in my native lands. I was met there by a small band of citizens who told me they had Rubina captured and asked what I wanted them to do. I told them, "I shall burn her over the remains of the prison she beat me in that prison, bring many trees, and place on it. Have the ground leveled by trees, lay on it another layer, and keep beside it two more levels. You are to tie Rubina to a post where she can see the fire, making sure the smoke does not kill her first before the fire. I will be there soon. Have a chain available that I may take her from the post and tie her to one of the giant cut trees.

I shall then slowly drop her into the fire. They did this perfectly and even created a rope pulley system which made it possible for me easily to maneuver the tree. The fire burned so high that we could see it, the instant they started it. I was only ten miles from my chamber of horrors when the fire began. When we arrived, my brothers, sisters, and their spouses, all ran to hide when they saw our mother. I walked up to her and said twirling around, "How do you like my body, mommy?" She said, "You look exactly like I left you." I then said, "Oh mommy, you know what happens to people who lie?" She asked me, "What?" I told her, "The bad liar's burn as you shall soon." I motioned for the guards to tie her to the chains attached to the tree and the said to her, "Oh behalf of my daddy, you shall now be punished for the misery and suffering you have given to New Venus." She began to beg and plead for mercy. I did not even know she knew these words. One of the guards asked me, "When do we remove her clothing?" I told them, "She shall not be given the same honors as me. Moreover, I did come from her womb thus she shared her shame that I may have life."

I slowly lifted her over the fire, and she began to scream and beg someone to save her. As the fire burned on her legs, large dark slimy creatures come out of her flesh and fell into the fire. We could hear these things also cry in agony. Before we completely burned her, over 100 of those black bags of slim escaped through her burning flesh. Boudica asked me, "Mommy, how can there be so many of them in one body?" I told her, "My baby, a thousand legions of evil demons can hide in a speck of dust. They use some physical thing in our world to create a portal to their chambers of evil. You must always be careful to stay in the light so that evil may not hurt you." As the fire started to burnout, I had them put the remaining trees on the fire. This kept it burning for two more days. Soon all we could see was red-hot coals. We continued to let them burn and four days later; I had the people bury the burning site so that the light would never see this terrible place again. I felt so good, Rubina, her demons, and her Empire had fallen. What should have been the greatest day of my life was to take one more hit, which would drop me to my knees. After the burning, my siblings and their spouses came out to ask me for a private meeting in the palace. As we all sat down, I told them, "If you worry about your future in our parents' lands have no fear, for each of you shall be given a province and be governor thereof in an Empire that Boudica shall set up."

My sister Ibrány now asked, "Tianshire, did you pick Boudica to be our next Queen?" I looked at her and said, "Sister Ibrány, I wish I had; however, our Lord selected her." Afterwards all my family began clapping saying, "She will make a Great Queen indeed, and we shall all serve her with all our hearts." Then Ibrány said to me, "Tianshire, Tolna told me you knew that Boudica is not your real daughter." I then told them, "This thing I do know." Ibrány asked again, "Did she tell you what happened to her real parents?" I next told Ibrány, "She believes raiders killed them." After that Tsarsko told me, "Tianshire, I know what happened to her parents, as I was there." I later asked Tsarsko, "Please tell me my favorite younger brother." He subsequently told me that it was a rainy cloudy day, as he was visiting little Boudica and her parents. I would tell her stories about you and Oi, which she loved so much, often times more than reality. One day, an army of raiders invaded her home, as she lived in the green lands not far from the border. I could hide her under the floor in this house in a special box we created if of an emergency such as this. The raiders came in, destroyed everything in this house, and killed Boudica's father. The raiders tied her mother and myself and took us away to Rubina's prison for her children."

I said, "Both of you, did she think you were married?" Tsarsko told me, "No Tianshire, she put her son and daughter in the prison. Boudica's mother is sitting at this table today." I afterwards began to cry, as they all came up to comfort me. I next told them, "As a fool I thought my punishments was over." Then Tsarsko told me, "Tianshire, her mother loves Boudica so much; nevertheless, she loves you more and has decided if you want to keep Boudica and this secret, she will swear her allegiance to you." I subsequently said, "Only a true mother would do that for little Boudica; notwithstanding, such a secret would be a lie. Such a mother should have her daughter. Now to know that my blood truly runs in her and that I was doing a holy duty by loving her is a great reward. I will abide by Boudica's mother wishes; her mother will not abide by my wishes. Her mother has that right knowing that from her womb, Boudica came forth. I can now see why she held onto us so strongly. She was holding onto your stories and her true mother, which is within its self a great story of love. May I talk with her mother now and see what she desires me to do?" Tsarsko then said, "Will you swear to the Lord that you will not hurt Boudica or her mother?" I answered, "Tsarsko, which is the easiest pledge that I can ever give.

They shall be safe, as I will give my blood to make sure they are. What manner of evil could kill a mother who offered to give her only baby if I desired her to do so?" They all looked at me and said, "Rubina!" Afterwards I said, "I did not burn our mother so that I may follow in her footsteps." Then all my brothers and sisters, except for one, got up and left the room. My sister Ibrány had been sitting beside me the entire day. I then asked Ibrány if she held me. She quickly lifted me up and gave me a long stern hug, saying repeatedly, "I love you so much Tianshire." I then started kissing her cheek and told her, "Of all my sisters, I was secretly hoping it was you, because I so much needed someone by my side today while meeting you all again." Ibrány told me, "The reason I was beside you was that I could feel Boudica's love flowing from your heart." I then said, "My love, my Ibrány, how do you want to do this? Do you know that my days are few?" Ibrány started crying saying, "We did not know. If we knew we never would have told you this." I then told her, "Oh Ibrány, it is therefore, good that you told me, because I will know when looking down from the heavens my niece is being loved by the womb, which that created her. Boudica so much deserves this." She then said, "Why must you go?" I told her, "The Lord gave me something that I must give back. I must give each of you your provinces and then go to my goodbye cliff."

Ibrány afterwards said, "Do you think the Lord would be angry if I did not take a province and instead served my daughter?" I then said, "Actually, that will be perfect; as he shorted me one province, and I could not figure out why." I will now ask you, as your sister, if you live with your daughter as her mother. Ibrány yelled, "Yes!" She then pushed me to the table and jumped on me, so much as Boudica had so many times convincing me that Boudica was hers, and started kissing me and screaming I love you; I love you. This startled our siblings as they came rushing in thinking I had betrayed them. Once they figured out that I was helpless in this situation, everyone started laughing and teasing Ibrány saying, "Ibrány, do not think that only you can kiss her, for this entire continent is packed with men who would love to be over her, kissing her, and telling her how much they love her." Ibrány next says aloud, "They can suffer, because I have her, and I will not share her!" After that, I looked at them, pretending to be starry-eyed and said, "Wow, once someone has been loved by Ibrány, why would they ever want, another?" Our sisters were laughing so hard now, since we had smoked our brothers' first class. Then my favorite lovely brother Tsarsko said, "Oh Lord, why do I have such crazy sisters?"

Now this one busted all of us, not knowing that this was the first time so much laughter had echoed from this palace. At this time, Boudica came in crying with Zala and Tolna behind her. Boudica now stuck her growing head between Ibrány and my heads and asked, "Are you okay mommy?" I then told her, "Your mommy is crazy." Boudica laughs and says, "I know that." I then look at Tsarsko and give him my eye signals to get everyone out of this room. This brings back so many memories of how Tsarsko and I would communicate using facial expressions as little children. He motioned everyone out as a couple of my sisters escorted Zala and Tolna out. Naturally, Boudica did not move, because once she got her, claws latched into me, which was it until breakfast time the next day. She helped Ibrány and me to get up. She paused and stared at Ibrány's eyes for a moment, then shook her head and said, "Wow; you look just like my mommy." Now was the time to take advantage of this comment, as Boudica meant the Ibrány looked like me, I would play it as her knowing Ibrány was her mother. I, therefore, said, "Boudica, that is because Ibrány is your actual birth mother." Boudica looked both shocked and relieved and said, "I hoped to find my real mother after you went away to be with the Lord. How long did you know?"

I told her, "Boudica, I just found out about 30 minutes ago. We have not left the room thus far. Your mother and I both love you so much. You will always be my 'only daughter' and your mother's daughter. She wants to give up her province, so she can live with, and love you. Would this be okay?" Boudica said, "Oh yes mommy, you will live with me and go everywhere with me, while you keep your clothes on." Ibrány afterwards said to Boudica, "Boudica, I think your aunt Tianshire looks sexy without any clothing on." Boudica next said, "That is the same thing all the boys are telling me, wonder why?" I then told her, "Well, her stay dressed and keep on wondering." We now sat Boudica down and told her the whole story. Then, for the first time since she left the prison, she could remember her daddy's face and that little safety room under the floor. Boudica after that asked Ibrány if she had any other children or had remarried. Ibrány told her that she had not remarried nor had any more children. She subsequently told Boudica, "When the Lord gives you such a wonderful one such as you, why would you ever want another?" Boudica later laughed and said, "I see; you can flatter as well as our Queen." When we went outside to meet our family, both Ibrány and I held one of Boudica's hands with her in the middle.

I winked at Zala and Tolna, and they rushed up to hug me and make sure I was okay. Then Boudica looked at them and said, "I hope you two do not think that you can get free of me." Zala and Tolna both looked at Ibrány, who gave her a heads up, and afterwards, they told Boudica, "Nor can you perpetually think that we would ever stop loving you. Zala and Tolna currently gave Ibrány a big hug and told her, "Welcome to our family." I now showed my siblings their provinces as we traveled to each province, and I declared them the brand-new governor. When we finished this, the five of us girls, returned to our new nation, which had a new name who described who described them as the Lord's people. When we arrived at our original borders, Ózdi and Égerszög were there to greet us. Égerszög asked me if it were okay if he invited the families of the guards to journey here. A scribe had now arrived, so I pulled my seal out and had Égerszög tell what he wanted to do, then when they gave it to me for my seal, I added, 'and anything else he so desires to do.' I sealed it and we decided to camp nearby tonight. I did a little sexy twirl for Égerszög and asked him, "Do you like my uniform?" He winked and said, "I love it Tianshire; I Tianshire; I never dreamed you were that perfect." Then I asked them to join us, as we had some news to share with them.

After I introduced them to Ibrány, and told the true story about Boudica, Ózdi afterwards explained the relationship they had with her. Ibrány then joked, "I think Boudica has the whole country loving her." We all laughed and Ibrány told Ózdi, nothing had changed, for I simply step in where my sister has left open. The next day, my favorite guard and my favorite "just a friend" confidantes were on their way. I truly did not know if they returned as their homeland was now building a wonderful future. We rode slowly to the Miskoldi mountains. Boudica was getting along so well with Ibrány; nevertheless, she always made sure to eat and sleep with me and her mother, which was special. She did not abandon me. While riding the next day, some high priests met us. I told them Boudica was The Queen now and that after that would be Tolna and Zala, and that they would pick their successor. The priests guided us to a nearby temple and conducted the coronation. I was so happy with this, I could see Boudica has become Queen. I told her, My Queen, you had much work to do fast for the heavens will call for you within a few years. I now told them that it was time for me to go on alone. Queen Boudica refused to let me go solely and quickly was at my side walking with me. Everyone considered this to be, 'the times of Queens.' We soon arrived at the cliff with a small cave hole not far from the top. No human has ever climbed this cliff.

I gave Boudica a big hug, kiss, and thanked her for giving me the only true love in my life. I then began to climb this cliff, and as I went up, I could hear Boudica crying and begging me to come back. She was begging the Lord not to take me. When I was about 1300 feet up, I could still hear Boudica going crazy. Her mother, Tolna, and Zala were working hard to comfort her. I feel so bad for her, as I remember the misery, I suffered with Oi had left, yet somehow life goes on with one less player. My hands and feet now turned to web as I climbed a straight wall cliff currently. I soon made it to the cave hole and crawled in, lying on the rock floor to catch my breath. Shortly thereafter I saw two bright lights appear in the hole. I looked again and saw it was Oi and the Lord.

Oi took my hand and said, "Welcome home to my wonderful sister." The Lord took my other hand and into the heavens we zipped. I was in heaven again and sitting at Oi's table. We discussed all the things that had happened since he departed. He told me that pride filled his heart in knowing he was my brother. I then told him, "Oi, now I can pester you for eternity." Oi afterwards told me, "We are being summoned to the throne; I wonder if Boudica is okay." I almost froze yet I was still able to rush to the throne. The Lord called me up to his throne and shocked me by saying, "My heavens, here is our guest of honor." I thought, how could I be a guest of honor, considering most of the great works I did, simply involve me watching him do all the work. Nevertheless, he called me up to the throne. As I was walking up the steps, I noticed that I was now wearing a nice long white evening gown. It was so nice to have clothing again, for I will appreciate this small treat all the days of my eternity. I then looked and saw two beautiful female Saints with crowns on their heads. I now think that I could be in trouble, because I do not know them. As I walk up to the stage, they come down and escort me up and then introduce themselves. The first beauty tells me her name is Supreme Queen Lablonta, and the second one tells me, I am your grandmother, Supreme Queen Eve. I was so happy finally to see my grandmother. I told her that my father had told me so many wonderful things about her. She then winked at me, and Lablonta motioned for me to be quiet. The Lord now said, "Let me introduce to my heavens, Supreme Queen Tianshire." I was so shocked at how the angels were playing such wonderful music, and the Saints were cheering. The only thing that is holding me together now is that my grandmother is with me. I had longed so much to meet her, yet never could because she lived in the garden her entire life. Her story is so wonderful. We sang songs and met different Saints. This was the first time I met the Earth Saint Enoch. He taught me so many things as my time flew quickly. I could visit with Boudica a couple of times; nevertheless, time changed us. Then one day, the horns blew as the throne faced a destroying enemy from another dimension or parallel universe. We needed someone who would be strong enough, brave, trustworthy, and loyal to the throne. It could not be a spirit, yet had to come from New Venus. Oi and I recommended Boudica. He refused to recruit her, as he declared, "None other walks as holy as Boudica." We all agreed on a short one-hour test for her loyalty and courage, and if she passed it, she would be asked, and if she said yes she could fight this battle. She passed, agreed to fight, and won, saving our heavens. The Lord immediately promoted her to Queen Boudica, and once again, she joined Oi and myself. She was home again. Eve was now so proud of Belcher, for his family had two of the four Heavenly Queens, plus High Saint Oi. Eve was my grandmother and Boudica's great-grandmother as Ibrány was a daughter of Belcher. Many ages passed as the throne suffered much from the total lambasting from evil. The Lord could put Boubica and me in hiding for our protection, and when Lilith promised to give us, a peaceful future in an Empire that had the largest known number of galaxies and still growing. Boudica was the last one to join us, as the Lord had to give her a kick in the butt to get her to go, she joined Lablonta, Eve, Oi, Belcher, Enoch and myself plus so many others in the greatest heavens for the good ever known. We rested in peace and love for eternity, with Boudica trailing Oi, our sister Ibrány, and myself for all the ages. She made heaven a great eternity for all of us. My story goes on and on for the rest of eternity. I still remember my days of New Venus and how much happened while I kept my life in the light.

INDEX

P

Q

R

S

T

U

V

W

Y

Z

The Adventures in This Series

Mempire, Born in Blood
Penance on Earth
Patmos Paradigm
Lord of New Venus
Rachmanism in Ereshkigal
Sisterhood, Blood of our Blood
Salvation, Showers of Blood

The Great Stories
Prikhodko, Dream of Nagykanizsai
Tianshire, Life in the Light

AUTHOR BIO

James Hendershot, D.D. was born in Marietta Ohio, finally settling in Caldwell, Ohio where he eventually graduated from high school. After graduating, he served four years in the Air Force and graduated, Magna Cum Laude, with three majors from the prestigious Marietta College. He then served until retirement in the US Army during which time he obtained his Masters of Science degree from Central Michigan University in Public Administration, and his third degree in Computer Programing from Central Texas College. His final degree was the honorary degree of Doctor of Divinity from Kingsway Bible College, which provided him with keen insight into the divine nature of man.

After retiring from the US Army, he accepted a visiting professor position with Korea University in Seoul, South Korea. He later moved to a suburb outside Seattle to finish his lifelong search for Mempire and the goddess Lilith, only to find them in his fingers and not with his eyes. It is now time for Earth to learn about the great mysteries not only deep in our universe but also in the dimensions beyond sharing these magnanimities with you.